THE DAY'S WORK

RUDYARD KIPLING

ZINC READ

Published by
1st Floor H49-A4 Mohan Garden 110059

Design and setting By Zinc Read
Email- zincread@gmail.com
ISBN-978-93-5885-938-6

CONTENTS

THE BRIDGEBUILDERS

The least that Findlayson, of the Public Works Department, expected was a C. I. E.; he dreamed of a C. S. I.: indeed, his friends told him that he deserved more. For three years he had endured heat and cold, disappointment, discomfort, danger, and disease, with responsibility almost too heavy for one pair of shoulders; and day by day, through that time, the great Kashi Bridge over the Ganges had grown under his charge. Now, in less than three months, if all went well, his Excellency the Viceroy would open the bridge in state, an archbishop would bless it, and the first trainload of soldiers would come over it, and there would be speeches.

Findlayson, C. E., sat in his trolley on a construction line that ran along one of the main revetments—the huge stone-faced banks that flared away north and south for three miles on either side of the river—and permitted himself to think of the end. With its approaches, his work was one mile and three-quarters fin length; a lattice-girder bridge, trussed with the Findlayson truss, standing on seven-and-twenty brick pies. Each one of those piers was twenty-four feet in diameter, capped with red Agra stone and sunk eighty feet below the shifting sand of the Ganges' bed. Above them was a railway-line fifteen feet broad; above that, again, a cart-road of eighteen feet, flanked with footpaths. At either end rose towers of red brick, loopholed for musketry and pierced for big guns, and the ramp of the road was being pushed forward to their haunches. The raw earth-ends were crawling and alive with hundreds upon hundreds of tiny asses climbing out of the yawning borrow-pit below with sackfuls of stuff; and the hot afternoon air was filled with the noise of hooves, the rattle of the drivers' sticks, and the swish and roll-down of the dirt. The river was very low, and on the dazzling white sand between the three centre piers stood squat cribs of railway-sleepers, filled within and daubed without with mud, to support the last of the girders as those were riveted up. In the little deep water left by the drought, an overhead-crane travelled to and fro along its spile-pier, jerking sections of iron into place, snorting and backing and grunting as an elephant grunts in the timber-yard. Riveters by the hundred swarmed about the lattice side-work and the iron roof of the railway-line, hung from invisible staging under the bellies of the girders, clustered round the throats of the piers, and rode on the overhang of the footpath-stanchions; their fire-pots and the spurts of flame that answered each hammer-stroke showing no more than pale yellow in the sun's glare. East and west and north and south the construction-trains rattled and shrieked up and down the embankments, the piled trucks of brown and white stone banging behind them till the side-boards were unpinned, and with a roar and a grumble a few thousand tons more material were flung out to hold the river in place.

Findlayson, C. E., turned on his trolley and looked over the face of the country that he had changed for seven miles around. Looked back on the humming village of five thousand workmen; up stream and down, along the vista of spurs and sand; across the river to the far piers, lessening in the haze; overhead to the guard-towers—and only he knew how strong those were—and with a sigh of contentment saw that his work was good. There stood his bridge before him in the sunlight, lacking only a few weeks' work on the girders of the three middle piers—his bridge, raw and ugly as original sin, but pukka—permanent—to endure when all memory of the builder, yea, even of the splendid Findlayson truss, had perished. Practically, the thing was done.

Hitchcock, his assistant, cantered along the line on a little switch-tailed Kabuli pony who through long practice could have trotted securely over a trestle, and nodded to his chief.

"All but," said he, with a smile.

"I've been thinking about it," the senior answered. "Not half a bad job for two men, is it?"

"One-and a half. Gad, what a Cooper's Hill cub I was when I came on the works!" Hitchcock felt very old in the crowded experiences of the past three years, that had taught him power and responsibility.

"You were rather a colt," said Findlayson. "I wonder how you'll like going back to office-work when this job's over."

"I shall hate it!" said the young man, and as he went on his eye followed Findlayson's, and he muttered, "Isn't it damned good?"

"I think we'll go up the service together," Findlayson said to himself. "You're too good a youngster to waste on another man. Cub thou wart; assistant thou art. Personal assistant, and at Simla, thou shalt be, if any credit comes to me out of the business!"

Indeed; the burden of the work had fallen altogether on Findlayson and his assistant, the young man whom he had chosen because of his rawness to break to his own needs. There were labour contractors by the half-hundred—fitters and riveters, European, borrowed from the railway workshops, with, perhaps, twenty white and half-caste subordinates to direct, under direction, the bevies of workmen—but none knew better than these two, who trusted each other, how the underlings were not to be trusted. They had been tried many times in sudden crises—by slipping of booms, by breaking of tackle, failure of cranes, and the wrath of the river—but no stress had brought to light any man among men whom Findlayson and Hitchcock would have honoured by working as remorselessly as they worked themselves.

Findlayson thought it over from the beginning: the months of office-work destroyed at a blow when the Government of India, at the last moment, added two feet to the width of the bridge, under the impression that bridges were cut out of paper, and so brought to ruin at least half an acre of calculations—and Hitchcock, new to disappointment, buried his head in his arms and wept; the heart-breaking delays over the filling of the contracts in England; the futile correspondences hinting at great wealth of commissions if one, only one, rather doubtful consignment were passed; the war that followed the refusal; the careful, polite obstruction at the other end that followed the war, till young Hitchcock, putting one month's leave to another month, and borrowing ten days from Findlayson, spent his poor little savings of a year in a wild dash to London, and there, as his own tongue asserted and the later consignments proved, put the fear of God into a man so great that he feared only Parliament and said so till Hitchcock wrought with him across his own dinner-table, and—he feared the Kashi Bridge and all who spoke in its name. Then there was the cholera that came in the night to the village by the bridge works; and after the cholera smote the Smallpox. The fever they had always with them. Hitchcock had been appointed a magistrate of the third class with whipping powers, for the better government of the community, and Findlayson watched him wield his powers temperately, learning what to overlook and what to look after. It was a long, long reverie, and it covered storm, sudden freshets, death in every manner and shape, violent and awful rage against red tape half frenzying a mind that knows it should be busy on other things; drought, sanitation, finance; birth, wedding, burial, and riot in the village of twenty warring castes; argument, expostulation, persuasion, and the blank despair that a man goes to bed upon, thankful that his rifle is all in pieces in the gun-case. Behind everything rose the black frame of the Kashi Bridge—plate by plate, girder by girder, span by span-and each pier of it recalled Hitchcock, the all-round man, who had stood by his chief without failing from the very first to this last.

So the bridge was two men's work—unless one counted Peroo, as Peroo certainly counted himself. He was a Lascar, a Kharva from Bulsar, familiar with every port between Rockhampton and London, who had risen to the rank of sarang on the British India boats, but wearying of routine musters and clean clothes, had thrown up the service and gone inland, where men of his calibre were sure of employment. For his knowledge of tackle and the handling of heavy weights, Peroo was worth almost any price he might have chosen to put upon his services; but custom decreed the wage of the overhead men, and Peroo was not within many silver pieces of his proper value. Neither running water nor extreme heights made him afraid; and, as an ex-serang, he knew how to hold authority. No piece of iron was so big or so badly placed that Peroo could not devise a tackle to lift it—a loose-ended, sagging arrangement, rigged with a scandalous amount of talking, but perfectly equal to the work in hand. It was Peroo who had saved the girder of Number Seven pier from destruction when the new wire rope jammed in the eye of the crane, and the huge plate tilted in its slings, threatening to slide out sideways. Then the native workmen lost their heads with great shoutings, and Hitchcock's right arm was broken by a falling T-plate, and he buttoned it up in his coat and swooned, and came to and directed for four hours till Peroo, from the top of the crane, reported "All's well," and the plate swung home. There was no one like Peroo, serang, to lash, and guy, and hold to control the donkey-engines, to hoist a fallen locomotive craftily out of the borrow-pit into which it had tumbled; to strip, and dive, if need be, to see how the concrete blocks round the piers stood the scouring of Mother Gunga, or to adventure up-stream on a monsoon night and report on the state of the embankment-facings. He would interrupt the field-councils of Findlayson and Hitchcock without fear, till his wonderful English, or his still more wonderful lingua franca, half Portuguese and half Malay, ran out and he was forced to take string and show the knots that he would recommend. He controlled his own gang of tacklemen—mysterious relatives from Kutch Mandvi gathered month by month and tried to the uttermost. No consideration of family or kin allowed Peroo to keep weak hands or a giddy head on the pay-roll. "My honour is the honour of this bridge," he would say to the about-to-be-dismissed. "What do I care for your honour? Go and work on a steamer. That is all you are fit for."

The little cluster of huts where he and his gang lived centred round the tattered dwelling of a sea-priest—one who had never set foot on black water, but had been chosen as ghostly counsellor by two generations of sea-rovers all unaffected by port missions or those creeds which are thrust upon sailors by agencies along Thames bank. The priest of the Lascara had nothing to do with their caste, or indeed with anything at all. He ate the offerings of his church, and slept and smoked, and slept again "for," said Peroo, who had haled him a thousand miles inland, "he is a very holy man. He never cares what you eat so long as you do not eat beef, and that is good, because on land we worship Shiva, we Kharvas; but at sea on the Kumpani's boats we attend strictly to the orders of the Burra Malum [the first mate], and on this bridge we observe what Finlinson Sahib says."

Finlinson Sahib had that day given orders to clear the scaffolding from the guard-tower on the right bank, and Peroo with his mates was casting loose and lowering down the bamboo poles and planks as swiftly as ever they had whipped the cargo out of a coaster.

From his trolley he could hear the whistle of the serang's silver pipe and the creak and clatter of the pulleys. Peroo was standing on the topmost coping of the tower, clad in the blue dungaree of his abandoned service, and as Findlayson motioned to him to be careful, for his was no life to throw away, he gripped the last pole, and, shading his eyes ship-fashion, answered with the long-drawn wail of the fo'c'sle lookout: "Ham dekhta hai" ("I am looking out"). Findlayson laughed and then sighed. It was years since he had seen a steamer, and he was sick for home. As his trolley passed under the tower, Peroo descended by a rope, ape-fashion, and cried: "It looks well now, Sahib. Our bridge is all but done. What think you Mother Gunga will say when the rail runs over?"

"She has said little so far. It was never Mother Gunga that delayed us."

"There is always time for her; and none the less there has been delay. Has the Sahib forgotten last autumn's flood, when the stoneboats were sunk without warning—or only a half-day's warning?"

"Yes, but nothing save a big flood could hurt us now. The spurs are holding well on the west bank."

"Mother Gunga eats great allowances. There is always room for more stone on the revetments. I tell this to the Chota Sahib"—he meant Hitchcock— "and he laughs."

"No matter, Peroo. Another year thou wilt be able to build a bridge in thine own fashion."

The Lascar grinned. "Then it will not be in this way—with stonework sunk under water, as the Quetta was sunk. I like sus-suspen-sheen bridges that fly from bank to bank, with one big step, like a gang-plank. Then no water can hurt. When does the Lord Sahib come to open the bridge?"

"In three months, when the weather is cooler."

"Ho! ho! He is like the Burra Malum. He sleeps below while the work is being done. Then he comes upon the quarter-deck and touches with his finger, and says: 'This is not clean! Dam jibboonwallah!'"

"But the Lord Sahib does not call me a dam jibboonwallah, Peroo."

"No, Sahib; but he does not come on deck till the work is all finished. Even the Burra Malum of the Nerbudda said once at Tuticorin—"

"Bah! Go! I am busy."

"I, also!" said Peroo, with an unshaken countenance. "May I take the light dinghy now and row along the spurs?"

"To hold them with thy hands? They are, I think, sufficiently heavy."

"Nay, Sahib. It is thus. At sea, on the Black Water, we have room to be blown up and down without care. Here we have no room at all. Look you, we have put the river into a dock, and run her between stone sills."
Findlayson smiled at the "we."
"We have bitted and bridled her. She is not like the sea, that can beat against a soft beach. She is Mother Gunga—in irons." His voice fell a little.
"Peroo, thou hast been up and down the world more even than I. Speak true talk, now. How much dolt thou in thy heart believe of Mother Gunga?"
"All that our priest says. London is London, Sahib. Sydney is Sydney, and Port Darwin is Port Darwin. Also Mother Gunga is Mother Gunga, and when I come back to her banks I know this and worship. In London I did poojah to the big temple by the river for the sake of the God within . . . . Yes, I will not take the cushions in the dinghy."
Findlayson mounted his horse and trotted to the shed of a bungalow that he shared with his assistant. The place had become home to him in the last three years. He had grilled in the heat, sweated in the rains, and shivered with fever under the rude thatch roof; the lime-wash beside the door was covered with rough drawings and formulae, and the sentry-path trodden in the matting of the verandah showed where he had walked alone. There is no eight-hour limit to an engineer's work, and the evening meal with Hitchcock was eaten booted and spurred: over their cigars they listened to the hum of the village as the gangs came up from the river-bed and the lights began to twinkle.
"Peroo has gone up the spurs in your dinghy. He's taken a couple of nephews with him, and he's lolling in the stern like a commodore," said Hitchcock.
"That's all right. He's got something on his mind. You'd think that ten years in the British India boats would have knocked most of his religion out of him."
"So it has," said Hitchcock, chuckling. "I overheard him the other day in the middle of a most atheistical talk with that fat old guru of theirs. Peroo denied the efficacy of prayer; and wanted the guru to go to sea and watch a gale out with him, and see if he could stop a monsoon."
"All the same, if you carried off his gurus he'd leave us like a shot. He was yarning away to me about praying to the dome of St. Paul's when he was in London."
"He told me that the first time he went into the engine-room of a steamer, when he was a boy, he prayed to the low-pressure cylinder."
"Not half a bad thing to pray to, either. He's propitiating his own Gods now, and he wants to know what Mother Gunga will think of a bridge

being run across her. Who's there?" A shadow darkened the doorway, and a telegram was put into Hitchcock's hand.

"She ought to be pretty well used to it by this time. Only a tar. It ought to be Ralli's answer about the new rivets. . . . Great Heavens!" Hitchcock jumped to his feet.

"What is it?" said the senior, and took the form. "That's what Mother Gunga thinks, is it," he said, reading. "Keep cool, young'un. We've got all our work cut out for us. Let's see. Muir wired half an hour ago: 'Floods on the Ramgunga. Look out.' Well, that gives us—one, two—nine and a half for the flood to reach Melipur Ghaut and seven's sixteen and a half to Lataoli—say fifteen hours before it comes down to us."

"Curse that hill-fed sewer of a Ramgunga! Findlayson, this is two months before anything could have been expected, and the left bank is littered up with stuff still. Two full months before the time!"

"That's why it comes. I've only known Indian rivers for five-and-twenty years, and I don't pretend to understand. Here comes another tar." Findlayson opened the telegram. "Cockran, this time, from the Ganges Canal: 'Heavy rains here. Bad.' He might have saved the last word. Well, we don't want to know any more. We've got to work the gangs all night and clean up the river-bed. You'll take the east bank and work out to meet me in the middle. Get every thing that floats below the bridge: we shall have quite enough rivercraft coming down adrift anyhow, without letting the stoneboats ram the piers. What have you got on the east bank that needs looking after."

"Pontoon—one big pontoon with the overhead crane on it. T'other overhead crane on the mended pontoon, with the cart-road rivets from Twenty to Twenty-three piers—two construction lines, and a turning-spur. The pilework must take its chance," said Hitchcock.

"All right. Roll up everything you can lay hands on. We'll give the gang fifteen minutes more to eat their grub."

Close to the verandah stood a big night-gong, never used except for flood, or fire in the village. Hitchcock had called for a fresh horse, and was off to his side of the bridge when Findlayson took the cloth-bound stick and smote with the rubbing stroke that brings out the full thunder of the metal.

Long before the last rumble ceased every night-gong in the village had taken up the warning. To these were added the hoarse screaming of conches in the little temples; the throbbing of drums and tom-toms; and, from the European quarters, where the riveters lived, McCartney's bugle, a weapon of offence on Sundays and festivals, brayed desperately, calling to "Stables." Engine after engine toiling home along the spurs at the end of her day's work whistled in answer till the whistles were answered from the far bank. Then the big gong thundered thrice for a sign that it was flood and not fire; conch, drum, and whistle echoed the call, and the village quivered to the sound of bare feet running upon soft earth. The order in all cases was to stand by the day's work and wait instructions. The gangs poured by in the dusk; men stopping to knot a loin-cloth or fasten a sandal; gang-foremen shouting to their subordinates as they ran or paused by the tool-issue sheds for bars and mattocks; locomotives creeping down their tracks wheel-deep in the crowd; till the brown torrent disappeared into the dusk of the river-bed, raced over the pilework, swarmed along the lattices, clustered by the cranes, and stood still each man in his place.

Then the troubled beating of the gong carried the order to take up everything and bear it beyond highwater mark, and the flare-lamps broke out by the hundred between the webs of dull iron as the riveters began a night's work, racing against the flood that was to come. The girders of the three centre piers—those that stood on the cribs—were all but in position. They needed just as many rivets as could be driven into them, for the flood would assuredly wash out their supports, and the ironwork would settle down on the caps of stone if they were not blocked at the ends. A hundred crowbars strained at the sleepers of the temporary line that fed the unfinished piers. It was heaved up in lengths, loaded into trucks, and backed up the bank beyond flood-level by the groaning locomotives. The tool-sheds on the sands melted away before the attack of shouting armies, and with them went the stacked ranks of Government stores, iron-bound boxes of rivets, pliers, cutters, duplicate parts of the riveting-machines, spare pumps and chains. The big crane would be the last to be shifted, for she was hoisting all the heavy stuff up to the main structure of the bridge. The concrete blocks on the fleet of stoneboats were dropped overside, where there was any depth of water, to guard the piers, and the empty boats themselves were poled under the bridge down-stream. It was here that Peroo's pipe shrilled loudest, for the first stroke of the big gong had brought the dinghy back at racing speed, and Peroo and his people were stripped to the waist, working for the honour and credit which are better than life.

"I knew she would speak," he cried. "I knew, but the telegraph gives us good warning. O sons of unthinkable begetting—children of unspeakable shame—are we here for the look of the thing?" It was two feet of wirerope frayed at the ends, and it did wonders as Peroo leaped from gunnel to gunnel, shouting the language of the sea.

Findlayson was more troubled for the stoneboats than anything else. McCartney, with his gangs, was blocking up the ends of the three doubtful spans, but boats adrift, if the flood chanced to be a high one, might endanger the girders; and there was a very fleet in the shrunken channel.

"Get them behind the swell of the guard-tower," he shouted down to Peroo. "It will be dead-water there. Get them below the bridge."

"Accha! [Very good.] I know; we are mooring them with wirerope," was the answer. "Heh! I Listen to the Chota Sahib. He is working hard."

From across the river came an almost continuous whistling of locomotives, backed by the rumble of stone. Hitchcock at the last minute was spending a few hundred more trucks of Tarakee stone in reinforcing his spurs and embankments.

"The bridge challenges Mother Gunga," said Peroo, with a laugh. "But when she talks I know whose voice will be the loudest."

For hours the naked men worked, screaming and shouting under the lights. It was a hot, moonless night; the end of it was darkened by clouds and a sudden squall that made Findlayson very grave.

"She moves!" said Peroo, just before the dawn. "Mother Gunga is awake! Hear!" He dipped his hand over the side of a boat and the current mumbled on it. A little wave hit the side of a pier with a crisp slap.

"Six hours before her time," said Findlayson, mopping his forehead savagely. "Now we can't depend on anything. We'd better clear all hands out of the river-bed."

Again the big gong beat, and a second time there was the rushing of naked feet on earth and ringing iron; the clatter of tools ceased. In the silence, men heard the dry yawn of water crawling over thirsty sand.

Foreman after foreman shouted to Findlayson, who had posted himself by the guard-tower, that his section of the river-bed had been cleaned out, and when the last voice dropped Findlayson hurried over the bridge till the iron plating of the permanent way gave place to the temporary plank-walk over the three centre piers, and there he met Hitchcock.

"All clear your side?" said Findlayson. The whisper rang in the box of latticework.

"Yes, and the east channel's filling now. We're utterly out of our reckoning. When is this thing down on us?"

"There's no saying. She's filling as fast as she can. Look!" Findlayson pointed to the planks below his feet, where the sand, burned and defiled by months of work, was beginning to whisper and fizz.

"What orders?" said Hitchcock.

"Call the roll—count stores—sit on your hunkers—and pray for the bridge. That's all I can think of. Good night. Don't risk your life trying to fish out anything that may go down-stream."

"Oh, I'll be as prudent as you are! 'Night. Heavens, how she's filling! Here's the rain in earnest!" Findlayson picked his way back to his bank, sweeping the last of McCartney's riveters before him. The gangs had spread themselves along the embankments, regardless of the cold rain of the dawn, and there they waited for the flood. Only Peroo kept his men together behind the swell of the guard-tower, where the stoneboats lay tied fore and aft with hawsers, wirerope, and chains.

A shrill wail ran along the line, growing to a yell, half fear and half wonder: the face of the river whitened from bank to bank between the stone facings, and the faraway spurs went out in spouts of foam. Mother Gunga had come bank-high in haste, and a wall of chocolate-coloured water was her messenger. There was a shriek above the roar of the water, the complaint of the spans coming down on their blocks as the cribs were whirled out from under their bellies. The stoneboats groaned and ground each other in the eddy that swung round the abutment, and their clumsy masts rose higher and higher against the dim sky-line.

"Before she was shut between these walls we knew what she would do. Now she is thus cramped God only knows what she will do!" said Peroo, watching the furious turmoil round the guard-tower. "Ohe! Fight, then! Fight hard, for it is thus that a woman wears herself out."

But Mother Gunga would not fight as Peroo desired. After the first down-stream plunge there came no more walls of water, but the river lifted herself bodily, as a snake when she drinks in midsummer, plucking and fingering along the revetments, and banking up behind the piers till even Findlayson began to recalculate the strength of his work.

When day came the village gasped. "Only last night," men said, turning to each other, "it was as a town in the river-bed! Look now!"

And they looked and wondered afresh at the deep water, the racing water that licked the throat of the piers. The farther bank was veiled by rain, into which the bridge ran out and vanished; the spurs up-stream were marked by no more than eddies and spoutings, and down-stream the pent river, once freed of her guide-lines, had spread like a sea to the horizon. Then hurried by, rolling in the water, dead men and oxen together, with here and there a patch of thatched roof that melted when it touched a pier.

"Big flood," said Peroo, and Findlayson nodded. It was as big a flood as he had any wish to watch. His bridge would stand what was upon her now, but not very much more, and if by any of a thousand chances there happened to be a weakness in the embankments, Mother Gunga would carry his honour to the sea with the other raffle. Worst of all, there was nothing to do except to sit still; and Findlayson sat still under his macintosh till his helmet became pulp on his head, and his boots were over-ankle in mire. He took no count of time, for the river was marking the hours, inch by inch and foot by foot, along the embankment, and he listened, numb and hungry, to the straining of the stoneboats, the hollow thunder under the piers, and the hundred noises that make the full note of a flood. Once a dripping servant brought him food, but he could not eat; and once he thought that he heard a faint toot from a locomotive across the river, and then he smiled. The bridge's failure would hurt his assistant not a little, but Hitchcock was a young man with his big work yet to do. For himself the crash meant everything—everything that made a hard life worth the living. They would say, the men of his own profession. . . he remembered the half pitying things that he himself had said when Lockhart's new waterworks burst and broke down in brickheaps and sludge, and Lockhart's spirit broke in him and he died. He remembered what he himself had said when the Sumao Bridge went out in the big cyclone by the sea; and most he remembered poor Hartopp's face three weeks later, when the shame had marked it. His bridge was twice the size of Hartopp's, and it carried the Findlayson truss as well as the new pier-shoe—the Findlayson bolted shoe. There were no excuses in his service. Government might listen, perhaps, but his own kind would judge him by his bridge, as that stood or fell. He went over it in his head, plate by plate, span by span, brick by brick, pier by pier, remembering, comparing, estimating, and recalculating, lest there should be any mistake; and through the long hours and through the flights of formulae that danced and wheeled before him a cold fear would come to pinch his heart. His side of the sum was beyond question; but what man knew Mother Gunga's arithmetic? Even as he was making all sure by the multiplication-table, the river might be scooping a pot-hole to the very bottom of any one of those eighty-foot piers that carried his reputation. Again a servant came to him with food, but his mouth was dry, and he could only drink and return to the decimals in his brain. And the river was still rising. Peroo, in a mat shelter-coat, crouched at his feet, watching now his face and now the face of the river, but saying nothing.

At last the Lascar rose and floundered through the mud towards the village, but he was careful to leave an ally to watch the boats.

Presently he returned, most irreverently driving before him the priest of his creed—a fat old man, with a grey beard that whipped the wind with the wet cloth that blew over his shoulder. Never was seen so lamentable a guru.

"What good are offerings and little kerosene lamps and dry grain," shouted Peroo, "if squatting in the mud is all that thou canst do? Thou hast dealt long with the Gods when they were contented and well-wishing. Now they are angry. Speak to them!"

"What is a man against the wrath of Gods?" whined the priest, cowering as the wind took him. "Let me go to the temple, and I will pray there."

"Son of a pig, pray here! Is there no return for salt fish and curry powder and dried onions? Call aloud! Tell Mother Gunga we have had enough.

Bid her be still for the night. I cannot pray, but I have been serving in the Kumpani's boats, and when men did not obey my orders I— " A flourish of the wirerope colt rounded the sentence, and the priest, breaking free from his disciple, fled to the village.

"Fat pig!" said Peroo. "After all that we have done for him! When the flood is down I will see to it that we get a new guru. Finlinson Sahib, it darkens for night now, and since yesterday nothing has been eaten. Be wise, Sahib. No man can endure watching and great thinking on an empty belly. Lie down, Sahib. The river will do what the river will do."

"The bridge is mine; I cannot leave it."

"Wilt thou hold it up with thy hands, then?" said Peroo, laughing. "I was troubled for my boats and sheers before the flood came. Now we are in the hands of the Gods. The Sahib will not eat and lie down? Take these, then. They are meat and good toddy together, and they kill all weariness, besides the fever that follows the rain. I have eaten nothing else to-day at all."

He took a small tin tobacco-box from his sodden waistbelt and thrust it into Findlayson's hand, saying, "Nay, do not be afraid. It is no more than opium—clean Malwa opium!"

Findlayson shook two or three of the dark-brown pellets into his hand, and hardly knowing what he did, swallowed them. The stuff was at least a good guard against fever—the fever that was creeping upon him out of the wet mud—and he had seen what Peroo could do in the stewing mists of autumn on the strength of a dose from the tin box.

Peroo nodded with bright eyes. "In a little—in a little the Sahib will find that he thinks well again. I too will— " He dived into his treasure-box, resettled the rain-coat over his head, and squatted down to watch the boats. It was too dark now to see beyond the first pier, and the night seemed to have given the river new strength. Findlayson stood with his chin on his chest, thinking. There was one point about one of the piers—the seventh—that he had not fully settled in his mind. The figures would not shape themselves to the eye except one by one and at enormous intervals of time. There was a sound rich and mellow in his ears like the deepest note of a double-bass—an entrancing sound upon which he pondered for several hours, as it seemed. Then Peroo was at his elbow, shouting that a wire hawser had snapped and the stoneboats were loose. Findlayson saw the fleet open and swing out fanwise to a long-drawn shriek of wire straining across gunnels.

"A tree hit them. They will all go," cried Peroo. "The main hawser has parted. What does the Sahib do?"

An immensely complex plan had suddenly flashed into Findlayson's mind. He saw the ropes running from boat to boat in straight lines and angles—each rope a line of white fire. But there was one rope which was the master rope. He could see that rope. If he could pull it once, it was absolutely and mathematically certain that the disordered fleet would reassemble itself in the backwater behind the guard-tower. But why, he wondered, was Peroo clinging so desperately to his waist as he hastened down the bank? It was necessary to put the Lascar aside, gently and slowly, because it was necessary to save the boats, and, further, to demonstrate the extreme ease of the problem that looked so difficult. And then—but it was of no conceivable importance—a wirerope raced through his hand, burning it, the high bank disappeared, and with it all the slowly dispersing factors of the problem. He was sitting in the rainy darkness—sitting in a boat that spun like a top, and Peroo was standing over him.

"I had forgotten," said the Lascar, slowly, "that to those fasting and unused, the opium is worse than any wine. Those who die in Gunga go to the Gods. Still, I have no desire to present myself before such great ones. Can the Sahib swim?"

"What need? He can fly—fly as swiftly as the wind," was the thick answer.

"He is mad!" muttered Peroo, under his breath. "And he threw me aside like a bundle of dung-cakes. Well, he will not know his death. The boat cannot live an hour here even if she strike nothing. It is not good to look at death with a clear eye."

He refreshed himself again from the tin box, squatted down in the bows of the reeling, pegged, and stitched craft, staring through the mist at the nothing that was there. A warm drowsiness crept over Findlayson, the Chief Engineer, whose duty was with his bridge. The heavy raindrops struck him with a thousand tingling little thrills, and the weight of all time since time was made hung heavy on his eyelids. He thought and perceived that he was perfectly secure, for the water was so solid that a man could surely step out upon it, and, standing still with his legs apart to keep his balance—this was the most important point—would be borne with great and easy speed to the shore. But yet a better plan came to him. It needed only an exertion of will for the soul to hurl the body ashore as wind drives paper, to waft it kite-fashion to the bank. Thereafter—the boat spun dizzily—suppose the high wind got under the freed body? Would it tower up like a kite and pitch headlong on the faraway sands, or would it duck about, beyond control, through all eternity? Findlayson gripped the gunnel to anchor himself, for it seemed that he was on the edge of taking the flight before he had settled all his plans. Opium has more effect on the white man than the black. Peroo was only comfortably indifferent to accidents. "She cannot live," he grunted. "Her seams open already. If she were even a dinghy with oars we could have ridden it out; but a box with holes is no good. Finlinson Sahib, she fills."

"Accha! I am going away. Come thou also."

In his mind, Findlayson had already escaped from the boat, and was circling high in air to find a rest for the sole of his foot. His body—he was really sorry for its gross helplessness—lay in the stern, the water rushing about its knees.

"How very ridiculous!" he said to himself, from his eyrie—"that is Findlayson—chief of the Kashi Bridge. The poor beast is going to be drowned, too. Drowned when it's close to shore. I'm—I'm onshore already. Why doesn't it come along."

To his intense disgust, he found his soul back in his body again, and that body spluttering and choking in deep water. The pain of the reunion was atrocious, but it was necessary, also, to fight for the body. He was conscious of grasping wildly at wet sand, and striding prodigiously, as one strides in a dream, to keep foothold in the swirling water, till at last he hauled himself clear of the hold of the river, and dropped, panting, on wet earth.

"Not this night," said Peroo, in his ear. "The Gods have protected us." The Lascar moved his feet cautiously, and they rustled among dried stumps. "This is some island of last year's indigo-crop," he went on. "We shall find no men here; but have great care, Sahib; all the snakes of a hundred miles have been flooded out. Here comes the lightning, on the heels of the wind. Now we shall be able to look; but walk carefully."

Findlayson was far and far beyond any fear of snakes, or indeed any merely human emotion. He saw, after he had rubbed the water from his eyes, with an immense clearness, and trod, so it seemed to himself, with world-encompassing strides. Somewhere in the night of time he had built a bridge—a bridge that spanned illimitable levels of shining seas; but the Deluge had swept it away, leaving this one island under heaven for Findlayson and his companion, sole survivors of the breed of Man.

An incessant lightning, forked and blue, showed all that there was to be seen on the little patch in the flood—a clump of thorn, a clump of swaying creaking bamboos, and a grey gnarled peepul overshadowing a Hindoo shrine, from whose dome floated a tattered red flag. The holy man whose summer resting-place it was had long since abandoned it, and the weather had broken the red-daubed image of his god. The two men stumbled, heavy limbed and heavy-eyed, over the ashes of a brick-set cooking-place, and dropped down under the shelter of the branches, while the rain and river roared together.

The stumps of the indigo crackled, and there was a smell of cattle, as a huge and dripping Brahminee bull shouldered his way under the tree. The flashes revealed the trident mark of Shiva on his flank, the insolence of head and hump, the luminous stag-like eyes, the brow crowned with a wreath of sodden marigold blooms, and the silky dewlap that almost swept the ground. There was a noise behind him of other beasts coming up from the floodline through the thicket, a sound of heavy feet and deep breathing.

"Here be more beside ourselves," said Findlayson, his head against the tree-pole, looking through half-shut eyes, wholly at ease.

"Truly," said Peroo, thickly, "and no small ones."

"What are they, then? I do not see clearly."

"The Gods. Who else? Look!"

"Ah, true! The Gods surely—the Gods." Findlayson smiled as his head fell forward on his chest. Peroo was eminently right. After the Flood, who should be alive in the land except the Gods that made it—the Gods to whom his village prayed nightly—the Gods who were in all men's mouths and about all men's ways. He could not raise his head or stir a finger for the trance that held him, and Peroo was smiling vacantly at the lightning.

The Bull paused by the shrine, his head lowered to the damp earth. A green Parrot in the branches preened his wet wings and screamed against the thunder as the circle under the tree filled with the shifting shadows of beasts. There was a black Buck at the Bull's heels—such a Buck as Findlayson in his faraway life upon earth might have seen in dreams—a Buck with a royal head, ebon back, silver belly, and gleaming straight horns. Beside him, her head bowed to the ground, the green eyes burning under the heavy brows, with restless tail switching the dead grass, paced a Tigress, full-bellied and deep-jowled.

The Bull crouched beside the shrine, and there leaped from the darkness a monstrous grey Ape, who seated himself man-wise in the place of the fallen image, and the rain spilled like jewels from the hair of his neck and shoulders.

Other shadows came and went behind the circle, among them a drunken Man flourishing staff and drinking-bottle. Then a hoarse bellow broke out from near the ground. "The flood lessens even now," it cried. "Hour by hour the water falls, and their bridge still stands!"

"My bridge," said Findlayson to himself. "That must be very old work now. What have the Gods to do with my bridge?"

His eyes rolled in the darkness following the roar. A Mugger—the blunt-nosed, ford-haunting Mugger of the Ganges—draggled herself before the beasts, lashing furiously to right and left with her tail.

"They have made it too strong for me. In all this night I have only torn away a handful of planks. The walls stand. The towers stand. They have chained my flood, and the river is not free any more. Heavenly Ones, take this yoke away! Give me clear water between bank and bank! It is I,

Mother Gunga, that speak. The Justice of the Gods! Deal me the Justice of the Gods!"

"What said I?" whispered Peroo. "This is in truth a Punchayet of the Gods. Now we know that all the world is dead, save you and I, Sahib."

The Parrot screamed and fluttered again, and the Tigress, her ears flat to her head, snarled wickedly.

Somewhere in the shadow, a great trunk and gleaming tusks swayed to and fro, and a low gurgle broke the silence that followed on the snarl.

"We be here," said a deep voice, "the Great Ones. One only and very many. Shiv, my father, is here, with Indra. Kali has spoken already. Hanuman listens also."

"Kashi is without her Kotwal tonight," shouted the Man with the drinking-bottle, flinging his staff to the ground, while the island rang to the baying of hounds. "Give her the Justice of the Gods."

"Ye were still when they polluted my waters," the great Crocodile bellowed. "Ye made no sign when my river was trapped between the walls. I had no help save my own strength, and that failed—the strength of Mother Gunga failed—before their guard-towers. What could I do? I have done everything. Finish now, Heavenly Ones!"

"I brought the death; I rode the spotted sickness from hut to hut of their workmen, and yet they would not cease." A nose-slitten, hide-worn Ass, lame, scissor-legged, and galled, limped forward. "I cast the death at them out of my nostrils, but they would not cease."

Peroo would have moved, but the opium lay heavy upon him.

"Bah!" he said, spitting. "Here is Sitala herself; Mata—the smallpox. Has the Sahib a handkerchief to put over his face?"

"Little help! They fed me the corpses for a month, and I flung them out on my sand-bars, but their work went forward. Demons they are, and sons of demons! And ye left Mother Gunga alone for their fire-carriage to make a mock of. The Justice of the Gods on the bridgebuilders!"

The Bull turned the cud in his mouth and answered slowly: "If the Justice of the Gods caught all who made a mock of holy things there would be many dark altars in the land, mother."

"But this goes beyond a mock," said the Tigress, darting forward a griping paw. "Thou knowest, Shiv, and ye, too, Heavenly Ones; ye know that they have defiled Gunga. Surely they must come to the Destroyer. Let Indra judge."

The Buck made no movement as he answered: "How long has this evil been?"

"Three years, as men count years," said the Mugger, close pressed to the earth.

"Does Mother Gunga die, then, in a year, that she is so anxious to see vengeance now? The deep sea was where she runs but yesterday, and tomorrow the sea shall cover her again as the Gods count that which men call time. Can any say that this their bridge endures till tomorrow?" said the Buck.

There was along hush, and in the clearing of the storm the full moon stood up above the dripping trees.

"Judge ye, then," said the River, sullenly. "I have spoken my shame. The flood falls still. I can do no more."

"For my own part"—it was the voice of the great Ape seated within the shrine—"it pleases me well to watch these men, remembering that I also builded no small bridge in the world's youth."

"They say, too," snarled the Tiger, "that these men came of the wreck of thy armies, Hanuman, and therefore thou hast aided—"

"They toil as my armies toiled in Lanka, and they believe that their toil endures. Indra is too high, but Shiv, thou knowest how the land is threaded with their fire-carriages."

"Yea, I know," said the Bull. "Their Gods instructed them in the matter."

A laugh ran round the circle.

"Their Gods! What should their Gods know? They were born yesterday, and those that made them are scarcely yet cold," said the Mugger, "tomorrow their Gods will die."

"Ho!" said Peroo. "Mother Gunga talks good talk. I told that to the padre-sahib who preached on the Mombassa, and he asked the Burra Malum to put me in irons for a great rudeness."

"Surely they make these things to please their Gods," said the Bull again.

"Not altogether," the Elephant rolled forth. "It is for the profit of my mahajuns fat money-lenders that worship me at each new year, when they draw my image at the head of the account-books. I, looking over their shoulders by lamplight, see that the names in the books are those of men in far places—for all the towns are drawn together by the fire-carriage, and the money comes and goes swiftly, and the account-books grow as fat as myself. And I, who am Ganesh of Good Luck, I bless my peoples."

"They have changed the face of the land-which is my land. They have killed and made new towns on my banks," said the Mugger.

"It is but the shifting of a little dirt. Let the dirt dig in the dirt if it pleases the dirt," answered the Elephant.

"But afterwards?" said the Tiger. "Afterwards they will see that Mother Gunga can avenge no insult, and they fall away from her first, and later from us all, one by one. In the end, Ganesh, we are left with naked altars."

The drunken Man staggered to his feet, and hiccupped vehemently.

"Kali lies. My sister lies. Also this my stick is the Kotwal of Kashi, and he keeps tally of my pilgrims. When the time comes to worship Bhairon—

and it is always time—the fire-carriages move one by one, and each hears a thousand pilgrims. They do not come afoot any more, but rolling upon wheels, and my honour is increased."

"Gunga, I have seen thy bed at Pryag black with the pilgrims," said the Ape, leaning forward, "and but for the fire-carriage they would have come slowly and in fewer numbers. Remember."

"They come to me always," Bhairon went on thickly. "By day and night they pray to me, all the Common People in the fields and the roads. Who is like Bhairon today? What talk is this of changing faiths? Is my staff Kotwal of Kashi for nothing? He keeps the tally, and he says that never were so many altars as today, and the fire carriage serves them well. Bhairon am I—Bhairon of the Common People, and the chiefest of tithe Heavenly Ones today. Also my staff says—"

"Peace, thou!" lowed the Bull. "The worship of the schools is mine, and they talk very wisely, asking whether I be one or many, as is the delight of my people, and ye know what I am. Kali, my wife, thou knowest also."

"Yea, I know," said the Tigress, with lowered head.

"Greater am I than Gunga also. For ye know who moved the minds of men that they should count Gunga holy among the rivers. Who die in that water—ye know how men say—come to us without punishment, and Gunga knows that the fire-carriage has borne to her scores upon scores of such anxious ones; and Kali knows that she has held her chiefest festivals among the pilgrimages that are fed by the fire-carriage. Who smote at Pooree, under the Image there, her thousands in a day and a night, and bound the sickness to the wheels of the fire-carriages, so that it ran from one end of the land to the other? Who but Kali? Before the fire-carriage came it was a heavy toil. The fire-carriages have served thee well, Mother of Death. But I speak for mine own altars, who am not Bhairon of the Common Folk, but Shiv. Men go to and fro, making words and telling talk of strange Gods, and I listen. Faith follows faith among my people in the schools, and I have no anger; for when all words are said, and the new talk is ended, to Shiv men return at the last."

"True. It is true," murmured Hanuman. "To Shiv and to the others, mother, they return. I creep from temple to temple in the North, where they worship one God and His Prophet; and presently my image is alone within their shrines."

"Small thanks," said the Buck, turning his head slowly. "I am that One and His Prophet also."

"Even so, father," said Hanuman. "And to the South I go who am the oldest of the Gods as men know the Gods, and presently I touch the shrines of the New 'Faith and the Woman whom we know is hewn twelve-armed, and still they call her Mary."

"Small thanks, brother," said the Tigress. "I am that Woman."

"Even so, sister; and I go West among the fire-carriages, and stand before the bridgebuilders in many shapes, and because of me they change their faiths and are very wise. Ho! ho! I am the builder of bridges, indeed—bridges between this and that, and each bridge leads surely to Us in the end. Be content, Gunga.

"Neither these men nor those that follow them mock thee at all."

"Am I alone, then, Heavenly Ones? Shall I smooth out my flood lest unhappily I bear away their walls? Will Indra dry my springs in the hills and make me crawl humbly between their wharfs? Shall I bury me in the sand ere I offend?"

"And all for the sake of a little iron bar with the fire-carriage atop. Truly, Mother Gunga is always young!" said Ganesh the Elephant. "A child had not spoken more foolishly. Let the dirt dig in the dirt ere it return to the dirt. I know only that my people grow rich and praise me. Shiv has said that the men of the schools do not forget; Bhairon is content for his crowd of the Common People; and Hanuman laughs."

"Surely I laugh," said the Ape. "My altars are few beside those of Ganesh or Bhairon, but the fire-carriages bring me new worshippers from beyond the Black Water—the men who believe that their God is toil. I run before them beckoning, and they follow Hanuman."

"Give them the toil that they desire, then," said the River. "Make a bar across my flood and throw the water back upon the bridge. Once thou wast strong in Lanka, Hanuman. Stoop and lift my bed."

"Who gives life can take life." The Ape scratched in the mud with a long forefinger. "And yet, who would profit by the killing? Very many would die."

There came up from the water a snatch of a love-song such as the boys sing when they watch their cattle in the noon heats of late spring. The Parrot screamed joyously, sidling along his branch with lowered head as the song grew louder, and in a patch of clear moonlight stood revealed the young herd, the darling of the Gopis, the idol of dreaming maids and of mothers ere their children are born—Krishna the Well-beloved. He stooped to knot up his long wet hair, and the parrot fluttered to his shoulder.

"Fleeting and singing, and singing and fleeting," hiccupped Bhairon. "Those make thee late for the council, brother."

"And then?" said Krishna, with a laugh, throwing back his head. "Ye can do little without me or Karma here." He fondled the Parrot's plumage and laughed again. "What is this sitting and talking together? I heard Mother Gunga roaring in the dark, and so came quickly from a but where I lay warm. And what have ye done to Karma, that he is so wet and silent? And what does Mother Gunga here? Are the heavens full that ye must come paddling in the mud beast-wise? Karma, what do they do?"

"Gunga has prayed for a vengeance on the bridgebuilders, and Kali is with her. Now she bids Hanuman whelm the bridge, that her honour may be made great," cried the Parrot. "I waited here, knowing that thou wouldst come, O my master!"

"And the Heavenly Ones said nothing? Did Gunga and the Mother of Sorrows out-talk them? Did none speak for my people?"

"Nay," said Ganesh, moving uneasily from foot to foot; "I said it was but dirt at play, and why should we stamp it flat?"

"I was content to let them toil—well content," said Hanuman.

"What had I to do with Gunga's anger?" said the Bull.

"I am Bhairon of the Common Folk, and this my staff is Kotwal of all Kashi. I spoke for the Common People."

"Thou?" The young God's eyes sparkled.

"Am I not the first of the Gods in their mouths today?" returned Bhairon, unabashed. "For the sake of the Common People I said very many wise things which I have now forgotten, but this my staff— "

Krishna turned impatiently, saw the Mugger at his feet, and kneeling, slipped an arm round the cold neck. "Mother," he said gently, "get thee to thy flood again. This matter is not for thee. What harm shall thy honour take of this live dirt? Thou hast given them their fields new year after year, and by thy flood they are made strong. They come all to thee at the last. What need to slay them now? Have pity, mother, for a little and it is only for a little."

"If it be only for a little— " the slow beast began.

"Are they Gods, then?" Krishna, returned with a laugh, his eyes looking into the dull eyes of the River. "Be certain that it is only for a little. The Heavenly Ones have heard thee, and presently justice will be done. Go now, mother, to the flood again. Men and cattle are thick on the waters—the banks fall—the villages melt because of thee."

"But the bridge-the bridge stands." The Mugger turned grunting into the undergrowth as Krishna rose.

"It is ended," said the Tigress, viciously. "There is no more justice from the Heavenly Ones. Ye have made shame and sport of Gunga, who asked no more than a few score lives."

"Of my people—who lie under the leaf-roofs of the village yonder—of the young girls, and the young men who sing to them in the dark of the child that will be born next morn—of that which was begotten tonight," said Krishna. "And when all is done, what profit? Tomorrow sees them at work. Ay, if ye swept the bridge out from end to end they would begin anew. Hear me! Bhairon is drunk always. Hanuman mocks his people with new riddles."

"Nay, but they are very old ones," the Ape said, laughing.

"Shiv hears the talk of the schools and the dreams of the holy men; Ganesh thinks only of his fat traders; but I—I live with these my people, asking for no gifts, and so receiving them hourly."

"And very tender art thou of thy people," said the Tigress.

"They are my own. The old women dream of me turning in their sleep; the maids look and listen for me when they go to fill their lotahs by the river. I walk by the young men waiting without the gates at dusk, and I call over my shoulder to the whitebeards. Ye know, Heavenly Ones, that I alone of us all walk upon the earth continually, and have no pleasure in our heavens so long as a green blade springs here, or there are two voices at twilight in the standing crops. Wise are ye, but ye live far off, forgetting whence ye came. So do I not forget. And the fire-carriage feeds your shrines, ye say? And the fire-carriages bring a thousand pilgrims where but ten came in the old years? True. That is true, today."

"But tomorrow they are dead, brother," said Ganesh.

"Peace!" said the Bull, as Hanuman leaned forward again. "And tomorrow, beloved—what of tomorrow?"

"This only. A new word creeping from mouth to mouth among the Common Folk—a word that neither man nor God can lay hold of—an evil word—a little lazy word among the Common Folk, saying (and none know who set that word afoot) that they weary of ye, Heavenly Ones."

The Gods laughed together softly. "And then, beloved?" they said.

"And to cover that weariness they, my people, will bring to thee, Shiv, and to thee, Ganesh, at first greater offerings and a louder noise of worship. But the word has gone abroad, and, after, they will pay fewer dues to our fat Brahmins. Next they will forget your altars, but so slowly that no man can say how his forgetfulness began.

"I knew—I knew! I spoke this also, but they would not hear," said the Tigress. "We should have slain—we should have slain!"

"It is too late now. Ye should have slain at the beginning when the men from across the water had taught our folk nothing. Now my people see their work, and go away thinking. They do not think of the Heavenly Ones altogether. They think of the fire-carriage and the other things that the bridgebuilders have done, and when your priests thrust forward hands asking alms, they give a little unwillingly. That is the beginning, among one or two, or five or ten—for I, moving among my people, know what is in their hearts."

"And the end, Jester of the Gods? What shall the end be?" said Ganesh.

"The end shall be as it was in the beginning, O slothful son of Shiv! The flame shall die upon the altars and the prayer upon the tongue till ye become little Gods again—Gods of the jungle—names that the hunters of rats and noosers of dogs whisper in the thicket and among the caves—rag-Gods, pot Godlings of the tree, and the villagemark, as ye were at the beginning. That is the end, Ganesh, for thee, and for Bhairon—Bhairon of the Common People."

"It is very far away," grunted Bhairon. "Also, it is a lie."

"Many women have kissed Krishna. They told him this to cheer their own hearts when the grey hairs came, and he has told us the tale," said the Bull, below his breath.

"Their Gods came, and we changed them. I took the Woman and made her twelve-armed. So shall we twist all their Gods," said Hanuman.

"Their Gods! This is no question of their Gods—one or three—man or woman. The matter is with the people. They move, and not the Gods of the bridgebuilders," said Krishna.

"So be it. I have made a man worship the fire-carriage as it stood still breathing smoke, and he knew not that he worshipped me," said Hanuman the Ape. "They will only change a little the names of their Gods. I shall lead the builders of the bridges as of old; Shiv shall be worshipped in the schools by such as doubt and despise their fellows; Ganesh shall have his mahajuns, and Bhairon the donkey-drivers, the pilgrims, and the sellers of toys. Beloved, they will do no more than change the names, and that we have seen a thousand times."

"Surely they will do no more than change the names," echoed Ganesh; but there was an uneasy movement among the Gods.

"They will change more than the names. Me alone they cannot kill, so long as a maiden and a man meet together or the spring follows the winter rains. Heavenly Ones, not for nothing have I walked upon the earth. My people know not now what they know; but I, who live with them, I read their hearts. Great Kings, the beginning of the end is born already. The fire-carriages shout the names of new Gods that are not the old under new names. Drink now and eat greatly! Bathe your faces in the smoke of the altars before they grow cold! Take dues and listen to the cymbals and the drums, Heavenly Ones, while yet there are flowers and songs. As men count time the end is far off; but as we who know reckon it is today. I have spoken."

The young God ceased, and his brethren looked at each other long in silence.

"This I have not heard before," Peroo whispered in his companion's ear. "And yet sometimes, when I oiled the brasses in the engine-room of the Goorkha, I have wondered if our priests were so wise—so wise. The day is coming, Sahib. They will be gone by the morning."

A yellow light broadened in the sky, and the tone of the river changed as the darkness withdrew.

Suddenly the Elephant trumpeted aloud as though man had goaded him.

"Let Indra judge. Father of all, speak thou! What of the things we have heard? Has Krishna lied indeed? Or— "

"Ye know," said the Buck, rising to his feet. "Ye know the Riddle of the Gods. When Brahm ceases to dream, the Heavens and the Hells and Earth disappear. Be content. Brahm dreams still. The dreams come and go, and the nature of the dreams changes, but still Brahm dreams. Krishna has walked too long upon earth, and yet I love him the more for the tale he has told. The Gods change, beloved-all save One!"

"Ay, all save one that makes love in the hearts of men," said Krishna, knotting his girdle. "It is but a little time to wait, and ye shall know if I lie."

"Truly it is but a little time, as thou sayest, and we shall know. Get thee to thy huts again, beloved, and make sport for the young things, for still Brahm dreams. Go, my children! Brahm dreams—and till he wakes the Gods die not."

"Whither went they?" said the Lascar, awe-struck, shivering a little with the cold.

"God knows!" said Findlayson. The river and the island lay in full daylight now, and there was never mark of hoof or pug on the wet earth under the peepul. Only a parrot screamed in the branches, bringing down showers of water-drops as he fluttered his wings.

"Up! We are cramped with cold! Has the opium died out? Canst thou move, Sahib?"

Findlayson staggered to his feet and shook himself. His head swam and ached, but the work of the opium was over, and, as he sluiced his forehead in a pool, the Chief Engineer of the Kashi Bridge was wondering how he had managed to fall upon the island, what chances the day offered of return, and, above all, how his work stood.

"Peroo, I have forgotten much. I was under the guard-tower watching the river; and then. . . . Did the flood sweep us away?"

"No. The boats broke loose, Sahib, and" (if the Sahib had forgotten about the opium, decidedly Peroo would not remind him) "in striving to retie them, so it seemed to me—but it was darka rope caught the Sahib and threw him upon a boat. Considering that we two, with Hitchcock Sahib, built, as it were, that bridge, I came also upon the boat, which came riding on horseback, as it were, on the nose of this island, and so, splitting, cast us ashore. I made a great cry when the boat left the wharf, and without doubt Hitchcock Sahib will come for us. As for the bridge, so many have died in the building that it cannot fall."

A fierce sun, that drew out all the smell of the sodden land, had followed the storm, and in that clear light there was no room for a man to think of the dreams of the dark. Findlayson stared up-stream, across the blaze of moving water, till his eyes ached. There was no sign of any bank to the Ganges, much less of a bridgeline.

"We came down far," he said. "It was wonderful that we were not drowned a hundred times."

"That was the least of the wonder, for no man dies before his time. I have seen Sydney, I have seen London, and twenty great ports, but"—Peroo looked at the damp, discoloured shrine under the peopul—"never man has seen that we saw here."

"What?"

"Has the Sahib forgotten; or do we black men only see the Gods?"

"There was a fever upon me." Findlayson was still looking uneasily across the water. "It seemed that the island was full of beasts and men talking, but I do not remember. A boat could live in this water now, I think."

"Oho! Then it is true. 'When Brahm ceases to dream, the Gods die.' Now I know, indeed, what he meant. Once, too, the guru said as much to me; but then I did not understand. Now I am wise."

"What?" said Findlayson, over his shoulder.

Peroo went on as if he were talking to himself. "Six-seven-ten monsoons since, I was watch on the fo'c'sle of the ehwah—the Kumpani's big boat-and there was a big tufan; green and black water beating, and I held fast to the life-lines, choking under the waters. Then I thought of the Gods—of Those whom we saw tonight"—he stared curiously at Findlayson's back, but the white man was looking across the flood. "Yes, I say of Those whom we saw this night past, and I called upon Them to protect me. And while I prayed, still keeping my lookout, a big wave came and threw me forward upon the ring of the great black bowanchor, and the Rewah rose high and high, leaning towards the lefthand side, and the water drew away from beneath her nose, and I lay upon my belly, holding the ring, and looking down into those great deeps. Then I thought, even in the face of death: If I lose hold I die, and for me neither the Rewah nor my place by the galley where the rice is cooked, nor Bombay, nor Calcutta, nor even London, will be any more for me. 'How shall I be sure,' I said, that the Gods to whom I pray will abide at all?' This I thought, and the Rewah dropped her nose as a hammer falls, and all the sea came in and slid me backwards along the fo'c'sle and over the break of the fo'c'sle, and I very badly bruised my shin against the donkey-engine: but I did not die, and I have seen the Gods. They are good for live men, but for the dead. . . They have spoken Themselves. Therefore, when I come to the village I will beat the guru for talking riddles which are no riddles. When Brahm ceases to dream the Gods go."

"Look up-stream. The light blinds. Is there smoke yonder?"

Peroo shaded his eyes with his hands. "He is a wise man and quick. Hitchcock Sahib would not trust a rowboat. He has borrowed the Rao Sahib's steam launch, and comes to look for us. I have always said that there should have been a steam-launch on the bridge works for us."

The territory of the Rao of Baraon lay within ten miles of the bridge; and Findlayson and Hitchcock had spent a fair portion of their scanty leisure in playing billiards and shooting black-buck with the young man. He had been bear-led by an English tutor of sporting tastes for some five or six years, and was now royally wasting the revenues accumulated during his minority by the Indian Government. His steam-launch, with its silverplated rails, striped silk awning, and mahogany decks, was a new toy which Findlayson had found horribly in the way when the Rao came to look at the bridge works.

"It's great luck," murmured Findlayson, but he was none the less afraid, wondering what news might be of the bridge.

The gaudy blue and white funnel came down-stream swiftly. They could see Hitchcock in the bows, with a pair of opera-glasses, and his face was unusually white. Then Peroo hailed, and the launch made for the tail of the island. The Rao Sahib, in tweed shooting-suit and a seven-hued turban, waved his royal hand, and Hitchcock shouted. But he need have asked no questions, for Findlayson's first demand was for his bridge.

"All serene! Gad, I never expected to see you again, Findlayson. You're seven koss down-stream. Yes; there's not a stone shifted anywhere; but how are you? I borrowed the Rao Sahib's launch, and he was good enough to come along. Jump in."

"Ah, Finlinson, you are very well, eh? That was most unprecedented calamity last night, eh? My royal palace, too, it leaks like the devil, and the crops will also be short all about my country. Now you shall back her out, Hitchcock. I—I do not understand steam engines. You are wet? You are cold, Finlinson? I have some things to eat here, and you will take a good drink."

"I'm immensely grateful, Rao Sahib. I believe you've saved my life. How did Hitchcock—"

"Oho! His hair was upon end. He rode to me in the middle of the night and woke me up in the arms of Morpheus. I was most truly concerned, Finlinson, so I came too. My head-priest he is very angry just now. We will go quick, Mister Hitchcock. I am due to attend at twelve forty-five in the state temple, where we sanctify some new idol. If not so I would have asked you to spend the day with me. They are dam-bore, these religious ceremonies, Finlinson, eh?"

Peroo, well known to the crew, had possessed himself of the inlaid wheel, and was taking the launch craftily up-stream. But while he steered he was, in his mind, handling two feet of partially untwisted wirerope; and the back upon which he beat was the back of his guru.

A WALKING DELEGATE

According to the custom of Vermont, Sunday afternoon is salting-time on the farm, and, unless something very important happens, we attend to the salting ourselves. Dave and Pete, the red oxen, are treated first; they stay in the home meadow ready for work on Monday. Then come the cows, with Pan, the calf, who should have been turned into veal long ago, but survived on account of his manners; and lastly the horses, scattered through the seventy acres of the Back Pasture.

You must go down by the brook that feeds the clicking, bubbling water-ram; up through the sugar-bush, where the young maple undergrowth closes round you like a shallow sea; next follow the faint line of an old county-road running past two green hollows fringed with wild rose that mark the cellars of two ruined houses; then by Lost Orchard, where nobody ever comes except in cider-time; then across another brook, and so into the Back Pasture. Half of it is pine and hemlock and Spruce, with sumach and little juniper bushes, and the other half is grey rock and boulder and moss, with green streaks of brake and swamp; but the horses like it well enough—our own, and the others that are turned down there to feed at fifty cents a week. Most people walk to the Back Pasture, and find it very rough work; but one can get there in a buggy, if the horse knows what is expected of him. The safest conveyance is our coupe. This began life as a buckboard, and we bought it for five dollars from a sorrowful man who had no other sort of possessions; and the seat came off one night when we were turning a corner in a hurry. After that alteration it made a beautiful salting-machine, if you held tight, because there was nothing to catch your feet when you fell out, and the slats rattled tunes.

One Sunday afternoon we went out with the salt as usual. It was a broiling hot day, and we could not find the horses anywhere till we let Tedda Gabler, the bobtailed mare who throws up the dirt with her big hooves exactly as a tedder throws hay, have her head. Clever as she is, she tipped the coupe over in a hidden brook before she came out on a ledge of rock where all the horses had gathered, and were switching flies. The Deacon was the first to call to her. He is a very dark iron-grey four-year-old, son of Grandee. He has been handled since he was two, was driven in a light cart before he was three, and now ranks as an absolutely steady lady's horse—proof against steam-rollers, grade-crossings, and street processions.

"Salt!" said the Deacon, joyfully. "You're dreffle late, Tedda."

"Any—any place to cramp the coupe?" Tedda panted. "It weighs turr'ble this weather. I'd 'a' come sooner, but they didn't know what they wanted—ner haow. Fell out twice, both of 'em. I don't understand sech foolishness."

"You look consider'ble het up. 'Guess you'd better cramp her under them pines, an' cool off a piece."

Tedda scrambled on the ledge, and cramped the coupe in the shade of a tiny little wood of pines, while my companion and I lay down among the brown, silky needles, and gasped. All the home horses were gathered round us, enjoying their Sunday leisure.

There were Rod and Rick, the seniors on the farm. They were the regular road-pair, bay with black points, full brothers, aged, sons of a Hambletonian sire and a Morgan dam. There were Nip and Tuck, seal-browns, rising six, brother and sister, Black Hawks by birth, perfectly matched, just finishing their education, and as handsome a pair as man could wish to find in a forty-mile drive. There was Muldoon, our ex-car-horse, bought at a venture, and any colour you choose that is not white; and Tweezy, who comes from Kentucky, with an affliction of his left hip, which makes him a little uncertain how his hind legs are moving. He and Muldoon had been hauling gravel all the week for our new road. The Deacon you know already. Last of all, and eating something, was our faithful Marcus Aurelius Antoninus, the black buggy-horse, who had seen us through every state of weather and road, the horse who was always standing in harness before some door or other—a philosopher with the appetite of a shark and the manners of an archbishop. Tedda Gabler was a new "trade," with a reputation for vice which was really the result of bad driving. She had one working gait, which she could hold till further notice; a Roman nose; a large, prominent eye; a shaving-brush of a tail; and an irritable temper. She took her salt through her bridle; but the others trotted up nuzzling and wickering for theirs, till we emptied it on the clean rocks. They were all standing at ease, on three legs for the most part, talking the ordinary gossip of the Back Pasture—about the scarcity of water, and gaps in the fence, and how the early windfalls tasted that season—when little Rick blew the last few grains of his allowance into a crevice, and said:

"Hurry, boys! 'Might ha' knowed that livery plug would be around."

We heard a clatter of hooves, and there climbed up from the ravine below a fifty-center transient—a wall-eyed, yellow frame-house of a horse, sent up to board from a livery-stable in town, where they called him "The Lamb," and never let him out except at night and to strangers. My companion, who knew and had broken most of the horses, looked at the ragged hammer-head as it rose, and said quietly:

"Ni-ice beast. Man-eater, if he gets the chance—see his eye. Kicker, too—see his hocks. Western horse."

The animal lumbered up, snuffling and grunting. His feet showed that he had not worked for weeks and weeks, and our creatures drew together significantly.

"As usual," he said, with an underhung sneer—"bowin' your heads before the Oppressor that comes to spend his leisure gloatin' over you."

"Mine's done," said the Deacon; he licked up the remnant of his salt, dropped his nose in his master's hand, and sang a little grace all to himself. The Deacon has the most enchanting manners of any one I know.

"An' fawnin' on them for what is your inalienable right. It's humiliatin'," said the yellow horse, sniffing to see if he could find a few spare grains.

"Go daown hill, then, Boney," the Deacon replied. "Guess you'll find somethin' to eat still, if yer hain't hogged it all. You've ett more'n any three of us to-day—an' day 'fore that—an' the last two months—sence you've been here."

"I am not addressin' myself to the young an' immature. I am speakin' to those whose opinion an' experience commands respect."

I saw Rod raise his head as though he were about to make a remark; then he dropped it again, and stood three-cornered, like a plough-horse. Rod can cover his mile in a shade under three minutes on an ordinary road to an ordinary buggy. He is tremendously powerful behind, but, like most Hambletonians, he grows a trifle sullen as he gets older. No one can love Rod very much; but no one can help respecting him.

"I wish to wake those," the yellow horse went on, "to an abidin' sense o' their wrongs an' their injuries an' their outrages."

"Haow's that?" said Marcus Aurelius Antoninus, dreamily. He thought Boney was talking of some kind of feed.

"An' when I say outrages and injuries"—Boney waved his tail furiously "I mean 'em, too. Great Oats! That's just what I do mean, plain an' straight."

"The gentleman talks quite earnest," said Tuck, the mare, to Nip, her brother. "There's no doubt thinkin' broadens the horizons o' the mind. His language is quite lofty."

"Hesh, sis," Nip answered.

"He hain't widened nothin' 'cep' the circle he's ett in pasture. They feed words fer beddin' where he comes from."

"It's elegant talkin', though," Tuck returned, with an unconvinced toss of her pretty, lean little head.

The yellow horse heard her, and struck an attitude which he meant to be extremely impressive. It made him look as though he had been badly stuffed.

"Now I ask you, I ask you without prejudice an' without favour,—what has Man the Oppressor ever done for you?—Are you not inalienably entitled to the free air o' heaven, blowin' acrost this boundless prairie?"

"Hev ye ever wintered here?" said the Deacon, merrily, while the others snickered. "It's kinder cool."

"Not yet," said Boney. "I come from the boundless confines o' Kansas, where the noblest of our kind have their abidin' place among the sunflowers on the threshold o' the settin' sun in his glory."

"An' they sent you ahead as a sample?" said Rick, with an amused quiver of his long, beautifully groomed tail, as thick and as fine and as wavy as a quadroon's back hair.

"Kansas, sir, needs no advertisement. Her native sons rely on themselves an' their native sires. Yes, sir."

Then Tweezy lifted up his wise and polite old head. His affliction makes him bashful as a rule, but he is ever the most courteous of horses.

"Excuse me, suh," he said slowly, "but, unless I have been misinfohmed, most of your prominent siahs, suh, are impo'ted from Kentucky; an' I'm from Paduky."

There was the least little touch of pride in the last words.

"Any horse dat knows beans," said Muldoon, suddenly (he had been standing with his hairy chin on Tweezy's broad quarters), "gits outer Kansas 'fore dey crip his shoes. I blew in dere from Ioway in de days o' me youth an' innocence, an' I wuz grateful when dey boxed me fer N' York. You can't tell me anything about Kansas I don't wanter fergit. De Belt Line stables ain't no Hoffman House, but dey're Vanderbilts 'longside o' Kansas."

"What the horses o' Kansas think to-day, the horses of America will think to-morrow; an' I tell you that when the horses of America rise in their might, the day o' the Oppressor is ended."

There was a pause, till Rick said, with a little grunt:

"Ef you put it that way, every one of us has riz in his might, 'cep' Marcus, mebbe. Marky, 'j ever rise in yer might?"

"Nope," said Marcus Aurelius Antoninus, thoughtfully quidding over a mouthful of grass. "I seen a heap o' fools try, though."

"You admit that you riz?" said the Kansas horse, excitedly. "Then why—why in Kansas did you ever go under again?"

"Horse can't walk on his hind legs all the time," said the Deacon.

"Not when he's jerked over on his back 'fore he knows what fetched him. We've all done it, Boney," said Rick. "Nip an' Tuck they tried it, spite o' what the Deacon told 'em; an' the Deacon he tried it, spite o' what me an' Rod told him; an' me an' Rod tried it, spite o' what Grandee told us; an' I guess Grandee he tried it, spite o' what his dam told him. It's the same old circus from generation to generation. 'Colt can't see why he's called on to back. Same old rearm' on end—straight up. Same old feelin' that you've bested 'em this time. Same old little yank at your mouth when you're up good an' tall. Same old Pegasus-act, wonderin' where you'll 'light. Same old wop when you hit the dirt with your head where your tail should be, and your in'ards shook up like a bran-mash. Same old voice in your ear: 'Waal, ye little fool, an' what did you reckon to make by that?' We're through with risin in our might on this farm. We go to pole er single, accordin' ez we're hitched."

"An' Man the Oppressor sets an' gloats over you, same as he's settin' now. Hain't that been your experience, madam?"

This last remark was addressed to Tedda; and any one could see with half an eye that poor, old anxious, fidgety Tedda, stamping at the flies, must have left a wild and tumultuous youth behind her.

"'Pends on the man," she answered, shifting from one foot to the other, and addressing herself to the home horses. "They abused me dreffle when I was young. I guess I was sperrity an' nervous some, but they didn't allow for that. 'Twas in Monroe County, Noo York, an' sence then till I come here, I've run away with more men than 'u'd fill a boardin'-house. Why, the man that sold me here he says to the boss, s' he: 'Mind, now, I've warned you. 'Twon't be none of my fault if she sheds you daown the road. Don't you drive her in a top-buggy, ner 'thout winkers,' s' he, 'ner 'thought this bit ef you look to come home behind her.' 'N' the fust thing the boss did was to git the top-buggy.

"Can't say as I like top-buggies," said Rick; "they don't balance good."

"Suit me to a ha'ar," said Marcus Aurelius Antoninus. "Top-buggy means the baby's in behind, an' I kin stop while she gathers the pretty flowers—yes, an' pick a maouthful, too. The women-folk all say I hev to be humoured, an' I don't kerry things to the sweatin'-point."

"'Course I've no prejudice against a top-buggy s' long's I can see it," Tedda went on quickly. "It's ha'f-seein' the pesky thing bobbin' an' balancn' behind the winkers gits on my nerves. Then the boss looked at the bit they'd sold with me, an' s' he: 'Jiminy Christmas! This 'u'd make a clothes-horse Stan' 'n end!' Then he gave me a plain bar bit, an' fitted it's if there was some feelin' to my maouth."

"Hain't ye got any, Miss Tedda?" said Tuck, who has a mouth like velvet, and knows it.

"Might 'a' had, Miss Tuck, but I've forgot. Then he give me an open bridle,—my style's an open bridle—an'—I dunno as I ought to tell this by rights—he—give—me—a kiss."

"My!" said Tuck, "I can't tell fer the shoes o' me what makes some men so fresh."

"Pshaw, sis," said Nip, "what's the sense in actin' so? You git a kiss reg'lar's hitchin'-up time."

"Well, you needn't tell, smarty," said Tuck, with a squeal and a kick.

"I'd heard o' kisses, o' course," Tedda went on, "but they hadn't come my way specially. I don't mind tellin' I was that took aback at that man's doin's he might ha' lit fire-crackers on my saddle. Then we went out jest's if a kiss was nothin', an' I wasn't three strides into my gait 'fore I felt the boss knoo his business, an' was trustin' me. So I studied to please him, an' he never took the whip from the dash—a whip drives me plumb distracted—an' the upshot was that—waal, I've come up the Back Pasture to-day, an' the coupe's tipped clear over twice, an' I've waited till 'twuz fixed each time. You kin judge for yourselves. I don't set up to be no better than my neighbours,—specially with my tail snipped off the way 'tis,—but I want you all to know Tedda's quit fightin' in harness or out of it, 'cep' when there's a born fool in the pasture, stuffin' his stummick with board that ain't rightly hisn, 'cause he hain't earned it."

"Meanin' me, madam?" said the yellow horse.

"Ef the shoe fits, clinch it," said Tedda, snorting. "I named no names, though, to be sure, some folks are mean enough an' greedy enough to do 'thout 'em."

"There's a deal to be forgiven to ignorance," said the yellow horse, with an ugly look in his blue eye.

"Seemin'ly, yes; or some folks 'u'd ha' been kicked raound the pasture 'bout onct a minute sence they came—board er no board."

"But what you do not understand, if you will excuse me, madam, is that the whole principle o' servitood, which includes keep an' feed, starts from a radically false basis; an' I am proud to say that me an' the majority o' the horses o' Kansas think the entire concern should be relegated to the limbo of exploded superstitions. I say we're too progressive for that. I say we're too enlightened for that. 'Twas good enough's long's we didn't think, but naow—but naow—a new loominary has arisen on the horizon!"

"Meanin' you?" said the Deacon.

"The horses o' Kansas are behind me with their multitoodinous thunderin' hooves, an' we say, simply but grandly, that we take our stand with all four feet on the inalienable rights of the horse, pure and simple,—the high-toned child o' nature, fed by the same wavin' grass, cooled by the same ripplin' brook—yes, an' warmed by the same gen'rous sun as falls impartially on the outside an' the inside of the pampered machine o' the trottin'-track, or the bloated coupe-horses o' these yere Eastern cities. Are we not the same flesh an' blood?"

"Not by a bushel an' a half," said the Deacon, under his breath. "Grandee never was in Kansas."

"My! Ain't that elegant, though, abaout the wavin' grass an' the ripplin' brooks?" Tuck whispered in Nip's ear. "The gentleman's real convincin' I think."

"I say we are the same flesh an' blood! Are we to be separated, horse from horse, by the artificial barriers of a trottin'-record, or are we to look down upon each other on the strength o' the gifts o' nature—an extry inch below the knee, or slightly more powerful quarters? What's the use o' them advantages to you? Man the Oppressor comes along, an' sees you're likely an' good-lookin', an' grinds you to the face o' the earth. What for? For his own pleasure: for his own convenience! Young an' old, black an' bay, white an' grey, there's no distinctions made between us. We're ground up together under the remorseless teeth o' the engines of oppression!"

"Guess his breechin' must ha' broke goin' daown-hill," said the Deacon. "Slippery road, maybe, an' the buggy come onter him, an' he didn't know 'nough to hold back. That don't feel like teeth, though. Maybe he busted a shaft, an' it pricked him."

"An' I come to you from Kansas, wavin' the tail o' friendship to all an' sundry, an' in the name of the uncounted millions o' pure-minded, high-toned horses now strugglin' towards the light o' freedom, I say to you, Rub noses with us in our sacred an' holy cause. The power is yourn. Without you, I say, Man the Oppressor cannot move himself from place to place. Without you he cannot reap, he cannot sow, he cannot plough."

"Mighty odd place, Kansas!" said Marcus Aurelius Antoninus. "Seemin'ly they reap in the spring an' plough in the fall. 'Guess it's right fer them, but 'twould make me kinder giddy."

"The produc's of your untirin' industry would rot on the ground if you did not weakly consent to help him. Let 'em rot, I say! Let him call you to the stables in vain an' nevermore! Let him shake his ensnarin' oats under your nose in vain! Let the Brahmas roost in the buggy, an' the rats run riot round the reaper! Let him walk on his two hind feet till they blame well drop off! Win no more soul-destroyn' races for his pleasure! Then, an' not till then, will Man the Oppressor know where he's at. Quit workin', fellow-sufferers an' slaves! Kick! Rear! Plunge! Lie down on the shafts, an' woller! Smash an' destroy! The conflict will be but short, an' the victory is certain. After that we can press our inalienable rights to eight quarts o' oats a day, two good blankets, an' a fly-net an' the best o' stablin'."

The yellow horse shut his yellow teeth with a triumphant snap; and Tuck said, with a sigh: "Seems's if somethin' ought to be done. Don't seem right, somehow,—oppressin' us an all,—to my way o' thinkin'."

Said Muldoon, in a far-away and sleepy voice:

"Who in Vermont's goin' to haul de inalienable oats? Dey weigh like Sam Hill, an' sixty bushel at dat allowance ain't goin' to last t'ree weeks here. An' dere's de winter hay for five mont's!"

"We can settle those minor details when the great cause is won," said the yellow horse. "Let us return simply but grandly to our inalienable rights—the right o' freedom on these yere verdant hills, an' no invijjus distinctions o' track an' pedigree:"

"What in stables 'jer call an invijjus distinction?" said the Deacon, stiffly.

"Fer one thing, bein' a bloated, pampered trotter jest because you happen to be raised that way, an' couldn't no more help trottin' than eatin'."

"Do ye know anythin' about trotters?" said the Deacon.

"I've seen 'em trot. That was enough for me. I don't want to know any more. Trottin''s immoral."

"Waal, I'll tell you this much. They don't bloat, an' they don't pamp—much. I don't hold out to be no trotter myself, though I am free to say I had hopes that way—onct. But I do say, fer I've seen 'em trained, that a trotter don't trot with his feet: he trots with his head; an' he does more work—ef you know what that is—in a week than you er your sire ever done in all your lives. He's everlastingly at it, a trotter is; an' when he isn't, he's studyin' haow. You seen 'em trot? Much you hev! You was hitched to a rail, back o' the stand, in a buckboard with a soap-box nailed on the slats, an' a frowzy buff'lo atop, while your man peddled rum fer lemonade to little boys as thought they was actin' manly, till you was both run off the track an' jailed—you intoed, shufflin', sway-backed, wind-suckin' skate, you!"

"Don't get het up, Deacon," said Tweezy, quietly. "Now, suh, would you consider a fox-trot, an' single-foot, an' rack, an' pace, an' amble, distinctions not worth distinguishin'? I assuah you, gentlemen, there was a time befo' I was afflicted in my hip, if you'll pardon me, Miss Tuck, when I was quite celebrated in Paduky for all those gaits; an in my opinion the Deacon's co'rect when he says that a ho'se of any position in society gets his gaits by his haid, an' not by—his, ah, limbs, Miss Tuck. I reckon I'm very little good now, but I'm rememberin' the things I used to do befo' I took to transpo'tin' real estate with the help an' assistance of this gentleman here." He looked at Muldoon.

"Invijjus arterficial hind legs!" said the ex-carhorse, with a grunt of contempt. "On de Belt Line we don't reckon no horse wuth his keep 'less he kin switch de car off de track, run her round on de cobbles, an' dump her in ag'in ahead o' de truck what's blockin' him. Dere is a way o' swingin' yer quarters when de driver says, 'Yank her out, boys!' dat takes a year to learn. Onct yer git onter it, youse kin yank a cable-car outer a manhole. I don't advertise myself for no circus-horse, but I knew dat trick better than most, an' dey was good to me in de stables, fer I saved time on de Belt—an' time's what dey hunt in N' York."

"But the simple child o' nature—" the yellow horse began.

"Oh, go an' unscrew yer splints! You're talkin' through yer bandages," said Muldoon, with a horse-laugh. "Dere ain't no loose-box for de simple child o' nature on de Belt Line, wid de Paris comin' in an' de Teutonic goin' out, an' de trucks an' de coupe's sayin' things, an' de heavy freight movin' down fer de Boston boat 'bout t'ree o'clock of an August afternoon, in de middle of a hot wave when de fat Kanucks an' Western horses drops dead on de block. De simple child o' nature had better chase himself inter de water. Every man at de end of his lines is mad or loaded or silly, an' de cop's madder an' loadeder an' sillier than de rest. Dey all take it outer de horses. Dere's no wavin' brooks ner ripplin' grass on de Belt Line. Run her out on de cobbles wid de sparks flyin', an' stop when de cop slugs you on de bone o' yer nose. Dat's N'York; see?

"I was always told s'ciety in Noo York was dreffle refined an' high-toned," said Tuck. "We're lookin' to go there one o' these days, Nip an' me."

"Oh, you won't see no Belt business where you'll go, miss. De man dat wants you'll want bad, an' he'll summer you on Long Island er at Newport, wid a winky-pinky silver harness an' an English coachman. You'll make a star-hitch, you an' yer brother, miss. But I guess you won't have no nice smooth bar bit. Dey checks 'em, an' dey bangs deir tails, an' dey bits 'em, de city folk, an' dey says it's English, ye know, an' dey darsen't cut a horse loose 'ca'se o' de cops. N' York's no place fer a horse, 'less he's on de Belt, an' can go round wid de boys. Wisht I was in de Fire Department!"

"But did you never stop to consider the degradin' servitood of it all?" said the yellow horse.

"You don't stop on de Belt, cully. You're stopped. An' we was all in de servitood business, man an' horse, an' Jimmy dat sold de papers. Guess de passengers weren't out to grass neither, by de way dey acted. I done my turn, an' I'm none o' Barnum's crowd; but any horse dat's worked on de Belt four years don't train wid no simple child o' nature—not by de whole length o' N' York."

"But can it be possible that with your experience, and at your time of life, you do not believe that all horses are free and equal?" said the yellow horse.

"Not till they're dead," Muldoon answered quietly. "An' den it depends on de gross total o' buttons an' mucilage dey gits outer youse at Barren Island."

"They tell me you're a prominent philosopher." The yellow horse turned to Marcus. "Can you deny a basic and pivotal statement such as this?"

"I don't deny anythin'," said Marcus Aurelius Antoninus, cautiously; "but ef you ast me, I should say 'twuz more different sorts o' clipped oats of a lie than anythin' I've had my teeth into sence I wuz foaled."

"Are you a horse?" said the yellow horse.

"Them that knows me best 'low I am."

"Ain't I a horse?"

"Yep; one kind of."

"Then ain't you an' me equal?"

"How fer kin you go in a day to a loaded buggy, drawin' five hundred pounds?" Marcus asked carelessly.

"That has nothing to do with the case," the yellow horse answered excitedly.

"There's nothing I know hez more to do with the case," Marcus replied.

"Kin ye yank a full car outer de tracks ten times in de mornin'?" said Muldoon.

"Kin ye go to Keene—forty-two mile in an afternoon—with a mate," said Rick; "an' turn out bright an' early next mornin'?"

"Was there evah any time in your careah, suh—I am not referrin' to the present circumstances, but our mutual glorious past—when you could carry a pretty girl to market hahnsome, an' let her knit all the way on account o' the smoothness o' the motion?" said Tweezy.

"Kin you keep your feet through the West River Bridge, with the narrer-gage comin' in on one side, an' the Montreal flyer the other, an' the old bridge teeterin' between?" said the Deacon. "Kin you put your nose down on the cow-catcher of a locomotive when you're waitin' at the depot an' let 'em play 'Curfew shall not ring to-night' with the big brass bell?"

"Kin you hold back when the brichin' breaks? Kin you stop fer orders when your nigh hind leg's over your trace an' ye feel good of a frosty mornin'?" said Nip, who had only learned that trick last winter, and thought it was the crown of horsely knowledge.

"What's the use o' talk in'?" said Tedda Gabler, scornfully. "What kin ye do?"

"I rely on my simple rights—the inalienable rights o' my unfettered horsehood. An' I am proud to say I have never, since my first shoes, lowered myself to obeyin' the will o' man."

"'Must ha' had a heap o' whips broke over yer yaller back," said Tedda. "Hev ye found it paid any?"

"Sorrer has been my portion since the day I was foaled. Blows an' boots an' whips an' insults—injury, outrage, an' oppression. I would not endoor the degradin' badges o' servitood that connect us with the buggy an' the farm-wagon."

"It's amazin' difficult to draw a buggy 'thout traces er collar er breast-strap er somefin'," said Marcus. "A Power-machine for sawin' wood is most the only thing there's no straps to. I've helped saw 's much as three cord in an afternoon in a Power-machine. Slep', too, most o' the time, I did; but 'tain't half as interestin' ez goin' daown-taown in the Concord."

"Concord don't hender you goin' to sleep any," said Nip. "My throat-lash! D'you remember when you lay down in the sharves last week, waitin' at the piazza?"

"Pshaw! That didn't hurt the sharves. They wuz good an' wide, an' I lay down keerful. The folks kep' me hitched up nigh an hour 'fore they started; an' larfed—why, they all but lay down themselves with larfin'. Say, Boney, if you've got to be hitched to anything that goes on wheels, you've got to be hitched with somefin'."

"Go an' jine a circus," said Muldoon, "an' walk on your hind legs. All de horses dat knows too much to work [he pronounced it 'woik,' New York fashion] jine de circus."

"I am not sayin' anythin' again' work," said the yellow horse; "work is the finest thing in the world."

"'Seems too fine fer some of us," Tedda snorted.

"I only ask that each horse should work for himself, an' enjoy the profit of his labours. Let him work intelligently, an' not as a machine."

"There ain't no horse that works like a machine," Marcus began.

"There's no way o' workin' that doesn't mean goin' to pole er single—they never put me in the Power-machine—er under saddle," said Rick.

"Oh, shucks! We're talkin' same ez we graze," said Nip, "raound an' raound in circles. Rod, we hain't heard from you yet, an' you've more know-how than any span here."

Rod, the off-horse of the pair, had been standing with one hip lifted, like a tired cow; and you could only tell by the quick flutter of the haw across his eye, from time to time, that he was paying any attention to the argument. He thrust his jaw out sidewise, as his habit is when he pulls, and changed his leg. His voice was hard and heavy, and his ears were close to his big, plain Hambletonian head.

"How old are you?" he said to the yellow horse.

"Nigh thirteen, I guess."

"Mean age; ugly age; I'm gettin' that way myself. How long hev ye been pawin' this firefanged stable-litter?"

"If you mean my principles, I've held 'em sence I was three."

"Mean age; ugly age; teeth give heaps o' trouble then. 'Set a colt to actin' crazy fer a while. You've kep' it up, seemin'ly. D'ye talk much to your neighbours fer a steady thing?"

"I uphold the principles o' the Cause wherever I am pastured."

"'Done a heap o' good, I guess?"

"I am proud to say I have taught a few of my companions the principles o' freedom an' liberty."

"Meanin' they ran away er kicked when they got the chanst?"

"I was talkin' in the abstrac', an' not in the concrete. My teachin's educated them."

"What a horse, specially a young horse, hears in the abstrac', he's liable to do in the Concord. You was handled late, I presoom."

"Four, risin' five."

"That's where the trouble began. Driv' by a woman, like ez not—eh?"

"Not fer long," said the yellow horse, with a snap of his teeth.

"Spilled her?"

"I heerd she never drove again."

"Any childern?"

"Buckboards full of 'em."

"Men too?"

"I have shed conside'ble men in my time."

"By kickin'?"

"Any way that come along. Fallin' back over the dash is as handy as most."

"They must be turr'ble afraid o' you daown taown?"

"They've sent me here to get rid o' me. I guess they spend their time talkin' over my campaigns."

"I wanter know!"

"Yes, sir. Now, all you gentlemen have asked me what I can do. I'll just show you. See them two fellers lyin' down by the buggy?"

"Yep; one of 'em owns me. T'other broke me," said Rod.

"Get 'em out here in the open, an' I'll show you something. Lemme hide back o' you peoples, so's they won't see what I'm at."

"Meanin' ter kill 'em?" Rod drawled. There was a shudder of horror through the others; but the yellow horse never noticed.

"I'll catch 'em by the back o' the neck, an' pile-drive 'em a piece. They can suit 'emselves about livin' when I'm through with 'em."

"'Shouldn't wonder ef they did," said Rod. The yellow horse had hidden himself very cleverly behind the others as they stood in a group, and was swaying his head close to the ground with a curious scythe-like motion, looking sidewise out of his wicked eyes. You can never mistake a man-eater getting ready to knock a man down. We had had one to pasture the year before.

"See that?" said my companion, turning over on the pine-needles. "Nice for a woman walking 'cross lots, wouldn't it be?"

"Bring 'em out!" said the yellow horse, hunching his sharp back. "There's no chance among them tall trees. Bring out the—oh! Ouch!"

It was a right-and-left kick from Muldoon. I had no idea that the old carhorse could lift so quickly. Both blows caught the yellow horse full and fair in the ribs, and knocked the breath out of him.

"What's that for?" he said angrily, when he recovered himself; but I noticed he did not draw any nearer to Muldoon than was necessary.

Muldoon never answered, but discoursed to himself in the whining grunt that he uses when he is going down-hill in front of a heavy load. We call it singing; but I think it's something much worse, really. The yellow horse blustered and squealed a little, and at last said that, if it was a horse-fly that had stung Muldoon, he would accept an apology.

"You'll get it," said Muldoon, "in de sweet by-and-bye—all de apology you've any use for. Excuse me interruptin' you, Mr. Rod, but I'm like Tweezy—I've a Southern drawback in me hind legs."

"Naow, I want you all here to take notice, an' you'll learn something," Rod went on. "This yaller-backed skate comes to our pastur'-"

"Not havin' paid his board," put in Tedda.

"Not havin' earned his board, an' talks smooth to us abaout ripplin' brooks an' wavin' grass, an' his high-toned, pure-souled horsehood, which don't hender him sheddin' women an' childern, an' fallin' over the dash onter men. You heard his talk, an' you thought it mighty fine, some o' you."

Tuck looked guilty here, but she did not say anything.

"Bit by bit he goes on ez you have heard."

"I was talkin' in the abstrac'," said the yellow horse, in an altered voice.

"Abstrac' be switched! Ez I've said, it's this yer blamed abstrac' business that makes the young uns cut up in the Concord; an' abstrac' or no abstrac', he crep' on an' on till he come to killin' plain an' straight—killin' them as never done him no harm, jest beca'se they owned horses."

"An' knowed how to manage 'em," said Tedda. "That makes it worse."

"Waal, he didn't kill 'em, anyway," said Marcus. "He'd ha' been half killed ef he had tried."

"'Makes no differ," Rod answered. "He meant to; an' ef he hadn't—s'pose we want the Back Pasture turned into a biffin'-ground on our only day er rest? 'S'pose we want our men walkin' round with bits er lead pipe an' a twitch, an' their hands full o' stones to throw at us, same's if we wuz hogs er hooky keows? More'n that, leavin' out Tedda here—an' I guess it's more her maouth than her manners stands in her light—there ain't a horse on this farm that ain't a woman's horse, an' proud of it. An' this yer bogspavined Kansas sunflower goes up an' daown the length o' the country, traded off an' traded on, boastin' as he's shed women—an' childern. I don't say as a woman in a buggy ain't a fool. I don't say as she ain't the lastin'est kind er fool, ner I don't say a child ain't worse—

spattin' the lines an' standin' up an' hollerin'—but I do say, 'tain't none of our business to shed 'em daown the road."

"We don't," said the Deacon. "The baby tried to git some o' my tail for a sooveneer last fall when I was up to the haouse, an' I didn't kick. Boney's talk ain't goin' to hurt us any. We ain't colts."

"Thet's what you think Bimeby you git into a tight corner, 'Lection day er Valley Fair, like's not, daown-taown, when you're all het an' lathery, an' pestered with flies, an' thirsty, an' sick o' bein' worked in an aout 'tween buggies. Then somethin' whispers inside o' your winkers, bringin' up all that talk abaout servitood an' inalienable truck an' sech like, an' jest then a Militia gun goes off; er your wheels hit, an'—waal, you're only another horse ez can't be trusted. I've been there time an' again. Boys—fer I've seen you all bought er broke—on my solemn repitation fer a three-minute clip, I ain't givin' you no bran-mash o' my own fixin'. I'm tellin' you my experiences, an' I've had ez heavy a load an' ez high a check's any horse here. I wuz born with a splint on my near fore ez big's a walnut, an' the cussed, three-cornered Hambletonian temper that sours up an' curdles daown ez you git older. I've favoured my splint; even little Rick he don't know what it's cost me to keep my end up sometimes; an' I've fit my temper in stall an' harness, hitched up an' at pasture, till the sweat trickled off my hooves, an' they thought I wuz off condition, an' drenched me."

"When my affliction came," said Tweezy, gently, "I was very near to losin' my manners. Allow me to extend to you my sympathy, suh."

Rick said nothing, but he looked at Rod curiously. Rick is a sunny-tempered child who never bears malice, and I don't think he quite understood. He gets his temper from his mother, as a horse should.

"I've been there too, Rod," said Tedda. "Open confession's good for the soul, an' all Monroe County knows I've had my experriences."

"But if you will excuse me, suh, that pusson"—Tweezy looked unspeakable things at the yellow horse—"that pusson who has insulted our intelligences comes from Kansas. An' what a ho'se of his position, an' Kansas at that, says cannot, by any stretch of the halter, concern gentlemen of our position. There's no shadow of equal'ty, suh, not even for one kick. He's beneath our contempt."

"Let him talk," said Marcus. "It's always interestin' to know what another horse thinks. It don't tech us."

"An' he talks so, too," said Tuck. "I've never heard anythin' so smart for a long time."

Again Rod stuck out his jaws sidewise, and went on slowly, as though he were slugging on a plain bit at the end of a thirty-mile drive:

"I want all you here ter understand thet ther ain't no Kansas, ner no Kentucky, ner yet no Vermont, in our business. There's jest two kind o' horse in the United States—them ez can an' will do their work after bein' properly broke an' handled, an' them as won't. I'm sick an' tired o' this everlastin' tail-switchin' an' wickerin' abaout one State er another. A horse kin be proud o' his State, an' swap lies abaout it in stall or when he's hitched to a block, ef he keers to put in fly-time that way; but he hain't no right to let that pride o' hisn interfere with his work, ner to make it an excuse fer claimin' he's different. That's colts' talk, an' don't you fergit it, Tweezy. An', Marcus, you remember that hem' a philosopher, an' anxious to save trouble,—fer you ate,—don't excuse you from jumpin' with all your feet on a slack-jawed, crazy clay-bank like Boney here. It's leavin' 'em alone that gives 'em their chance to ruin colts an' kill folks. An', Tuck, waal, you're a mare anyways—but when a horse comes along an' covers up all his talk o' killin' with ripplin' brooks, an wavin grass, an' eight quarts of oats a day free, after killn' his man, don't you be run away with by his yap. You're too young an' too nervous."

"I'll—I'll have nervous prostration sure ef there's a fight here," said Tuck, who saw what was in Rod's eye; "I'm—I'm that sympathetic I'd run away clear to next caounty."

"Yep; I know that kind o' sympathy. Jest lasts long enough to start a fuss, an' then lights aout to make new trouble. I hain't been ten years in harness fer nuthin'. Naow, we're goin' to keep school with Boney fer a spell."

"Say, look a-here, you ain't goin' to hurt me, are you? Remember, I belong to a man in town," cried the yellow horse, uneasily. Muldoon kept behind him so that he could not run away.

"I know it. There must be some pore delooded fool in this State hez a right to the loose end o' your hitchin'-strap. I'm blame sorry fer him, but he shall hev his rights when we're through with you," said Rod.

"If it's all the same, gentlemen, I'd ruther change pasture. Guess I'll do it now."

"'Can't always have your 'druthers. 'Guess you won't," said Rod.

"But look a-here. All of you ain't so blame unfriendly to a stranger. S'pose we count noses."

"What in Vermont fer?" said Rod, putting up his eyebrows. The idea of settling a question by counting noses is the very last thing that ever enters the head of a well-broken horse.

"To see how many's on my side. Here's Miss Tuck, anyway; an' Colonel Tweezy yonder's neutral; an' Judge Marcus, an' I guess the Reverend [the yellow horse meant the Deacon] might see that I had my rights. He's the likeliest-lookin' Trotter I've ever set eyes on. Pshaw. Boys. You ain't goin' to pound me, be you? Why, we've gone round in pasture, all colts together, this month o' Sundays, hain't we, as friendly as could be. There ain't a horse alive I don't care who he is—has a higher opinion o' you, Mr. Rod, than I have. Let's do it fair an' true an' above the exe. Let's count noses same's they do in Kansas." Here he dropped his voice a little and turned to Marcus: "Say, Judge, there's some green food I know, back o' the brook, no one hain't touched yet. After this little fracas is fixed up, you an' me'll make up a party an' 'tend to it."

Marcus did not answer for a long time, then he said: "There's a pup up to the haouse 'bout eight weeks old. He'll yap till he gits a lickin', an' when he sees it comin' he lies on his back, an' yowls. But he don't go through no cirkituous nose-countin' first. I've seen a noo light sence Rod spoke. You'll better stand up to what's served. I'm goin' to philosophise all over your carcass."

"I'm goin' to do yer up in brown paper," said Muldoon. "I can fit you on apologies."

"Hold on. Ef we all biffed you now, these same men you've been so dead anxious to kill 'u'd call us off. 'Guess we'll wait till they go back to the haouse, an' you'll have time to think cool an' quiet," said Rod.

"Have you no respec' whatever fer the dignity o' our common horsehood?" the yellow horse squealed.

"Nary respec' onless the horse kin do something. America's paved with the kind er horse you are—jist plain yaller-dog horse—waitin' ter be whipped inter shape. We call 'em yearlings an' colts when they're young. When they're aged we pound 'em—in this pastur'. Horse, sonny, is what you start from. We know all about horse here, an' he ain't any high-toned, pure souled child o' nature. Horse, plain horse, same ez you, is chock-full o' tricks, an' meannesses, an' cussednesses, an' shirkin's, an' monkey-shines, which he's took over from his sire an' his dam, an' thickened up with his own special fancy in the way o' goin' crooked. Thet's horse, an' thet's about his dignity an' the size of his soul 'fore he's been broke an' rawhided a piece. Now we ain't goin' to give ornery unswitched horse, that hain't done nawthin' wuth a quart of oats sence he wuz foaled, pet names that would be good enough fer Nancy Hanks, or Alix, or Directum, who hev. Don't you try to back off acrost them rocks. Wait where you are! Ef I let my Hambletonian temper git the better o' me I'd frazzle you out finer than rye-straw inside o' three minutes, you woman-scarin', kid-killin', dash-breakin', unbroke, unshod, ungaited, pastur'-hoggin', saw-backed, shark-mouthed, hair-trunk-thrown-in-in-trade son of a bronco an' a sewin'-machine!"

"I think we'd better get home," I said to my companion, when Rod had finished; and we climbed into the coupe, Tedda whinnying, as we bumped over the ledges: "Well, I'm dreffle sorry I can't stay fer the sociable; but I hope an' trust my friends'll take a ticket fer me."

"Bet your natchul!" said Muldoon, cheerfully, and the horses scattered before us, trotting into the ravine.

Next morning we sent back to the livery-stable what was left of the yellow horse. It seemed tired, but anxious to go.

THE SHIP THAT FOUND HERSELF

It was her first voyage, and though she was but a cargo-steamer of twenty-five hundred tons, she was the very best of her kind, the outcome of forty years of experiments and improvements in framework and machinery; and her designers and owner thought as much of her as though she had been the Lucania. Any one can make a floating hotel that will pay expenses, if he puts enough money into the saloon, and charges for private baths, suites of rooms, and such like; but in these days of competition and low freights every square inch of a cargo-boat must be built for cheapness, great hold-capacity, and a certain steady speed. This boat was, perhaps, two hundred and forty feet long and thirty-two feet wide, with arrangements that enabled her to carry cattle on her main and sheep on her upper deck if she wanted to; but her great glory was the amount of cargo that she could store away in her holds. Her owners—they were a very well known Scotch firm—came round with her from the north, where she had been launched and christened and fitted, to Liverpool, where she was to take cargo for New York; and the owner's daughter, Miss Frazier, went to and fro on the clean decks, admiring the new paint and the brass work, and the patent winches, and particularly the strong, straight bow, over which she had cracked a bottle of champagne when she named the steamer the Dimbula. It was a beautiful September afternoon, and the boat in all her newness—she was painted lead-colour with a red funnel—looked very fine indeed. Her house-flag was flying, and her whistle from time to time acknowledged the salutes of friendly boats, who saw that she was new to the High and Narrow Seas and wished to make her welcome.

"And now," said Miss Frazier, delightedly, to the captain, "she's a real ship, isn't she? It seems only the other day father gave the order for her, and now—and now—isn't she a beauty!" The girl was proud of the firm, and talked as though she were the controlling partner.

"Oh, she's no so bad," the skipper replied cautiously. "But I'm sayin' that it takes more than christenin' to mak' a ship. In the nature o' things, Miss Frazier, if ye follow me, she's just irons and rivets and plates put into the form of a ship. She has to find herself yet."

"I thought father said she was exceptionally well found."

"So she is," said the skipper, with a laugh. "But it's this way wi' ships, Miss Frazier. She's all here, but the parrts of her have not learned to work together yet. They've had no chance."

"The engines are working beautifully. I can hear them."

"Yes, indeed. But there's more than engines to a ship. Every inch of her, ye'll understand, has to be livened up and made to work wi' its neighbour—sweetenin' her, we call it, technically."

"And how will you do it?" the girl asked.

"We can no more than drive and steer her and so forth; but if we have rough weather this trip—it's likely—she'll learn the rest by heart! For a ship, ye'll obsairve, Miss Frazier, is in no sense a reegid body closed at both ends. She's a highly complex structure o' various an' conflictin' strains, wi' tissues that must give an' tak' accordin' to her personal modulus of elasteecity." Mr. Buchanan, the chief engineer, was coming towards them. "I'm sayin' to Miss Frazier, here, that our little Dimbula has to be sweetened yet, and nothin' but a gale will do it. How's all wi' your engines, Buck?"

"Well enough—true by plumb an' rule, o' course; but there's no spontaneeity yet." He turned to the girl. "Take my word, Miss Frazier, and maybe ye'll comprehend later; even after a pretty girl's christened a ship it does not follow that there's such a thing as a ship under the men that work her."

"I was sayin' the very same, Mr. Buchanan," the skipper interrupted.

"That's more metaphysical than I can follow," said Miss Frazier, laughing.

"Why so? Ye're good Scotch, an'—I knew your mother's father, he was fra' Dumfries—ye've a vested right in metapheesics, Miss Frazier, just as ye have in the Dimbula," the engineer said.

"Eh, well, we must go down to the deep watters, an' earn Miss Frazier her deevidends. Will you not come to my cabin for tea?" said the skipper. "We'll be in dock the night, and when you're goin' back to Glasgie ye can think of us loadin' her down an' drivin' her forth—all for your sake."

In the next few days they stowed some four thousand tons dead-weight into the Dimbula, and took her out from Liverpool. As soon as she met the lift of the open water, she naturally began to talk. If you lay your ear to the side of the cabin, the next time you are in a steamer, you will hear hundreds of little voices in every direction, thrilling and buzzing, and whispering and popping, and gurgling and sobbing and squeaking exactly like a telephone in a thunder-storm. Wooden ships shriek and growl and grunt, but iron vessels throb and quiver through all their hundreds of ribs and thousands of rivets. The Dimbula was very strongly built, and every piece of her had a letter or a number, or both, to describe it; and every piece had been hammered, or forged, or rolled, or punched by man, and had lived in the roar and rattle of the shipyard for months. Therefore, every piece had its own separate voice, in exact proportion to the amount of trouble spent upon it. Cast-iron, as a rule, says very little; but mild steel plates and wrought-iron, and ribs and beams that have been much bent and welded and riveted, talk continuously. Their conversation, of course, is not half as wise as our human talk, because they are all, though they do not know it, bound down one to the other in a black darkness, where they cannot tell what is happening near them, nor what will overtake them next.

As soon as she had cleared the Irish coast, a sullen, grey-headed old wave of the Atlantic climbed leisurely over her straight bows, and sat down on the steam-capstan used for hauling up the anchor. Now the capstan and the engine that drove it had been newly painted red and green; besides which, nobody likes being ducked.

"Don't you do that again," the capstan sputtered through the teeth of his cogs. "Hi! Where's the fellow gone?"

The wave had slouched overside with a plop and a chuckle; but "Plenty more where he came from," said a brother-wave, and went through and over the capstan, who was bolted firmly to an iron plate on the iron deckbeams below.

"Can't you keep still up there?" said the deckbeams. "What's the matter with you? One minute you weigh twice as much as you ought to, and the next you don't!"

"It isn't my fault," said the capstan. "There's a green brute outside that comes and hits me on the head."

"Tell that to the shipwrights. You've been in position for months and you've never wriggled like this before. If you aren't careful you'll strain us."

"Talking of strain," said a low, rasping, unpleasant voice, "are any of you fellows—you deckbeams, we mean—aware that those exceedingly ugly knees of yours happen to be riveted into our structure—ours?"

"Who might you be?" the deckbeams inquired.

"Oh, nobody in particular," was the answer. "We're only the port and starboard upper-deck stringers; and if you persist in heaving and hiking like this, we shall be reluctantly compelled to take steps."

Now the stringers of the ship are long iron girders, so to speak, that run lengthways from stern to bow. They keep the iron frames (what are called ribs in a wooden ship) in place, and also help to hold the ends of the deckbeams, which go from side to side of the ship. Stringers always consider themselves most important, because they are so long.

"You will take steps—will you?" This was a long echoing rumble. It came from the frames—scores and scores of them, each one about eighteen inches distant from the next, and each riveted to the stringers in four places. "We think you will have a certain amount of trouble in that"; and thousands and thousands of the little rivets that held everything together whispered: "You Will! You will! Stop quivering and be quiet. Hold on, brethren! Hold on! Hot Punches! What's that?"

Rivets have no teeth, so they cannot chatter with fright; but they did their best as a fluttering jar swept along the ship from stern to bow, and she shook like a rat in a terrier's mouth.

An unusually severe pitch, for the sea was rising, had lifted the big throbbing screw nearly to the surface, and it was spinning round in a kind of soda-water—half sea and half air—going much faster than was proper, because there was no deep water for it to work in. As it sank again, the engines—and they were triple expansion, three cylinders in a row—snorted through all their three pistons. "Was that a joke, you fellow outside? It's an uncommonly poor one. How are we to do our work if you fly off the handle that way?"

"I didn't fly off the handle," said the screw, twirling huskily at the end of the screw-shaft. "If I had, you'd have been scrap-iron by this time. The sea dropped away from under me, and I had nothing to catch on to. That's all."

"That's all, d'you call it?" said the thrust-block, whose business it is to take the push of the screw; for if a screw had nothing to hold it back it would crawl right into the engine-room. (It is the holding back of the screwing action that gives the drive to a ship.) "I know I do my work deep down and out of sight, but I warn you I expect justice. All I ask for is bare justice. Why can't you push steadily and evenly, instead of whizzing like a whirligig, and making me hot under all my collars?" The thrust-block had six collars, each faced with brass, and he did not wish to get them heated.

All the bearings that supported the fifty feet of screw-shaft as it ran to the stern whispered: "Justice—give us justice."

"I can only give you what I can get," the screw answered. "Look out! It's coming again!"

He rose with a roar as the Dimbula plunged, and "whack—flack—whack— whack" went the engines, furiously, for they had little to check them.

"I'm the noblest outcome of human ingenuity—Mr. Buchanan says so," squealed the high-pressure cylinder. "This is simply ridiculous!" The piston went up savagely, and choked, for half the steam behind it was mixed with dirty water. "Help! Oiler! Fitter! Stoker! Help I'm choking," it gasped. "Never in the history of maritime invention has such a calamity over-taken one so young and strong. And if I go, who's to drive the ship?"

"Hush! oh, hush!" whispered the Steam, who, of course, had been to sea many times before. He used to spend his leisure ashore in a cloud, or a gutter, or a flower-pot, or a thunder-storm, or anywhere else where water was needed. "That's only a little priming, a little carrying-over, as they call it. It'll happen all night, on and off. I don't say it's nice, but it's the best we can do under the circumstances."

"What difference can circumstances make? I'm here to do my work—on clean, dry steam. Blow circumstances!" the cylinder roared.

"The circumstances will attend to the blowing. I've worked on the North Atlantic run a good many times—it's going to be rough before morning."

"It isn't distressingly calm now," said the extra strong frames—they were called web-frames—in the engine-room. "There's an upward thrust that we don't understand, and there's a twist that is very bad for our brackets and diamond-plates, and there's a sort of west-northwesterly pull, that follows the twist, which seriously annoys us. We mention this because we happened to cost a good deal of money, and we feel sure that the owner would not approve of our being treated in this frivolous way."

"I'm afraid the matter is out of owner's hands for the present," said the Steam, slipping into the condenser. "You're left to your own devices till the weather betters."

"I wouldn't mind the weather," said a flat bass voice below; "it's this confounded cargo that's breaking my heart. I'm the garboard-strake, and I'm twice as thick as most of the others, and I ought to know something."

The garboard-strake is the lowest plate in the bottom of a ship, and the Dimbula's garboard-strake was nearly three-quarters of an inch mild steel.

"The sea pushes me up in a way I should never have expected," the strake grunted, "and the cargo pushes me down, and, between the two, I don't know what I'm supposed to do."

"When in doubt, hold on," rumbled the Steam, making head in the boilers.

"Yes; but there's only dark, and cold, and hurry, down here; and how do I know whether the other plates are doing their duty? Those bulwark-plates up above, I've heard, ain't more than five-sixteenths of an inch thick—scandalous, I call it."

"I agree with you," said a huge web-frame, by the main cargo-hatch. He was deeper and thicker than all the others, and curved half-way across the ship in the shape of half an arch, to support the deck where deckbeams would have been in the way of cargo coming up and down. "I work entirely unsupported, and I observe that I am the sole strength of this vessel, so far as my vision extends. The responsibility, I assure you, is enormous. I believe the money-value of the cargo is over one hundred and fifty thousand pounds. Think of that!"

"And every pound of it is dependent on my personal exertions." Here spoke a sea-valve that communicated directly with the water outside, and was seated not very far from the garboard-strake. "I rejoice to think that I am a Prince-Hyde Valve, with best Para rubber facings. Five patents cover me—I mention this without pride—five separate and several patents, each one finer than the other. At present I am screwed fast. Should I open, you would immediately be swamped. This is incontrovertible!"

Patent things always use the longest words they can. It is a trick that they pick up from their inventors.

"That's news," said a big centrifugal bilge-pump. "I had an idea that you were employed to clean decks and things with. At least, I've used you for that more than once. I forget the precise number, in thousands, of gallons which I am guaranteed to throw per hour; but I assure you, my complaining friends, that there is not the least danger. I alone am capable of clearing any water that may find its way here. By my Biggest Deliveries, we pitched then!"

The sea was getting up in workmanlike style. It was a dead westerly gale, blown from under a ragged opening of green sky, narrowed on all sides by fat, grey clouds; and the wind bit like pincers as it fretted the spray into lacework on the flanks of the waves.

"I tell you what it is," the foremast telephoned down its wire-stays. "I'm up here, and I can take a dispassionate view of things. There's an organised conspiracy against us. I'm sure of it, because every single one of these waves is heading directly for our bows. The whole sea is concerned in it—and so's the wind. It's awful!"

"What's awful?" said a wave, drowning the capstan for the hundredth time.

"This organised conspiracy on your part," the capstan gurgled, taking his cue from the mast. "Organised bubbles and spindrift! There has been a depression in the Gulf of Mexico. Excuse me!" He leaped overside; but his friends took up the tale one after another.

"Which has advanced— " That wave hove green water over the funnel.

"As far as Cape Hatteras— " He drenched the bridge.

"And is now going out to sea—to sea—to sea!" The third went out in three surges, making a clean sweep of a boat, which turned bottom up and sank in the darkening troughs alongside, while the broken falls whipped the davits.

"That's all there is to it," seethed the white water roaring through the scuppers. "There's no animus in our proceedings. We're only meteorological corollaries."

"Is it going to get any worse?" said the bow-anchor chained down to the deck, where he could only breathe once in five minutes.

"Not knowing, can't say. Wind may blow a bit by midnight. Thanks awfully. Good-bye."

The wave that spoke so politely had travelled some distance aft, and found itself all mixed up on the deck amidships, which was a well-deck sunk between high bulwarks. One of the bulwark-plates, which was hung on hinges to open outward, had swung out, and passed the bulk of the water back to the sea again with a clean smack.

"Evidently that's what I'm made for," said the plate, closing again with a sputter of pride. "Oh, no, you don't, my friend!" The top of a wave was trying to get in from the outside, but as the plate did not open in that direction, the defeated water spurted back.

"Not bad for five-sixteenths of an inch," said the bulwark-plate. "My work, I see, is laid down for the night"; and it began opening and shutting, as it was designed to do, with the motion of the ship.

"We are not what you might call idle," groaned all the frames together, as the Dimbula climbed a big wave, lay on her side at the top, and shot into the next hollow, twisting in the descent. A huge swell pushed up exactly under her middle, and her bow and stern hung free with nothing to support them. Then one joking wave caught her up at the bow, and another at the stern, while the rest of the water slunk away from under her just to see how she would like it; so she was held up at her two ends only, and the weight of the cargo and the machinery fell on the groaning iron keels and bilge-stringers.

"Ease off! Ease off; there!" roared the garboard-strake. "I want one-eighth of an inch fair play. D' you hear me, you rivets!"

"Ease off! Ease off!" cried the bilge-stringers. "Don't hold us so tight to the frames!"

"Ease off!" grunted the deckbeams, as the Dimbula rolled fearfully. "You've cramped our knees into the stringers, and we can't move. Ease off; you flat-headed little nuisances."

Then two converging seas hit the bows, one on each side, and fell away in torrents of streaming thunder.

"Ease off!" shouted the forward collision-bulkhead. "I want to crumple up, but I'm stiffened in every direction. Ease off; you dirty little forge-filings. Let me breathe!"

All the hundreds of plates that are riveted to the frames, and make the outside skin of every steamer, echoed the call, for each plate wanted to shift and creep a little, and each plate, according to its position, complained against the rivets.

"We can't help it! We can't help it!" they murmured in reply. "We're put here to hold you, and we're going to do it; you never pull us twice in the same direction. If you'd say what you were going to do next, we'd try to meet your views.

"As far as I could feel," said the upper-deck planking, and that was four inches thick, "every single iron near me was pushing or pulling in opposite directions. Now, what's the sense of that? My friends, let us all pull together."

"Pull any way you please," roared the funnel, "so long as you don't try your experiments on me. I need fourteen wire-ropes, all pulling in different directions, to hold me steady. Isn't that so?"

"We believe you, my boy!" whistled the funnel-stays through their clinched teeth, as they twanged in the wind from the top of the funnel to the deck.

"Nonsense! We must all pull together," the decks repeated. "Pull lengthways."

"Very good," said the stringers; "then stop pushing sideways when you get wet. Be content to run gracefully fore and aft, and curve in at the ends as we do."

"No—no curves at the end. A very slight workmanlike curve from side to side, with a good grip at each knee, and little pieces welded on," said the deckbeams.

"Fiddle!" cried the iron pillars of the deep, dark hold. "Who ever heard of curves? Stand up straight; be a perfectly round column, and carry tons of good solid weight—like that! There!" A big sea smashed on the deck above, and the pillars stiffened themselves to the load.

"Straight up and down is not bad," said the frames, who ran that way in the sides of the ship, "but you must also expand yourselves sideways. Expansion is the law of life, children. Open out! open out!"

"Come back!" said the deckbeams, savagely, as the upward heave of the sea made the frames try to open. "Come back to your bearings, you slack-jawed irons!"

"Rigidity! Rigidity! Rigidity!" thumped the engines. "Absolute, unvarying rigidity—rigidity!"

"You see!" whined the rivets, in chorus. "No two of you will ever pull alike, and—and you blame it all on us. We only know how to go through a plate and bite down on both sides so that it can't, and mustn't, and sha'n't move."

"I've got one fraction of an inch play, at any rate," said the garboard-strake, triumphantly. So he had, and all the bottom of the ship felt the easier for it.

"Then we're no good," sobbed the bottom rivets. "We were ordered—we were ordered—never to give; and we've given, and the sea will come in, and we'll all go to the bottom together! First we're blamed for everything unpleasant, and now we haven't the consolation of having done our work."

"Don't say I told you," whispered the Steam, consolingly; "but, between you and me and the last cloud I came from, it was bound to happen sooner or later. You had to give a fraction, and you've given without knowing it. Now, hold on, as before."

"What's the use?" a few hundred rivets chattered. "We've given—we've given; and the sooner we confess that we can't keep the ship together, and go off our little heads, the easier it will be. No rivet forged can stand this strain."

"No one rivet was ever meant to. Share it among you," the Steam answered.

"The others can have my share. I'm going to pull out," said a rivet in one of the forward plates.

"If you go, others will follow," hissed the Steam. "There's nothing so contagious in a boat as rivets going. Why, I knew a little chap like you—he was an eighth of an inch fatter, though—on a steamer—to be sure, she was only twelve hundred tons, now I come to think of it in exactly the same place as you are. He pulled out in a bit of a bobble of a sea, not half as bad as this, and he started all his friends on the same butt-strap, and the plates opened like a furnace door, and I had to climb into the nearest fog-bank, while the boat went down."

"Now that's peculiarly disgraceful," said the rivet. "Fatter than me, was he, and in a steamer not half our tonnage? Reedy little peg! I blush for the family, sir." He settled himself more firmly than ever in his place, and the Steam chuckled.

"You see," he went on, quite gravely, "a rivet, and especially a rivet in your position, is really the one indispensable part of the ship."

The Steam did not say that he had whispered the very same thing to every single piece of iron aboard. There is no sense in telling too much.

And all that while the little Dimbula pitched and chopped, and swung and slewed, and lay down as though she were going to die, and got up as though she had been stung, and threw her nose round and round in circles half a dozen times as she dipped, for the gale was at its worst. It was inky black, in spite of the tearing white froth on the waves, and, to top everything, the rain began to fall in sheets, so that you could not see your hand before your face. This did not make much difference to the ironwork below, but it troubled the foremast a good deal.

"Now it's all finished," he said dismally. "The conspiracy is too strong for us. There is nothing left but to— "

"Hurraar! Brrrraaah! Brrrrrrp!" roared the Steam through the fog-horn, till the decks quivered. "Don't be frightened, below. It's only me, just throwing out a few words, in case any one happens to be rolling round to-night."

"You don't mean to say there's any one except us on the sea in such weather?" said the funnel, in a husky snuffle.

"Scores of 'em," said the Steam, clearing its throat. "Rrrrrraaa! Brraaaaa! Prrrrp! It's a trifle windy up here; and, Great Boilers! how it rains!"

"We're drowning," said the scuppers. They had been doing nothing else all night, but this steady thrash of rain above them seemed to be the end of the world.

"That's all right. We'll be easier in an hour or two. First the wind and then the rain. Soon you may make sail again! Grrraaaaaah! Drrrraaaa! Drrrp! I have a notion that the sea is going down already. If it does you'll learn something about rolling. We've only pitched till now. By the way, aren't you chaps in the hold a little easier than you were?"

There was just as much groaning and straining as ever, but it was not so loud or squeaky in tone; and when the ship quivered she did not jar stiffly, like a poker hit on the floor, but gave with a supple little waggle, like a perfectly balanced golf-club.

"We have made a most amazing discovery," said the stringers, one after another. "A discovery that entirely changes the situation. We have found, for the first time in the history of ship-building, that the inward pull of the deckbeams and the outward thrust of the frames locks us, as it were, more closely in our places, and enables us to endure a strain which is entirely without parallel in the records of marine architecture."

The Steam turned a laugh quickly into a roar up the fog-horn. "What massive intellects you great stringers have," he said softly, when he had finished.

"We also," began the deckbeams, "are discoverers and geniuses. We are of opinion that the support of the hold-pillars materially helps us. We find that we lock up on them when we are subjected to a heavy and singular weight of sea above."

Here the Dimbula shot down a hollow, lying almost on her side; righting at the bottom with a wrench and a spasm.

"In these cases—are you aware of this, Steam?—the plating at the bows, and particularly at the stern—we would also mention the floors beneath us—help us to resist any tendency to spring." The frames spoke, in the solemn awed voice which people use when they have just come across something entirely new for the very first time.

"I'm only a poor puffy little flutterer," said the Steam, "but I have to stand a good deal of pressure in my business. It's all tremendously interesting. Tell us some more. You fellows are so strong."

"Watch us and you'll see," said the bow-plates, proudly. "Ready, behind there! Here's the father and mother of waves coming! Sit tight, rivets all!"

A great sluicing comber thundered by, but through the scuffle and confusion the Steam could hear the low, quick cries of the ironwork as the various strains took them—cries like these: "Easy, now—easy! Now push for all your strength! Hold out! Give a fraction! Hold up! Pull in!

Shove crossways! Mind the strain at the ends! Grip, now! Bite tight! Let the water get away from under—and there she goes!"

The wave raced off into the darkness, shouting, "Not bad, that, if it's your first run!" and the drenched and ducked ship throbbed to the beat of the engines inside her. All three cylinders were white with the salt spray that had come down through the engine-room hatch; there was white fur on the canvas-bound steam-pipes, and even the bright-work deep below was speckled and soiled; but the cylinders had learned to make the most of steam that was half water, and were pounding along cheerfully.

"How's the noblest outcome of human ingenuity hitting it?" said the Steam, as he whirled through the engine-room.

"Nothing for nothing in this world of woe," the cylinders answered, as though they had been working for centuries, "and precious little for seventy-five pounds head. We've made two knots this last hour and a quarter! Rather humiliating for eight hundred horse-power, isn't it?"

"Well, it's better than drifting astern, at any rate. You seem rather less—how shall I put it—stiff in the back than you were."

"If you'd been hammered as we've been this night, you wouldn't be stiff—iff—iff; either. Theoreti—retti—retti—cally, of course, rigidity is the thing. Purrr—purr—practically, there has to be a little give and take. We found that out by working on our sides for five minutes at a stretch—chch—chh. How's the weather?"

"Sea's going down fast," said the Steam.

"Good business," said the high-pressure cylinder. "Whack her up, boys. They've given us five pounds more steam"; and he began humming the first bars of "Said the young Obadiah to the old Obadiah," which, as you may have noticed, is a pet tune among engines not built for high speed. Racing-liners with twin-screws sing "The Turkish Patrol" and the overture to the "Bronze Horse," and "Madame Angot," till something goes wrong, and then they render Gounod's "Funeral March of a Marionette," with variations.

"You'll learn a song of your own some fine day," said the Steam, as he flew up the fog-horn for one last bellow.

Next day the sky cleared and the sea dropped a little, and the Dimbula began to roll from side to side till every inch of iron in her was sick and giddy. But luckily they did not all feel ill at the same time: otherwise she would have opened out like a wet paper box.

The Steam whistled warnings as he went about his business: it is in this short, quick roll and tumble that follows a heavy sea that most of the accidents happen, for then everything thinks that the worst is over and goes off guard. So he orated and chattered till the beams and frames and floors and stringers and things had learned how to lock down and lock up on one another, and endure this new kind of strain.

They found ample time to practise, for they were sixteen days at sea, and it was foul weather till within a hundred miles of New York. The Dimbula picked up her pilot, and came in covered with salt and red rust. Her funnel was dirty-grey from top to bottom; two boats had been carried away; three copper ventilators looked like hats after a fight with the police; the bridge had a dimple in the middle of it; the house that covered the steam steering-gear was split as with hatchets; there was a bill for small repairs in the engine-room almost as long as the screw-shaft; the forward cargo-hatch fell into bucket-staves when they raised the iron cross-bars; and the steam-capstan had been badly wrenched on its bed. Altogether, as the skipper said, it was "a pretty general average."

"But she's soupled," he said to Mr. Buchanan. "For all her dead-weight she rode like a yacht. Ye mind that last blow off the Banks—I am proud of her, Buck."

"It's vera good," said the chief engineer, looking along the dishevelled decks. "Now, a man judgin' superfeecially would say we were a wreck, but we know otherwise—by experience."

Naturally everything in the Dimbula fairly stiffened with pride, and the foremast and the forward collision-bulkhead, who are pushing creatures, begged the Steam to warn the Port of New York of their arrival. "Tell those big boats all about us," they said. "They seem to take us quite as a matter of course."

It was a glorious, clear, dead calm morning, and in single file, with less than half a mile between each, their bands playing and their tugboats shouting and waving handkerchiefs, were the Majestic, the Paris, the Touraine, the Servia, the Kaiser Wilhelm II, and the Werkendam, all statelily going out to sea. As the Dimbula shifted her helm to give the great boats clear way, the Steam (who knows far too much to mind making an exhibition of himself now and then) shouted:

"Oyez! Oyez! Oyez! Princes, Dukes, and Barons of the High Seas! Know ye by these presents, we are the Dimbula, fifteen days nine hours from Liverpool, having crossed the Atlantic with four thousand ton of cargo for the first time in our career! We have not foundered. We are here. 'Eer! 'Eer! We are not disabled. But we have had a time wholly unparalleled in the annals of ship-building! Our decks were swept! We pitched; we rolled! We thought we were going to die! Hi! Hi! But we didn't. We wish to give notice that we have come to New York all the way across the Atlantic, through the worst weather in the world; and we are the Dimbula! We are—arr—ha—ha—ha-r-r-r!"

The beautiful line of boats swept by as steadily as the procession of the Seasons. The Dimbula heard the Majestic say, "Hmph!" and the Paris grunted, "How!" and the Touraine said, "Oui!" with a little coquettish flicker of steam; and the Servia said, "Haw!" and the Kaiser and the Werkendam said, "Hoch!" Dutch fashion—and that was absolutely all.

"I did my best," said the Steam, gravely, "but I don't think they were much impressed with us, somehow. Do you?"

"It's simply disgusting," said the bow-plates. "They might have seen what we've been through. There isn't a ship on the sea that has suffered as we have—is there, now?"

"Well, I wouldn't go so far as that," said the Steam, "because I've worked on some of those boats, and sent them through weather quite as bad as the fortnight that we've had, in six days; and some of them are a little over ten thousand tons, I believe. Now I've seen the Majestic, for instance, ducked from her bows to her funnel; and I've helped the Arizona, I think she was, to back off an iceberg she met with one dark night; and I had to run out of the Paris's engine-room, one day, because there was thirty foot of water in it. Of course, I don't deny—" The Steam shut off suddenly, as a tugboat, loaded with a political club and a brass band, that had been to see a New York Senator off to Europe, crossed their bows, going to Hoboken. There was a long silence that reached, without a break, from the cut-water to the propeller-blades of the Dimbula.

Then a new, big voice said slowly and thickly, as though the owner had just waked up: "It's my conviction that I have made a fool of myself."

The Steam knew what had happened at once; for when a ship finds herself all the talking of the separate pieces ceases and melts into one voice, which is the soul of the ship.

"Who are you?" he said, with a laugh. "I am the Dimbula, of course. I've never been anything else except that—and a fool!"

The tugboat, which was doing its very best to be run down, got away just in time; its band playing clashily and brassily a popular but impolite air:

In the days of old Rameses—are you on?

In the days of old Rameses—are you on?

In the days of old Rameses,

That story had paresis,

Are you on—are you on—are you on?

"Well, I'm glad you've found yourself," said the Steam. "To tell the truth, I was a little tired of talking to all those ribs and stringers. Here's

Quarantine. After that we'll go to our wharf and clean up a little, and—next month we'll do it all over again."

THE TOMB OF HIS ANCESTORS

Some people will tell you that if there were but a single loaf of bread in all India it would be divided equally between the Plowdens, the Trevors, the Beadons, and the Rivett-Carnacs. That is only one way of saying that certain families serve India generation after generation, as dolphins follow in line across the open sea.

Let us take a small and obscure case. There has been at least one representative of the Devonshire Chinns in or near Central India since the days of Lieutenant-Fireworker Humphrey Chinn, of the Bombay European Regiment, who assisted at the capture of Seringapatam in 1799. Alfred Ellis Chinn, Humphrey's younger brother, commanded a regiment of Bombay grenadiers from 1804 to 1813, when he saw some mixed fighting; and in 1834 John Chinn of the same family—we will call him John Chinn the First—came to light as a level-headed administrator in time of trouble at a place called Mundesur. He died young, but left his mark on the new country, and the Honourable the Board of Directors of the Honourable the East India Company embodied his virtues in a stately resolution, and paid for the expenses of his tomb among the Satpura hills.

He was succeeded by his son, Lionel Chinn, who left the little old Devonshire home just in time to be severely wounded in the Mutiny. He spent his working life within a hundred and fifty miles of John Chinn's grave, and rose to the command of a regiment of small, wild hill-men, most of whom had known his father. His son John was born in the small thatched-roofed, mud-walled cantonment, which is even to-day eighty miles from the nearest railway, in the heart of a scrubby, tigerish country. Colonel Lionel Chinn served thirty years and retired. In the Canal his steamer passed the outward-bound troop-ship, carrying his son eastward to the family duty.

The Chinns are luckier than most folk, because they know exactly what they must do. A clever Chinn passes for the Bombay Civil Service, and gets away to Central India, where everybody is glad to see him. A dull Chinn enters the Police Department or the Woods and Forest, and sooner or later he, too, appears in Central India, and that is what gave rise to the saying, "Central India is inhabited by Bhils, Mairs, and Chinns, all very much alike." The breed is small-boned, dark, and silent, and the stupidest of them are good shots. John Chinn the Second was rather clever, but as the eldest son he entered the army, according to Chinn tradition. His duty was to abide in his father's regiment for the term of his natural life, though the corps was one which most men would have paid heavily to avoid. They were irregulars, small, dark, and blackish, clothed in rifle-green with black-leather trimmings; and friends called them the "Wuddars," which means a race of low-caste people who dig up rats to eat. But the Wuddars did not resent it. They were the only Wuddars, and their points of pride were these:

Firstly, they had fewer English officers than any native regiment. Secondly, their subalterns were not mounted on parade, as is the general rule, but walked at the head of their men. A man who can hold his own with the Wuddars at their quickstep must be sound in wind and limb. Thirdly, they were the most pukka shikarries (out-and-out hunters) in all India. Fourthly-up to one-hundredthly—they were the Wuddars—Chinn's Irregular Bhil Levies of the old days, but now, henceforward and for ever, the Wuddars.

No Englishman entered their mess except for love or through family usage. The officers talked to their soldiers in a tongue not two hundred white folk in India understood; and the men were their children, all drawn from the Bhils, who are, perhaps, the strangest of the many strange races in India. They were, and at heart are, wild men, furtive, shy, full of untold superstitions. The races whom we call natives of the country found the Bhil in possession of the land when they first broke into that part of the world thousands of years ago. The books call them Pre-Aryan, Aboriginal, Dravidian, and so forth; and, in other words, that is what the Bhils call themselves. When a Rajput chief whose bards can sing his pedigree backwards for twelve hundred years is set on the throne, his investiture is not complete till he has been marked on the forehead with blood from the veins of a Bhil. The Rajputs say the ceremony has no meaning, but the Bhil knows that it is the last, last shadow of his old rights as the long-ago owner of the soil.

Centuries of oppression and massacre made the Bhil a cruel and half-crazy thief and cattle-stealer, and when the English came he seemed to be almost as open to civilisation as the tigers of his own jungles. But John Chinn the First, father of Lionel, grandfather of our John, went into his country, lived with him, learned his language, shot the deer that stole his poor crops, and won his confidence, so that some Bhils learned to plough and sow, while others were coaxed into the Company's service to police their friends.

When they understood that standing in line did not mean instant execution, they accepted soldiering as a cumbrous but amusing kind of sport, and were zealous to keep the wild Bhils under control. That was the thin edge of the wedge. John Chinn the First gave them written promises that, if they were good from a certain date, the Government would overlook previous offences; and since John Chinn was never known to break his word—he promised once to hang a Bhil locally esteemed invulnerable, and hanged him in front of his tribe for seven proved murders—the Bhils settled down as steadily as they knew how. It was slow, unseen work, of the sort that is being done all over India to-day; and though John Chinn's only reward came, as I have said, in the shape of a grave at Government expense, the little people of the hills never forgot him.

Colonel Lionel Chinn knew and loved them, too, and they were very fairly civilised, for Bhils, before his service ended. Many of them could hardly be distinguished from low-caste Hindoo farmers; but in the south, where John Chinn the First was buried, the wildest still clung to the Satpura ranges, cherishing a legend that some day Jan Chinn, as they called him, would return to his own. In the mean time they mistrusted the white man and his ways. The least excitement would stampede them, plundering, at random, and now and then killing; but if they were handled discreetly they grieved like children, and promised never to do it again.

The Bhils of the regiment—the uniformed men—were virtuous in many ways, but they needed humouring. They felt bored and homesick unless taken after tiger as beaters; and their cold-blooded daring—all Wuddars shoot tigers on foot: it is their caste-mark—made even the officers wonder. They would follow up a wounded tiger as unconcernedly as though it were a sparrow with a broken wing; and this through a country full of caves and rifts and pits, where a wild beast could hold a dozen men at his mercy. Now and then some little man was brought to barracks with his head smashed in or his ribs torn away; but his companions never learned caution; they contented themselves with settling the tiger.

Young John Chinn was decanted at the verandah of the Wuddars' lonely mess-house from the back seat of a two-wheeled cart, his gun-cases cascading all round him. The slender little, hookey-nosed boy looked forlorn as a strayed goat when he slapped the white dust off his knees, and the cart jolted down the glaring road. But in his heart he was contented. After all, this was the place where he had been born, and things were not much changed since he had been sent to England, a child, fifteen years ago.

There were a few new buildings, but the air and the smell and the sunshine were the same; and the little green men who crossed the parade-ground looked very familiar. Three weeks ago John Chinn would have said he did not remember a word of the Bhil tongue, but at the mess door he found his lips moving in sentences that he did not understand—bits of old nursery rhymes, and tail-ends of such orders as his father used to give the men.

The Colonel watched him come up the steps, and laughed.

"Look!" he said to the Major. "No need to ask the young un's breed. He's a pukka Chinn. 'Might be his father in the Fifties over again."
"'Hope he'll shoot as straight," said the Major. "He's brought enough ironmongery with him."
"'Wouldn't be a Chinn if he didn't. Watch him blowin' his nose. 'Regular Chinn beak. 'Flourishes his handkerchief like his father. It's the second edition—line for line."
"'Fairy tale, by Jove!" said the Major, peering through the slats of the jalousies. "If he's the lawful heir, he'll.... Now old Chinn could no more pass that chick without fiddling with it than...."
"His son!" said the Colonel, jumping up.
"Well, I be blowed!" said the Major. The boy's eye had been caught by a split-reed screen that hung on a slew between the veranda pillars, and, mechanically, he had tweaked the edge to set it level. Old Chinn had sworn three times a day at that screen for many years; he could never get it to his satisfaction.
His son entered the anteroom in the middle of a fivefold silence. They made him welcome for his father's sake and, as they took stock of him, for his own. He was ridiculously like the portrait of the Colonel on the wall, and when he had washed a little of the dust from his throat he went to his quarters with the old man's short, noiseless jungle-step.
"So much for heredity," said the Major. "That comes of four generations among the Bhils."
"And the men know it," said a Wing officer. "They've been waiting for this youth with their tongues hanging out. I am persuaded that, unless he absolutely beats 'em over the head, they'll lie down by companies and worship him."
"Nothin' like havin' a father before you," said the Major. "I'm a parvenu with my chaps. I've only been twenty years in the regiment, and my revered parent he was a simple squire. There's no getting at the bottom of a Bhil's mind. Now, why is the superior bearer that young Chinn brought with him fleeing across country with his bundle?" He stepped into the verandah, and shouted after the man—a typical new-joined subaltern's servant who speaks English and cheats in proportion.
"What is it?" he called.
"Plenty bad man here. I going, sar," was the reply. "Have taken Sahib's keys, and say will shoot."
"Doocid lucid—doocid convincin'. How those up-country thieves can leg it! He has been badly frightened by some one." The Major strolled to his quarters to dress for mess.
Young Chinn, walking like a man in a dream, had fetched a compass round the entire cantonment before going to his own tiny cottage. The captain's quarters, in which he had been born, delayed him for a little;

then he looked at the well on the parade-ground, where he had sat of evenings with his nurse, and at the ten-by-fourteen church, where the officers went to service if a chaplain of any official creed happened to come along. It seemed very small as compared with the gigantic buildings he used to stare up at, but it was the same place.

From time to time he passed a knot of silent soldiers, who saluted. They might have been the very men who had carried him on their backs when he was in his first knickerbockers. A faint light burned in his room, and, as he entered, hands clasped his feet, and a voice murmured from the floor.

"Who is it?" said young Chinn, not knowing he spoke in the Bhil tongue.

"I bore you in my arms, Sahib, when I was a strong man and you were a small one—crying, crying, crying! I am your servant, as I was your father's before you. We are all your servants."

Young Chinn could not trust himself to reply, and the voice went on:

"I have taken your keys from that fat foreigner, and sent him away; and the studs are in the shirt for mess. Who should know, if I do not know? And so the baby has become a man, and forgets his nurse; but my nephew shall make a good servant, or I will beat him twice a day."

Then there rose up, with a rattle, as straight as a Bhil arrow, a little white-haired wizened ape of a man, with medals and orders on his tunic, stammering, saluting, and trembling. Behind him a young and wiry Bhil, in uniform, was taking the trees out of Chinn's mess-boots.

Chinn's eyes were full of tears. The old man held out his keys.

"Foreigners are bad people. He will never come back again. We are all servants of your father's son. Has the Sahib forgotten who took him to see the trapped tiger in the village across the river, when his mother was so frightened and he was so brave?"

The scene came back to Chinn in great magic-lantern flashes. "Bukta!" he cried; and all in a breath: "You promised nothing should hurt me. Is it Bukta?"

The man was at his feet a second time. "He has not forgotten. He remembers his own people as his father remembered. Now can I die. But first I will live and show the Sahib how to kill tigers. That that yonder is my nephew. If he is not a good servant, beat him and send him to me, and I will surely kill him, for now the Sahib is with his own people. Ai, Jan haba—Jan haba! My Jan haba! I will stay here and see that this does his work well. Take off his boots, fool. Sit down upon the bed, Sahib, and let me look. It is Jan haba."

He pushed forward the hilt of his sword as a sign of service, which is an honour paid only to viceroys, governors, generals, or to little children whom one loves dearly. Chinn touched the hilt mechanically with three fingers, muttering he knew not what. It happened to be the old answer of his childhood, when Bukta in jest called him the little General Sahib.

The Major's quarters were opposite Chinn's, and when he heard his servant gasp with surprise he looked across the room. Then the Major sat on the bed and whistled; for the spectacle of the senior native commissioned officer of the regiment, an "unmixed" Bhil, a Companion of the Order of British India, with thirty-five years' spotless service in the army, and a rank among his own people superior to that of many Bengal princelings, valeting the last-joined subaltern, was a little too much for his nerves.

The throaty bugles blew the Mess-call that has a long legend behind it. First a few piercing notes like the shrieks of beaters in a far-away cover, and next, large, full, and smooth, the refrain of the wild song: "And oh, and oh, the green pulse of Mundore—Mundore!"

"All little children were in bed when the Sahib heard that call last," said Bukta, passing Chinn a clean handkerchief. The call brought back memories of his cot under the mosquito-netting, his mother's kiss, and the sound of footsteps growing fainter as he dropped asleep among his men. So he hooked the dark collar of his new mess-jacket, and went to dinner like a prince who has newly inherited his father's crown.

Old Bukta swaggered forth curling his whiskers. He knew his own value, and no money and no rank within the gift of the Government would have induced him to put studs in young officers' shirts, or to hand them clean ties. Yet, when he took off his uniform that night, and squatted among his fellows for a quiet smoke, he told them what he had done, and they said that he was entirely right. Thereat Bukta propounded a theory which to a white mind would have seemed raving insanity; but the whispering, level-headed little men of war considered it from every point of view, and thought that there might be a great deal in it.

At mess under the oil-lamps the talk turned as usual to the unfailing subject of shikar—big game-shooting of every kind and under all sorts of conditions. Young Chinn opened his eyes when he understood that each one of his companions had shot several tigers in the Wuddar style—on foot, that is—making no more of the business than if the brute had been a dog.

"In nine cases out of ten," said the Major, "a tiger is almost as dangerous as a porcupine. But the tenth time you come home feet first."

That set all talking, and long before midnight Chinn's brain was in a whirl with stories of tigers—man-eaters and cattle-killers each pursuing his own business as methodically as clerks in an office; new tigers that had lately come into such-and-such a district; and old, friendly beasts of great cunning, known by nicknames in the mess-such as "Puggy," who was lazy, with huge paws, and "Mrs. Malaprop," who turned up when you never expected her, and made female noises. Then they spoke of Bhil superstitions, a wide and picturesque field, till young Chinn hinted that they must be pulling his leg.

"'Deed, we aren't," said a man on his left. "We know all about you. You're a Chinn and all that, and you've a sort of vested right here; but if you don't believe what we're telling you, what will you do when old Bukta begins his stories? He knows about ghost-tigers, and tigers that go to a hell of their own; and tigers that walk on their hind feet; and your grandpapa's riding-tiger, as well. 'Odd he hasn't spoken of that yet."

"You know you've an ancestor buried down Satpura way, don't you?" said the Major, as Chinn smiled irresolutely.

"Of course I do," said Chinn, who had the chronicle of the Book of Chinn by heart. It lies in a worn old ledger on the Chinese lacquer table behind the piano in the Devonshire home, and the children are allowed to look at it on Sundays.

"Well, I wasn't sure. Your revered ancestor, my boy, according to the Bhils, has a tiger of his own—a saddle-tiger that he rides round the country whenever he feels inclined. I don't call it decent in an ex-Collector's ghost; but that is what the Southern Bhils believe. Even our men, who might be called moderately cool, don't care to beat that country if they hear that Jan Chinn is running about on his tiger. It is supposed to be a clouded animal—not stripy, but blotchy, like a tortoise-shell tom-cat. No end of a brute, it is, and a sure sign of war or pestilence or—or something. There's a nice family legend for you."

"What's the origin of it, d' you suppose?" said Chinn.

"Ask the Satpura Bhils. Old Jan Chinn was a mighty hunter before the Lord. Perhaps it was the tiger's revenge, or perhaps he's huntin' 'em still. You must go to his tomb one of these days and inquire. Bukta will probably attend to that. He was asking me before you came whether by any ill-luck you had already bagged your tiger. If not, he is going to enter you under his own wing. Of course, for you of all men it's imperative. You'll have a first-class time with Bukta."

The Major was not wrong. Bukta kept an anxious eye on young Chinn at drill, and it was noticeable that the first time the new officer lifted up his voice in an order the whole line quivered. Even the Colonel was taken aback, for it might have been Lionel Chinn returned from Devonshire with a new lease of life. Bukta had continued to develop his peculiar theory among his intimates, and it was accepted as a matter of faith in the lines, since every word and gesture on young Chinn's part so confirmed it.

The old man arranged early that his darling should wipe out the reproach of not having shot a tiger; but he was not content to take the first or any beast that happened to arrive. In his own villages he dispensed the high, low, and middle justice, and when his people—naked and fluttered—came to him with word of a beast marked down, he bade them send spies to the kills and the watering-places, that he might be sure the quarry was such an one as suited the dignity of such a man.

Three or four times the reckless trackers returned, most truthfully saying that the beast was mangy, undersized—a tigress worn with nursing, or a broken-toothed old male—and Bukta would curb young Chinn's impatience.

At last, a noble animal was marked down—a ten-foot cattle-killer with a huge roll of loose skin along the belly, glossy-hided, full-frilled about the neck, whiskered, frisky, and young. He had slain a man in pure sport, they said.

"Let him be fed," quoth Bukta, and the villagers dutifully drove out a cow to amuse him, that he might lie up near by.

Princes and potentates have taken ship to India and spent great moneys for the mere glimpse of beasts one-half as fine as this of Bukta's.

"It is not good," said he to the Colonel, when he asked for shooting-leave, "that my Colonel's son who may be—that my Colonel's son should lose his maidenhead on any small jungle beast. That may come after. I have waited long for this which is a tiger. He has come in from the Mair country. In seven days we will return with the skin."

The mess gnashed their teeth enviously. Bukta, had he chosen, might have invited them all. But he went out alone with Chinn, two days in a shooting-cart and a day on foot, till they came to a rocky, glary valley with a pool of good water in it. It was a parching day, and the boy very naturally stripped and went in for a bathe, leaving Bukta by the clothes. A white skin shows far against brown jungle, and what Bukta beheld on Chinn's back and right shoulder dragged him forward step by step with staring eyeballs.

"I'd forgotten it isn't decent to strip before a man of his position," said Chinn, flouncing in the water. "How the little devil stares! What is it, Bukta?" "The Mark!" was the whispered answer.

"It is nothing. You know how it is with my people!" Chinn was annoyed. The dull-red birth-mark on his shoulder, something like a conventionalised Tartar cloud, had slipped his memory or he would not have bathed. It occurred, so they said at home, in alternate generations, appearing, curiously enough, eight or nine years after birth, and, save that it was part of the Chinn inheritance, would not be considered pretty. He hurried ashore, dressed again, and went on till they met two or three Bhils, who promptly fell on their faces. "My people," grunted Bukta, not condescending to notice them. "And so your people, Sahib.

When I was a young man we were fewer, but not so weak. Now we are many, but poor stock. As may be remembered. How will you shoot him, Sahib? From a tree; from a shelter which my people shall build; by day or by night?"

"On foot and in the daytime," said young Chinn.

"That was your custom, as I have heard," said Bukta to himself "I will get news of him. Then you and I will go to him. I will carry one gun. You have yours. There is no need of more. What tiger shall stand against thee?"

He was marked down by a little water-hole at the head of a ravine, full-gorged and half asleep in the May sunlight. He was walked up like a partridge, and he turned to do battle for his life. Bukta made no motion to raise his rifle, but kept his eyes on Chinn, who met the shattering roar of the charge with a single shot—it seemed to him hours as he sighted—which tore through the throat, smashing the backbone below the neck and between the shoulders. The brute couched, choked, and fell, and before Chinn knew well what had happened Bukta bade him stay still while he paced the distance between his feet and the ringing jaws.

"Fifteen," said Bukta. "Short paces. No need for a second shot, Sahib. He bleeds cleanly where he lies, and we need not spoil the skin. I said there would be no need of these, but they came—in case."

Suddenly the sides of the ravine were crowned with the heads of Bukta's people—a force that could have blown the ribs out of the beast had Chinn's shot failed; but their guns were hidden, and they appeared as interested beaters, some five or six waiting the word to skin. Bukta watched the life fade from the wild eyes, lifted one hand, and turned on his heel.

"No need to show that we care," said he. "Now, after this, we can kill what we choose. Put out your hand, Sahib."

Chinn obeyed. It was entirely steady, and Bukta nodded. "That also was your custom. My men skin quickly. They will carry the skin to cantonments. Will the Sahib come to my poor village for the night and, perhaps, forget that I am his officer?"

"But those men—the beaters. They have worked hard, and perhaps—"

"Oh, if they skin clumsily, we will skin them. They are my people. In the lines I am one thing. Here I am another."

This was very true. When Bukta doffed uniform and reverted to the fragmentary dress of his own people, he left his civilisation of drill in the next world. That night, after a little talk with his subjects, he devoted to an orgie; and a Bhil orgie is a thing not to be safely written about. Chinn, flushed with triumph, was in the thick of it, but the meaning of the mysteries was hidden. Wild folk came and pressed about his knees with offerings. He gave his flask to the elders of the village. They grew eloquent, and wreathed him about with flowers. Gifts and loans, not all seemly, were thrust upon him, and infernal music rolled and maddened round red fires, while singers sang songs of the ancient times, and danced peculiar dances. The aboriginal liquors are very potent, and Chinn was compelled to taste them often, but, unless the stuff had been drugged, how came he to fall asleep suddenly, and to waken late the next day—half a march from the village?

"The Sahib was very tired. A little before dawn he went to sleep," Bukta explained. "My people carried him here, and now it is time we should go back to cantonments."

The voice, smooth and deferential, the step, steady and silent, made it hard to believe that only a few hours before Bukta was yelling and capering with naked fellow-devils of the scrub.

"My people were very pleased to see the Sahib. They will never forget. When next the Sahib goes out recruiting, he will go to my people, and they will give him as many men as we need."

Chinn kept his own counsel, except as to the shooting of the tiger, and Bukta embroidered that tale with a shameless tongue. The skin was certainly one of the finest ever hung up in the mess, and the first of many. When Bukta could not accompany his boy on shooting-trips, he took care to put him in good hands, and Chinn learned more of the mind and desire of the wild Bhil in his marches and campings, by talks at twilight or at wayside pools, than an uninstructed man could have come at in a lifetime.

Presently his men in the regiment grew bold to speak of their relatives—mostly in trouble—and to lay cases of tribal custom before him. They would say, squatting in his verandah at twilight, after the easy, confidential style of the Wuddars, that such-and-such a bachelor had run away with such-and-such a wife at a far-off village. Now, how many cows would Chinn Sahib consider a just fine? Or, again, if written order came from the Government that a Bhil was to repair to a walled city of the plains to give evidence in a law-court, would it be wise to disregard that order? On the other hand, if it were obeyed, would the rash voyager return alive?

"But what have I to do with these things?" Chinn demanded of Bukta, impatiently. "I am a soldier. I do not know the law."

"Hoo! Law is for fools and white men. Give them a large and loud order, and they will abide by it. Thou art their law."

"But wherefore?"

Every trace of expression left Bukta's countenance. The idea might have smitten him for the first time. "How can I say?" he replied. "Perhaps it is on account of the name. A Bhil does not love strange things. Give them orders, Sahib—two, three, four words at a time such as they can carry away in their heads. That is enough."

Chinn gave orders then, valiantly, not realising that a word spoken in haste before mess became the dread unappealable law of villages beyond the smoky hills was, in truth, no less than the Law of Jan Chinn the First, who, so the whispered legend ran, had come back to earth, to oversee the third generation, in the body and bones of his grandson.

There could be no sort of doubt in this matter. All the Bhils knew that Jan Chinn reincarnated had honoured Bukta's village with his presence after slaying his first—in this life—tiger; that he had eaten and drunk with the people, as he was used; and—Bukta must have drugged Chinn's liquor very deeply—upon his back and right shoulder all men had seen the same angry red Flying Cloud that the high Gods had set on the flesh of Jan Chinn the First when first he came to the Bhil. As concerned the foolish white world which has no eyes, he was a slim and young officer in the Wuddars; but his own people knew he was Jan Chinn, who had made the Bhil a man; and, believing, they hastened to carry his words, careful never to alter them on the way.

Because the savage and the child who plays lonely games have one horror of being laughed at or questioned, the little folk kept their convictions to themselves; and the Colonel, who thought he knew his regiment, never guessed that each one of the six hundred quick-footed, beady-eyed rank-and-file, to attention beside their rifles, believed serenely and unshakenly that the subaltern on the left flank of the line was a demi-god twice born—tutelary deity of their land and people. The Earth-gods themselves had stamped the incarnation, and who would dare to doubt the handiwork of the Earth-gods?

Chinn, being practical above all things, saw that his family name served him well in the lines and in camp. His men gave no trouble—one does not commit regimental offences with a god in the chair of justice—and he was sure of the best beaters in the district when he needed them. They believed that the protection of Jan Chinn the First cloaked them, and were bold in that belief beyond the utmost daring of excited Bhils.

His quarters began to look like an amateur natural-history museum, in spite of duplicate heads and horns and skulls that he sent home to Devonshire. The people, very humanly, learned the weak side of their god. It is true he was unbribable, but bird-skins, butterflies, beetles, and, above all, news of big game pleased him. In other respects, too, he lived up to the Chinn tradition. He was fever-proof. A night's sitting out over a tethered goat in a damp valley, that would have filled the Major with a month's malaria, had no effect on him. He was, as they said, "salted before he was born."

Now in the autumn of his second year's service an uneasy rumour crept out of the earth and ran about among the Bhils. Chinn heard nothing of it till a brother-officer said across the mess-table: "Your revered ancestor's on the rampage in the Satpura country. You'd better look him up."

"I don't want to be disrespectful, but I'm a little sick of my revered ancestor. Bukta talks of nothing else. What's the old boy supposed to be doing now?"

"Riding cross-country by moonlight on his processional tiger. That's the story. He's been seen by about two thousand Bhils, skipping along the tops of the Satpuras, and scaring people to death. They believe it devoutly, and all the Satpura chaps are worshipping away at his shrine—tomb, I mean—like good uns. You really ought to go down there. Must be a queer thing to see your grandfather treated as a god."

"What makes you think there's any truth in the tale?" said Chinn.

"Because all our men deny it. They say they've never heard of Chinn's tiger. Now that's a manifest lie, because every Bhil has."

"There's only one thing you've overlooked," said the Colonel, thoughtfully. "When a local god reappears on earth, it's always an excuse for trouble of some kind; and those Satpura Bhils are about as wild as your grandfather left them, young un. It means something."

"Meanin' they may go on the war-path?" said Chinn.

"'Can't say—as yet. 'Shouldn't be surprised a little bit."

"I haven't been told a syllable."

"Proves it all the more. They are keeping something back."

"Bukta tells me everything, too, as a rule. Now, why didn't he tell me that?"

Chinn put the question directly to the old man that night, and the answer surprised him.

"Why should I tell what is well known? Yes, the Clouded Tiger is out in the Satpura country."

"What do the wild Bhils think that it means?"

"They do not know. They wait. Sahib, what is coming? Say only one little word, and we will be content."

"We? What have tales from the south, where the jungly Bhils live, to do with drilled men?"

"When Jan Chinn wakes is no time for any Bhil to be quiet."

"But he has not waked, Bukta."

"Sahib"—the old man's eyes were full of tender reproof—"if he does not wish to be seen, why does he go abroad in the moonlight? We know he is awake, but we do not know what he desires. Is it a sign for all the Bhils, or one that concerns the Satpura folk alone? Say one little word, Sahib, that I may carry it to the lines, and send on to our villages. Why does Jan Chinn ride out? Who has done wrong? Is it pestilence? Is it murrain? Will our children die? Is it a sword? Remember, Sahib, we are thy people and thy servants, and in this life I bore thee in my arms—not knowing."

"Bukta has evidently looked on the cup this evening," Chinn thought; "but if I can do anything to soothe the old chap I must. It's like the Mutiny rumours on a small scale."

He dropped into a deep wicker chair, over which was thrown his first tiger-skin, and his weight on the cushion flapped the clawed paws over his shoulders. He laid hold of them mechanically as he spoke, drawing the painted hide, cloak-fashion, about him.

"Now will I tell the truth, Bukta," he said, leaning forward, the dried muzzle on his shoulder, to invent a specious lie.

"I see that it is the truth," was the answer, in a shaking voice.

"Jan Chinn goes abroad among the Satpuras, riding on the Clouded Tiger, ye say? Be it so. Therefore the sign of the wonder is for the Satpura Bhils only, and does not touch the Bhils who plough in the north and east, the Bhils of the Khandesh, or any others, except the Satpura Bhils, who, as we know, are wild and foolish."

"It is, then, a sign for them. Good or bad?"

"Beyond doubt, good. For why should Jan Chinn make evil to those whom he has made men? The nights over yonder are hot; it is ill to lie in one bed over-long without turning, and Jan Chinn would look again upon his people. So he rises, whistles his Clouded Tiger, and goes abroad a little to breathe the cool air. If the Satpura Bhils kept to their villages, and did not wander after dark, they would not see him. Indeed, Bukta, it is no more than that he would see the light again in his own country. Send this news south, and say that it is my word."

Bukta bowed to the floor. "Good Heavens!" thought Chinn, "and this blinking pagan is a first-class officer, and as straight as a die! I may as well round it off neatly." He went on:

"If the Satpura Bhils ask the meaning of the sign, tell them that Jan Chinn would see how they kept their old promises of good living. Perhaps they have plundered; perhaps they mean to disobey the orders of the Government; perhaps there is a dead man in the jungle; and so Jan Chinn has come to see."

"Is he, then, angry?"

"Bah! Am I ever angry with my Bhils? I say angry words, and threaten many things. Thou knowest, Bukta. I have seen thee smile behind the hand. I know, and thou knowest. The Bhils are my children. I have said it many times."

"Ay. We be thy children," said Bukta.

"And no otherwise is it with Jan Chinn, my father's father. He would see the land he loved and the people once again. It is a good ghost, Bukta. I say it. Go and tell them. And I do hope devoutly," he added, "that it will calm 'em down." Flinging back the tiger-skin, he rose with a long, unguarded yawn that showed his well-kept teeth.

Bukta fled, to be received in the lines by a knot of panting inquirers.

"It is true," said Bukta. "He wrapped himself in the skin, and spoke from it. He would see his own country again. The sign is not for us; and, indeed, he is a young man. How should he lie idle of nights? He says his bed is too hot and the air is bad. He goes to and fro for the love of night-running. He has said it."

The grey-whiskered assembly shuddered.

"He says the Bhils are his children. Ye know he does not lie. He has said it to me."

"But what of the Satpura Bhils? What means the sign for them?"

"Nothing. It is only night-running, as I have said. He rides to see if they obey the Government, as he taught them to do in his first life."

"And what if they do not?"

"He did not say."

The light went out in Chinn's quarters.

"Look," said Bukta. "Now he goes away. None the less it is a good ghost, as he has said. How shall we fear Jan Chinn, who made the Bhil a man? His protection is on us; and ye know Jan Chinn never broke a protection spoken or written on paper. When he is older and has found him a wife he will lie in his bed till morning."

A commanding officer is generally aware of the regimental state of mind a little before the men; and this is why the Colonel said, a few days later, that some one had been putting the Fear of God into the Wuddars. As he was the only person officially entitled to do this, it distressed him to see such unanimous virtue. "It's too good to last," he said. "I only wish I could find out what the little chaps mean."

The explanation, as it seemed to him, came at the change of the moon, when he received orders to hold himself in readiness to "allay any possible excitement" among the Satpura Bhils, who were, to put it mildly, uneasy because a paternal Government had sent up against them a Mahratta State-educated vaccinator, with lancets, lymph, and an officially registered calf. In the language of State, they had "manifested a strong objection to all prophylactic measures," had "forcibly detained the vaccinator," and "were on the point of neglecting or evading their tribal obligations."

"That means they are in a blue funk—same as they were at census-time," said the Colonel; "and if we stampede them into the hills we'll never catch 'em, in the first place, and, in the second, they'll whoop off plundering till further orders. 'Wonder who the God-forsaken idiot is who is trying to vaccinate a Bhil. I knew trouble was coming. One good thing is that they'll only use local corps, and we can knock up something we'll call a campaign, and let them down easy. Fancy us potting our best beaters because they don't want to be vaccinated! They're only crazy with fear."

"Don't you think, sir," said Chinn, the next day, "that perhaps you could give me a fortnight's shooting-leave?"

"Desertion in the face of the enemy, by Jove!" The Colonel laughed. "I might, but I'd have to antedate it a little, because we're warned for service, as you might say. However, we'll assume that you applied for leave three days ago, and are now well on your way south."

"I'd like to take Bukta with me."

"Of course, yes. I think that will be the best plan. You've some kind of hereditary influence with the little chaps, and they may listen to you when a glimpse of our uniforms would drive them wild. You've never been in that part of the world before, have you? Take care they don't send you to your family vault in your youth and innocence. I believe you'll be all right if you can get 'em to listen to you."

"I think so, sir; but if—if they should accidentally put an—make asses of 'emselves—they might, you know—I hope you'll represent that they were only frightened. There isn't an ounce of real vice in 'em, and I should never forgive myself if any one of—of my name got them into trouble."

The Colonel nodded, but said nothing.

Chinn and Bukta departed at once. Bukta did not say that, ever since the official vaccinator had been dragged into the hills by indignant Bhils, runner after runner had skulked up to the lines, entreating, with forehead in the dust, that Jan Chinn should come and explain this unknown horror that hung over his people.

The portent of the Clouded Tiger was now too clear. Let Jan Chinn comfort his own, for vain was the help of mortal man. Bukta toned down these beseechings to a simple request for Chinn's presence. Nothing would have pleased the old man better than a rough-and-tumble campaign against the Satpuras, whom he, as an "unmixed" Bhil, despised; but he had a duty to all his nation as Jan Chinn's interpreter; and he devoutly believed that forty plagues would fall on his village if he tampered with that obligation. Besides, Jan Chinn knew all things, and he rode the Clouded Tiger.

They covered thirty miles a day on foot and pony, raising the blue wall-like line of the Satpuras as swiftly as might be. Bukta was very silent.

They began the steep climb a little after noon, but it was near sunset ere they reached the stone platform clinging to the side of a rifted, jungle-covered hill, where Jan Chinn the First was laid, as he had desired, that he might overlook his people. All India is full of neglected graves that date from the beginning of the eighteenth century—tombs of forgotten colonels of corps long since disbanded; mates of East India men who went on shooting expeditions and never came back; factors, agents, writers, and ensigns of the Honourable the East India Company by hundreds and thousands and tens of thousands. English folk forget quickly, but natives have long memories, and if a man has done good in his life it is remembered after his death. The weathered marble four-square tomb of Jan Chinn was hung about with wild flowers and nuts, packets of wax and honey, bottles of native spirits, and infamous cigars, with buffalo horns and plumes of dried grass. At one end was a rude clay image of a white man, in the old-fashioned top-hat, riding on a bloated tiger.

Bukta salamed reverently as they approached. Chinn bared his head and began to pick out the blurred inscription. So far as he could read it ran thus—word for word, and letter for letter:

To the Memory of JOHN CHINN, Esq.

Late Collector of............

....ithout Bloodshed or...error of Authority

Employ.only..cans of Conciliat...and Confiden.

accomplished the...tire Subjection...

a Lawless and Predatory Peop...

....taching them to...ish Government

by a Conquest over....Minds

The most perma...and rational Mode of Domini..

...Governor General and Counc...engal

have ordered thi.....erected

....arted this Life Aug. 19, 184..Ag...

On the other side of the grave were ancient verses, also very worn. As much as Chinn could decipher said:

....the savage band

Forsook their Haunts and b.....is Command

....mended..rais check a...st for spoil.

And.s.ing Hamlets prove his gene....toil.

Humanit...survey......ights restor..

A Nation..ield..subdued without a Sword.

For some little time he leaned on the tomb thinking of this dead man of his own blood, and of the house in Devonshire; then, nodding to the plains: "Yes; it's a big work all of it even my little share. He must have been worth knowing.... Bukta, where are my people?"

"Not here, Sahib. No man comes here except in full sun. They wait above. Let us climb and see."

But Chinn, remembering the first law of Oriental diplomacy, in an even voice answered: "I have come this far only because the Satpura folk are foolish, and dared not visit our lines. Now bid them wait on me here. I am not a servant, but the master of Bhils."

"I go—I go," clucked the old man. Night was falling, and at any moment Jan Chinn might whistle up his dreaded steed from the darkening scrub. Now for the first time in a long life Bukta disobeyed a lawful command and deserted his leader; for he did not come back, but pressed to the flat table-top of the hill, and called softly. Men stirred all about him—little trembling men with bows and arrows who had watched the two since noon.

"Where is he?" whispered one.

"At his own place. He bids you come," said Bukta.

"Now?"

"Now."

"Rather let him loose the Clouded Tiger upon us. We do not go."

"Nor I, though I bore him in my arms when he was a child in this his life. Wait here till the day."

"But surely he will be angry."

"He will be very angry, for he has nothing to eat. But he has said to me many times that the Bhils are his children. By sunlight I believe this, but—by moonlight I am not so sure. What folly have ye Satpura pigs compassed that ye should need him at all?"

"One came to us in the name of the Government with little ghost-knives and a magic calf, meaning to turn us into cattle by the cutting off of our arms. We were greatly afraid, but we did not kill the man. He is here, bound—a black man; and we think he comes from the west. He said it was an order to cut us all with knives—especially the women and the children. We did not hear that it was an order, so we were afraid, and kept to our hills. Some of our men have taken ponies and bullocks from the plains, and others pots and cloths and ear-rings."

"Are any slain?"

"By our men? Not yet. But the young men are blown to and fro by many rumours like flames upon a hill. I sent runners asking for Jan Chinn lest worse should come to us. It was this fear that he foretold by the sign of the Clouded Tiger."

"He says it is otherwise," said Bukta; and he repeated, with amplifications, all that young Chinn had told him at the conference of the wicker chair.

"Think you," said the questioner, at last, "that the Government will lay hands on us?"

"Not I," Bukta rejoined. "Jan Chinn will give an order, and ye will obey. The rest is between the Government and Jan Chinn. I myself know something of the ghost-knives and the scratching. It is a charm against the Smallpox. But how it is done I cannot tell. Nor need that concern you."

"If he stands by us and before the anger of the Government we will most strictly obey Jan Chinn, except—except we do not go down to that place to-night."

They could hear young Chinn below them shouting for Bukta; but they cowered and sat still, expecting the Clouded Tiger. The tomb had been holy ground for nearly half a century. If Jan Chinn chose to sleep there, who had better right? But they would not come within eyeshot of the place till broad day.

At first Chinn was exceedingly angry, till it occurred to him that Bukta most probably had a reason (which, indeed, he had), and his own dignity might suffer if he yelled without answer. He propped himself against the foot of the grave, and, alternately dozing and smoking, came through the warm night proud that he was a lawful, legitimate, fever-proof Chinn.

He prepared his plan of action much as his grandfather would have done; and when Bukta appeared in the morning with a most liberal supply of food, said nothing of the overnight desertion. Bukta would have been relieved by an outburst of human anger; but Chinn finished his victual leisurely, and a cheroot, ere he made any sign.

"They are very much afraid," said Bukta, who was not too bold himself. "It remains only to give orders. They said they will obey if thou wilt only stand between them and the Government."

"That I know," said Chinn, strolling slowly to the table-land. A few of the elder men stood in an irregular semicircle in an open glade; but the ruck of people—women and children were hidden in the thicket. They had no desire to face the first anger of Jan Chinn the First.

Seating himself on a fragment of split rock, he smoked his cheroot to the butt, hearing men breathe hard all about him. Then he cried, so suddenly that they jumped:

"Bring the man that was bound!"

A scuffle and a cry were followed by the appearance of a Hindoo vaccinator, quaking with fear, bound hand and foot, as the Bhils of old were accustomed to bind their human sacrifices. He was pushed cautiously before the presence; but young Chinn did not look at him.

"I said—the man that was bound. Is it a jest to bring me one tied like a buffalo? Since when could the Bhil bind folk at his pleasure? Cut!"

Half a dozen hasty knives cut away the thongs, and the man crawled to Chinn, who pocketed his case of lancets and tubes of lymph. Then, sweeping the semicircle with one comprehensive forefinger, and in the voice of compliment, he said, clearly and distinctly: "Pigs!

"Ai!" whispered Bukta. "Now he speaks. Woe to foolish people!"

"I have come on foot from my house" (the assembly shuddered) "to make clear a matter which any other Satpura Bhil would have seen with both eyes from a distance. Ye know the Smallpox who pits and scars your children so that they look like wasp-combs. It is an order of the Government that whoso is scratched on the arm with these little knives which I hold up is charmed against her. All Sahibs are thus charmed, and very many Hindoos. This is the mark of the charm. Look!"

He rolled back his sleeve to the armpit and showed the white scars of the vaccination-mark on his white skin. "Come, all, and look."

A few daring spirits came up, and nodded their heads wisely. There was certainly a mark, and they knew well what other dread marks were hidden by the shirt. Merciful was Jan Chinn, that then and there proclaimed his godhead!

"Now all these things the man whom ye bound told you."

"I did—a hundred times; but they answered with blows," groaned the operator, chafing his wrists and ankles.

"But, being pigs, ye did not believe; and so came I here to save you, first from Smallpox, next from a great folly of fear, and lastly, it may be, from the rope and the jail. It is no gain to me; it is no pleasure to me: but for the sake of that one who is yonder, who made the Bhil a man"—he pointed down the hill—"I, who am of his blood, the son of his son, come to turn your people. And I speak the truth, as did Jan Chinn."

The crowd murmured reverently, and men stole out of the thicket by twos and threes to join it. There was no anger in their god's face.

"These are my orders. (Heaven send they'll take 'em, but I seem to have impressed 'em so far!) I myself will stay among you while this man scratches your arms with the knives, after the order of the Government. In three, or it may be five or seven, days, your arms will swell and itch and burn. That is the power of Smallpox fighting in your base blood against the orders of the Government I will therefore stay among you till I see that Smallpox is conquered, and I will not go away till the men and the women and the little children show me upon their arms such marks as I have even now showed you. I bring with me two very good guns, and a man whose name is known among beasts and men. We will hunt together, I and he and your young men, and the others shall eat and lie still. This is my order."

There was a long pause while victory hung in the balance. A white-haired old sinner, standing on one uneasy leg, piped up:

"There are ponies and some few bullocks and other things for which we need a kowl [protection]. They were not taken in the way of trade."

The battle was won, and John Chinn drew a breath of relief. The young Bhils had been raiding, but if taken swiftly all could be put straight.

"I will write a kowl so soon as the ponies, the bullocks, and the other things are counted before me and sent back whence they came. But first we will put the Government mark on such as have not been visited by Smallpox." In an undertone, to the vaccinator: "If you show you are afraid you'll never see Poona again, my friend."

"There is not sufficient ample supply of vaccination for all this population," said the man. "They destroyed the offeecial calf."

"They won't know the difference. Scrape 'em and give me a couple of lancets; I'll attend to the elders."

The aged diplomat who had demanded protection was the first victim. He fell to Chinn's hand and dared not cry out. As soon as he was freed he dragged up a companion, and held him fast, and the crisis became, as it were, a child's sport; for the vaccinated chased the unvaccinated to treatment, vowing that all the tribe must suffer equally. The women shrieked, and the children ran howling; but Chinn laughed, and waved the pink-tipped lancet.

"It is an honour," he cried. "Tell them, Bukta, how great an honour it is that I myself mark them. Nay, I cannot mark every one—the Hindoo must also do his work—but I will touch all marks that he makes, so there will be an equal virtue in them. Thus do the Rajputs stick pigs. Ho, brother with one eye! Catch that girl and bring her to me. She need not run away yet, for she is not married, and I do not seek her in marriage. She will not come? Then she shall be shamed by her little brother, a fat boy, a bold boy. He puts out his arm like a soldier. Look! He does not flinch at the blood. Some day he shall be in my regiment. And now, mother of many, we will lightly touch thee, for Smallpox has been before us here. It is a true thing, indeed, that this charm breaks the power of Mata. There will be no more pitted faces among the Satpuras, and so ye can ask many cows for each maid to be wed."

And so on and so on—quick-poured showman's patter, sauced in the Bhil hunting-proverbs and tales of their own brand of coarse humour till the lancets were blunted and both operators worn out.

But, nature being the same the world over, the unvaccinated grew jealous of their marked comrades, and came near to blows about it. Then Chinn declared himself a court of justice, no longer a medical board, and made formal inquiry into the late robberies.

"We are the thieves of Mahadeo," said the Bhils, simply. "It is our fate, and we were frightened. When we are frightened we always steal."

Simply and directly as children, they gave in the tale of the plunder, all but two bullocks and some spirits that had gone amissing (these Chinn promised to make good out of his own pocket), and ten ringleaders were despatched to the lowlands with a wonderful document, written on the leaf of a note-book, and addressed to an Assistant District Superintendent of Police. There was warm calamity in that note, as Jan Chinn warned them, but anything was better than loss of liberty.

Armed with this protection, the repentant raiders went down-hill. They had no desire whatever to meet Mr. Dundas Fawne of the Police, aged twenty-two, and of a cheerful countenance, nor did they wish to revisit the scene of their robberies. Steering a middle course, they ran into the camp of the one Government chaplain allowed to the various irregular corps through a district of some fifteen thousand square miles, and stood before him in a cloud of dust. He was by way of being a priest, they knew, and, what was more to the point, a good sportsman who paid his beaters generously.

When he read Chinn's note he laughed, which they deemed a lucky omen, till he called up policemen, who tethered the ponies and the bullocks by the piled house-gear, and laid stern hands upon three of that smiling band of the thieves of Mahadeo. The chaplain himself addressed them magisterially with a riding-whip. That was painful, but Jan Chinn had prophesied it. They submitted, but would not give up the written protection, fearing the jail. On their way back they met Mr. D. Fawne, who had heard about the robberies, and was not pleased.

"Certainly," said the eldest of the gang, when the second interview was at an end, "certainly Jan Chinn's protection has saved us our liberty, but it is as though there were many beatings in one small piece of paper. Put it away."

One climbed into a tree, and stuck the letter into a cleft forty feet from the ground, where it could do no harm. Warmed, sore, but happy, the ten returned to Jan Chinn next day, where he sat among uneasy Bhils, all looking at their right arms, and all bound under terror of their god's disfavour not to scratch.

"It was a good kowl," said the leader. "First the chaplain, who laughed, took away our plunder, and beat three of us, as was promised. Next, we meet Fawne Sahib, who frowned, and asked for the plunder. We spoke the truth, and so he beat us all, one after another, and called us chosen names. He then gave us these two bundles"—they set down a bottle of whisky and a box of cheroots—"and we came away. The kowl is left in a tree, because its virtue is that so soon as we show it to a Sahib we are beaten."

"But for that kowl" said Jan Chinn, sternly, "ye would all have been marching to jail with a policeman on either side. Ye come now to serve as beaters for me. These people are unhappy, and we will go hunting till they are well. To-night we will make a feast."

It is written in the chronicles of the Satpura Bhils, together with many other matters not fit for print, that through five days, after the day that he had put his mark upon them, Jan Chinn the First hunted for his people; and on the five nights of those days the tribe was gloriously and entirely drunk. Jan Chinn bought country spirits of an awful strength, and slew wild pig and deer beyond counting, so that if any fell sick they might have two good reasons.

Between head—and stomach-aches they found no time to think of their arms, but followed Jan Chinn obediently through the jungles, and with each day's returning confidence men, women, and children stole away to their villages as the little army passed by. They carried news that it was good and right to be scratched with ghost-knives; that Jan Chinn was indeed reincarnated as a god of free food and drink, and that of all nations the Satpura Bhils stood first in his favour, if they would only refrain from scratching. Henceforward that kindly demi-god would be connected in their minds with great gorgings and the vaccine and lancets of a paternal Government.

"And to-morrow I go back to my home," said Jan Chinn to his faithful few, whom neither spirits, overeating, nor swollen glands could conquer. It is hard for children and savages to behave reverently at all times to the idols of their make-belief; and they had frolicked excessively with Jan Chinn. But the reference to his home cast a gloom on the people.

"And the Sahib will not come again?" said he who had been vaccinated first.

"That is to be seen," answered Chinn, warily.

"Nay, but come as a white man—come as a young man whom we know and love; for, as thou alone knowest, we are a weak people. If we again saw thy—thy horse—" They were picking up their courage.

"I have no horse. I came on foot with Bukta, yonder. What is this?"

"Thou knowest—the thing that thou hast chosen for a night-horse." The little men squirmed in fear and awe.

"Night-horses? Bukta, what is this last tale of children?"

Bukta had been a silent leader in Chinn's presence since the night of his desertion, and was grateful for a chance-flung question.

"They know, Sahib," he whispered. "It is the Clouded Tiger. That that comes from the place where thou didst once sleep. It is thy horse—as it has been these three generations."

"My horse! That was a dream of the Bhils."

"It is no dream. Do dreams leave the tracks of broad pugs on earth? Why make two faces before thy people? They know of the night-ridings, and they—and they—"

"Are afraid, and would have them cease."

Bukta nodded. "If thou hast no further need of him. He is thy horse."

"The thing leaves a trail, then?" said Chinn.

"We have seen it. It is like a village road under the tomb."

"Can ye find and follow it for me?"

"By daylight—if one comes with us, and, above all, stands near by."

"I will stand close, and we will see to it that Jan Chinn does not ride any more."

The Bhils shouted the last words again and again.

From Chinn's point of view the stalk was nothing more than an ordinary one—down-hill, through split and crannied rocks, unsafe, perhaps, if a man did not keep his wits by him, but no worse than twenty others he had undertaken. Yet his men—they refused absolutely to beat, and would only trail—dripped sweat at every move. They showed the marks of enormous pugs that ran, always down-hill, to a few hundred feet below Jan Chinn's tomb, and disappeared in a narrow-mouthed cave. It was an insolently open road, a domestic highway, beaten without thought of concealment.

"The beggar might be paying rent and taxes," Chinn muttered ere he asked whether his friend's taste ran to cattle or man.

"Cattle," was the answer. "Two heifers a week. We drive them for him at the foot of the hill. It is his custom. If we did not, he might seek us."

"Blackmail and piracy," said Chinn. "I can't say I fancy going into the cave after him. What's to be done?"

The Bhils fell back as Chinn lodged himself behind a rock with his rifle ready. Tigers, he knew, were shy beasts, but one who had been long cattle-fed in this sumptuous style might prove overbold.

"He speaks!" some one whispered from the rear. "He knows, too."

"Well, of all the infernal cheek!" said Chinn. There was an angry growl from the cave—a direct challenge.

"Come out, then," Chinn shouted. "Come out of that. Let's have a look at you." The brute knew well enough that there was some connection between brown nude Bhils and his weekly allowance; but the white helmet in the sunlight annoyed him, and he did not approve of the voice that broke his rest. Lazily as a gorged snake, he dragged himself out of the cave, and stood yawning and blinking at the entrance. The sunlight fell upon his flat right side, and Chinn wondered. Never had he seen a tiger marked after this fashion. Except for his head, which was staringly barred, he was dappled—not striped, but dappled like a child's rocking-horse in rich shades of smoky black on red gold. That portion of his belly and throat which should have been white was orange, and his tail and paws were black.

He looked leisurely for some ten seconds, and then deliberately lowered his head, his chin dropped and drawn in, staring intently at the man. The effect of this was to throw forward the round arch of his skull, with two broad bands across it, while below the bands glared the unwinking eyes; so that, head on, as he stood, he showed something like a diabolically scowling pantomime-mask. It was a piece of natural mesmerism that he had practised many times on his quarry, and though Chinn was by no means a terrified heifer, he stood for a while, held by the extraordinary oddity of the attack. The head—the body seemed to have been packed away behind it—the ferocious, skull-like head, crept nearer to the switching of an angry tail-tip in the grass. Left and right the Bhils had scattered to let John Chinn subdue his own horse.

"My word!" he thought. "He's trying to frighten me!" and fired between the saucer-like eyes, leaping aside upon the shot.

A big coughing mass, reeking of carrion, bounded past him up the hill, and he followed discreetly. The tiger made no attempt to turn into the jungle; he was hunting for sight and breath—nose up, mouth open, the tremendous fore-legs scattering the gravel in spurts.

"Scuppered!" said John Chinn, watching the flight. "Now if he was a partridge he'd tower. Lungs must be full of blood."

The brute had jerked himself over a boulder and fallen out of sight the other side. John Chinn looked over with a ready barrel. But the red trail led straight as an arrow even to his grandfather's tomb, and there, among the smashed spirit-bottles and the fragments of the mud image, the life left, with a flurry and a grunt.

"If my worthy ancestor could see that," said John Chinn, "he'd have been proud of me. Eyes, lower jaw, and lungs. A very nice shot." He whistled for Bukta as he drew the tape over the stiffening bulk.

"Ten—six—eight—by Jove! It's nearly eleven—call it eleven. Fore-arm, twenty-four—five—seven and a half. A short tail, too: three feet one. But what a skin! Oh, Bukta! Bukta! The men with the knives swiftly."

"Is he beyond question dead?" said an awe-stricken voice behind a rock.

"That was not the way I killed my first tiger," said Chinn. "I did not think that Bukta would run. I had no second gun."

"It—it is the Clouded Tiger," said Bukta, un-heeding the taunt.

"He is dead."

Whether all the Bhils, vaccinated and unvaccinated, of the Satpuras had lain by to see the kill, Chinn could not say; but the whole hill's flank rustled with little men, shouting, singing, and stamping. And yet, till he had made the first cut in the splendid skin, not a man would take a knife; and, when the shadows fell, they ran from the red-stained tomb, and no persuasion would bring them back till dawn. So Chinn spent a second night in the open, guarding the carcass from jackals, and thinking about his ancestor.

He returned to the lowlands to the triumphal chant of an escorting army three hundred strong, the Mahratta vaccinator close at his elbow, and the rudely dried skin a trophy before him. When that army suddenly and noiselessly disappeared, as quail in high corn, he argued he was near civilisation, and a turn in the road brought him upon the camp of a wing of his own corps. He left the skin on a cart-tail for the world to see, and sought the Colonel.

"They're perfectly right," he explained earnestly. "There isn't an ounce of vice in 'em. They were only frightened. I've vaccinated the whole boiling, and they like it awfully. What are—what are we doing here, sir?"

"That's what I'm trying to find out," said the Colonel. "I don't know yet whether we're a piece of a brigade or a police force. However, I think we'll call ourselves a police force. How did you manage to get a Bhil vaccinated?"

"Well, sir," said Chinn, "I've been thinking it over, and, as far as I can make out, I've got a sort of hereditary influence over 'em."

"So I know, or I wouldn't have sent you; but what, exactly?"

"It's rather rummy. It seems, from what I can make out, that I'm my own grandfather reincarnated, and I've been disturbing the peace of the country by riding a pad-tiger of nights. If I hadn't done that, I don't think they'd have objected to the vaccination; but the two together were more than they could stand. And so, sir, I've vaccinated 'em, and shot my tiger-horse as a sort o' proof of good faith. You never saw such a skin in your life."

The Colonel tugged his moustache thoughtfully. "Now, how the deuce," said he, "am I to include that in my report?"

Indeed, the official version of the Bhils' anti-vaccination stampede said nothing about Lieutenant John Chinn, his godship. But Bukta knew, and the corps knew, and every Bhil in the Satpura hills knew.

And now Bukta is zealous that John Chinn shall swiftly be wedded and impart his powers to a son; for if the Chinn succession fails, and the little Bhils are left to their own imaginings, there will be fresh trouble in the Satpuras.

THE DEVIL AND THE DEEP SEA

All supplies very bad and dear, and there are no facilities for even the smallest repairs. —Sailing Directions.

Her nationality was British, but you will not find her house-flag in the list of our mercantile marine. She was a nine-hundred-ton, iron, schooner-rigged, screw cargo-boat, differing externally in no way from any other tramp of the sea. But it is with steamers as it is with men. There are those who will for a consideration sail extremely close to the wind; and, in the present state of a fallen world, such people and such steamers have their use. From the hour that the Aglaia first entered the Clyde—new, shiny, and innocent, with a quart of cheap champagne trickling down her cut-water—Fate and her owner, who was also her captain, decreed that she should deal with embarrassed crowned heads, fleeing Presidents, financiers of over-extended ability, women to whom change of air was imperative, and the lesser law-breaking Powers. Her career led her sometimes into the Admiralty Courts, where the sworn statements of her skipper filled his brethren with envy. The mariner cannot tell or act a lie in the face of the sea, or mis-lead a tempest; but, as lawyers have discovered, he makes up for chances withheld when he returns to shore, an affidavit in either hand.

The Aglaia figured with distinction in the great Mackinaw salvage-case. It was her first slip from virtue, and she learned how to change her name, but not her heart, and to run across the sea. As the Guiding Light she was very badly wanted in a South American port for the little matter of entering harbour at full speed, colliding with a coal-hulk and the State's only man-of-war, just as that man-of-war was going to coal. She put to sea without explanations, though three forts fired at her for half an hour. As the Julia M'Gregor she had been concerned in picking up from a raft certain gentlemen who should have stayed in Noumea, but who preferred making themselves vastly unpleasant to authority in quite another quarter of the world; and as the Shah-in-Shah she had been overtaken on the high seas, indecently full of munitions of war, by the cruiser of an agitated Power at issue with its neighbour. That time she was very nearly sunk, and her riddled hull gave eminent lawyers of two countries great profit. After a season she reappeared as the Martin Hunt painted a dull slate-colour, with pure saffron funnel, and boats of robin's-egg blue, engaging in the Odessa trade till she was invited (and the invitation could not well be disregarded) to keep away from Black Sea ports altogether.

She had ridden through many waves of depression. Freights might drop out of sight, Seamen's Unions throw spanners and nuts at certificated masters, or stevedores combine till cargo perished on the dock-head; but the boat of many names came and went, busy, alert, and inconspicuous always. Her skipper made no complaint of hard times, and port officers observed that her crew signed and signed again with the regularity of Atlantic liner boatswains. Her name she changed as occasion called; her well-paid crew never; and a large percentage of the profits of her voyages was spent with an open hand on her engine-room. She never troubled the underwriters, and very seldom stopped to talk with a signal-station, for her business was urgent and private.

But an end came to her tradings, and she perished in this manner. Deep peace brooded over Europe, Asia, Africa, America, Australasia, and Polynesia. The Powers dealt together more or less honestly; banks paid their depositors to the hour; diamonds of price came safely to the hands of their owners; Republics rested content with their Dictators; diplomats found no one whose presence in the least incommoded them; monarchs lived openly with their lawfully wedded wives. It was as though the whole earth had put on its best Sunday bib and tucker; and business was very bad for the Martin Hunt. The great, virtuous calm engulfed her, slate sides, yellow funnel, and all, but cast up in another hemisphere the steam whaler Haliotis, black and rusty, with a manure-coloured funnel, a litter of dingy white boats, and an enormous stove, or furnace, for boiling blubber on her forward well-deck. There could be no doubt that her trip was successful, for she lay at several ports not too well known, and the smoke of her trying-out insulted the beaches.

Anon she departed, at the speed of the average London four-wheeler, and entered a semi-inland sea, warm, still, and blue, which is, perhaps, the most strictly preserved water in the world. There she stayed for a certain time, and the great stars of those mild skies beheld her playing puss-in-the-corner among islands where whales are never found. All that while she smelt abominably, and the smell, though fishy, was not whalesome. One evening calamity descended upon her from the island of Pygang-Watai, and she fled, while her crew jeered at a fat black-and-brown gunboat puffing far behind. They knew to the last revolution the capacity of every boat, on those seas, that they were anxious to avoid. A British ship with a good conscience does not, as a rule, flee from the man-of-war of a foreign Power, and it is also considered a breach of etiquette to stop and search British ships at sea. These things the skipper of the Haliotis did not pause to prove, but held on at an inspiriting eleven knots an hour till nightfall. One thing only he overlooked.

The Power that kept an expensive steam-patrol moving up and down those waters (they had dodged the two regular ships of the station with an ease that bred contempt) had newly brought up a third and a fourteen-knot boat with a clean bottom to help the work; and that was why the Haliotis, driving hard from the east to the west, found herself at daylight in such a position that she could not help seeing an arrangement of four flags, a mile and a half behind, which read: "Heave to, or take the consequences!"

She had her choice, and she took it. The end came when, presuming on her lighter draught, she tried to draw away northward over a friendly shoal. The shell that arrived by way of the Chief Engineer's cabin was some five inches in diameter, with a practice, not a bursting, charge. It had been intended to cross her bows, and that was why it knocked the framed portrait of the Chief Engineer's wife—and she was a very pretty girl—on to the floor, splintered his wash-hand stand, crossed the alleyway into the engine-room, and striking on a grating, dropped directly in front of the forward engine, where it burst, neatly fracturing both the bolts that held the connecting-rod to the forward crank.

What follows is worth consideration. The forward engine had no more work to do. Its released piston-rod, therefore, drove up fiercely, with nothing to check it, and started most of the nuts of the cylinder-cover. It came down again, the full weight of the steam behind it, and the foot of the disconnected connecting-rod, useless as the leg of a man with a sprained ankle, flung out to the right and struck the starboard, or right-hand, cast-iron supporting-column of the forward engine, cracking it clean through about six inches above the base, and wedging the upper portion outwards three inches towards the ship's side. There the connecting-rod jammed. Meantime, the after-engine, being as yet unembarrassed, went on with its work, and in so doing brought round at its next revolution the crank of the forward engine, which smote the already jammed connecting-rod, bending it and therewith the piston-rod cross-head—the big cross-piece that slides up and down so smoothly.

The cross-head jammed sideways in the guides, and, in addition to putting further pressure on the already broken starboard supporting-column, cracked the port, or left-hand, supporting-column in two or three places. There being nothing more that could be made to move, the engines brought up, all standing, with a hiccup that seemed to lift the Haliotis a foot out of the water; and the engine-room staff, opening every steam outlet that they could find in the confusion, arrived on deck somewhat scalded, but calm. There was a sound below of things happening—a rushing, clicking, purring, grunting, rattling noise that did not last for more than a minute. It was the machinery adjusting itself, on the spur of the moment, to a hundred altered conditions. Mr. Wardrop, one foot on the upper grating, inclined his ear sideways, and groaned. You cannot stop engines working at twelve knots an hour in three seconds without disorganising them. The Haliotis slid forward in a cloud of steam, shrieking like a wounded horse. There was nothing more to do. The five-inch shell with a reduced charge had settled the situation. And when you are full, all three holds, of strictly preserved pearls; when you have cleaned out the Tanna Bank, the Sea-Horse Bank, and four other banks from one end to the other of the Amanala Sea—when you have ripped out the very heart of a rich Government monopoly so that five years will not repair your wrong-doings—you must smile and take what is in store. But the skipper reflected, as a launch put out from the man-of-war, that he had been bombarded on the high seas, with the British flag—several of them—picturesquely disposed above him, and tried to find comfort from the thought.

"Where," said the stolid naval lieutenant hoisting himself aboard, "where are those dam' pearls?"

They were there beyond evasion. No affidavit could do away with the fearful smell of decayed oysters, the diving-dresses, and the shell-littered hatches. They were there to the value of seventy thousand pounds, more or less; and every pound poached.

The man-of-war was annoyed; for she had used up many tons of coal, she had strained her tubes, and, worse than all, her officers and crew had been hurried. Every one on the Haliotis was arrested and rearrested several times, as each officer came aboard; then they were told by what they esteemed to be the equivalent of a midshipman that they were to consider themselves prisoners, and finally were put under arrest.

"It's not the least good," said the skipper, suavely. "You'd much better send us a tow—"

"Be still—you are arrest!" was the reply.

"Where the devil do you expect we are going to escape to? We're helpless. You've got to tow us into somewhere, and explain why you fired on us. Mr. Wardrop, we're helpless, aren't we?"

"Ruined from end to end," said the man of machinery. "If she rolls, the forward cylinder will come down and go through her bottom. Both columns are clean cut through. There's nothing to hold anything up."

The council of war clanked off to see if Mr. Wardrop's words were true. He warned them that it was as much as a man's life was worth to enter the engine-room, and they contented themselves with a distant inspection through the thinning steam. The Haliotis lifted to the long, easy swell, and the starboard supporting-column ground a trifle, as a man grits his teeth under the knife. The forward cylinder was depending on that unknown force men call the pertinacity of materials, which now and then balances that other heartbreaking power, the perversity of inanimate things.

"You see!" said Mr. Wardrop, hurrying them away. "The engines aren't worth their price as old iron."

"We tow," was the answer. "Afterwards we shall confiscate."

The man-of-war was short-handed, and did not see the necessity for putting a prize-crew aboard the Haliotis. So she sent one sublieutenant, whom the skipper kept very drunk, for he did not wish to make the tow too easy, and, moreover, he had an inconspicuous little rope hanging from the stem of his ship.

Then they began to tow at an average speed of four knots an hour. The Haliotis was very hard to move, and the gunnery-lieutenant, who had fired the five-inch shell, had leisure to think upon consequences. Mr. Wardrop was the busy man. He borrowed all the crew to shore up the cylinders with spars and blocks from the bottom and sides of the ship. It was a day's risky work; but anything was better than drowning at the end of a tow-rope; and if the forward cylinder had fallen, it would have made its way to the sea-bed, and taken the Haliotis after.

"Where are we going to, and how long will they tow us?" he asked of the skipper.

"God knows! and this prize-lieutenant's drunk. What do you think you can do?"

"There's just the bare chance," Mr. Wardrop whispered, though no one was within hearing—"there's just the bare chance o' repairin' her, if a man knew how. They've twisted the very guts out of her, bringing her up with that jerk; but I'm saying that, with time and patience, there's just the chance o' making steam yet. We could do it."

The skipper's eye brightened. "Do you mean," he began, "that she is any good?"

"Oh, no," said Mr. Wardrop. "She'll need three thousand pounds in repairs, at the lowest, if she's to take the sea again, an' that apart from any injury to her structure. She's like a man fallen down five pair o' stairs. We can't tell for months what has happened; but we know she'll never be good again without a new inside. Ye should see the condenser-tubes an' the steam connections to the donkey, for two things only. I'm not afraid of them repairin' her. I'm afraid of them stealin' things."

"They've fired on us. They'll have to explain that."

"Our reputation's not good enough to ask for explanations. Let's take what we have and be thankful. Ye would not have consuls remembern' the Guidin' Light, an' the Shah-in-Shah, an' the Aglaia, at this most alarmin' crisis. We've been no better than pirates these ten years. Under Providence we're no worse than thieves now. We've much to be thankful for—if we e'er get back to her."

"Make it your own way, then," said the skipper. "If there's the least chance—"

"I'll leave none," said Mr. Wardrop—"none that they'll dare to take. Keep her heavy on the tow, for we need time."

The skipper never interfered with the affairs of the engine-room, and Mr. Wardrop—an artist in his profession—turned to and composed a work terrible and forbidding. His background was the dark-grained sides of the engine-room; his material the metals of power and strength, helped out with spars, baulks, and ropes. The man-of-war towed sullenly and viciously. The Haliotis behind her hummed like a hive before swarming. With extra and totally unneeded spars her crew blocked up the space round the forward engine till it resembled a statue in its scaffolding, and the butts of the shores interfered with every view that a dispassionate eye might wish to take. And that the dispassionate mind might be swiftly shaken out of its calm, the well-sunk bolts of the shores were wrapped round untidily with loose ends of ropes, giving a studied effect of most dangerous insecurity. Next, Mr. Wardrop took up a collection from the after-engine, which, as you will remember, had not been affected in the general wreck. The cylinder escape-valve he abolished with a flogging-hammer. It is difficult in far-off ports to come by such valves, unless, like Mr. Wardrop, you keep duplicates in store. At the same time men took off the nuts of two of the great holding-down bolts that serve to keep the engines in place on their solid bed. An engine violently arrested in mid-career may easily jerk off the nut of a holding-down bolt, and this accident looked very natural.

Passing along the tunnel, he removed several shaft coupling-bolts and—nuts, scattering other and ancient pieces of iron underfoot. Cylinder-bolts he cut off to the number of six from the after-engine cylinder, so that it might match its neighbour, and stuffed the bilge—and feed-pumps with cotton-waste. Then he made up a neat bundle of the various odds and ends that he had gathered from the engines—little things like nuts and valve-spindles, all carefully tallowed—and retired with them under the floor of the engine-room, where he sighed, being fat, as he passed from manhole to manhole of the double bottom, and in a fairly dry submarine compartment hid them. Any engineer, particularly in an unfriendly port, has a right to keep his spare stores where he chooses; and the foot of one of the cylinder shores blocked all entrance into the regular store-room, even if that had not been already closed with steel wedges. In conclusion, he disconnected the after-engine, laid piston and connecting-rod, carefully tallowed, where it would be most inconvenient to the casual visitor, took out three of the eight collars of the thrust-block, hid them where only he could find them again, filled the boilers by hand, wedged the sliding doors of the coal-bunkers, and rested from his labours. The engine-room was a cemetery, and it did not need the contents of the ash-lift through the skylight to make it any worse.

He invited the skipper to look at the completed work.

"Saw ye ever such a forsaken wreck as that?" said he, proudly. "It almost frights me to go under those shores. Now, what d' you think they'll do to us?"

"Wait till we see," said the skipper. "It'll be bad enough when it comes."

He was not wrong. The pleasant days of towing ended all too soon, though the Haliotis trailed behind her a heavily weighted jib stayed out into the shape of a pocket; and Mr. Wardrop was no longer an artist of imagination, but one of seven-and-twenty prisoners in a prison full of insects. The man-of-war had towed them to the nearest port, not to the headquarters of the colony, and when Mr. Wardrop saw the dismal little harbour, with its ragged line of Chinese junks, its one crazy tug, and the boat-building shed that, under the charge of a philosophical Malay, represented a dockyard, he sighed and shook his head.

"I did well," he said. "This is the habitation o' wreckers an' thieves. We're at the uttermost ends of the earth. Think you they'll ever know in England?"

"Doesn't look like it," said the skipper.

They were marched ashore with what they stood up in, under a generous escort, and were judged according to the customs of the country, which, though excellent, are a little out of date. There were the pearls; there were the poachers; and there sat a small but hot Governor. He consulted for a while, and then things began to move with speed, for he did not wish to keep a hungry crew at large on the beach, and the man-of-war had gone up the coast. With a wave of his hand—a stroke of the pen was not necessary—he consigned them to the black gang-tana, the back-country, and the hand of the Law removed them from his sight and the knowledge of men. They were marched into the palms, and the back-country swallowed them up—all the crew of the Haliotis.

Deep peace continued to brood over Europe, Asia, Africa, America, Australasia, and Polynesia.

It was the firing that did it. They should have kept their counsel; but when a few thousand foreigners are bursting with joy over the fact that a ship under the British flag has been fired at on the high seas, news travels quickly; and when it came out that the pearl-stealing crew had not been allowed access to their consul (there was no consul within a few hundred miles of that lonely port) even the friendliest of Powers has a right to ask questions. The great heart of the British public was beating furiously on account of the performance of a notorious race-horse, and had not a throb to waste on distant accidents; but somewhere deep in the hull of the ship of State there is machinery which more or less accurately takes charge of foreign affairs. That machinery began to revolve, and who so shocked and surprised as the Power that had captured the Haliotis? It explained that colonial governors and far-away men-of-war were difficult to control, and promised that it would most certainly make an example both of the Governor and the vessel. As for the crew reported to be pressed into military service in tropical climes, it would produce them as soon as possible, and it would apologise, if necessary. Now, no apologies were needed. When one nation apologises to another, millions of amateurs who have no earthly concern with the difficulty hurl themselves into the strife and embarrass the trained specialist. It was requested that the crew be found, if they were still alive—they had been eight months beyond knowledge—and it was promised that all would be forgotten.

The little Governor of the little port was pleased with himself. Seven-and-twenty white men made a very compact force to throw away on a war that had neither beginning nor end—a jungle and stockade fight that flickered and smouldered through the wet hot years in the hills a hundred miles away, and was the heritage of every wearied official. He had, he thought, deserved well of his country; and if only some one would buy the unhappy Haliotis, moored in the harbour below his verandah, his cup would be full. He looked at the neatly silvered lamps that he had taken from her cabins, and thought of much that might be turned to account. But his countrymen in that moist climate had no spirit. They would peep into the silent engine-room, and shake their heads. Even the men-of-war would not tow her further up the coast, where the Governor believed that she could be repaired. She was a bad bargain; but her cabin carpets were undeniably beautiful, and his wife approved of her mirrors.

Three hours later cables were bursting round him like shells, for, though he knew it not, he was being offered as a sacrifice by the nether to the upper millstone, and his superiors had no regard for his feelings. He had, said the cables, grossly exceeded his power, and failed to report on events. He would, therefore—at this he cast himself back in his hammock—produce the crew of the Haliotis. He would send for them, and, if that failed, he would put his dignity on a pony and fetch them himself. He had no conceivable right to make pearl-poachers serve in any war. He would be held responsible.

Next morning the cables wished to know whether he had found the crew of the Haliotis. They were to be found, freed and fed—he was to feed them—till such time as they could be sent to the nearest English port in a man-of-war. If you abuse a man long enough in great words flashed over the sea-beds, things happen. The Governor sent inland swiftly for his prisoners, who were also soldiers; and never was a militia regiment more anxious to reduce its strength. No power short of death could make these mad men wear the uniform of their service. They would not fight, except with their fellows, and it was for that reason the regiment had not gone to war, but stayed in a stockade, reasoning with the new troops. The autumn campaign had been a fiasco, but here were the Englishmen. All the regiment marched back to guard them, and the hairy enemy, armed with blow-pipes, rejoiced in the forest. Five of the crew had died, but there lined up on the Governor's verandah two-and-twenty men marked about the legs with the scars of leech-bites. A few of them wore fringes that had once been trousers; the others used loin-cloths of gay patterns; and they existed beautifully but simply in the Governor's verandah, and when he came out they sang at him. When you have lost seventy thousand pounds' worth of pearls, your pay, your ship, and all your clothes, and have lived in bondage for five months beyond the faintest pretences of civilisation, you know what true independence means, for you become the happiest of created things—natural man.

The Governor told the crew that they were evil, and they asked for food. When he saw how they ate, and when he remembered that none of the pearl patrol-boats were expected for two months, he sighed. But the crew of the Haliotis lay down in the verandah, and said that they were pensioners of the Governor's bounty. A grey-bearded man, fat and bald-headed, his one garment a green-and-yellow loin-cloth, saw the Haliotis in the harbour, and bellowed for joy. The men crowded to the verandah-rail, kicking aside the long cane chairs. They pointed, gesticulated, and argued freely, without shame. The militia regiment sat down in the Governor's garden. The Governor retired to his hammock—it was as easy to be killed lying as standing—and his women squeaked from the shuttered rooms.

"She sold?" said the grey-bearded man, pointing to the Haliotis. He was Mr. Wardrop.

"No good," said the Governor, shaking his head. "No one come buy."

"He's taken my lamps, though," said the skipper. He wore one leg of a pair of trousers, and his eye wandered along the verandah. The Governor quailed. There were cuddy camp-stools and the skipper's writing-table in plain sight.

"They've cleaned her out, o' course," said Mr. Wardrop. "They would. We'll go aboard and take an inventory. See!" He waved his hands over the harbour. "We—live—there—now. Sorry?"

The Governor smiled a smile of relief.

"He's glad of that," said one of the crew, reflectively. "I shouldn't wonder."

They flocked down to the harbour-front, the militia regiment clattering behind, and embarked themselves in what they found—it happened to be the Governor's boat. Then they disappeared over the bulwarks of the Haliotis, and the Governor prayed that they might find occupation inside.

Mr. Wardrop's first bound took him to the engine-room; and when the others were patting the well-remembered decks, they heard him giving God thanks that things were as he had left them. The wrecked engines stood over his head untouched; no inexpert hand had meddled with his shores; the steel wedges of the store-room were rusted home; and, best of all, the hundred and sixty tons of good Australian coal in the bunkers had not diminished.

"I don't understand it," said Mr. Wardrop. "Any Malay knows the use o' copper. They ought to have cut away the pipes. And with Chinese junks coming here, too. It's a special interposition o' Providence."

"You think so," said the skipper, from above. "There's only been one thief here, and he's cleaned her out of all my things, anyhow."

Here the skipper spoke less than the truth, for under the planking of his cabin, only to be reached by a chisel, lay a little money which never drew any interest—his sheet-anchor to windward. It was all in clean sovereigns that pass current the world over, and might have amounted to more than a hundred pounds.

"He's left me alone. Let's thank God," repeated Mr. Wardrop.

"He's taken everything else; look!"

The Haliotis, except as to her engine-room, had been systematically and scientifically gutted from one end to the other, and there was strong evidence that an unclean guard had camped in the skipper's cabin to regulate that plunder. She lacked glass, plate, crockery, cutlery, mattresses, cuddy carpets and chairs, all boats, and her copper ventilators. These things had been removed, with her sails and as much of the wire rigging as would not imperil the safety of the masts.

"He must have sold those," said the skipper. "The other things are in his house, I suppose."

Every fitting that could be pried or screwed out was gone. Port, starboard, and masthead lights; teak gratings; sliding sashes of the deckhouse; the captain's chest of drawers, with charts and chart-table; photographs, brackets, and looking-glasses; cabin doors; rubber cuddy mats; hatch-irons; half the funnel-stays; cork fenders; carpenter's grindstone and tool-chest; holystones, swabs, squeegees; all cabin and pantry lamps; galley-fittings en bloc; flags and flag-locker; clocks, chronometers; the forward compass and the ship's bell and belfry, were among the missing.

There were great scarred marks on the deck-planking over which the cargo-derricks had been hauled. One must have fallen by the way, for the bulwark-rails were smashed and bent and the side-plates bruised.

"It's the Governor," said the skipper "He's been selling her on the instalment plan."

"Let's go up with spanners and shovels, and kill 'em all," shouted the crew. "Let's drown him, and keep the woman!"

"Then we'll be shot by that black-and-tan regiment—our regiment. What's the trouble ashore? They've camped our regiment on the beach."

"We're cut off; that's all. Go and see what they want," said Mr. Wardrop. "You've the trousers."

In his simple way the Governor was a strategist. He did not desire that the crew of the Haliotis should come ashore again, either singly or in detachments, and he proposed to turn their steamer into a convict-hulk. They would wait—he explained this from the quay to the skipper in the barge—and they would continue to wait till the man-of-war came along, exactly where they were. If one of them set foot ashore, the entire regiment would open fire, and he would not scruple to use the two cannon of the town. Meantime food would be sent daily in a boat under an armed escort. The skipper, bare to the waist, and rowing, could only grind his teeth; and the Governor improved the occasion, and revenged himself for the bitter words in the cables, by saying what he thought of the morals and manners of the crew. The barge returned to the Haliotis in silence, and the skipper climbed aboard, white on the cheek-bones and blue about the nostrils.

"I knew it," said Mr. Wardrop; "and they won't give us good food, either. We shall have bananas morning, noon, and night, an' a man can't work on fruit. We know that."

Then the skipper cursed Mr. Wardrop for importing frivolous side-issues into the conversation; and the crew cursed one another, and the Haliotis, the voyage, and all that they knew or could bring to mind. They sat down in silence on the empty decks, and their eyes burned in their heads. The green harbour water chuckled at them overside. They looked at the palm-fringed hills inland, at the white houses above the harbour road, at the single tier of native craft by the quay, at the stolid soldiery sitting round the two cannon, and, last of all, at the blue bar of the horizon. Mr. Wardrop was buried in thought, and scratched imaginary lines with his untrimmed finger-nails on the planking.

"I make no promise," he said, at last, "for I can't say what may or may not have happened to them. But here's the ship, and here's us."

There was a little scornful laughter at this, and Mr. Wardrop knitted his brows. He recalled that in the days when he wore trousers he had been Chief Engineer of the Haliotis.

"Harland, Mackesy, Noble, Hay, Naughton, Fink, O'Hara, Trumbull."

"Here, sir!" The instinct of obedience waked to answer the roll-call of the engine-room.

"Below!"

They rose and went.

"Captain, I'll trouble you for the rest of the men as I want them. We'll get my stores out, and clear away the shores we don't need, and then we'll patch her up. My men will remember that they're in the Haliotis,—under me."

He went into the engine-room, and the others stared. They were used to the accidents of the sea, but this was beyond their experience. None who had seen the engine-room believed that anything short of new engines from end to end could stir the Haliotis from her moorings.

The engine-room stores were unearthed, and Mr. Wardrop's face, red with the filth of the bilges and the exertion of travelling on his stomach, lit with joy. The spare gear of the Haliotis had been unusually complete, and two-and-twenty men, armed with screw-jacks, differential blocks, tackle, vices, and a forge or so, can look Kismet between the eyes without winking. The crew were ordered to replace the holding-down and shaft-bearing bolts, and return the collars of the thrust-block. When they had finished, Mr. Wardrop delivered a lecture on repairing compound engines without the aid of the shops, and the men sat about on the cold machinery. The cross-head jammed in the guides leered at them drunkenly, but offered no help. They ran their fingers hopelessly into the cracks of the starboard supporting-column, and picked at the ends of the ropes round the shores, while Mr. Wardrop's voice rose and fell echoing, till the quick tropic night closed down over the engine-room skylight.

Next morning the work of reconstruction began. It has been explained that the foot of the connecting-rod was forced against the foot of the starboard supporting-column, which it had cracked through and driven outward towards the ship's skin. To all appearance the job was more than hopeless, for rod and column seemed to have been welded into one. But herein Providence smiled on them for one moment to hearten them through the weary weeks ahead. The second engineer—more reckless than resourceful—struck at random with a cold chisel into the cast-iron of the column, and a greasy, grey flake of metal flew from under the imprisoned foot of the connecting-rod, while the rod itself fell away slowly, and brought up with a thunderous clang somewhere in the dark of the crank-pit. The guides-plates above were still jammed fast in the guides, but the first blow had been struck. They spent the rest of the day grooming the donkey-engine, which stood immediately forward of the engine-room hatch. Its tarpaulin, of course, had been stolen, and eight warm months had not improved the working parts. Further, the last dying hiccup of the Haliotis seemed—or it might have been the Malay from the boat-house—to have lifted the thing bodily on its bolts, and set it down inaccurately as regarded its steam connections.

"If we only had one single cargo-derrick!" Mr. Wardrop sighed. "We can take the cylinder-cover off by hand, if we sweat; but to get the rod out o' the piston's not possible unless we use steam. Well, there'll be steam the morn, if there's nothing else. She'll fizzle!"

Next morning men from the shore saw the Haliotis through a cloud, for it was as though the deck smoked. Her crew were chasing steam through the shaken and leaky pipes to its work in the forward donkey-engine; and where oakum failed to plug a crack, they stripped off their loin-cloths for lapping, and swore, half-boiled and mother-naked. The donkey-engine worked—at a price—the price of constant attention and furious stoking—worked long enough to allow a wire-rope (it was made up of a funnel and a foremast-stay) to be led into the engine-room and made fast on the cylinder-cover of the forward engine. That rose easily enough, and was hauled through the skylight and on to the deck, many hands assisting the doubtful steam. Then came the tug of war, for it was necessary to get to the piston and the jammed piston-rod. They removed two of the piston junk-ring studs, screwed in two strong iron eye-bolts by way of handles, doubled the wire-rope, and set half a dozen men to smite with an extemporised battering-ram at the end of the piston-rod, where it peered through the piston, while the donkey-engine hauled upwards on the piston itself. After four hours of this furious work, the piston-rod suddenly slipped, and the piston rose with a jerk, knocking one or two men over into the engine-room. But when Mr. Wardrop declared that the piston had not split, they cheered, and thought nothing of their wounds; and the donkey-engine was hastily stopped; its boiler was nothing to tamper with.

And day by day their supplies reached them by boat. The skipper humbled himself once more before the Governor, and as a concession had leave to get drinking-water from the Malay boat-builder on the quay. It was not good drinking-water, but the Malay was anxious to supply anything in his power, if he were paid for it.

Now when the jaws of the forward engine stood, as it were, stripped and empty, they began to wedge up the shores of the cylinder itself. That work alone filled the better part of three days—warm and sticky days, when the hands slipped and sweat ran into the eyes. When the last wedge was hammered home there was no longer an ounce of weight on the supporting-columns; and Mr. Wardrop rummaged the ship for boiler-plate three-quarters of an inch thick, where he could find it. There was not much available, but what there was was more than beaten gold to him. In one desperate forenoon the entire crew, naked and lean, haled back, more or less into place, the starboard supporting-column, which, as you remember, was cracked clean through. Mr. Wardrop found them asleep where they had finished the work, and gave them a day's rest, smiling upon them as a father while he drew chalk-marks about the cracks. They woke to new and more trying labour; for over each one of those cracks a plate of three-quarter-inch boiler-iron was to be worked hot, the rivet-holes being drilled by hand. All that time they were fed on fruits, chiefly bananas, with some sago.

Those were the days when men swooned over the ratchet-drill and the hand-forge, and where they fell they had leave to lie unless their bodies were in the way of their fellows' feet. And so, patch upon patch, and a patch over all, the starboard supporting-column was clouted; but when they thought all was secure, Mr. Wardrop decreed that the noble patchwork would never support working engines; at the best, it could only hold the guide-bars approximately true, he deadweight of the cylinders must be borne by vertical struts; and, therefore, a gang would repair to the bows, and take out, with files, the big bow-anchor davits, each of which was some three inches in diameter. They threw hot coals at Wardrop, and threatened to kill him, those who did not weep (they were ready to weep on the least provocation); but he hit them with iron bars heated at the end, and they limped forward, and the davits came with them when they returned. They slept sixteen hours on the strength of it, and in three days two struts were in place, bolted from the foot of the starboard supporting-column to the under side of the cylinder. There remained now the port, or condenser-column, which, though not so badly cracked as its fellow, had also been strengthened in four places with boiler-plate patches, but needed struts. They took away the main stanchions of the bridge for that work, and, crazy with toil, did not see till all was in place that the rounded bars of iron must be flattened from top to bottom to allow the air-pump levers to clear them. It was Wardrop's oversight, and he wept bitterly before the men as he gave the order to unbolt the struts and flatten them with hammer and the flame. Now the broken engine was underpinned firmly, and they took away the wooden shores from under the cylinders, and gave them to the robbed bridge, thanking God for even half a day's work on gentle, kindly wood instead of the iron that had entered into their souls. Eight months in the back-country among the leeches, at a temperature of 84 degrees moist, is very bad for the nerves.

They had kept the hardest work to the last, as boys save Latin prose, and, worn though they were, Mr. Wardrop did not dare to give them rest. The piston-rod and connecting-rod were to be straightened, and this was a job for a regular dockyard with every appliance. They fell to it, cheered by a little chalk showing of work done and time consumed which Mr. Wardrop wrote up on the engine-room bulkhead. Fifteen days had gone—fifteen days of killing labour—and there was hope before them.

It is curious that no man knows how the rods were straightened. The crew of the Haliotis remember that week very dimly, as a fever patient remembers the delirium of a long night. There were fires everywhere, they say; the whole ship was one consuming furnace, and the hammers were never still. Now, there could not have been more than one fire at the most, for Mr. Wardrop distinctly recalls that no straightening was done except under his own eye. They remember, too, that for many years voices gave orders which they obeyed with their bodies, but their minds were abroad on all the seas. It seems to them that they stood through days and nights slowly sliding a bar backwards and forwards through a white glow that was part of the ship. They remember an intolerable noise in their burning heads from the walls of the stoke-hole, and they remember being savagely beaten by men whose eyes seemed asleep. When their shift was over they would draw straight lines in the air, anxiously and repeatedly, and would question one another in their sleep, crying, "Is she straight?"

At last—they do not remember whether this was by day or by night—Mr. Wardrop began to dance clumsily, and wept the while; and they too danced and wept, and went to sleep twitching all over; and when they woke, men said that the rods were straightened, and no one did any work for two days, but lay on the decks and ate fruit. Mr. Wardrop would go below from time to time, and pat the two rods where they lay, and they heard him singing hymns.

Then his trouble of mind went from him, and at the end of the third day's idleness he made a drawing in chalk upon the deck, with letters of the alphabet at the angles. He pointed out that, though the piston-rod was more or less straight, the piston-rod cross-head—the thing that had been jammed sideways in the guides—had been badly strained, and had cracked the lower end of the piston-rod. He was going to forge and shrink a wrought-iron collar on the neck of the piston-rod where it joined the cross-head, and from the collar he would bolt a Y-shaped piece of iron whose lower arms should be bolted into the cross-head. If anything more were needed, they could use up the last of the boiler-plate.

So the forges were lit again, and men burned their bodies, but hardly felt the pain. The finished connection was not beautiful, but it seemed strong enough—at least, as strong as the rest of the machinery; and with that job their labours came to an end. All that remained was to connect up the engines, and to get food and water. The skipper and four men dealt with the Malay boat-builder by night chiefly; it was no time to haggle over the price of sago and dried fish. The others stayed aboard and replaced piston, piston-rod, cylinder-cover, cross-head, and bolts, with the aid of the faithful donkey-engine. The cylinder-cover was hardly steam-proof, and the eye of science might have seen in the connecting-rod a flexure something like that of a Christmas-tree candle which has melted and been straightened by hand over a stove, but, as Mr. Wardrop said, "She didn't hit anything."

As soon as the last bolt was in place, men tumbled over one another in their anxiety to get to the hand starting-gear, the wheel and worm, by which some engines can be moved when there is no steam aboard. They nearly wrenched off the wheel, but it was evident to the blindest eye that the engines stirred. They did not revolve in their orbits with any enthusiasm, as good machines should; indeed, they groaned not a little; but they moved over and came to rest in a way which proved that they still recognised man's hand. Then Mr. Wardrop sent his slaves into the darker bowels of the engine-room and the stoke-hole, and followed them with a flare-lamp. The boilers were sound, but would take no harm from a little scaling and cleaning. Mr. Wardrop would not have any one over-zealous, for he feared what the next stroke of the tool might show. "The less we know about her now," said he, "the better for us all, I'm thinkin'. Ye'll understand me when I say that this is in no sense regular engineerin'."

As his raiment, when he spoke, was his grey beard and uncut hair, they believed him. They did not ask too much of what they met, but polished and tallowed and scraped it to a false brilliancy.

"A lick of paint would make me easier in my mind," said Mr. Wardrop, plaintively. "I know half the condenser-tubes are started; and the propeller-shaftin"s God knows how far out of the true, and we'll need a new air-pump, an' the main-steam leaks like a sieve, and there's worse each way I look; but—paint's like clothes to a man, 'an ours is near all gone."

The skipper unearthed some stale ropy paint of the loathsome green that they used for the galleys of sailing-ships, and Mr. Wardrop spread it abroad lavishly to give the engines self-respect.

His own was returning day by day, for he wore his loin-cloth continuously; but the crew, having worked under orders, did not feel as he did. The completed work satisfied Mr. Wardrop. He would at the last have made shift to run to Singapore, and gone home without vengeance taken to show his engines to his brethren in the craft; but the others and the captain forbade him. They had not yet recovered their self-respect.

"It would be safer to make what ye might call a trial trip, but beggars mustn't be choosers; an if the engines will go over to the hand-gear, the probability—I'm only saying it's a probability—the chance is that they'll hold up when we put steam on her."

"How long will you take to get steam?" said the skipper.

"God knows! Four hours—a day—half a week. If I can raise sixty pound I'll not complain."

"Be sure of her first; we can't afford to go out half a mile, and break down."

"My soul and body, man, we're one continuous breakdown, fore an' aft! We might fetch Singapore, though."

"We'll break down at Pygang-Watai, where we can do good," was the answer, in a voice that did not allow argument. "She's my boat, and—I've had eight months to think in."

No man saw the Haliotis depart, though many heard her. She left at two in the morning, having cut her moorings, and it was none of her crew's pleasure that the engines should strike up a thundering half-seas-over chanty that echoed among the hills. Mr. Wardrop wiped away a tear as he listened to the new song.

"She's gibberin'—she's just gibberin'," he whimpered. "Yon's the voice of a maniac."

And if engines have any soul, as their masters believe, he was quite right. There were outcries and clamours, sobs and bursts of chattering laughter, silences where the trained ear yearned for the clear note, and torturing reduplications where there should have been one deep voice. Down the screw-shaft ran murmurs and warnings, while a heart-diseased flutter without told that the propeller needed re-keying.

"How does she make it?" said the skipper.

"She moves, but—but she's breakin' my heart. The sooner we're at Pygang-Watai, the better. She's mad, and we're waking the town."

"Is she at all near safe?"

"What do I care how safe she is? She's mad. Hear that, now! To be sure, nothing's hittin' anything, and the bearin's are fairly cool, but—can ye not hear?"

"If she goes," said the skipper, "I don't care a curse. And she's my boat, too."

She went, trailing a fathom of weed behind her. From a slow two knots an hour she crawled up to a triumphant four. Anything beyond that made the struts quiver dangerously, and filled the engine-room with steam. Morning showed her out of sight of land, and there was a visible ripple under her bows; but she complained bitterly in her bowels, and, as though the noise had called it, there shot along across the purple sea a swift, dark proa, hawk-like and curious, which presently ranged alongside and wished to know if the Haliotis were helpless. Ships, even the steamers of the white men, had been known to break down in those waters, and the honest Malay and Javanese traders would sometimes aid them in their own peculiar way. But this ship was not full of lady passengers and well-dressed officers. Men, white, naked and savage, swarmed down her sides—some with red-hot iron bars, and others with large hammers—threw themselves upon those innocent inquiring strangers, and, before any man could say what had happened, were in full possession of the proa, while the lawful owners bobbed in the water overside. Half an hour later the proa's cargo of sago and trepang, as well as a doubtful-minded compass, was in the Haliotis. The two huge triangular mat sails, with their seventy-foot yards and booms, had followed the cargo, and were being fitted to the stripped masts of the steamer.

They rose, they swelled, they filled, and the empty steamer visibly laid over as the wind took them. They gave her nearly three knots an hour, and what better could men ask? But if she had been forlorn before, this new purchase made her horrible to see. Imagine a respectable charwoman in the tights of a ballet-dancer rolling drunk along the streets, and you will come to some faint notion of the appearance of that nine-hundred-ton, well-decked, once schooner-rigged cargo-boat as she staggered under her new help, shouting and raving across the deep. With steam and sail that marvellous voyage continued; and the bright-eyed crew looked over the rail, desolate, unkempt, unshorn, shamelessly clothed beyond the decencies.

At the end of the third week she sighted the island of Pygang-Watai, whose harbour is the turning-point of a pearl sea-patrol. Here the gunboats stay for a week ere they retrace their line. There is no village at Pygang-Watai; only a stream of water, some palms, and a harbour safe to rest in till the first violence of the southeast monsoon has blown itself out.

They opened up the low coral beach, with its mound of whitewashed coal ready for supply, the deserted huts for the sailors, and the flagless flagstaff.

Next day there was no Haliotis—only a little proa rocking in the warm rain at the mouth of the harbour, whose crew watched with hungry eyes the smoke of a gunboat on the horizon.

Months afterwards there were a few lines in an English newspaper to the effect that some gunboat of some foreign Power had broken her back at the mouth of some far-away harbour by running at full speed into a sunken wreck.

WILLIAM THE CONQUEROR. PART I

I have done one braver thing
Than all the worthies did;

And yet a braver thence doth spring,

Which is to keep that hid.

The Undertaking.

"Is it officially declared yet?"
"They've gone as far as to admit 'extreme local scarcity,' and they've started relief-works in one or two districts, the paper says."
"That means it will be declared as soon as they can make sure of the men and the rolling-stock. Shouldn't wonder if it were as bad as the '78 Famine."
"'Can't be," said Scott, turning a little in the long cane chair.
"We've had fifteen-anna crops in the north, and Bombay and Bengal report more than they know what to do with. They'll be able to check it before it gets out of hand. It will only be local."
Martyn picked the "Pioneer" from the table, read through the telegrams once more, and put up his feet on the chair-rests. It was a hot, dark, breathless evening, heavy with the smell of the newly watered Mall. The flowers in the Club gardens were dead and black on their stalks, the little lotus-pond was a circle of caked mud, and the tamarisk-trees were white with the dust of weeks. Most of the men were at the band-stand in the public gardens—from the Club verandah you could hear the native Police band hammering stale waltzes—or on the polo-ground, or in the high-walled fives-court, hotter than a Dutch oven. Half a dozen grooms, squatted at the heads of their ponies, waited their masters' return. From time to time a man would ride at a foot-pace into the Club compound, and listlessly loaf over to the whitewashed barracks beside the main building. These were supposed to be chambers. Men lived in them, meeting the same white faces night after night at dinner, and drawing out their office-work till the latest possible hour, that they might escape that doleful company.
"What are you going to do?" said Martyn, with a yawn. "Let's have a swim before dinner."
"Water's hot. I was at the bath to-day."
"Play you game o' billiards—fifty up."

"It's a hundred and five in the hall now. Sit still and don't be so abominably energetic."

A grunting camel swung up to the porch, his badged and belted rider fumbling a leather pouch.

"Kubber-kargaz-ki-yektraaa," the man whined, handing down the newspaper extra—a slip printed on one side only, and damp from the press. It was pinned up on the green-baize board, between notices of ponies for sale and fox-terriers missing.

Martyn rose lazily, read it, and whistled. "It's declared!" he cried. "One, two, three—eight districts go under the operations of the Famine Code ek dum. They've put Jimmy Hawkins in charge."

"Good business!" said Scott, with the first sign of interest he had shown. "When in doubt hire a Punjabi. I worked under Jimmy when I first came out and he belonged to the Punjab. He has more bundobust than most men."

"Jimmy's a Jubilee Knight now," said Martyn. "He's a good chap, even though he is a thrice-born civilian and went to the Benighted Presidency. What unholy names these Madras districts rejoice in—all ungas or rungas or pillays or polliums!"

A dog-cart drove up in the dusk, and a man entered, mopping his head. He was editor of the one daily paper at the capital of a Province of twenty-five million natives and a few hundred white men: as his staff was limited to himself and one assistant, his office-hours ran variously from ten to twenty a day.

"Hi, Raines; you're supposed to know everything," said Martyn, stopping him. "How's this Madras 'scarcity' going to turn out?"

"No one knows as yet. There's a message as long as your arm coming in on the telephone. I've left my cub to fill it out. Madras has owned she can't manage it alone, and Jimmy seems to have a free hand in getting all the men he needs. Arbuthnot's warned to hold himself in readiness."

"'Badger' Arbuthnot?"

"The Peshawur chap. Yes: and the Pi wires that Ellis and Clay have been moved from the Northwest already, and they've taken half a dozen Bombay men, too. It's pukka famine, by the looks of it."

"They're nearer the scene of action than we are; but if it comes to indenting on the Punjab this early, there's more in this than meets the eye," said Martyn.

"Here to-day and gone to-morrow. 'Didn't come to stay for ever," said Scott, dropping one of Marryat's novels, and rising to his feet. "Martyn, your sister's waiting for you."

A rough grey horse was backing and shifting at the edge of the verandah, where the light of a kerosene lamp fell on a brown-calico habit and a white face under a grey-felt hat.

"Right, O!" said Martyn. "I'm ready. Better come and dine with us, if you've nothing to do, Scott. William, is there any dinner in the house?"

"I'll go home and see," was the rider's answer. "You can drive him over—at eight, remember."

Scott moved leisurely to his room, and changed into the evening-dress of the season and the country: spotless white linen from head to foot, with a broad silk cummerbund. Dinner at the Martyns' was a decided improvement on the goat-mutton, twiney-tough fowl, and tinned entrees of the Club. But it was a great pity that Martyn could not afford to send his sister to the hills for the hot weather. As an Acting District Superintendent of Police, Martyn drew the magnificent pay of six hundred depreciated silver rupees a month, and his little four-roomed bungalow said just as much. There were the usual blue-and-white-striped jail-made rugs on the uneven floor; the usual glass-studded Amritsar phulkaris draped on nails driven into the flaking whitewash of the walls; the usual half-dozen chairs that did not match, picked up at sales of dead men's effects; and the usual streaks of black grease where the leather punka-thong ran through the wall. It was as though everything had been unpacked the night before to be repacked next morning. Not a door in the house was true on its hinges. The little windows, fifteen feet up, were darkened with wasp-nests, and lizards hunted flies between the beams of the wood-ceiled roof. But all this was part of Scott's life. Thus did people live who had such an income; and in a land where each man's pay, age, and position are printed in a book, that all may read, it is hardly worth while to play at pretence in word or deed. Scott counted eight years' service in the Irrigation Department, and drew eight hundred rupees a month, on the understanding that if he served the State faithfully for another twenty-two years he could retire on a pension of some four hundred rupees a month. His working-life, which had been spent chiefly under canvas or in temporary shelters where a man could sleep, eat, and write letters, was bound up with the opening and guarding of irrigation canals, the handling of two or three thousand workmen of all castes and creeds, and the payment of vast sums of coined silver.

He had finished that spring, not without credit, the last section of the great Mosuhl Canal, and—much against his will, for he hated office-work—had been sent in to serve during the hot weather on the accounts and supply side of the Department, with sole charge of the sweltering sub-office at the capital of the Province. Martyn knew this; William, his sister, knew it; and everybody knew it. Scott knew, too, as well as the rest of the world, that Miss Martyn had come out to India four years ago to keep house for her brother, who, as every one knew, had borrowed the money to pay for her passage, and that she ought, as all the world said, to have married at once. In stead of this, she had refused some half a dozen subalterns, a Civilian twenty years her senior, one Major, and a man in the Indian Medical Department. This, too, was common property. She had "stayed down three hot weathers," as the saying is, because her brother was in debt and could not afford the expense of her keep at even a cheap hill-station. Therefore her face was white as bone, and in the centre of her forehead was a big silvery scar about the size of a shilling—the mark of a Delhi sore, which is the same as a "Bagdad date." This comes from drinking bad water, and slowly eats into the flesh till it is ripe enough to be burned out.

None the less William had enjoyed herself hugely in her four years. Twice she had been nearly drowned while fording a river; once she had been run away with on a camel; had witnessed a midnight attack of thieves on her brother's camp; had seen justice administered, with long sticks, in the open under trees; could speak Urdu and even rough Punjabi with a fluency that was envied by her seniors; had entirely fallen out of the habit of writing to her aunts in England, or cutting the pages of the English magazines; had been through a very bad cholera year, seeing sights unfit to be told; and had wound up her experiences by six weeks of typhoid fever, during which her head had been shaved and hoped to keep her twenty-third birthday that September. It is conceivable that the aunts would not have approved of a girl who never set foot on the ground if a horse were within hail; who rode to dances with a shawl thrown over her skirt; who wore her hair cropped and curling all over her head; who answered indifferently to the name of William or Bill; whose speech was heavy with the flowers of the vernacular; who could act in amateur theatricals, play on the banjo, rule eight servants and two horses, their accounts and their diseases, and look men slowly and deliberately between the eyes—even after they had proposed to her and been rejected.

"I like men who do things," she had confided to a man in the Educational Department, who was teaching the sons of cloth-merchants and dyers the beauty of Wordsworth's "Excursion" in annotated cram-books; and when he grew poetical, William explained that she "didn't understand poetry very much; it made her head ache," and another broken heart took refuge at the Club. But it was all William's fault. She delighted in hearing men talk of their own work, and that is the most fatal way of bringing a man to your feet.

Scott had known her for some three years, meeting her, as a rule, under canvass, when his camp and her brother's joined for a day on the edge of the Indian Desert. He had danced with her several times at the big Christmas gatherings, when as many as five hundred white people came in to the station; and had always a great respect for her housekeeping and her dinners.

She looked more like a boy than ever when, the meal ended, she sat, rolling cigarettes, her low forehead puckered beneath the dark curls as she twiddled the papers and stuck out her rounded chin when the tobacco stayed in place, or, with a gesture as true as a school-boy's throwing a stone, tossed the finished article across the room to Martyn, who caught it with one hand, and continued his talk with Scott. It was all "shop,"—canals and the policing of canals; the sins of villagers who stole more water than they had paid for, and the grosser sin of native constables who connived at the thefts; of the transplanting bodily of villages to newly irrigated ground, and of the coming fight with the desert in the south when the Provincial funds should warrant the opening of the long-surveyed Luni Protective Canal System. And Scott spoke openly of his great desire to be put on one particular section of the work where he knew the land and the people; and Martyn sighed for a billet in the Himalayan foot-hills, and said his mind of his superiors, and William rolled cigarettes and said nothing, but smiled gravely on her brother because he was happy.

At ten Scott's horse came to the door, and the evening was ended. The lights of the two low bungalows in which the daily paper was printed showed bright across the road. It was too early to try to find sleep, and Scott drifted over to the editor. Raines, stripped to the waist like a sailor at a gun, lay half asleep in a long chair, waiting for night telegrams. He had a theory that if a man did not stay by his work all day and most of the night he laid himself open to fever: so he ate and slept among his files.

"Can you do it?" he said drowsily. "I didn't mean to bring you over."

"About what? I've been dining at the Martyns'."

"The Madras famine, of course. Martyn's warned, too. They're taking men where they can find 'em. I sent a note to you at the Club just now, asking if you could do us a letter once a week from the south—between two and three columns, say. Nothing sensational, of course, but just plain facts about who is doing what, and so forth. Our regular rates—ten rupees a column."

"'Sorry, but it's out of my line," Scott answered, staring absently at the map of India on the wall. "It's rough on Martyn—very. 'Wonder what he'll do with his sister? 'Wonder what the deuce they'll do with me? I've no famine experience. This is the first I've heard of it. Am I ordered?"

"Oh, yes. Here's the wire. They'll put you on to relief-works," Raines said, "with a horde of Madrassis dying like flies; one native apothecary and half a pint of cholera-mixture among the ten thousand of you. It comes of your being idle for the moment. Every man who isn't doing two men's work seems to have been called upon. Hawkins evidently believes in Punjabis. It's going to be quite as bad as anything they have had in the last ten years."

"It's all in the day's work, worse luck. I suppose I shall get my orders officially some time to-morrow. I'm awfully glad I happened to drop in. Better go and pack my kit now. Who relieves me here—do you know?"

Raines turned over a sheaf of telegrams. "McEuan," said he, "from Murree."

Scott chuckled. "He thought he was going to be cool all summer. He'll be very sick about this. Well, no good talking. 'Night."

Two hours later, Scott, with a clear conscience, laid himself down to rest on a string cot in a bare room. Two worn bullock trunks, a leather water-bottle, a tin ice-box, and his pet saddle sewed up in sacking were piled at the door, and the Club secretary's receipt for last month's bill was under his pillow. His orders came next morning, and with them an unofficial telegram from Sir James Hawkins; who was not in the habit of forgetting good men when he had once met them, bidding him report himself with all speed at some unpronounceable place fifteen hundred miles to the south, for the famine was sore in the land, and white men were needed.

A pink and fattish youth arrived in the red-hot noonday, whimpering a little at fate and famines, which never allowed any one three months' peace. He was Scott's successor—another cog in the machinery, moved forward behind his fellow whose services, as the official announcement ran, "were placed at the disposal of the Madras Government for famine duty until further orders." Scott handed over the funds in his charge, showed him the coolest corner in the office, warned him against excess of zeal, and, as twilight fell, departed from the Club in a hired carriage, with his faithful body-servant, Faiz Ullah, and a mound of disordered baggage atop, to catch the southern mail at the loopholed and bastioned railway-station. The heat from the thick brick walls struck him across the face as if it had been a hot towel; and he reflected that there were at least five nights and four days of this travel before him. Faiz Ullah, used to the chances of service, plunged into the crowd on the stone platform, while Scott, a black cheroot between his teeth, waited till his compartment should be set away. A dozen native policemen, with their rifles and bundles, shouldered into the press of Punjabi farmers, Sikh craftsmen, and greasy-locked Afreedee pedlars, escorting with all pomp Martyn's uniform-case, water-bottles, ice-box, and bedding-roll. They saw Faiz Ullah's lifted hand, and steered for it.

"My Sahib and your Sahib," said Faiz Ullah to Martyn's man, "will travel together. Thou and I, O brother, will thus secure the servants' places close by; and because of our masters' authority none will dare to disturb us."

When Faiz Ullah reported all things ready, Scott settled down at full length, coatless and bootless, on the broad leather-covered bunk. The heat under the iron-arched roof of the station might have been anything over a hundred degrees. At the last moment Martyn entered, dripping.

"Don't swear," said Scott, lazily; "it's too late to change your carriage; and we'll divide the ice."

"What are you doing here?" said the police-man.

"I'm lent to the Madras Government, same as you. By Jove, it's a bender of a night! Are you taking any of your men down?"

"A dozen. I suppose I shall have to superintend relief distributions. 'Didn't know you were under orders too."

"I didn't till after I left you last night. Raines had the news first. My orders came this morning. McEuan relieved me at four, and I got off at once. 'Shouldn't wonder if it wouldn't be a good thing—this famine—if we come through it alive."

"Jimmy ought to put you and me to work together," said Martyn; and then, after a pause: "My sister's here."

"Good business," said Scott, heartily. "Going to get off at Umballa, I suppose, and go up to Simla. Who'll she stay with there?"

"No-o; that's just the trouble of it. She's going down with me."

Scott sat bolt upright under the oil-lamps as the train jolted past Tarn-Taran. "What! You don't mean you couldn't afford—"

"'Tain't that. I'd have scraped up the money somehow."

"You might have come to me, to begin with," said Scott, stiffly; "we aren't altogether strangers."

"Well, you needn't be stuffy about it. I might, but—you don't know my sister. I've been explaining and exhorting and all the rest of it all day—lost my temper since seven this morning, and haven't got it back yet—but she wouldn't hear of any compromise. A woman's entitled to travel with her husband if she wants to; and William says she's on the same footing. You see, we've been together all our lives, more or less, since my people died. It isn't as if she were an ordinary sister."

"All the sisters I've ever heard of would have stayed where they were well off."

She's as clever as a man, confound—Martyn went on. "She broke up the bungalow over my head while I was talking at her. 'Settled the whole thing in three hours—servants, horses, and all. I didn't get my orders till nine."

"Jimmy Hawkins won't be pleased," said Scott "A famine's no place for a woman."

"Mrs. Jim—I mean Lady Jim's in camp with him. At any rate, she says she will look after my sister. William wired down to her on her own responsibility, asking if she could come, and knocked the ground from under me by showing me her answer."

Scott laughed aloud. "If she can do that she can take care of herself, and Mrs. Jim won't let her run into any mischief. There aren't many women, sisters or wives, who would walk into a famine with their eyes open. It isn't as if she didn't know what these things mean. She was through the Jalo cholera last year."

The train stopped at Amritsar, and Scott went back to the ladies' compartment, immediately behind their carriage. William, with a cloth riding-cap on her curls, nodded affably.

"Come in and have some tea," she said. "'Best thing in the world for heat-apoplexy."

"Do I look as if I were going to have heat-apoplexy?"

"'Never can tell," said William, wisely. "It's always best to be ready."

She had arranged her compartment with the knowledge of an old campaigner. A felt-covered water-bottle hung in the draught of one of the shuttered windows; a tea-set of Russian china, packed in a wadded basket, stood on the seat; and a travelling spirit-lamp was clamped against the woodwork above it.

William served them generously, in large cups, hot tea, which saves the veins of the neck from swelling inopportunely on a hot night. It was characteristic of the girl that, her plan of action once settled, she asked for no comments on it. Life among men who had a great deal of work to do, and very little time to do it in, had taught her the wisdom of effacing, as well as of fending for, herself. She did not by word or deed suggest that she would be useful, comforting, or beautiful in their travels, but continued about her business serenely: put the cups back without clatter when tea was ended, and made cigarettes for her guests.

"This time last night," said Scott, "we didn't expect—er—this kind of thing, did we?"

"I've learned to expect anything," said William. "You know, in our service, we live at the end of the telegraph; but, of course, this ought to be a good thing for us all, departmentally—if we live."

"It knocks us out of the running in our own Province," Scott replied, with equal gravity. "I hoped to be put on the Luni Protective Works this cold weather, but there's no saying how long the famine may keep us."

"Hardly beyond October, I should think," said Martyn. "It will be ended, one way or the other, then."

"And we've nearly a week of this," said William. "Sha'n't we be dusty when it's over?"

For a night and a day they knew their surroundings, and for a night and a day, skirting the edge of the great Indian Desert on a narrow-gauge railway, they remembered how in the days of their apprenticeship they had come by that road from Bombay. Then the languages in which the names of the stations were written changed, and they launched south into a foreign land, where the very smells were new. Many long and heavily laden grain-trains were in front of them, and they could feel the hand of Jimmy Hawkins from far off. They waited in extemporised sidings while processions of empty trucks returned to the north, and were coupled on to slow, crawling trains, and dropped at midnight, Heaven knew where; but it was furiously hot, and they walked to and fro among sacks, and dogs howled. Then they came to an India more strange to them than to the untravelled Englishman—the flat, red India of palm-tree, palmyra-palm, and rice—the India of the picture-books, of "Little Harry and His Bearer"—all dead and dry in the baking heat. They had left the incessant passenger-traffic of the north and west far and far behind them. Here the people crawled to the side of the train, holding their little ones in their arms; and a loaded truck would be left behind, the men and women clustering round it like ants by spilled honey. Once in the twilight they saw on a dusty plain a regiment of little brown men, each bearing a body over his shoulder; and when the train stopped to leave yet another truck, they perceived that the burdens were not corpses, but only foodless folk picked up beside dead oxen by a corps of Irregular troops. Now they met more white men, here one and there two, whose tents stood close to the line, and who came armed with written authorities and angry words to cut off a truck. They were too busy to do more than nod at Scott and Martyn, and stare curiously at William, who could do nothing except make tea, and watch how her men staved off the rush of wailing, walking skeletons, putting them down three at a time in heaps, with their own hands uncoupling the marked trucks, or taking receipts from the hollow-eyed, weary white men, who spoke another argot than theirs. They ran out of ice, out of soda-water, and out of tea; for they were six days and seven nights on the road, and it seemed to them like seven times seven years.

At last, in a dry, hot dawn, in a land of death, lit by long red fires of railway-sleepers, where they were burning the dead, they came to their destination, and were met by Jim Hawkins, the Head of the Famine, unshaven, unwashed, but cheery, and entirely in command of affairs.

Martyn, he decreed then and there, was to live on trains till further orders; was to go back with empty trucks, filling them with starving people as he found them, and dropping them at a famine-camp on the edge of the Eight Districts. He would pick up supplies and return, and his constables would guard the loaded grain-cars, also picking up people, and would drop them at a camp a hundred miles south. Scott—Hawkins was very glad to see Scott again—would that same hour take charge of a convoy of bullock-carts, and would go south, feeding as he went, to yet another famine-camp, where he would leave his starving—there would be no lack of starving on the route—and wait for orders by telegraph. Generally, Scott was in all small things to act as he thought best.

William bit her under lip. There was no one in the wide world like her one brother, but Martyn's orders gave him no discretion.

She came out on the platform, masked with dust from head to foot, a horse-shoe wrinkle on her forehead, put here by much thinking during the past week, but as self-possessed as ever. Mrs. Jim—who should have been Lady Jim but that no one remembered the title—took possession of her with a little gasp.

"Oh, I'm so glad you're here," she almost sobbed. "You oughtn't to, of course, but there—there isn't another woman in the place, and we must help each other, you know; and we've all the wretched people and the little babies they are selling."

"I've seen some," said William.

"Isn't it ghastly? I've bought twenty; they're in our camp; but won't you have something to eat first? We've more than ten people can do here; and I've got a horse for you. Oh, I'm so glad you've come, dear. You're a Punjabi, too, you know."

"Steady, Lizzie," said Hawkins, over his shoulder. "We'll look after you, Miss Martyn. 'Sorry I can't ask you to breakfast, Martyn. You'll have to eat as you go. Leave two of your men to help Scott. These poor devils can't stand up to load carts. Saunders" (this to the engine-driver, who was half asleep in the cab), "back down and get those empties away. You've 'line clear' to Anundrapillay; they'll give you orders north of that. Scott, load up your carts from that B. P. P. truck, and be off as soon as you can. The Eurasian in the pink shirt is your interpreter and guide. You'll find an apothecary of sorts tied to the yoke of the second wagon. He's been trying to bolt; you'll have to look after him. Lizzie, drive Miss Martyn to camp, and tell them to send the red horse down here for me."

Scott, with Faiz Ullah and two policemen, was already busied with the carts, backing them up to the truck and unbolting the sideboards quietly, while the others pitched in the bags of millet and wheat. Hawkins watched him for as long as it took to fill one cart.

"That's a good man," he said. "If all goes well I shall work him hard." This was Jim Hawkins's notion of the highest compliment one human being could pay another.

An hour later Scott was under way; the apothecary threatening him with the penalties of the law for that he, a member of the Subordinate

Medical Department, had been coerced and bound against his will and all laws governing the liberty of the subject; the pink-shirted Eurasian begging leave to see his mother, who happened to be dying some three miles away: "Only verree, verree short leave of absence, and will presently return, sar—"; the two constables, armed with staves, bringing up the rear; and Faiz Ullah, a Mohammedan's contempt for all Hindoos and foreigners in every line of his face, explaining to the drivers that though Scott Sahib was a man to be feared on all fours, he, Faiz Ullah, was Authority Itself.

The procession creaked past Hawkins's camp—three stained tents under a clump of dead trees, behind them the famine-shed, where a crowd of hopeless ones tossed their arms around the cooking-kettles.

"'Wish to Heaven William had kept out of it," said Scott to himself, after a glance. "We'll have cholera, sure as a gun, when the Rains break."

But William seemed to have taken kindly to the operations of the Famine Code, which, when famine is declared, supersede the workings of the ordinary law. Scott saw her, the centre of a mob of weeping women, in a calico riding-habit, and a blue-grey felt hat with a gold puggaree.

"I want fifty rupees, please. I forgot to ask Jack before he went away. Can you lend it me? It's for condensed-milk for the babies," said she.

Scott took the money from his belt, and handed it over without a word. "For goodness sake, take care of yourself," he said.

"Oh, I shall be all right. We ought to get the milk in two days. By the way, the orders are, I was to tell you, that you're to take one of Sir Jim's horses. There's a grey Cabuli here that I thought would be just your style, so I've said you'd take him. Was that right?"

"That's awfully good of you. We can't either of us talk much about style, I am afraid."

Scott was in a weather-stained drill shooting-kit, very white at the seams and a little frayed at the wrists. William regarded him thoughtfully, from his pith helmet to his greased ankle-boots. "You look very nice, I think. Are you sure you've everything you'll need—quinine, chlorodyne, and so on?"

"'Think so," said Scott, patting three or four of his shooting-pockets as he mounted and rode alongside his convoy.

"Good-bye," he cried.

"Good-bye, and good luck," said William. "I'm awfully obliged for the money." She turned on a spurred heel and disappeared into the tent, while the carts pushed on past the famine-sheds, past the roaring lines of the thick, fat fires, down to the baked Gehenna of the South.

WILLIAM THE CONQUEROR. PART II

So let us melt and make no noise,
No tear-floods nor sigh-tempests move;

'Twere profanation of our joys

To tell the Laity our love.

A Valediction.

It was punishing work, even though he travelled by night and camped by day; but within the limits of his vision there was no man whom Scott could call master. He was as free as Jimmy Hawkins—freer, in fact, for the Government held the Head of the Famine tied neatly to a telegraph-wire, and if Jimmy had ever regarded telegrams seriously, the death-rate of that famine would have been much higher than it was.

At the end of a few days' crawling Scott learned something of the size of the India which he served, and it astonished him. His carts, as you know, were loaded with wheat, millet, and barley, good food-grains needing only a little grinding. But the people to whom he brought the life-giving stuffs were rice-eaters. They could hull rice in their mortars, but they knew nothing of the heavy stone querns of the North, and less of the material that the white man convoyed so laboriously. They clamoured for rice—unhusked paddy, such as they were accustomed to—and, when they found that there was none, broke away weeping from the sides of the cart. What was the use of these strange hard grains that choked their throats? They would die. And then and there very many of them kept their word. Others took their allowance, and bartered enough millet to feed a man through a week for a few handfuls of rotten rice saved by some less unfortunate. A few put their share into the rice-mortars, pounded it, and made a paste with foul water; but they were very few. Scott understood dimly that many people in the India of the South ate rice, as a rule, but he had spent his service in a grain Province, had seldom seen rice in the blade or ear, and least of all would have believed that in time of deadly need men could die at arm's length of plenty, sooner than touch food they did not know. In vain the interpreters interpreted; in vain his two policemen showed in vigorous pantomime what should be done. The starving crept away to their bark and weeds, grubs, leaves, and clay, and left the open sacks untouched.

But sometimes the women laid their phantoms of children at Scott's feet, looking back as they staggered away.

Faiz Ullah opined it was the will of God that these foreigners should die, and it remained only to give orders to burn the dead. None the less there was no reason why the Sahib should lack his comforts, and Faiz Ullah, a campaigner of experience, had picked up a few lean goats and had added them to the procession. That they might give milk for the morning meal, he was feeding them on the good grain that these imbeciles rejected. "Yes," said Faiz Ullah; "if the Sahib thought fit, a little milk might be given to some of the babies"; but, as the Sahib well knew, babies were cheap, and, for his own part, Faiz Ullah held that there was no Government order as to babies. Scott spoke forcefully to Faiz Ullah and the two policemen, and bade them capture goats where they could find them. This they most joyfully did, for it was a recreation, and many ownerless goats were driven in. Once fed, the poor brutes were willing enough to follow the carts, and a few days' good food—food such as human beings died for lack of—set them in milk again.

"But I am no goatherd," said Faiz Ullah. "It is against my izzat [my honour]."

"When we cross the Bias River again we will talk of izzat," Scott replied. "Till that day thou and the policemen shall be sweepers to the camp, if I give the order."

"Thus, then, it is done," grunted Faiz Ullah, "if the Sahib will have it so"; and he showed how a goat should be milked, while Scott stood over him.

"Now we will feed them," said Scott; "twice a day we will feed them"; and he bowed his back to the milking, and took a horrible cramp.

When you have to keep connection unbroken between a restless mother of kids and a baby who is at the point of death, you suffer in all your system. But the babies were fed. Each morning and evening Scott would solemnly lift them out one by one from their nest of gunny-bags under the cart-tilts. There were always many who could do no more than breathe, and the milk was dropped into their toothless mouths drop by drop, with due pauses when they choked. Each morning, too, the goats were fed; and since they would straggle without a leader, and since the natives were hirelings, Scott was forced to give up riding, and pace slowly at the head of his flocks, accommodating his step to their weaknesses. All this was sufficiently absurd, and he felt the absurdity keenly; but at least he was saving life, and when the women saw that their children did not die, they made shift to eat a little of the strange foods, and crawled after the carts, blessing the master of the goats.

"Give the women something to live for," said Scott to himself, as he sneezed in the dust of a hundred little feet, "and they'll hang on somehow. This beats William's condensed-milk trick all to pieces. I shall never live it down, though."

He reached his destination very slowly, found that a rice-ship had come in from Burmah, and that stores of paddy were available; found also an overworked Englishman in charge of the shed, and, loading the carts, set back to cover the ground he had already passed. He left some of the children and half his goats at the famine-shed. For this he was not thanked by the Englishman, who had already more stray babies than he knew what to do with. Scott's back was suppled to stooping now, and he went on with his wayside ministrations in addition to distributing the paddy. More babies and more goats were added unto him; but now some of the babies wore rags, and beads round their wrists or necks. "That" said the interpreter, as though Scott did not know, "signifies that their mothers hope in eventual contingency to resume them offeecially."

"The sooner, the better," said Scott; but at the same time he marked, with the pride of ownership, how this or that little Ramasawmy was putting on flesh like a bantam. As the paddy-carts were emptied he headed for Hawkins's camp by the railway, timing his arrival to fit in with the dinner-hour, for it was long since he had eaten at a cloth. He had no desire to make any dramatic entry, but an accident of the sunset ordered it that when he had taken off his helmet to get the evening breeze, the low light should fall across his forehead, and he could not see what was before him; while one waiting at the tent door beheld with new eyes a young man, beautiful as Paris, a god in a halo of golden dust, walking slowly at the head of his flocks, while at his knee ran small naked Cupids. But she laughed—William, in a slate-coloured blouse, laughed consumedly till Scott, putting the best face he could upon the matter, halted his armies and bade her admire the kindergarten. It was an unseemly sight, but the proprieties had been left ages ago, with the tea-party at Amritsar Station, fifteen hundred miles to the north.

"They are coming on nicely," said William. "We've only five-and-twenty here now. The women are beginning to take them away again."

"Are you in charge of the babies, then?"

"Yes—Mrs. Jim and I. We didn't think of goats, though. We've been trying condensed-milk and water."

"Any losses?"

"More than I care to think of;" said William, with a shudder. "And you?"

Scott said nothing. There had been many little burials along his route—one cannot burn a dead baby—many mothers who had wept when they did not find again the children they had trusted to the care of the Government.

Then Hawkins came out carrying a razor, at which Scott looked hungrily, for he had a beard that he did not love. And when they sat down to dinner in the tent he told his tale in few words, as it might have been an official report. Mrs. Jim snuffled from time to time, and Jim bowed his head judicially; but William's grey eyes were on the clean-shaven face, and it was to her that Scott seemed to appeal.

"Good for the Pauper Province!" said William, her chin on her hand, as she leaned forward among the wine-glasses. Her cheeks had fallen in, and the scar on her forehead was more prominent than ever, but the well-turned neck rose roundly as a column from the ruffle of the blouse which was the accepted evening-dress in camp.

"It was awfully absurd at times," said Scott. "You see, I didn't know much about milking or babies. They'll chaff my head off, if the tale goes up North."

"Let 'em," said William, haughtily. "We've all done coolie-work since we came. I know Jack has." This was to Hawkins's address, and the big man smiled blandly.

"Your brother's a highly efficient officer, William," said he, "and I've done him the honour of treating him as he deserves. Remember, I write the confidential reports."

"Then you must say that William's worth her weight in gold," said Mrs. Jim. "I don't know what we should have done without her. She has been everything to us." She dropped her hand upon William's, which was rough with much handling of reins, and William patted it softly. Jim beamed on the company. Things were going well with his world. Three of his more grossly incompetent men had died, and their places had been filled by their betters. Every day brought the Rains nearer. They had put out the famine in five of the Eight Districts, and, after all, the death-rate had not been too heavy—things considered. He looked Scott over carefully, as an ogre looks over a man, and rejoiced in his thews and iron-hard condition.

"He's just the least bit in the world tucked up," said Jim to himself, "but he can do two men's work yet." Then he was aware that Mrs. Jim was telegraphing to him, and according to the domestic code the message ran: "A clear case. Look at them!"

He looked and listened. All that William was saying was: "What can you expect of a country where they call a bhistee [a water-carrier] a tunni-cutch?" and all that Scott answered was: "I shall be glad to get back to the Club. Save me a dance at the Christmas Ball, won't you?"

"It's a far cry from here to the Lawrence Hall," said Jim. "Better turn in early, Scott. It's paddy-carts to-morrow; you'll begin loading at five."

"Aren't you going to give Mr. Scott a single day's rest?"

"'Wish I could, Lizzie, but I'm afraid I can't. As long as he can stand up we must use him."

"Well, I've had one Europe evening, at least. By Jove, I'd nearly forgotten! What do I do about those babies of mine?"

"Leave them here," said William—"we are in charge of that—and as many goats as you can spare. I must learn how to milk now."

"If you care to get up early enough to-morrow I'll show you. I have to milk, you see. Half of 'em have beads and things round their necks. You must be careful not to take 'em off; in case the mothers turn up."

"You forget I've had some experience here."

"I hope to goodness you won't overdo." Scott's voice was unguarded.

"I'll take care of her," said Mrs. Jim, telegraphing hundred-word messages as she carried William off; while Jim gave Scott his orders for the coming campaign. It was very late—nearly nine o'clock.

"Jim, you're a brute," said his wife, that night; and the Head of the Famine chuckled.

"Not a bit of it, dear. I remember doing the first Jandiala Settlement for the sake of a girl in a crinoline, and she was slender, Lizzie. I've never done as good a piece of work since. He'll work like a demon."

"But you might have given him one day."

"And let things come to a head now? No, dear; it's their happiest time."

"I don't believe either of the darlings know what's the matter with them. Isn't it beautiful? Isn't it lovely?"

"Getting up at three to learn to milk, bless her heart! Oh, ye Gods, why must we grow old and fat?"

"She's a darling. She has done more work under me—"

"Under you? The day after she came she was in charge and you were her subordinate. You've stayed there ever since; she manages you almost as well as you manage me."

"She doesn't, and that's why I love her. She's as direct as a man—as her brother."

"Her brother's weaker than she is. He's always to me for orders; but he's honest, and a glutton for work. I confess I'm rather fond of William, and if I had a daughter—"

The talk ended. Far away in the Derajat was a child's grave more than twenty years old, and neither Jim nor his wife spoke of it any more.

"All the same, you're responsible," Jim added, a moment's silence.

"Bless 'em!" said Mrs. Jim, sleepily.

Before the stars paled, Scott, who slept in an empty cart, waked and went about his work in silence; it seemed at that hour unkind to rouse Faiz Ullah and the interpreter. His head being close to the ground, he did not hear William till she stood over him in the dingy old riding-habit, her eyes still heavy with sleep, a cup of tea and a piece of toast in her hands. There was a baby on the ground, squirming on a piece of blanket, and a six-year-old child peered over Scott's shoulder.

"Hai, you little rip," said Scott, "how the deuce do you expect to get your rations if you aren't quiet?"

A cool white hand steadied the brat, who forthwith choked as the milk gurgled into his mouth.

"'Mornin'," said the milker. "You've no notion how these little fellows can wriggle."

"Oh, yes, I have." She whispered, because the world was asleep. "Only I feed them with a spoon or a rag. Yours are fatter than mine. And you've been doing this day after day?" The voice was almost lost.

"Yes; it was absurd. Now you try," he said, giving place to the girl. "Look out! A goat's not a cow."

The goat protested against the amateur, and there was a scuffle, in which Scott snatched up the baby. Then it was all to do over again, and William laughed softly and merrily. She managed, however, to feed two babies, and a third.

"Don't the little beggars take it well?" said Scott. "I trained 'em."

They were very busy and interested, when lo! it was broad daylight, and before they knew, the camp was awake, and they kneeled among the goats, surprised by the day, both flushed to the temples. Yet all the round world rolling up out of the darkness might have heard and seen all that had passed between them.

"Oh," said William, unsteadily, snatching up the tea and toast, "I had this made for you. It's stone-cold now. I thought you mightn't have anything ready so early. 'Better not drink it. It's—it's stone-cold."

"That's awfully kind of you. It's just right. It's awfully good of you, really. I'll leave my kids and goats with you and Mrs. Jim, and, of course, any one in camp can show you about the milking."

"Of course," said William; and she grew pinker and pinker and statelier and more stately, as she strode back to her tent, fanning herself with the saucer.

There were shrill lamentations through the camp when the elder children saw their nurse move off without them. Faiz Ullah unbent so far as to jest with the policemen, and Scott turned purple with shame because Hawkins, already in the saddle, roared.

A child escaped from the care of Mrs. Jim, and, running like a rabbit, clung to Scott's boot, William pursuing with long, easy strides.

"I will not go—I will not go!" shrieked the child, twining his feet round Scott's ankle. "They will kill me here. I do not know these people."

"I say," said Scott, in broken Tamil, "I say, she will do you no harm. Go with her and be well fed."

"Come!" said William, panting, with a wrathful glance at Scott, who stood helpless and, as it were, hamstrung.

"Go back," said Scott quickly to William. "I'll send the little chap over in a minute."

The tone of authority had its effect, but in a way Scott did not exactly intend. The boy loosened his grasp, and said with gravity: "I did not know the woman was thine. I will go." Then he cried to his companions, a mob of three-, four-, and five-year-olds waiting on the success of his venture ere they stampeded: "Go back and eat. It is our man's woman. She will obey his orders."

Jim collapsed where he sat; Faiz Ullah and the two policemen grinned; and Scott's orders to the cartmen flew like hail.

"That is the custom of the Sahibs when truth is told in their presence," said Faiz Ullah. "The time comes that I must seek new service. Young wives, especially such as speak our language and have knowledge of the ways of the Police, make great trouble for honest butlers in the matter of weekly accounts."

What William thought of it all she did not say, but when her brother, ten days later, came to camp for orders, and heard of Scott's performances, he said, laughing: "Well, that settles it. He'll be Bakri Scott to the end of his days." (Bakri in the Northern vernacular, means a goat.) "What a lark! I'd have given a month's pay to have seen him nursing famine babies. I fed some with conjee [rice-water], but that was all right."

"It's perfectly disgusting," said his sister, with blazing eyes. "A man does something like—like that—and all you other men think of is to give him an absurd nickname, and then you laugh and think it's funny."

"Ah," said Mrs. Jim, sympathetically.

"Well, you can't talk, William. You christened little Miss Demby the Button-quail, last cold weather; you know you did. India's the land of nicknames."

"That's different," William replied. "She was only a girl, and she hadn't done anything except walk like a quail, and she does. But it isn't fair to make fun of a man."

"Scott won't care," said Martyn. "You can't get a rise out of old Scotty. I've been trying for eight years, and you've only known him for three. How does he look?"

"He looks very well," said William, and went away with a flushed cheek. "Bakri Scott, indeed!" Then she laughed to herself, for she knew her country. "But it will he Bakri all the same"; and she repeated it under her breath several times slowly, whispering it into favour.

When he returned to his duties on the railway, Martyn spread the name far and wide among his associates, so that Scott met it as he led his paddy-carts to war. The natives believed it to be some English title of honour, and the cart-drivers used it in all simplicity till Faiz Ullah, who did not approve of foreign japes, broke their heads. There was very little time for milking now, except at the big camps, where Jim had extended Scott's idea and was feeding large flocks on the useless northern grains. Sufficient paddy had come now into the Eight Districts to hold the people safe, if it were only distributed quickly, and for that purpose no one was better than the big Canal officer, who never lost his temper, never gave an unnecessary order, and never questioned an order given. Scott pressed on, saving his cattle, washing their galled necks daily, so that no time should be lost on the road; reported himself with his rice at the minor famine-sheds, unloaded, and went back light by forced night-march to the next distributing centre, to find Hawkins's unvarying telegram: "Do it again." And he did it again and again, and yet again, while Jim Hawkins, fifty miles away, marked off on a big map the tracks of his wheels gridironing the stricken lands. Others did well—Hawkins reported at the end they all did well—but Scott was the most excellent, for he kept good coined rupees by him, settled for his own cart-repairs on the spot, and ran to meet all sorts of unconsidered extras, trusting to be recouped later on. Theoretically, the Government should have paid for every shoe and linchpin, for every hand employed in the loading; but Government vouchers cash themselves slowly, and intelligent and efficient clerks write at great length, contesting unauthorised expenditures of eight annas. The man who wants to make his work a success must draw on his own bank-account of money or other things as he goes.

"I told you he'd work," said Jimmy to his wife, at the end of six weeks. "He's been in sole charge of a couple of thousand men up north, on the Mosuhl Canal, for a year; but he gives less trouble than young Martyn with his ten constables; and I'm morally certain—only Government doesn't recognise moral obligations—he's spent about half his pay to grease his wheels. Look at this, Lizzie, for one week's work! Forty miles in two days with twelve carts; two days' halt building a famine-shed for young Rogers. (Rogers ought to have built it himself, the idiot!) Then forty miles back again, loading six carts on the way, and distributing all Sunday. Then in the evening he pitches in a twenty-page Demi-Official to me, saying the people where he is might be 'advantageously employed on relief-work,' and suggesting that he put 'em to work on some broken-down old reservoir he's discovered, so as to have a good water-supply when the Rains break. 'Thinks he can cauk the dam in a fortnight. Look at his marginal sketches—aren't they clear and good? I knew he was pukka, but I didn't know he was as pukka as this."

"I must show these to William," said Mrs. Jim. "The child's wearing herself out among the babies."

"Not more than you are, dear. Well, another two months ought to see us out of the wood. I'm sorry it's not in my power to recommend you for a V. C."

William sat late in her tent that night, reading through page after page of the square handwriting, patting the sketches of proposed repairs to the reservoir, and wrinkling her eyebrows over the columns of figures of estimated water-supply. "And he finds time to do all this," she cried to herself, "and—well, I also was present. I've saved one or two babies."

She dreamed for the twentieth time of the god in the golden dust, and woke refreshed to feed loathsome black children, scores of them, wastrels picked up by the wayside, their bones almost breaking their skin, terrible and covered with sores.

Scott was not allowed to leave his cart-work, but his letter was duly forwarded to the Government, and he had the consolation, not rare in India, of knowing that another man was reaping where he had sown. That also was discipline profitable to the soul.

"He's much too good to waste on canals," said Jimmy. "Any one can oversee coolies. You needn't be angry, William; he can—but I need my pearl among bullock-drivers, and I've transferred him to the Khanda district, where he'll have it all to do over again. He should be marching now.

"He's not a coolie," said William, furiously. "He ought to be doing his regulation work."

"He's the best man in his service, and that's saying a good deal; but if you must use razors to cut grindstones, why, I prefer the best cutlery."

"Isn't it almost time we saw him again?" said Mrs. Jim. "I'm sure the poor boy hasn't had a respectable meal for a month. He probably sits on a cart and eats sardines with his fingers."

"All in good time, dear. Duty before decency—wasn't it Mr. Chucks said that?"

"No; it was Midshipman Easy," William laughed. "I sometimes wonder how it will feel to dance or listen to a band again, or sit under a roof. I can't believe I ever wore a ball-frock in my life."

"One minute," said Mrs. Jim, who was thinking. "If he goes to Khanda, he passes within five miles of us. Of course he'll ride in."

"Oh, no, he won't," said William.

"How do you know, dear?"

"It will take him off his work. He won't have time."

"He'll make it," said Mrs. Jim, with a twinkle.

"It depends on his own judgment. There's absolutely no reason why he shouldn't, if he thinks fit," said Jim.

"He won't see fit," William replied, without sorrow or emotion. "It wouldn't be him if he did."

"One certainly gets to know people rather well in times like these," said Jim, drily; but William's face was serene as ever, and even as she prophesied, Scott did not appear.

The Rains fell at last, late, but heavily; and the dry, gashed earth was red mud, and servants killed snakes in the camp, where every one was weather-bound for a fortnight—all except Hawkins, who took horse and plashed about in the wet, rejoicing. Now the Government decreed that seed-grain should be distributed to the people, as well as advances of money for the purchase of new oxen; and the white men were doubly worked for this new duty, while William skipped from brick to brick laid down on the trampled mud, and dosed her charges with warming medicines that made them rub their little round stomachs; and the milch goats throve on the rank grass. There was never a word from Scott in the Khanda district, away to the southeast, except the regular telegraphic report to Hawkins. The rude country roads had disappeared; his drivers were half mutinous; one of Martyn's loaned policemen had died of cholera; and Scott was taking thirty grains of quinine a day to fight the fever that comes with the rain: but those were things Scott did not consider necessary to report. He was, as usual, working from a base of supplies on a railway line, to cover a circle of fifteen miles radius, and since full loads were impossible, he took quarter-loads, and toiled four times as hard by consequence; for he did not choose to risk an epidemic which might have grown uncontrollable by assembling villagers in thousands at the relief-sheds. It was cheaper to take Government bullocks, work them to death, and leave them to the crows in the wayside sloughs.

That was the time when eight years of clean living and hard condition told, though a man's head were ringing like a bell from the cinchona, and the earth swayed under his feet when he stood and under his bed when he slept. If Hawkins had seen fit to make him a bullock-driver, that, he thought, was entirely Hawkins's own affair. There were men in the North who would know what he had done; men of thirty years' service in his own department who would say that it was "not half bad"; and above, immeasurably above, all men of all grades, there was William in the thick of the fight, who would approve because she understood. He had so trained his mind that it would hold fast to the mechanical routine of the day, though his own voice sounded strange in his own ears, and his hands, when he wrote, grew large as pillows or small as peas at the end of his wrists. That steadfastness bore his body to the telegraph-office at the railway-station, and dictated a telegram to Hawkins saying that the Khanda district was, in his judgment, now safe, and he "waited further orders."

The Madrassee telegraph-clerk did not approve of a large, gaunt man falling over him in a dead faint, not so much because of the weight as because of the names and blows that Faiz Ullah dealt him when he found the body rolled under a bench. Then Faiz Ullah took blankets, quilts, and coverlets where he found them, and lay down under them at his master's side, and bound his arms with a tent-rope, and filled him with a horrible stew of herbs, and set the policeman to fight him when he wished to escape from the intolerable heat of his coverings, and shut the door of the telegraph-office to keep out the curious for two nights and one day; and when a light engine came down the line, and Hawkins kicked in the door, Scott hailed him weakly but in a natural voice, and Faiz Ullah stood back and took all the credit.

"For two nights, Heaven-born, he was pagal" said Faiz Ullah. "Look at my nose, and consider the eye of the policeman. He beat us with his bound hands; but we sat upon him, Heaven-born, and though his words were tez, we sweated him. Heaven-born, never has been such a sweat! He is weaker now than a child; but the fever has gone out of him, by the grace of God. There remains only my nose and the eye of the constabeel. Sahib, shall I ask for my dismissal because my Sahib has beaten me?" And Faiz Ullah laid his long thin hand carefully on Scott's chest to be sure that the fever was all gone, ere he went out to open tinned soups and discourage such as laughed at his swelled nose.

"The district's all right," Scott whispered. "It doesn't make any difference. You got my wire? I shall be fit in a week. 'Can't understand how it happened. I shall be fit in a few days."

"You're coming into camp with us," said Hawkins.

"But look here—but—"

"It's all over except the shouting. We sha'n't need you Punjabis any more. On my honour, we sha'n't. Martyn goes back in a few weeks; Arbuthnot's returned already; Ellis and Clay are putting the last touches to a new feeder-line the Government's built as relief-work. Morten's dead—he was a Bengal man, though; you wouldn't know him. 'Pon my word, you and Will—Miss Martyn—seem to have come through it as well as anybody."

"Oh, how is she, by-the-way?" The voice went up and down as he spoke.

"Going strong when I left her. The Roman Catholic Missions are adopting the unclaimed babies to turn them into little priests; the Basil Mission is taking some, and the mothers are taking the rest. You should hear the little beggars howl when they're sent away from William. She's pulled down a bit, but so are we all. Now, when do you suppose you'll be able to move?"

"I can't come into camp in this state. I won't," he replied pettishly.

"Well, you are rather a sight, but from what I gathered there it seemed to me they'd be glad to see you under any conditions. I'll look over your work here, if you like, for a couple of days, and you can pull yourself together while Faiz Ullah feeds you up."

Scott could walk dizzily by the time Hawkins's inspection was ended, and he flushed all over when Jim said of his work that it was "not half bad," and volunteered, further, that he had considered Scott his right-hand man through the famine, and would feel it his duty to say as much officially.

So they came back by rail to the old camp; but there were no crowds near it; the long fires in the trenches were dead and black, and the famine-sheds were almost empty.

"You see!" said Jim. "There isn't much more to do. 'Better ride up and see the wife. They've pitched a tent for you. Dinner's at seven. I've some work here."

Riding at a foot-pace, Faiz Ullah by his stirrup, Scott came to William in the brown-calico riding-habit, sitting at the dining-tent door, her hands in her lap, white as ashes, thin and worn, with no lustre in her hair. There did not seem to be any Mrs. Jim on the horizon, and all that William could say was: "My word, how pulled down you look!"

"I've had a touch of fever. You don't look very well yourself."

"Oh, I'm fit enough. We've stamped it out. I suppose you know?"

Scott nodded. "We shall all be returned in a few weeks. Hawkins told me."

"Before Christmas, Mrs. Jim says. Sha'n't you be glad to go back? I can smell the wood-smoke already"; William sniffed. "We shall be in time for all the Christmas doings. I don't suppose even the Punjab Government would be base enough to transfer Jack till the new year?"

"It seems hundreds of years ago—the Punjab and all that—doesn't it? Are you glad you came?"

"Now it's all over, yes. It has been ghastly here, though. You know we had to sit still and do nothing, and Sir Jim was away so much."

"Do nothing! How did you get on with the milking?"

"I managed it somehow—after you taught me. 'Remember?"

Then the talk stopped with an almost audible jar. Still no Mrs. Jim.

"That reminds me, I owe you fifty rupees for the condensed-milk. I thought perhaps you'd be coming here when you were transferred to the Khanda district, and I could pay you then; but you didn't."

"I passed within five miles of the camp, but it was in the middle of a march, you see, and the carts were breaking down every few minutes, and I couldn't get 'em over the ground till ten o'clock that night. I wanted to come awfully. You knew I did, didn't you?"

"I—believe—I—did," said William, facing him with level eyes. "She was no longer white."

"Did you understand?"

"Why you didn't ride in? Of course I did."

"Why?"

"Because you couldn't, of course. I knew that."

"Did you care?"

"If you had come in—but I knew you wouldn't—but if you had, I should have cared a great deal. You know I should."

"Thank God I didn't! Oh, but I wanted to! I couldn't trust myself to ride in front of the carts, because I kept edging 'em over here, don't you know?"

"I knew you wouldn't," said William, contentedly. "Here's your fifty."

Scott bent forward and kissed the hand that held the greasy notes. Its fellow patted him awkwardly but very tenderly on the head.

"And you knew, too, didn't you?" said William, in a new voice.

"No, on my honour, I didn't. I hadn't the—the cheek to expect anything of the kind, except... I say, were you out riding anywhere the day I passed by to Khanda?"

William nodded, and smiled after the manner of an angel surprised in a good deed.

"Then it was just a speck I saw of your habit in the—"

"Palm-grove on the Southern cart-road. I saw your helmet when you came up from the mullah by the temple—just enough to be sure that you were all right. D' you care?"

This time Scott did not kiss her hand, for they were in the dusk of the dining-tent, and, because William's knees were trembling under her, she had to sit down in the nearest chair, where she wept long and happily, her head on her arms; and when Scott imagined that it would be well to comfort her, she needing nothing of the kind, she ran to her own tent; and Scott went out into the world, and smiled upon it largely and idiotically. But when Faiz Ullah brought him a drink, he found it necessary to support one hand with the other, or the good whisky and soda would have been spilled abroad. There are fevers and fevers.

But it was worse—much worse—the strained, eye-shirking talk at dinner till the servants had withdrawn, and worst of all when Mrs. Jim, who had been on the edge of weeping from the soup down, kissed Scott and William, and they drank one whole bottle of champagne, hot, because there was no ice, and Scott and William sat outside the tent in the starlight till Mrs. Jim drove them in for fear of more fever.

Apropos of these things and some others William said: "Being engaged is abominable, because, you see, one has no official position. We must be thankful we've lots of things to do."

"Things to do!" said Jim, when that was reported to him. "They're neither of them any good any more. I can't get five hours' work a day out of Scott. He's in the clouds half the time."

"Oh, but they're so beautiful to watch, Jimmy. It will break my heart when they go. Can't you do anything for him?"

"I've given the Government the impression—at least, I hope I have—that he personally conducted the entire famine. But all he wants is to get on to the Luni Canal Works, and William's just as bad. Have you ever heard 'em talking of barrage and aprons and waste-water? It's their style of spooning, I suppose."

Mrs. Jim smiled tenderly. "Ah, that's in the intervals—bless 'em."

And so Love ran about the camp unrebuked in broad daylight, while men picked up the pieces and put them neatly away of the Famine in the Eight Districts.

Morning brought the penetrating chill of the Northern December, the layers of wood-smoke, the dusty grey-blue of the tamarisks, the domes of ruined tombs, and all the smell of the white Northern plains, as the mail-train ran on to the mile-long Sutlej Bridge. William, wrapped in a poshteen—a silk-embroidered sheepskin jacket trimmed with rough astrakhan—looked out with moist eyes and nostrils that dilated joyously. The South of pagodas and palm-trees, the overpopulated Hindu South, was done with. Here was the land she knew and loved, and before her lay the good life she understood, among folk of her own caste and mind.

They were picking them up at almost every station now—men and women coming in for the Christmas Week, with racquets, with bundles of polo-sticks, with dear and bruised cricket-bats, with fox-terriers and saddles. The greater part of them wore jackets like William's, for the Northern cold is as little to be trifled with as the Northern heat. And William was among them and of them, her hands deep in her pockets, her collar turned up over her ears, stamping her feet on the platforms as she walked up and down to get warm, visiting from carriage to carriage and everywhere being congratulated. Scott was with the bachelors at the far end of the train, where they chaffed him mercilessly about feeding babies and milking goats; but from time to time he would stroll up to William's window, and murmur: "Good enough, isn't it?" and William would answer with sighs of pure delight: "Good enough, indeed." The large open names of the home towns were good to listen to. Umballa, Ludianah, Phillour, Jullundur, they rang like the coming marriage-bells in her ears, and William felt deeply and truly sorry for all strangers and outsiders—visitors, tourists, and those fresh-caught for the service of the country.

It was a glorious return, and when the bachelors gave the Christmas Ball, William was, unofficially, you might say, the chief and honoured guest among the Stewards, who could make things very pleasant for their friends.

She and Scott danced nearly all the dances together, and sat out the rest in the big dark gallery overlooking the superb teak floor, where the uniforms blazed, and the spurs clinked, and the new frocks and four hundred dancers went round and round till the draped flags on the pillars flapped and bellied to the whirl of it.

About midnight half a dozen men who did not care for dancing came over from the Club to play "Waits," and that was a surprise the Stewards had arranged—before any one knew what had happened, the band stopped, and hidden voices broke into "Good King Wenceslaus," and William in the gallery hummed and beat time with her foot:

"Mark my footsteps well, my page,

Tread thou in them boldly.

Thou shalt feel the winter's rage

Freeze thy blood less coldly!"

"Oh, I hope they are going to give us another! Isn't it pretty, coming out of the dark in that way? Look—look down. There's Mrs. Gregory wiping her eyes!"

"It's like Home, rather," said Scott. "I remember— "

"Hsh! Listen!—dear." And it began again:

"When shepherds watched their flocks by night— "

"A-h-h!" said William, drawing closer to Scott.

"All seated on the ground,

The Angel of the Lord came down,

And glory shone around.

'Fear not,' said he (for mighty dread

Had seized their troubled mind);

'Glad tidings of great joy I bring

To you and all mankind.'"

This time it was William that wiped her eyes.

.007

A locomotive is, next to a marine engine, the most sensitive thing man ever made; and No. .007, besides being sensitive, was new. The red paint was hardly dry on his spotless bumper-bar, his headlight shone like a fireman's helmet, and his cab might have been a hard-wood-finish parlour. They had run him into the roundhouse after his trial—he had said good-bye to his best friend in the shops, the overhead travelling-crane—the big world was just outside; and the other locos were taking stock of him. He looked at the semicircle of bold, unwinking headlights, heard the low purr and mutter of the steam mounting in the gauges—scornful hisses of contempt as a slack valve lifted a little—and would have given a month's oil for leave to crawl through his own driving-wheels into the brick ash-pit beneath him. .007 was an eight-wheeled "American" loco, slightly different from others of his type, and as he stood he was worth ten thousand dollars on the Company's books. But if you had bought him at his own valuation, after half an hour's waiting in the darkish, echoing roundhouse, you would have saved exactly nine thousand nine hundred and ninety-nine dollars and ninety-eight cents.

A heavy Mogul freight, with a short cow-catcher and a fire-box that came down within three inches of the rail, began the impolite game, speaking to a Pittsburgh Consolidation, who was visiting.

"Where did this thing blow in from?" he asked, with a dreamy puff of light steam.

"it's all I can do to keep track of our makes," was the answer, "without lookin' after your back-numbers. Guess it's something Peter Cooper left over when he died."

.007 quivered; his steam was getting up, but he held his tongue. Even a hand-car knows what sort of locomotive it was that Peter Cooper experimented upon in the far-away Thirties. It carried its coal and water in two apple-barrels, and was not much bigger than a bicycle.

Then up and spoke a small, newish switching-engine, with a little step in front of his bumper-timber, and his wheels so close together that he looked like a broncho getting ready to buck.

"Something's wrong with the road when a Pennsylvania gravel-pusher tells us anything about our stock, I think. That kid's all right. Eustis designed him, and Eustis designed me. Ain't that good enough?"

.007 could have carried the switching-loco round the yard in his tender, but he felt grateful for even this little word of consolation.

"We don't use hand-cars on the Pennsylvania," said the Consolidation. "That—er—peanut-stand is old enough and ugly enough to speak for himself."

"He hasn't bin spoken to yet. He's bin spoke at. Hain't ye any manners on the Pennsylvania?" said the switching-loco.

"You ought to be in the yard, Poney," said the Mogul, severely. "We're all long-haulers here."

"That's what you think," the little fellow replied. "You'll know more 'fore the night's out. I've bin down to Track 17, and the freight there—oh, Christmas!"

"I've trouble enough in my own division," said a lean, light suburban loco with very shiny brake-shoes. "My commuters wouldn't rest till they got a parlourcar. They've hitched it back of all, and it hauls worsen a snow-plough. I'll snap her off someday sure, and then they'll blame every one except their foolselves. They'll be askin' me to haul a vestibuled next!"

"They made you in New Jersey, didn't they?" said Poney. "Thought so. Commuters and truck-wagons ain't any sweet haulin', but I tell you they're a heap better 'n cuttin' out refrigerator-cars or oil-tanks. Why, I've hauled— "

"Haul! You?" said the Mogul, contemptuously. "It's all you can do to bunt a cold-storage car up the yard. Now, I— " he paused a little to let the words sink in—"I handle the Flying Freight—e-leven cars worth just anything you please to mention. On the stroke of eleven I pull out; and I'm timed for thirty-five an hour. Costly-perishable-fragile, immediate—that's me! Suburban traffic's only but one degree better than switching. Express freight's what pays."

"Well, I ain't given to blowing, as a rule," began the Pittsburgh Consolidation.

"No? You was sent in here because you grunted on the grade," Poney interrupted.

"Where I grunt, you'd lie down, Poney: but, as I was saying, I don't blow much. Notwithstandin', if you want to see freight that is freight moved lively, you should see me warbling through the Alleghanies with thirty-seven ore-cars behind me, and my brakemen fightin' tramps so's they can't attend to my tooter. I have to do all the holdin' back then, and, though I say it, I've never had a load get away from me yet. No, sir. Haulin's's one thing, but judgment and discretion's another. You want judgment in my business."

"Ah! But—but are you not paralysed by a sense of your overwhelming responsibilities?" said a curious, husky voice from a corner.

"Who's that?".007 whispered to the Jersey commuter.

"Compound-experiment-N.G. She's bin switchin' in the B. & A. yards for six months, when she wasn't in the shops. She's economical (I call it mean) in her coal, but she takes it out in repairs. Ahem! I presume you found Boston somewhat isolated, madam, after your New York season?"

"I am never so well occupied as when I am alone." The Compound seemed to be talking from half-way up her smoke-stack.
"Sure," said the irreverent Poney, under his breath. "They don't hanker after her any in the yard."
"But, with my constitution and temperament—my work lies in Boston—I find your outrecuidance—"
"Outer which?" said the Mogul freight. "Simple cylinders are good enough for me."
"Perhaps I should have said faroucherie," hissed the Compound.
"I don't hold with any make of papier-mache wheel," the Mogul insisted.
The Compound sighed pityingly, and said no more.
"Git 'em all shapes in this world, don't ye?" said Poney, "that's Mass'chusetts all over. They half start, an' then they stick on a dead-centre, an' blame it all on other folk's ways o' treatin' them. Talkin' o' Boston, Comanche told me, last night, he had a hot-box just beyond the Newtons, Friday. That was why, he says, the Accommodation was held up. Made out no end of a tale, Comanche did."
"If I'd heard that in the shops, with my boiler out for repairs, I'd know 't was one o' Comanche's lies," the New Jersey commuter snapped. "Hot-box! Him! What happened was they'd put an extra car on, and he just lay down on the grade and squealed. They had to send 127 to help him through. Made it out a hotbox, did he? Time before that he said he was ditched! Looked me square in the headlight and told me that as cool as—as a water-tank in a cold wave. Hot-box! You ask 127 about Comanche's hot-box. Why, Comanche he was side-tracked, and 127 (he was just about as mad as they make 'em on account o' being called out at ten o'clock at night) took hold and snapped her into Boston in seventeen minutes. Hot-box! Hot fraud! that's what Comanche is."
Then.007 put both drivers and his pilot into it, as the saying is, for he asked what sort of thing a hot-box might be?
"Paint my bell sky-blue!" said Poney, the switcher. "Make me a surface-railroad loco with a hard-wood skirtin'-board round my wheels. Break me up and cast me into five-cent sidewalk-fakirs' mechanical toys! Here's an eight-wheel coupled 'American' don't know what a hot-box is! Never heard of an emergency-stop either, did ye? Don't know what ye carry jack-screws for? You're too innocent to be left alone with your own tender. Oh, you—you flatcar!"
There was a roar of escaping steam before any one could answer, and .007 nearly blistered his paint off with pure mortification.
"A hot-box," began the Compound, picking and choosing her words as though they were coal, "a hotbox is the penalty exacted from inexperience by haste. Ahem!"

"Hot-box!" said the Jersey Suburban. "It's the price you pay for going on the tear. It's years since I've had one. It's a disease that don't attack shorthaulers, as a rule."

"We never have hotboxes on the Pennsylvania," said the Consolidation. "They get 'em in New York—same as nervous prostration."

"Ah, go home on a ferry-boat," said the Mogul. "You think because you use worse grades than our road 'u'd allow, you're a kind of Alleghany angel. Now, I'll tell you what you... Here's my folk. Well, I can't stop. See you later, perhaps."

He rolled forward majestically to the turn-table, and swung like a man-of-war in a tideway, till he picked up his track. "But as for you, you pea-green swiveling' coffee-pot (this to.007'), you go out and learn something before you associate with those who've made more mileage in a week than you'll roll up in a year. Costly-perishable-fragile immediate—that's me! S' long."

"Split my tubes if that's actin' polite to a new member o' the Brotherhood," said Poney. "There wasn't any call to trample on ye like that. But manners was left out when Moguls was made. Keep up your fire, kid, an' burn your own smoke. 'Guess we'll all be wanted in a minute."

Men were talking rather excitedly in the roundhouse. One man, in a dingy jersey, said that he hadn't any locomotives to waste on the yard. Another man, with a piece of crumpled paper in his hand, said that the yard-master said that he was to say that if the other man said anything, he (the other man) was to shut his head. Then the other man waved his arms, and wanted to know if he was expected to keep locomotives in his hip-pocket. Then a man in a black Prince Albert, without a collar, came up dripping, for it was a hot August night, and said that what he said went; and between the three of them the locomotives began to go, too—first the Compound; then the Consolidation; then.007.

Now, deep down in his fire-box, .007 had cherished a hope that as soon as his trial was done, he would be led forth with songs and shoutings, and attached to a green-and-chocolate vestibuled flyer, under charge of a bold and noble engineer, who would pat him on his back, and weep over him, and call him his Arab steed. (The boys in the shops where he was built used to read wonderful stories of railroad life, and .007 expected things to happen as he had heard.) But there did not seem to be many vestibuled fliers in the roaring, rumbling, electric-lighted yards, and his engineer only said:

"Now, what sort of a fool-sort of an injector has Eustis loaded on to this rig this time?" And he put the lever over with an angry snap, crying: "Am I supposed to switch with this thing, hey?"

The collarless man mopped his head, and replied that, in the present state of the yard and freight and a few other things, the engineer would switch and keep on switching till the cows came home. .007 pushed out gingerly, his heart in his headlight, so nervous that the clang of his own bell almost made him jump the track. Lanterns waved, or danced up and down, before and behind him; and on every side, six tracks deep, sliding backward and forward, with clashings of couplers and squeals of hand-brakes, were cars—more cars than .007 had dreamed of. There were oil-cars, and hay-cars, and stock-cars full of lowing beasts, and ore-cars, and potato-cars with stovepipe-ends sticking out in the middle; cold-storage and refrigerator cars dripping ice water on the tracks; ventilated fruit—and milk-cars; flatcars with truck-wagons full of market-stuff; flatcars loaded with reapers and binders, all red and green and gilt under the sizzling electric lights; flatcars piled high with strong-scented hides, pleasant hemlock-plank, or bundles of shingles; flatcars creaking to the weight of thirty-ton castings, angle-irons, and rivet-boxes for some new bridge; and hundreds and hundreds and hundreds of box-cars loaded, locked, and chalked. Men—hot and angry—crawled among and between and under the thousand wheels; men took flying jumps through his cab, when he halted for a moment; men sat on his pilot as he went forward, and on his tender as he returned; and regiments of men ran along the tops of the box-cars beside him, screwing down brakes, waving their arms, and crying curious things.

He was pushed forward a foot at a time; whirled backward, his rear drivers clinking and clanking, a quarter of a mile; jerked into a switch (yard-switches are very stubby and unaccommodating), bunted into a Red D, or Merchant's Transport car, and, with no hint or knowledge of the weight behind him, started up anew. When his load was fairly on the move, three or four cars would be cut off, and .007 would bound forward, only to be held hiccupping on the brake. Then he would wait a few minutes, watching the whirled lanterns, deafened with the clang of the bells, giddy with the vision of the sliding cars, his brake-pump panting forty to the minute, his front coupler lying sideways on his cow-catcher, like a tired dog's tongue in his mouth, and the whole of him covered with half-burnt coal-dust.

"'Tisn't so easy switching with a straight-backed tender," said his little friend of the roundhouse, bustling by at a trot. "But you're comin' on pretty fair. 'Ever seen a flyin' switch? No? Then watch me."

Poney was in charge of a dozen heavy flatcars. Suddenly he shot away from them with a sharp "Whutt!" A switch opened in the shadows ahead; he turned up it like a rabbit as it snapped behind him, and the long line of twelve-foot-high lumber jolted on into the arms of a full-sized road-loco, who acknowledged receipt with a dry howl.

"My man's reckoned the smartest in the yard at that trick," he said, returning. "Gives me cold shivers when another fool tries it, though. That's where my short wheel-base comes in. Like as not you'd have your tender scraped off if you tried it."

.007 had no ambitions that way, and said so.

"No? Of course this ain't your regular business, but say, don't you think it's interestin'? Have you seen the yard-master? Well, he's the greatest man on earth, an' don't you forget it. When are we through? Why, kid, it's always like this, day an' night—Sundays an' week-days. See that thirty-car freight slidin' in four, no, five tracks off? She's all mixed freight, sent here to be sorted out into straight trains. That's why we're cuttin' out the cars one by one." He gave a vigorous push to a westbound car as he spoke, and started back with a little snort of surprise, for the car was an old friend—an M. T. K. box-car.

"Jack my drivers, but it's Homeless Kate! Why, Kate, ain't there no gettin' you back to your friends? There's forty chasers out for you from your road, if there's one. Who's holdin' you now?"

"Wish I knew," whimpered Homeless Kate. "I belong in Topeka, but I've bin to Cedar Rapids; I've bin to Winnipeg; I've bin to Newport News; I've bin all down the old Atlanta and West Point; an' I've bin to Buffalo. Maybe I'll fetch up at Haverstraw. I've only bin out ten months, but I'm homesick—I'm just achin' homesick."

"Try Chicago, Katie," said the switching-loco; and the battered old car lumbered down the track, jolting: "I want to be in Kansas when the sunflowers bloom."

"'Yard's full o' Homeless Kates an' Wanderin' Willies," he explained to.007. "I knew an old Fitchburg flatcar out seventeen months; an' one of ours was gone fifteen 'fore ever we got track of her. Dunno quite how our men fix it. 'Swap around, I guess. Anyway, I've done my duty. She's on her way to Kansas, via Chicago; but I'll lay my next boilerful she'll be held there to wait consignee's convenience, and sent back to us with wheat in the fall."

Just then the Pittsburgh Consolidation passed, at the head of a dozen cars.

"I'm goin' home," he said proudly.

"Can't get all them twelve on to the flat. Break 'em in half, Dutchy!" cried Poney. But it was.007 who was backed down to the last six cars, and he nearly blew up with surprise when he found himself pushing them on to a huge ferry-boat. He had never seen deep water before, and shivered as the flat drew away and left his bogies within six inches of the black, shiny tide.

After this he was hurried to the freight-house, where he saw the yard-master, a smallish, white-faced man in shirt, trousers, and slippers, looking down upon a sea of trucks, a mob of bawling truckmen, and squadrons of backing, turning, sweating, spark-striking horses.

"That's shippers' carts loadin' on to the receivin' trucks," said the small engine, reverently. "But he don't care. He lets 'em cuss. He's the Czar-King-Boss! He says 'Please,' and then they kneel down an' pray. There's three or four strings o' today's freight to be pulled before he can attend to them. When he waves his hand that way, things happen."

A string of loaded cars slid out down the track, and a string of empties took their place. Bales, crates, boxes, jars, carboys, frails, cases, and packages flew into them from the freight-house as though the cars had been magnets and they iron filings.

"Ki-yah!" shrieked little Poney. "Ain't it great?"

A purple-faced truckman shouldered his way to the yard-master, and shook his fist under his nose. The yard-master never looked up from his bundle of freight receipts. He crooked his forefinger slightly, and a tall young man in a red shirt, lounging carelessly beside him, hit the truckman under the left ear, so that he dropped, quivering and clucking, on a hay-bale.

"Eleven, seven, ninety-seven, L. Y. S.; fourteen ought ought three; nineteen thirteen; one one four; seventeen ought twenty-one M. B.; and the ten westbound. All straight except the two last. Cut 'em off at the junction. An' that's all right. Pull that string." The yard-master, with mild blue eyes, looked out over the howling truckmen at the waters in the moonlight beyond, and hummed:

"All things bright and beautiful,

All creatures great and small,

All things wise and wonderful,

The Lawd Gawd He made all!"

.007 moved out the cars and delivered them to the regular road-engine. He had never felt quite so limp in his life before.

"Curious, ain't it?" said Poney, puffing, on the next track. "You an' me, if we got that man under our bumpers, we'd work him into red waste an' not know what we'd done; but-up there—with the steam hummin' in his boiler that awful quiet way..."

"I know," said.007. "Makes me feel as if I'd dropped my Fire an' was getting cold. He is the greatest man on earth."

They were at the far north end of the yard now, under a switchtower, looking down on the four-track way of the main traffic. The Boston Compound was to haul .007's string to some far-away northern junction over an indifferent road-bed, and she mourned aloud for the ninety-six pound rails of the B. & A.

"You're young; you're young," she coughed. "You don't realise your responsibilities."

"Yes, he does," said Poney, sharply; "but he don't lie down under 'em." Then, with aside-spurt of steam, exactly like a tough spitting: "There ain't more than fifteen thousand dollars' worth o' freight behind her anyway, and she goes on as if 't were a hundred thousand—same as the Mogul's. Excuse me, madam, but you've the track.... She's stuck on a dead-centre again—bein' specially designed not to."

The Compound crawled across the tracks on a long slant, groaning horribly at each switch, and moving like a cow in a snow-drift. There was a little pause along the yard after her tail-lights had disappeared; switches locked crisply, and every one seemed to be waiting.

"Now I'll show you something worth," said Poney. "When the Purple Emperor ain't on time, it's about time to amend the Constitution. The first stroke of twelve is—"

"Boom!" went the clock in the big yard-tower, and far away.007 heard a full, vibrating "Yah! Yah! Yah!" A headlight twinkled on the horizon like a star, grew an overpowering blaze, and whooped up the humming track to the roaring music of a happy giant's song:

"With a michnai—ghignai—shtingal! Yah! Yah! Yah!

Ein—zwei—drei—Mutter! Yah! Yah! Yah!

She climb upon der shteeple,

Und she frighten all der people.

Singin' michnai—ghignai—shtingal! Yah! Yah!"

The last defiant "yah! yah!" was delivered a mile and a half beyond the passenger-depot; but .007 had caught one glimpse of the superb six-wheel-coupled racing-locomotive, who hauled the pride and glory of the road—the gilt-edged Purple Emperor, the millionaires' south-bound express, laying the miles over his shoulder as a man peels a shaving from a soft board. The rest was a blur of maroon enamel, a bar of white light from the electrics in the cars, and a flicker of nickel-plated hand-rail on the rear platform.

"Ooh!" said.007.

"Seventy-five miles an hour these five miles. Baths, I've heard; barber's shop; ticker; and a library and the rest to match. Yes, sir; seventy-five an hour! But he'll talk to you in the roundhouse just as democratic as I would. And I—cuss my wheel-base!—I'd kick clean off the track at half his gait. He's the Master of our Lodge. Cleans up at our house. I'll introdooce you some day. He's worth knowin'! There ain't many can sing that song, either."

.007 was too full of emotions to answer. He did not hear a raging of telephone-bells in the switchtower, nor the man, as he leaned out and called to .007's engineer: "Got any steam?"

"'Nough to run her a hundred mile out o' this, if I could," said the engineer, who belonged to the open road and hated switching.

"Then get. The Flying Freight's ditched forty mile out, with fifty rod o' track ploughed up. No; no one's hurt, but both tracks are blocked. Lucky the wreckin'-car an' derrick are this end of the yard. Crew 'll be along in a minute. Hurry! You've the track."

"Well, I could jest kick my little sawed-off self," said Poney, as .007 was backed, with a bang, on to a grim and grimy car like a caboose, but full of tools—a flatcar and a derrick behind it. "Some folks are one thing, and some are another; but you're in luck, kid. They push a wrecking-car. Now, don't get rattled. Your wheel-base will keep you on the track, and there ain't any curves worth mentionin'. Oh, say! Comanche told me there's one section o' sawedged track that's liable to jounce ye a little. Fifteen an' a half out, after the grade at Jackson's crossin'. You'll know it by a farmhouse an' a windmill an' five maples in the dooryard. Windmill's west o' the maples. An' there's an eighty-foot iron bridge in the middle o' that section with no guard-rails. See you later. Luck!"

Before he knew well what had happened, .007 was flying up the track into the dumb, dark world. Then fears of the night beset him. He remembered all he had ever heard of landslides, rain-piled boulders, blown trees, and strayed cattle, all that the Boston Compound had ever said of responsibility, and a great deal more that came out of his own head. With a very quavering voice he whistled for his first grade-crossing (an event in the life of a locomotive), and his nerves were in no way restored by the sight of a frantic horse and a white-faced man in a buggy less than a yard from his right shoulder. Then he was sure he would jump the track; felt his flanges mounting the rail at every curve; knew that his first grade would make him lie down even as Comanche had done at the Newtons. He whirled down the grade to Jackson's crossing, saw the windmill west of the maples, felt the badly laid rails spring under him, and sweated big drops all over his boiler. At each jarring bump he believed an axle had smashed, and he took the eighty-foot bridge without the guard-rail like a hunted cat on the top of a fence. Then a wet leaf stuck against the glass of his headlight and threw a flying shadow on the track, so that he thought it was some little dancing animal that would feel soft if he ran over it; and anything soft underfoot frightens a locomotive as it does an elephant. But the men behind seemed quite calm. The wrecking-crew were climbing carelessly from the caboose to the tender—even jesting with the engineer, for he heard a shuffling of feet among the coal, and the snatch of a song, something like this:

"Oh, the Empire State must learn to wait,

And the Cannon-ball go hang!

When the Westbound's ditched, and the tool-car's hitched,

And it's 'way for the Breakdown Gang (Tare-ra!)

'Way for the Breakdown Gang!"

"Say! Eustis knew what he was doin' when he designed this rig. She's a hummer. New, too."

"Snff! Phew! She is new. That ain't paint, that's— "

A burning pain shot through .007's right rear driver—a crippling, stinging pain.

"This," said .007, as he flew, "is a hot-box. Now I know what it means. I shall go to pieces, I guess. My first road-run, too!"

"Het a bit, ain't she?" the fireman ventured to suggest to the engineer.

"She'll hold for all we want of her. We're 'most there. Guess you chaps back had better climb into your car," said the engineer, his hand on the brake lever. "I've seen men snapped off— "

But the crew fled back with laughter. They had no wish to be jerked on to the track. The engineer half turned his wrist, and .007 found his drivers pinned firm.

"Now it's come!" said .007, as he yelled aloud, and slid like a sleigh. For the moment he fancied that he would jerk bodily from off his underpinning.

"That must be the emergency-stop that Poney guyed me about," he gasped, as soon as he could think. "Hot-box-emergency-stop. They both hurt; but now I can talk back in the roundhouse."

He was halted, all hissing hot, a few feet in the rear of what doctors would call a compound-comminuted car. His engineer was kneeling down among his drivers, but he did not call.007 his "Arab steed," nor cry over him, as the engineers did in the newspapers. He just bad worded.007, and pulled yards of charred cotton-waste from about the axles, and hoped he might some day catch the idiot who had packed it. Nobody else attended to him, for Evans, the Mogul's engineer, a little cut about the head, but very angry, was exhibiting, by lantern-light, the mangled corpse of a slim blue pig.

"T were n't even a decent-sized hog," he said. "'T were a shote."

"Dangerousest beasts they are," said one of the crew. "Get under the pilot an' sort o' twiddle ye off the track, don't they?"

"Don't they?" roared Evans, who was a red-headed Welshman. "You talk as if I was ditched by a hog every fool-day o' the week. I ain't friends with all the cussed half-fed shotes in the State o' New York. No, indeed! Yes, this is him—an' look what he's done!"

It was not a bad night's work for one stray piglet. The Flying Freight seemed to have flown in every direction, for the Mogul had mounted the rails and run diagonally a few hundred feet from right to left, taking with him such cars as cared to follow. Some did not. They broke their couplers and lay down, while rear cars frolicked over them. In that game, they had ploughed up and removed and twisted a good deal of the left-hand track. The Mogul himself had waddled into a corn-field, and there he knelt—fantastic wreaths of green twisted round his crankpins; his pilot covered with solid clods of field, on which corn nodded drunkenly; his fire put out with dirt (Evans had done that as soon as he recovered his senses); and his broken headlight half full of half-burnt moths. His tender had thrown coal all over him, and he looked like a disreputable buffalo who had tried to wallow in a general store. For there lay scattered over the landscape, from the burst cars, type-writers, sewing-machines, bicycles in crates, a consignment of silver-plated imported harness, French dresses and gloves, a dozen finely moulded hard-wood mantels, a fifteen-foot naphtha-launch, with a solid brass bedstead crumpled around her bows, a case of telescopes and microscopes, two coffins, a case of very best candies, some gilt-edged dairy produce, butter and eggs in an omelette, a broken box of expensive toys, and a few hundred other luxuries. A camp of tramps hurried up from nowhere, and generously volunteered to help the crew. So the brakemen, armed with coupler-pins, walked up and down on one side, and the freight-conductor and the fireman patrolled the other with their hands in their hip-pockets. A long-bearded man came out of a house beyond the corn-field, and told Evans that if the accident had happened a little later in the year, all his corn would have been burned, and accused Evans of carelessness. Then he ran away, for Evans was at his heels shrieking: "'T was his hog done it—his hog done it! Let me kill him! Let me kill him!" Then the wrecking-crew laughed; and the farmer put his head out of a window and said that Evans was no gentleman.

But .007 was very sober. He had never seen a wreck before, and it frightened him. The crew still laughed, but they worked at the same time; and 007 forgot horror in amazement at the way they handled the

Mogul freight. They dug round him with spades; they put ties in front of his wheels, and jack-screws under him; they embraced him with the derrick-chain and tickled him with crowbars; while .007 was hitched on to wrecked cars and backed away till the knot broke or the cars rolled clear of the track. By dawn thirty or forty men were at work, replacing and ramming down the ties, gauging the rails and spiking them. By daylight all cars who could move had gone on in charge of another loco; the track was freed for traffic; and 007 had hauled the old Mogul over a small pavement of ties, inch by inch, till his flanges bit the rail once more, and he settled down with a clank. But his spirit was broken, and his nerve was gone.

"'T weren't even a hog," he repeated dolefully; "'t were a shote; and you—you of all of 'em—had to help me on."

"But how in the whole long road did it happen?" asked 007, sizzling with curiosity.

"Happen! It didn't happen! It just come! I sailed right on top of him around that last curve—thought he was a skunk. Yes; he was all as little as that. He hadn't more 'n squealed once 'fore I felt my bogies lift (he'd rolled right under the pilot), and I couldn't catch the track again to save me. Swivelled clean off, I was. Then I felt him sling himself along, all greasy, under my left leadin' driver, and, oh, Boilers! that mounted the rail. I heard my flanges zippin' along the ties, an' the next I knew I was playin' 'Sally, Sally Waters' in the corn, my tender shuckin' coal through my cab, an' old man Evans lyin' still an' bleedin' in front o' me. Shook? There ain't a stay or a bolt or a rivet in me that ain't sprung to glory somewhere."

"Umm!" said 007. "What d' you reckon you weigh?"

"Without these lumps o' dirt I'm all of a hundred thousand pound."

"And the shote?"

"Eighty. Call him a hundred pound at the outside. He's worth about four 'n' a half dollars. Ain't it awful? Ain't it enough to give you nervous prostration? Ain't it paralysin'? Why, I come just around that curve—" and the Mogul told the tale again, for he was very badly shaken.

"Well, it's all in the day's run, I guess," said 007, soothingly; "an'—an' a corn-field's pretty soft fallin'."

"If it had bin a sixty-foot bridge, an' I could ha' slid off into deep water an' blown up an' killed both men, same as others have done, I wouldn't ha' cared; but to be ditched by a shote—an' you to help me out—in a corn-field—an' an old hayseed in his nightgown cussin' me like as if I was a sick truck-horse!... Oh, it's awful! Don't call me Mogul! I'm a sewin'-machine, they'll guy my sand-box off in the yard."

And 007, his hot-box cooled and his experience vastly enlarged, hauled the Mogul freight slowly to the roundhouse.

"Hello, old man! Bin out all night, hain't ye?" said the irrepressible Poney, who had just come off duty. "Well, I must say you look it. Costly-perishable-fragile-immediate—that's you! Go to the shops, take them vine-leaves out o' your hair, an' git 'em to play the hose on you."

"Leave him alone, Poney," said 007 severely, as he was swung on the turn-table, "or I'll—"

"'Didn't know the old granger was any special friend o' yours, kid. He wasn't over-civil to you last time I saw him."

"I know it; but I've seen a wreck since then, and it has about scared the paint off me. I'm not going to guy anyone as long as I steam—not when they're new to the business an' anxious to learn. And I'm not goin' to guy the old Mogul either, though I did find him wreathed around with roastin'-ears. 'T was a little bit of a shote—not a hog—just a shote, Poney—no bigger'n a lump of anthracite—I saw it—that made all the mess. Anybody can be ditched, I guess."

"Found that out already, have you? Well, that's a good beginnin'." It was the Purple Emperor, with his high, tight, plate-glass cab and green velvet cushion, waiting to be cleaned for his next day's fly.

"Let me make you two gen'lemen acquainted," said Poney. "This is our Purple Emperor, kid, whom you were admirin' and, I may say, envyin' last night. This is a new brother, worshipful sir, with most of his mileage ahead of him, but, so far as a serving-brother can, I'll answer for him.'

"'Happy to meet you," said the Purple Emperor, with a glance round the crowded roundhouse. "I guess there are enough of us here to form a full meetin'. Ahem! By virtue of the authority vested in me as Head of the Road, I hereby declare and pronounce No..007 a full and accepted Brother of the Amalgamated Brotherhood of Locomotives, and as such entitled to all shop, switch, track, tank, and roundhouse privileges throughout my jurisdiction, in the Degree of Superior Flier, it bein' well known and credibly reported to me that our Brother has covered forty-one miles in thirty-nine minutes and a half on an errand of mercy to the afflicted. At a convenient time, I myself will communicate to you the Song and Signal of this Degree whereby you may be recognised in the darkest night. Take your stall, newly entered Brother among Locomotives!"

****

Now, in the darkest night, even as the Purple Emperor said, if you will stand on the bridge across the freightyard, looking down upon the four-track way, at 2:30 A. M., neither before nor after, when the White Moth, that takes the overflow from the Purple Emperor, tears south with her seven vestibuled cream-white cars, you will hear, as the yard-clock makes the half-hour, a far-away sound like the bass of a violoncello, and then, a hundred feet to each word,

"With a michnai—ghignai—shtingal! Yah! Yah! Yah!

Ein—zwei—drei—Mutter! Yah! Yah! Yah!

She climb upon der shteeple,

Und she frighten all der people,

Singin' michnai—ghignai—shtingal! Yah! Yah!"

That is 007 covering his one hundred and fifty-six miles in two hundred and twenty-one minutes.

THE MALTESE CAT

They had good reason to be proud, and better reason to be afraid, all twelve of them; for though they had fought their way, game by game, up the teams entered for the polo tournament, they were meeting the Archangels that afternoon in the final match; and the Archangels men were playing with half a dozen ponies apiece. As the game was divided into six quarters of eight minutes each, that meant a fresh pony after every halt. The Skidars' team, even supposing there were no accidents, could only supply one pony for every other change; and two to one is heavy odds. Again, as Shiraz, the grey Syrian, pointed out, they were meeting the pink and pick of the polo-ponies of Upper India, ponies that had cost from a thousand rupees each, while they themselves were a cheap lot gathered, often from country-carts, by their masters, who belonged to a poor but honest native infantry regiment.

"Money means pace and weight," said Shiraz, rubbing his black-silk nose dolefully along his neat-fitting boot, "and by the maxims of the game as I know it—"

"Ah, but we aren't playing the maxims," said The Maltese Cat. "We're playing the game; and we've the great advantage of knowing the game. Just think a stride, Shiraz! We've pulled up from bottom to second place in two weeks against all those fellows on the ground here. That's because we play with our heads as well as our feet."

"It makes me feel undersized and unhappy all the same," said Kittiwynk, a mouse-coloured mare with a red brow-band and the cleanest pair of legs that ever an aged pony owned. "They've twice our style, these others."

Kittiwynk looked at the gathering and sighed. The hard, dusty pologround was lined with thousands of soldiers, black and white, not counting hundreds and hundreds of carriages and drags and dogcarts, and ladies with brilliant-coloured parasols, and officers in uniform and out of it, and crowds of natives behind them; and orderlies on camels, who had halted to watch the game, instead of carrying letters up and down the station; and native horse-dealers running about on thin-eared Biluchi mares, looking for a chance to sell a few first-class polo-ponies. Then there were the ponies of thirty teams that had entered for the Upper India Free-for-All Cup—nearly every pony of worth and dignity, from Mhow to Peshawar, from Allahabad to Multan; prize ponies, Arabs, Syrian, Barb, country-bred, Deccanee, Waziri, and Kabul ponies of every colour and shape and temper that you could imagine. Some of them were in mat-roofed stables, close to the pologround, but most were under saddle, while their masters, who had been defeated in the earlier games, trotted in and out and told the world exactly how the game should be played.

It was a glorious sight, and the come and go of the little, quick hooves, and the incessant salutations of ponies that had met before on other pologrounds or race-courses were enough to drive a four-footed thing wild.

But the Skidars' team were careful not to know their neighbours, though half the ponies on the ground were anxious to scrape acquaintance with the little fellows that had come from the North, and, so far, had swept the board.

"Let's see," said a soft gold-coloured Arab, who had been playing very badly the day before, to The Maltese Cat; "didn't we meet in Abdul Rahman's stable in Bombay, four seasons ago? I won the Paikpattan Cup next season, you may remember?"

"Not me," said The Maltese Cat, politely. "I was at Malta then, pulling a vegetable-cart. I don't race. I play the game."

"Oh!" said the Arab, cocking his tail and swaggering off.

"Keep yourselves to yourselves," said The Maltese Cat to his companions. "We don't want to rub noses with all those goose-rumped half-breeds of Upper India. When we've won this Cup they'll give their shoes to know us."

"We sha'n't win the Cup," said Shiraz. "How do you feel?"

"Stale as last night's feed when a muskrat has run over it," said Polaris, a rather heavy-shouldered grey; and the rest of the team agreed with him.

"The sooner you forget that the better," said The Maltese Cat, cheerfully. "They've finished tiffin in the big tent. We shall be wanted now. If your saddles are not comfy, kick. If your bits aren't easy, rear, and let the saises know whether your boots are tight."

Each pony had his sais, his groom, who lived and ate and slept with the animal, and had betted a good deal more than he could afford on the result of the game. There was no chance of anything going wrong, but to make sure, each sais was shampooing the legs of his pony to the last minute. Behind the saises sat as many of the Skidars' regiment as had leave to attend the match—about half the native officers, and a hundred or two dark, black-bearded men with the regimental pipers nervously fingering the big, beribboned bagpipes. The Skidars were what they call a Pioneer regiment, and the bagpipes made the national music of half their men. The native officers held bundles of polo-sticks, long cane-handled mallets, and as the grand stand filled after lunch they arranged themselves by ones and twos at different points round the ground, so that if a stick were broken the player would not have far to ride for a new one. An impatient British Cavalry Band struck up "If you want to know the time, ask a p'leeceman!" and the two umpires in light dust-coats danced out on two little excited ponies. The four players of the Archangels' team followed, and the sight of their beautiful mounts made Shiraz groan again.

"Wait till we know," said The Maltese Cat. "Two of 'em are playing in blinkers, and that means they can't see to get out of the way of their own side, or they may shy at the umpires' ponies. They've all got white web-reins that are sure to stretch or slip!"

"And," said Kittiwynk, dancing to take the stiffness out of her, "they carry their whips in their hands instead of on their wrists. Hah!"

"True enough. No man can manage his stick and his reins and his whip that way," said The Maltese Cat. "I've fallen over every square yard of the Malta ground, and I ought to know."

He quivered his little, flea-bitten withers just to show how satisfied he felt; but his heart was not so light. Ever since he had drifted into India on a troop-ship, taken, with an old rifle, as part payment for a racing debt, The Maltese Cat had played and preached polo to the Skidars' team on the Skidars' stony pologround. Now a polo-pony is like a poet. If he is born with a love for the game, he can be made. The Maltese Cat knew that bamboos grew solely in order that poloballs might be turned from their roots, that grain was given to ponies to keep them in hard condition, and that ponies were shod to prevent them slipping on a turn. But, besides all these things, he knew every trick and device of the finest game in the world, and for two seasons had been teaching the others all he knew or guessed.

"Remember," he said for the hundredth time, as the riders came up, "you must play together, and you must play with your heads. Whatever happens, follow the ball. Who goes out first?"

Kittiwynk, Shiraz, Polaris, and a short high little bay fellow with tremendous hocks and no withers worth speaking of (he was called Corks) were being girthed up, and the soldiers in the background stared with all their eyes.

"I want you men to keep quiet," said Lutyens, the captain of the team, "and especially not to blow your pipes."

"Not if we win, Captain Sahib?" asked the piper.

"If we win you can do what you please," said Lutyens, with a smile, as he slipped the loop of his stick over his wrist, and wheeled to canter to his place. The Archangels' ponies were a little bit above themselves on account of the many-coloured crowd so close to the ground. Their riders were excellent players, but they were a team of crack players instead of a crack team; and that made all the difference in the world. They honestly meant to play together, but it is very hard for four men, each the best of the team he is picked from, to remember that in polo no brilliancy in hitting or riding makes up for playing alone. Their captain shouted his orders to them by name, and it is a curious thing that if you call his name aloud in public after an Englishman you make him hot and fretty. Lutyens said nothing to his men, because it had all been said before. He pulled up Shiraz, for he was playing "back," to guard the goal. Powell on Polaris was half-back, and Macnamara and Hughes on Corks and Kittiwynk were forwards. The tough, bamboo ball was set in the middle of the ground, one hundred and fifty yards from the ends, and Hughes crossed sticks, heads up, with the Captain of the Archangels, who saw fit to play forward; that is a place from which you cannot easily control your team. The little click as the cane-shafts met was heard all over the ground, and then Hughes made some sort of quick wrist-stroke that just dribbled the ball a few yards. Kittiwynk knew that stroke of old, and followed as a cat follows a mouse. While the Captain of the Archangels was wrenching his pony round, Hughes struck with all his strength, and next instant Kittiwynk was away, Corks following close behind her, their little feet pattering like raindrops on glass.

"Pull out to the left," said Kittiwynk between her teeth; "it's coming your way, Corks!"

The back and half-back of the Archangels were tearing down on her just as she was within reach of the ball. Hughes leaned forward with a loose rein, and cut it away to the left almost under Kittiwynk's foot, and it hopped and skipped off to Corks, who saw that, if he was not quick it would run beyond the boundaries. That long bouncing drive gave the Archangels time to wheel and send three men across the ground to head off Corks. Kittiwynk stayed where she was; for she knew the game. Corks was on the ball half a fraction of a second before the others came up, and Macnamara, with a backhanded stroke, sent it back across the ground to Hughes, who saw the way clear to the Archangels' goal, and smacked the ball in before any one quite knew what had happened.

"That's luck," said Corks, as they changed ends. "A goal in three minutes for three hits, and no riding to speak of."

"'Don't know," said Polaris. "We've made 'em angry too soon. Shouldn't wonder if they tried to rush us off our feet next time."

"Keep the ball hanging, then," said Shiraz. "That wears out every pony that is not used to it."

Next time there was no easy galloping across the ground. All the Archangels closed up as one man, but there they stayed, for Corks, Kittiwynk, and Polaris were somewhere on the top of the ball, marking time among the rattling sticks, while Shiraz circled about outside, waiting for a chance.

"We can do this all day," said Polaris, ramming his quarters into the side of another pony. "Where do you think you're shoving to?"

"I'll—I'll be driven in an ekka if I know," was the gasping reply, "and I'd give a week's feed to get my blinkers off. I can't see anything."

"The dust is rather bad. Whew! That was one for my off-hock. Where's the ball, Corks?"

"Under my tail. At least, the man's looking for it there! This is beautiful. They can't use their sticks, and it's driving 'em wild. Give old Blinkers a push and then he'll go over."

"Here, don't touch me! I can't see. I'll—I'll back out, I think," said the pony in blinkers, who knew that if you can't see all round your head, you cannot prop yourself against the shock.

Corks was watching the ball where it lay in the dust, close to his near fore-leg, with Macnamara's shortened stick tap-tapping it from time to time. Kittiwynk was edging her way out of the scrimmage, whisking her stump of a tail with nervous excitement.

"Ho! They've got it," she snorted. "Let me out!" and she galloped like a rifle-bullet just behind a tall lanky pony of the Archangels, whose rider was swinging up his stick for a stroke.

"Not to-day, thank you," said Hughes, as the blow slid off his raised stick, and Kittiwynk laid her shoulder to the tall pony's quarters, and shoved him aside just as Lutyens on Shiraz sent the ball where it had come from, and the tall pony went skating and slipping away to the left. Kittiwynk, seeing that Polaris had joined Corks in the chase for the ball up the ground, dropped into Polaris' place, and then "time" was called.

The Skidars' ponies wasted no time in kicking or fuming. They knew that each minute's rest meant so much gain, and trotted off to the rails, and their saises began to scrape and blanket and rub them at once.

"Whew!" said Corks, stiffening up to get all the tickle of the big vulcanite scraper. "If we were playing pony for pony, we would bend those Archangels double in half an hour. But they'll bring up fresh ones and fresh ones and fresh ones after that—you see."

"Who cares?" said Polaris. "We've drawn first blood. Is my hock swelling?"

"Looks puffy," said Corks. "You must have had rather a wipe. Don't let it stiffen. You 'll be wanted again in half an hour."

"What's the game like?" said The Maltese Cat.

"Ground's like your shoe, except where they put too much water on it," said Kittiwynk. "Then it's slippery. Don't play in the centre. There's a bog there. I don't know how their next four are going to behave, but we kept the ball hanging, and made 'em lather for nothing. Who goes out? Two Arabs and a couple of country-breds! That's bad. What a comfort it is to wash your mouth out!"

Kitty was talking with a neck of a lather-covered soda-water bottle between her teeth, and trying to look over her withers at the same time. This gave her a very coquettish air.

"What's bad?" said Grey Dawn, giving to the girth and admiring his well-set shoulders.

"You Arabs can't gallop fast enough to keep yourselves warm—that's what Kitty means," said Polaris, limping to show that his hock needed attention. "Are you playing back, Grey Dawn?"

"'Looks like it," said Grey Dawn, as Lutyens swung himself up. Powell mounted The Rabbit, a plain bay country-bred much like Corks, but with mulish ears. Macnamara took Faiz-Ullah, a handy, short-backed little red Arab with a long tail, and Hughes mounted Benami, an old and sullen brown beast, who stood over in front more than a polo-pony should.

"Benami looks like business," said Shiraz. "How's your temper, Ben?" The old campaigner hobbled off without answering, and The Maltese Cat looked at the new Archangel ponies prancing about on the ground. They were four beautiful blacks, and they saddled big enough and strong enough to eat the Skidars' team and gallop away with the meal inside them.

"Blinkers again," said The Maltese Cat. "Good enough!"

"They're chargers-cavalry chargers!" said Kittiwynk, indignantly. "They'll never see thirteen-three again."

"They've all been fairly measured, and they've all got their certificates," said The Maltese Cat, "or they wouldn't be here. We must take things as they come along, and keep your eyes on the ball."

The game began, but this time the Skidars were penned to their own end of the ground, and the watching ponies did not approve of that.

"Faiz-Ullah is shirking—as usual," said Polaris, with a scornful grunt.

"Faiz-Ullah is eating whip," said Corks. They could hear the leather-thonged polo-quirt lacing the little fellow's well-rounded barrel. Then The Rabbit's shrill neigh came across the ground.

"I can't do all the work," he cried, desperately.

"Play the game—don't talk," The Maltese Cat whickered; and all the ponies wriggled with excitement, and the soldiers and the grooms gripped the railings and shouted. A black pony with blinkers had singled out old Benami, and was interfering with him in every possible way. They could see Benami shaking his head up and down, and flapping his under lip.

"There'll be a fall in a minute," said Polaris. "Benami is getting stuffy."

The game flickered up and down between goalpost and goalpost, and the black ponies were getting more confident as they felt they had the legs of the others. The ball was hit out of a little scrimmage, and Benami and The Rabbit followed it, Faiz-Ullah only too glad to be quiet for an instant.

The blinkered black pony came up like a hawk, with two of his own side behind him, and Benami's eye glittered as he raced. The question was which pony should make way for the other, for each rider was perfectly willing to risk a fall in a good cause. The black, who had been driven nearly crazy by his blinkers, trusted to his weight and his temper; but Benami knew how to apply his weight and how to keep his temper. They met, and there was a cloud of dust. The black was lying on his side, all the breath knocked out of his body. The Rabbit was a hundred yards up the ground with the ball, and Benami was sitting down. He had slid nearly ten yards on his tail, but he had had his revenge, and sat cracking his nostrils till the black pony rose.

"That's what you get for interfering. Do you want any more?" said Benami, and he plunged into the game. Nothing was done that quarter, because Faiz-Ullah would not gallop, though Macnamara beat him whenever he could spare a second. The fall of the black pony had impressed his companions tremendously, and so the Archangels could not profit by Faiz-Ullah's bad behaviour.

But as The Maltese Cat said when "time" was called, and the four came back blowing and dripping, Faiz-Ullah ought to have been kicked all round Umballa. If he did not behave better next time The Maltese Cat promised to pull out his Arab tail by the roots and—eat it.

There was no time to talk, for the third four were ordered out.

The third quarter of a game is generally the hottest, for each side thinks that the others must be pumped; and most of the winning play in a game is made about that time.

Lutyens took over The Maltese Cat with a pat and a hug, for Lutyens valued him more than anything else in the world; Powell had Shikast, a little grey rat with no pedigree and no manners outside polo; Macnamara mounted Bamboo, the largest of the team; and Hughes Who's Who, alias The Animal. He was supposed to have Australian blood in his veins, but he looked like a clothes-horse, and you could whack his legs with an iron crow-bar without hurting him.

They went out to meet the very flower of the Archangels' team; and when Who's Who saw their elegantly booted legs and their beautiful satin skins, he grinned a grin through his light, well-worn bridle.

"My word!" said Who's Who. "We must give 'em a little football. These gentlemen need a rubbing down."

"No biting," said The Maltese Cat, warningly; for once or twice in his career Who's Who had been known to forget himself in that way.

"Who said anything about biting? I'm not playing tiddly-winks. I'm playing the game."

The Archangels came down like a wolf on the fold, for they were tired of football, and they wanted polo. They got it more and more. Just after the game began, Lutyens hit a ball that was coming towards him rapidly, and it rolled in the air, as a ball sometimes will, with the whirl of a frightened partridge. Shikast heard, but could not see it for the minute, though he looked everywhere and up into the air as The Maltese Cat had taught him. When he saw it ahead and overhead he went forward with Powell as fast as he could put foot to ground. It was then that Powell, a quiet and level-headed man, as a rule, became inspired, and played a stroke that sometimes comes off successfully after long practice. He took his stick in both hands, and, standing up in his stirrups, swiped at the ball in the air, Munipore fashion. There was one second of paralysed astonishment, and then all four sides of the ground went up in a yell of applause and delight as the ball flew true (you could see the amazed Archangels ducking in their saddles to dodge the line of flight, and looking at it with open mouths), and the regimental pipes of the Skidars squealed from the railings as long as the pipers had breath. Shikast heard the stroke; but he heard the head of the stick fly off at the same time. Nine hundred and ninety-nine ponies out of a thousand would have gone tearing on after the ball with a useless player pulling at their heads; but Powell knew him, and he knew Powell; and the instant he felt Powell's right leg shift a trifle on the saddle-flap, he headed to the boundary, where a native officer was frantically waving a new stick. Before the shouts had ended, Powell was armed again.

Once before in his life The Maltese Cat had heard that very same stroke played off his own back, and had profited by the confusion it wrought. This time he acted on experience, and leaving Bamboo to guard the goal in case of accidents, came through the others like a flash, head and tail low—Lutyens standing up to ease him—swept on and on before the other side knew what was the matter, and nearly pitched on his head between the Archangels' goalpost as Lutyens kicked the ball in after a straight scurry of a hundred and fifty yards. If there was one thing more than another upon which The Maltese Cat prided himself, it was on this quick, streaking kind of run half across the ground. He did not believe in taking balls round the field unless you were clearly overmatched. After this they gave the Archangels five-minuted football; and an expensive fast pony hates football because it rumples his temper. Who's Who showed himself even better than Polaris in this game. He did not permit any wriggling away, but bored joyfully into the scrimmage as if he had his nose in a feed-box and was looking for something nice. Little Shikast jumped on the ball the minute it got clear, and every time an Archangel pony followed it, he found Shikast standing over it, asking what was the matter.

"If we can live through this quarter," said The Maltese Cat, "I sha'n't care. Don't take it out of yourselves. Let them do the lathering."

So the ponies, as their riders explained afterwards, "shut-up." The Archangels kept them tied fast in front of their goal, but it cost the Archangels' ponies all that was left of their tempers; and ponies began to kick, and men began to repeat compliments, and they chopped at the legs of Who's Who, and he set his teeth and stayed where he was, and the dust stood up like a tree over the scrimmage until that hot quarter ended.

They found the ponies very excited and confident when they went to their saises; and The Maltese Cat had to warn them that the worst of the game was coming.

"Now we are all going in for the second time," said he, "and they are trotting out fresh ponies. You think you can gallop, but you'll find you can't; and then you'll be sorry."

"But two goals to nothing is a halter-long lead," said Kittiwynk, prancing.

"How long does it take to get a goal?" The Maltese Cat answered. "For pity's sake, don't run away with a notion that the game is half-won just because we happen to be in luck now! They'll ride you into the grand stand, if they can; you must not give 'em a chance. Follow the ball."

"Football, as usual?" said Polaris. "My hock's half as big as a nose-bag."

"Don't let them have a look at the ball, if you can help it. Now leave me alone. I must get all the rest I can before the last quarter."

He hung down his head and let all his muscles go slack, Shikast, Bamboo, and Who's Who copying his example.

"Better not watch the game," he said. "We aren't playing, and we shall only take it out of ourselves if we grow anxious. Look at the ground and pretend it's fly-time."

They did their best, but it was hard advice to follow. The hooves were drumming and the sticks were rattling all up and down the ground, and yells of applause from the English troops told that the Archangels were pressing the Skidars hard. The native soldiers behind the ponies groaned and grunted, and said things in undertones, and presently they heard a long-drawn shout and a clatter of hurrahs!

"One to the Archangels," said Shikast, without raising his head. "Time's nearly up. Oh, my sire and dam!"

"Faiz-Ullah," said The Maltese Cat, "if you don't play to the last nail in your shoes this time, I'll kick you on the ground before all the other ponies."

"I'll do my best when my time comes," said the little Arab, sturdily.

The saises looked at each other gravely as they rubbed their ponies' legs. This was the time when long purses began to tell, and everybody knew it. Kittiwynk and the others came back, the sweat dripping over their hooves and their tails telling sad stories.

"They're better than we are," said Shiraz. "I knew how it would be."

"Shut your big head," said The Maltese Cat; "we've one goal to the good yet."

"Yes; but it's two Arabs and two country-breds to play now," said Corks. "Faiz-Ullah, remember!" He spoke in a biting voice.

As Lutyens mounted Grey Dawn he looked at his men, and they did not look pretty. They were covered with dust and sweat in streaks. Their yellow boots were almost black, their wrists were red and lumpy, and their eyes seemed two inches deep in their heads; but the expression in the eyes was satisfactory.

"Did you take anything at tiffin?" said Lutyens; and the team shook their heads. They were too dry to talk.

"All right. The Archangels did. They are worse pumped than we are."

"They've got the better ponies," said Powell. "I sha'n't be sorry when this business is over."

That fifth quarter was a painful one in every way. Faiz-Ullah played like a little red demon, and The Rabbit seemed to be everywhere at once, and Benami rode straight at anything and everything that came in his way; while the umpires on their ponies wheeled like gulls outside the shifting game. But the Archangels had the better mounts,—they had kept their racers till late in the game,—and never allowed the Skidars to play football. They hit the ball up and down the width of the ground till Benami and the rest were outpaced. Then they went forward, and time and again Lutyens and Grey Dawn were just, and only just, able to send the ball away with a long, spitting backhander. Grey Dawn forgot that he was an Arab; and turned from grey to blue as he galloped. Indeed, he forgot too well, for he did not keep his eyes on the ground as an Arab should, but stuck out his nose and scuttled for the dear honour of the game. They had watered the ground once or twice between the quarters, and a careless waterman had emptied the last of his skinful all in one place near the Skidars' goal. It was close to the end of the play, and for the tenth time Grey Dawn was bolting after the ball, when his near hind-foot slipped on the greasy mud, and he rolled over and over, pitching Lutyens just clear of the goalpost; and the triumphant Archangels made their goal. Then "time" was called-two goals all; but Lutyens had to be helped up, and Grey Dawn rose with his near hind-leg strained somewhere.

"What's the damage?" said Powell, his arm around Lutyens.

"Collar-bone, of course," said Lutyens, between his teeth. It was the third time he had broken it in two years, and it hurt him.

Powell and the others whistled.

"Game's up," said Hughes.

"Hold on. We've five good minutes yet, and it isn't my right hand. We 'll stick it out."

"I say," said the Captain of the Archangels, trotting up, "are you hurt, Lutyens? We'll wait if you care to put in a substitute. I wish—I mean—the fact is, you fellows deserve this game if any team does. 'Wish we could give you a man, or some of our ponies—or something."

"You 're awfully good, but we'll play it to a finish, I think."

The Captain of the Archangels stared for a little. "That's not half bad," he said, and went back to his own side, while Lutyens borrowed a scarf from one of his native officers and made a sling of it. Then an Archangel galloped up with a big bath-sponge, and advised Lutyens to put it under his armpit to ease his shoulder, and between them they tied up his left arm scientifically; and one of the native officers leaped forward with four long glasses that fizzed and bubbled.

The team looked at Lutyens piteously, and he nodded. It was the last quarter, and nothing would matter after that. They drank out the dark golden drink, and wiped their moustaches, and things looked more hopeful.

The Maltese Cat had put his nose into the front of Lutyens' shirt and was trying to say how sorry he was.

"He knows," said Lutyens, proudly. "The beggar knows. I've played him without a bridle before now—for fun."

"It's no fun now," said Powell. "But we haven't a decent substitute."

"No," said Lutyens. "It's the last quarter, and we've got to make our goal and win. I'll trust The Cat."

"If you fall this time, you'll suffer a little," said Macnamara.

"I'll trust The Cat," said Lutyens.

"You hear that?" said The Maltese Cat, proudly, to the others. "It's worth while playing polo for ten years to have that said of you. Now then, my sons, come along. We'll kick up a little bit, just to show the Archangels this team haven't suffered."

And, sure enough, as they went on to the ground, The Maltese Cat, after satisfying himself that Lutyens was home in the saddle, kicked out three or four times, and Lutyens laughed. The reins were caught up anyhow in the tips of his strapped left hand, and he never pretended to rely on them. He knew The Cat would answer to the least pressure of the leg, and by way of showing off—for his shoulder hurt him very much—he bent the little fellow in a close figure-of-eight in and out between the goalposts. There was a roar from the native officers and men, who dearly loved a piece of dugabashi (horse-trick work), as they called it, and the pipes very quietly and scornfully droned out the first bars of a common bazaar tune called "Freshly Fresh and Newly New," just as a warning to the other regiments that the Skidars were fit. All the natives laughed.

"And now," said The Maltese Cat, as they took their place, "remember that this is the last quarter, and follow the ball!"

"Don't need to be told," said Who's Who.

"Let me go on. All those people on all four sides will begin to crowd in—just as they did at Malta. You'll hear people calling out, and moving forward and being pushed back; and that is going to make the Archangel ponies very unhappy. But if a ball is struck to the boundary, you go after it, and let the people get out of your way. I went over the pole of a four-in-hand once, and picked a game out of the dust by it. Back me up when I run, and follow the ball."

There was a sort of an all-round sound of sympathy and wonder as the last quarter opened, and then there began exactly what The Maltese Cat had foreseen. People crowded in close to the boundaries, and the Archangels' ponies kept looking sideways at the narrowing space. If you know how a man feels to be cramped at tennis—not because he wants to run out of the court, but because he likes to know that he can at a pinch—you will guess how ponies must feel when they are playing in a box of human beings.

"I'll bend some of those men if I can get away," said Who's Who, as he rocketed behind the ball; and Bamboo nodded without speaking. They were playing the last ounce in them, and The Maltese Cat had left the goal undefended to join them. Lutyens gave him every order that he could to bring him back, but this was the first time in his career that the little wise grey had ever played polo on his own responsibility, and he was going to make the most of it.

"What are you doing here?" said Hughes, as The Cat crossed in front of him and rode off an Archangel.

"The Cat's in charge—mind the goal!" shouted Lutyens, and bowing forward hit the ball full, and followed on, forcing the Archangels towards their own goal.

"No football," said The Maltese Cat. "Keep the ball by the boundaries and cramp 'em. Play open order, and drive 'em to the boundaries."

Across and across the ground in big diagonals flew the ball, and whenever it came to a flying rush and a stroke close to the boundaries the Archangel ponies moved stiffly. They did not care to go headlong at a wall of men and carriages, though if the ground had been open they could have turned on a sixpence.

"Wriggle her up the sides," said The Cat. "Keep her close to the crowd. They hate the carriages. Shikast, keep her up this side."

Shikast and Powell lay left and right behind the uneasy scuffle of an open scrimmage, and every time the ball was hit away Shikast galloped on it at such an angle that Powell was forced to hit it towards the boundary; and when the crowd had been driven away from that side, Lutyens would send the ball over to the other, and Shikast would slide desperately after it till his friends came down to help. It was billiards, and no football, this time—billiards in a corner pocket; and the cues were not well chalked.

"If they get us out in the middle of the ground they'll walk away from us. Dribble her along the sides," cried The Maltese Cat.

So they dribbled all along the boundary, where a pony could not come on their right-hand side; and the Archangels were furious, and the umpires had to neglect the game to shout at the people to get back, and several blundering mounted policemen tried to restore order, all close to the scrimmage, and the nerves of the Archangels' ponies stretched and broke like cob-webs.

Five or six times an Archangel hit the ball up into the middle of the ground, and each time the watchful Shikast gave Powell his chance to send it back, and after each return, when the dust had settled, men could see that the Skidars had gained a few yards.

Every now and again there were shouts of "Side! Off side!" from the spectators; but the teams were too busy to care, and the umpires had all they could do to keep their maddened ponies clear of the scuffle.

At last Lutyens missed a short easy stroke, and the Skidars had to fly back helter-skelter to protect their own goal, Shikast leading. Powell stopped the ball with a backhander when it was not fifty yards from the goalposts, and Shikast spun round with a wrench that nearly hoisted Powell out of his saddle.

"Now's our last chance," said The Cat, wheeling like a cockchafer on a pin. "We've got to ride it out. Come along."

Lutyens felt the little chap take a deep breath, and, as it were, crouch under his rider. The ball was hopping towards the right-hand boundary, an Archangel riding for it with both spurs and a whip; but neither spur nor whip would make his pony stretch himself as he neared the crowd. The Maltese Cat glided under his very nose, picking up his hind legs sharp, for there was not a foot to spare between his quarters and the other pony's bit. It was as neat an exhibition as fancy figure-skating. Lutyens hit with all the strength he had left, but the stick slipped a little in his hand, and the ball flew off to the left instead of keeping close to the boundary. Who's Who was far across the ground, thinking hard as he galloped. He repeated stride for stride The Cat's manoeuvres with another Archangel pony, nipping the ball away from under his bridle, and clearing his opponent by half a fraction of an inch, for Who's Who was clumsy behind. Then he drove away towards the right as The Maltese Cat came up from the left; and Bamboo held a middle course exactly between them. The three were making a sort of Government-broad-arrow-shaped attack; and there was only the Archangels' back to guard the goal; but immediately behind them were three Archangels racing all they knew, and mixed up with them was Powell sending Shikast along on what he felt was their last hope. It takes a very good man to stand up to the rush of seven crazy ponies in the last quarters of a Cup game, when men are riding with their necks for sale, and the ponies are delirious. The Archangels' back missed his stroke and pulled aside just in time to let the rush go by. Bamboo and Who's Who shortened stride to give The Cat room, and Lutyens got the goal with a clean, smooth, smacking stroke that was heard all over the field. But there was no stopping the ponies. They poured through the goalposts in one mixed mob, winners and losers together, for the pace had been terrific. The Maltese Cat knew by experience what would happen, and, to save Lutyens, turned to the right with one last effort, that strained a back-sinew beyond hope of repair. As he did so he heard the right-hand goalpost crack as a pony cannoned into it—crack, splinter and fall like a mast. It had been sawed three parts through in case of accidents, but it upset the pony nevertheless, and he blundered into another, who blundered into the left-hand post, and then there was confusion and dust and wood. Bamboo was lying on the ground, seeing stars; an Archangel pony rolled beside him, breathless and angry; Shikast had sat down dog-fashion to avoid falling over the others, and was sliding along on his little bobtail in a cloud of dust; and Powell was sitting on the ground, hammering with his stick and trying to cheer. All the others were shouting at the top of what was left of their voices, and the men who had been spilt were shouting too. As soon as the people saw no one was hurt, ten thousand native and English shouted and clapped and yelled, and before any one could stop them the pipers of the Skidars broke on to the ground, with all the native officers and men behind them, and marched up and down, playing a wild Northern tune called "Zakhme Began," and through the insolent blaring of the pipes and the high-pitched native yells you could hear the Archangels' band hammering, "For they are all jolly good fellows," and then reproachfully to the losing team, "Ooh, Kafoozalum! Kafoozalum! Kafoozalum!"

Besides all these things and many more, there was a Commander-in-chief, and an Inspector-General of Cavalry, and the principal veterinary officer of all India standing on the top of a regimental coach, yelling like school-boys; and brigadiers and colonels and commissioners, and hundreds of pretty ladies joined the chorus. But The Maltese Cat stood with his head down, wondering how many legs were left to him; and Lutyens watched the men and ponies pick themselves out of the wreck of the two goalposts, and he patted The Maltese Cat very tenderly.

"I say," said the Captain of the Archangels, spitting a pebble out of his mouth, "will you take three thousand for that pony—as he stands?"

"No thank you. I've an idea he's saved my life," said Lutyens, getting off and lying down at full length. Both teams were on the ground too, waving their boots in the air, and coughing and drawing deep breaths, as the saises ran up to take away the ponies, and an officious water-carrier sprinkled the players with dirty water till they sat up.

"My aunt!" said Powell, rubbing his back, and looking at the stumps of the goalposts, "That was a game!"

They played it over again, every stroke of it, that night at the big dinner, when the Free-for-All Cup was filled and passed down the table, and emptied and filled again, and everybody made most eloquent speeches. About two in the morning, when there might have been some singing, a wise little, plain little, grey little head looked in through the open door.

"Hurrah! Bring him in," said the Archangels; and his sais, who was very happy indeed, patted The Maltese Cat on the flank, and he limped in to the blaze of light and the glittering uniforms, looking for Lutyens. He was used to messes, and men's bedrooms, and places where ponies are not usually encouraged, and in his youth had jumped on and off a mess-table for a bet. So he behaved himself very politely, and ate bread dipped in salt, and was petted all round the table, moving gingerly; and they drank his health, because he had done more to win the Cup than any man or horse on the ground.

That was glory and honour enough for the rest of his days, and The Maltese Cat did not complain much when the veterinary surgeon said that he would be no good for polo any more. When Lutyens married, his wife did not allow him to play, so he was forced to be an umpire; and his pony on these occasions was a flea-bitten grey with a neat polo-tail, lame all round, but desperately quick on his feet, and, as everybody knew, Past Pluperfect Prestissimo Player of the Game.

"BREAD UPON THE WATERS"

If you remember my improper friend Brugglesmith, you will also bear in mind his friend McPhee, Chief Engineer of the Breslau, whose dingey Brugglesmith tried to steal. His apologies for the performances of Brugglesmith may one day be told in their proper place: the tale before us concerns McPhee. He was never a racing engineer, and took special pride in saying as much before the Liverpool men; but he had a thirty-two years' knowledge of machinery and the humours of ships. One side of his face had been wrecked through the bursting of a pressure-gauge in the days when men knew less than they do now, and his nose rose grandly out of the wreck, like a club in a public riot. There were cuts and lumps on his head, and he would guide your forefinger through his short iron-grey hair and tell you how he had come by his trade-marks. He owned all sorts of certificates of extra-competency, and at the bottom of his cabin chest of drawers, where he kept the photograph of his wife, were two or three Royal Humane Society medals for saving lives at sea. Professionally—it was different when crazy steerage-passengers jumped overboard—professionally, McPhee does not approve of saving life at sea, and he has often told me that a new Hell awaits stokers and trimmers who sign for a strong man's pay and fall sick the second day out. He believes in throwing boots at fourth and fifth engineers when they wake him up at night with word that a bearing is redhot, all because a lamp's glare is reflected red from the twirling metal. He believes that there are only two poets in the world; one being Robert Burns, of course, and the other Gerald Massey. When he has time for novels he reads Wilkie Collins and Charles Reade chiefly the latter—and knows whole pages of "Very Hard Cash" by heart. In the saloon his table is next to the captain's, and he drinks only water while his engines work. He was good to me when we first met, because I did not ask questions, and believed in Charles Reade as a most shamefully neglected author. Later he approved of my writings to the extent of one pamphlet of twenty-four pages that I wrote for Holdock, Steiner & Chase, owners of the line, when they bought some ventilating patent and fitted it to the cabins of the Breslau, Spandau, and Koltzau. The purser of the Breslau recommended me to Holdock's secretary for the job; and Holdock, who is a Wesleyan Methodist, invited me to his house, and gave me dinner with the governess when the others had finished, and placed the plans and specifications in my hand, and I wrote the pamphlet that same afternoon. It was called "Comfort in the Cabin," and brought me seven pound ten, cash down—an important sum of money in those days; and the governess, who was teaching Master John Holdock his scales, told me that Mrs. Holdock had told her to keep an eye on me, in case I went away with coats from the hatrack. McPhee liked that pamphlet enormously, for it was composed in the Bouverie-Byzantine style, with baroque and rococo embellishments; and afterwards he introduced me to Mrs. McPhee, who succeeded Dinah in my heart; for Dinah was half a world away, and it is wholesome and antiseptic to love such a woman as Janet McPhee. They lived in a little twelve-pound house, close to the shipping. When McPhee was away Mrs. McPhee read the Lloyds column in the papers, and called on the wives of senior engineers of equal social standing. Once or twice, too, Mrs. Holdock visited Mrs. McPhee in a brougham with celluloid fittings, and I have reason to believe that, after she had played owner's wife long enough, they talked scandal. The Holdocks lived in an old-fashioned house with a big brick garden not a mile from the McPhees, for they stayed by their money as their money stayed by them; and in summer you met their brougham solemnly junketing by Theydon Bois or Loughton. But I was Mrs. McPhee's friend, for she allowed me to convoy her westward, sometimes, to theatres where she sobbed or laughed or shivered with a simple heart; and she introduced me to a new world of doctors' wives, captains' wives, and engineers' wives, whose whole talk and thought centred in and about ships and lines of ships you have never heard of. There were sailing-ships, with stewards and mahogany and maple saloons, trading to Australia, taking cargoes of consumptives and hopeless drunkards for whom a sea-voyage was recommended; there were frowzy little West African boats, full of rats and cockroaches, where men died anywhere but in their bunks; there were Brazilian boats whose cabins could be hired for merchandise, that went out loaded nearly awash; there were Zanzibar and Mauritius steamers and wonderful reconstructed boats that plied to the other tide of Borneo. These were loved and known, for they earned our bread and a little butter, and we despised the big Atlantic boats, and made fun of the P. & O. and Orient liners, and swore by our respective owners—Wesleyan, Baptist, or Presbyterian, as the case might be.

I had only just come back to England when Mrs. McPhee invited me to dinner at three o'clock in the afternoon, and the notepaper was almost bridal in its scented creaminess. When I reached the house I saw that there were new curtains in the window that must have cost forty-five shillings a pair; and as Mrs. McPhee drew me into the little marble-papered hall, she looked at me keenly, and cried:

"Have ye not heard? What d' ye think o' the hatrack?"

Now, that hatrack was oak-thirty shillings, at least. McPhee came down-stairs with a sober foot—he steps as lightly as a cat, for all his weight, when he is at sea—and shook hands in a new and awful manner—a parody of old Holdock's style when he says good-bye to his skippers. I perceived at once that a legacy had come to him, but I held my peace, though Mrs. McPhee begged me every thirty seconds to eat a great deal and say nothing. It was rather a mad sort of meal, because McPhee and his wife took hold of hands like little children (they always do after voyages), and nodded and winked and choked and gurgled, and hardly ate a mouthful.

A female servant came in and waited; though Mrs. McPhee had told me time and again that she would thank no one to do her housework while she had her health. But this was a servant with a cap, and I saw Mrs. McPhee swell and swell under her garance-coloured gown. There is no small free-board to Janet McPhee, nor is garance any subdued tint; and with all this unexplained pride and glory in the air I felt like watching fireworks without knowing the festival. When the maid had removed the cloth she brought a pineapple that would have cost half a guinea at that season (only McPhee has his own way of getting such things), and a Canton china bowl of dried lichis, and a glass plate of preserved ginger, and a small jar of sacred and Imperial chow-chow that perfumed the room. McPhee gets it from a Dutchman in Java, and I think he doctors it with liqueurs. But the crown of the feast was some Madeira of the kind you can only come by if you know the wine and the man. A little maize-wrapped fig of clotted Madeira cigars went with the wine, and the rest was a pale blue smoky silence; Janet, in her splendour, smiling on us two, and patting McPhee's hand.

"We'll drink," said McPhee, slowly, rubbing his chin, "to the eternal damnation o' Holdock, Steiner & Chase."

Of course I answered "Amen," though I had made seven pound ten shillings out of the firm. McPhee's enemies were mine, and I was drinking his Madeira.

"Ye've heard nothing?" said Janet. "Not a word, not a whisper?"

"Not a word, nor a whisper. On my word, I have not."

"Tell him, Mac," said she; and that is another proof of Janet's goodness and wifely love. A smaller woman would have babbled first, but Janet is five feet nine in her stockings.

"We're rich," said McPhee. I shook hands all round.

"We're damned rich," he added. I shook hands all round a second time.

"I'll go to sea no more—unless—there's no sayin'—a private yacht, maybe—wi' a small an' handy auxiliary."

"It's not enough for that," said Janet. "We're fair rich—well-to-do, but no more. A new gown for church, and one for the theatre. We'll have it made west."

"How much is it?" I asked.

"Twenty-five thousand pounds." I drew a long breath. "An' I've been earnin' twenty-five an' twenty pound a month!"

The last words came away with a roar, as though the wide world was conspiring to beat him down.

"All this time I'm waiting," I said. "I know nothing since last September. Was it left you?"

They laughed aloud together. "It was left," said McPhee, choking. "Ou, ay, it was left. That's vara good. Of course it was left. Janet, d' ye note that? It was left. Now if you'd put that in your pamphlet it would have been vara jocose. It was left." He slapped his thigh and roared till the wine quivered in the decanter.

The Scotch are a great people, but they are apt to hang over a joke too long, particularly when no one can see the point but themselves.

"When I rewrite my pamphlet I'll put it in, McPhee. Only I must know something more first."

McPhee thought for the length of half a cigar, while Janet caught my eye and led it round the room to one new thing after another—the new vine-pattern carpet, the new chiming rustic clock between the models of the Colombo outrigger-boats, the new inlaid sideboard with a purple cut-glass flower-stand, the fender of gilt and brass, and last, the new black-and-gold piano.

"In October o' last year the Board sacked me," began McPhee. "In October o' last year the Breslau came in for winter overhaul. She'd been runnin' eight months—two hunder an' forty days—an' I was three days makin' up my indents, when she went to drydock. All told, mark you, it was this side o' three hunder pound—to be preceese, two hunder an' eighty-six pound four shillings. There's not another man could ha' nursed the Breslau for eight months to that tune. Never again—never again! They may send their boats to the bottom, for aught I care."

"There's no need," said Janet, softly. "We're done wi' Holdock, Steiner & Chase."

"It's irritatin', Janet, it's just irritatin'. I ha' been justified from first to last, as the world knows, but—but I canna forgie 'em. Ay, wisdom is justified o' her children; an' any other man than me wad ha' made the indent eight hunder. Hay was our skipper—ye'll have met him. They shifted him to the Torgau, an' bade me wait for the Breslau under young Bannister. Ye'll obsairve there'd been a new election on the Board. I heard the shares were sellin' hither an' yon, an' the major part of the Board was new to me. The old Board would ne'er ha' done it. They trusted me. But the new Board were all for reorganisation. Young Steiner—Steiner's son—the Jew, was at the bottom of it, an' they did not think it worth their while to send me word. The first I knew—an' I was Chief Engineer—was the notice of the line's winter sailin's, and the

Breslau timed for sixteen days between port an' port! Sixteen days, man! She's a good boat, but eighteen is her summer time, mark you. Sixteen was sheer flytin', kitin' nonsense, an' so I told young Bannister.

"We've got to make it,' he said. 'Ye should not ha' sent in a three hunder pound indent.'

"Do they look for their boats to be run on air?' I said. 'The Board's daft.'

"'E'en tell 'em so,' he says. 'I'm a married man, an' my fourth's on the ways now, she says.'"

"A boy—wi' red hair," Janet put in. Her own hair is the splendid red-gold that goes with a creamy complexion.

"My word, I was an angry man that day! Forbye I was fond o' the old Breslau, I looked for a little consideration from the Board after twenty years' service. There was Board-meetin' on Wednesday, an' I slept overnight in the engine-room, takin' figures to support my case. Well, I put it fair and square before them all. 'Gentlemen,' I said, 'I've run the Breslau eight seasons, an' I believe there's no fault to find wi' my wark. But if ye haud to this'—I waggled the advertisement at 'em—'this that I've never heard of it till I read it at breakfast, I do assure you on my professional reputation, she can never do it. That is to say, she can for a while, but at a risk no thinkin' man would run.'

"'What the deil d' ye suppose we pass your indents for?' says old Holdock. 'Man, we're spendin' money like watter.'

"'I'll leave it in the Board's hands,' I said, 'if two hunder an' eighty-seven pound is anything beyond right and reason for eight months.' I might ha' saved my breath, for the Board was new since the last election, an' there they sat, the damned deevidend-huntin' ship-chandlers, deaf as the adders o' Scripture.

"'We must keep faith wi' the public,' said young Steiner.

"'Keep faith wi' the Breslau, then,' I said. 'She's served you well, an' your father before you. She'll need her bottom restiffenin', an' new bed-plates, an' turnin' out the forward boilers, an' re-turnin' all three cylinders, an' refacin' all guides, to begin with. It's a three months' job.'

"'Because one employee is afraid? 'says young Steiner. 'Maybe a piano in the Chief Engineer's cabin would be more to the point.'

"I crushed my cap in my hands, an' thanked God we'd no bairns an' a bit put by.

"'Understand, gentlemen,' I said. 'If the Breslau is made a sixteen-day boat, ye'll find another engineer.'

"'Bannister makes no objection,' said Holdock.

"'I'm speakin' for myself,' I said. 'Bannister has bairns. 'An' then I lost my temper. 'Ye can run her into Hell an' out again if ye pay pilotage,' I said, 'but ye run without me.'

"'That's insolence,' said young Steiner.

"'At your pleasure,' I said, turnin' to go.

"'Ye can consider yourself dismissed. We must preserve discipline among our employees,' said old Holdock, an' he looked round to see that the Board was with him. They knew nothin'—God forgie 'em—an' they nodded me out o' the line after twenty years—after twenty years.

"I went out an' sat down by the hall porter to get my wits again. I'm thinkin' I swore at the Board. Then auld McRimmon—o' McNaughten & McRimmon—came, oot o' his office, that's on the same floor, an' looked at me, proppin' up one eyelid wi' his forefinger. Ye know they call him the Blind Deevil, forbye he onythin' but blind, an' no deevil in his dealin's wi' me—McRimmon o' the Black Bird Line.

"'What's here, Mister McPhee?' said he.

"I was past prayin' for by then. 'A Chief Engineer sacked after twenty years' service because he'll not risk the Breslau on the new timin', an' be damned to ye, McRimmon,' I said.

"The auld man sucked in his lips an' whistled. 'AH,' said he, 'the new timin'. I see!' He doddered into the Board-room I'd just left, an' the Dandie-dog that is just his blind man's leader stayed wi' me. That was providential. In a minute he was back again. 'Ye've cast your bread on the watter, McPhee, an' be damned to you,' he says. 'Whaur's my dog? My word, is he on your knee? There's more discernment in a dog than a Jew. What garred ye curse your Board, McPhee? It's expensive.'

"'They'll pay more for the Breslau,' I said. 'Get off my knee, ye smotherin' beast.'

"'Bearin's hot, eh?' said McRimmon. 'It's thirty year since a man daur curse me to my face. Time was I'd ha' cast ye doon the stairway for that.'

"'Forgie's all!' I said. He was wearin' to eighty, as I knew. 'I was wrong, McRimmon; but when a man's shown the door for doin' his plain duty he's not always ceevil.'

"'So I hear,' says McRimmon. 'Ha' ye ony objection to a tramp freighter? It's only fifteen a month, but they say the Blind Deevil feeds a man better than others. She's my Kite. Come ben. Ye can thank Dandie, here. I'm no used to thanks. An' noo,' says he, 'what possessed ye to throw up your berth wi' Holdock?'

"'The new timin',' said I. 'The Breslau will not stand it.'

"'Hoot, oot,' said he. 'Ye might ha' crammed her a little—enough to show ye were drivin' her—an' brought her in twa days behind. What's easier than to say ye slowed for bearin's, eh? All my men do it, and—I believe 'em.'

"'McRimmon,' says I, 'what's her virginity to a lassie?'

"He puckered his dry face an' twisted in his chair. 'The warld an' a',' says he. 'My God, the vara warld an' a' (But what ha' you or me to do wi' virginity, this late along?)'

"'This,' I said. 'There's just one thing that each one of us in his trade or profession will not do for ony consideration whatever. If I run to time I run to time barrio' always the risks o' the high seas. Less than that, under God, I have not done. More than that, by God, I will not do! There's no trick o' the trade I'm not acquaint wi'—'

"'So I've heard,' says McRimmon, dry as a biscuit.

"'But yon matter o' fair rennin' s just my Shekinah, ye'll understand. I daurna tamper wi' that. Nursing weak engines is fair craftsmanship; but what the Board ask is cheatin', wi' the risk o' manslaughter addeetional.' Ye'll note I know my business.

"There was some more talk, an' next week I went aboard the Kite, twenty-five hunder ton, simple compound, a Black Bird tramp. The deeper she rode, the better she'd steam. I've snapped as much as eleven out of her, but eight point three was her fair normal. Good food forward an' better aft, all indents passed wi'out marginal remarks, the best coal, new donkeys, and good crews. There was nothin' the old man would not do, except paint. That was his deeficulty. Ye could no more draw paint than his last teeth from him. He'd come down to dock, an' his boats a scandal all along the watter, an' he'd whine an' cry an' say they looked all he could desire. Every owner has his non plus ultra, I've obsairved. Paint was McRimmon's. But you could get round his engines without riskin' your life, an', for all his blindness, I've seen him reject five flawed intermediates, one after the other, on a nod from me; an' his cattle-fittin's were guaranteed for North Atlantic winter weather. Ye ken what that means? McRimmon an' the Black Bird Line, God bless him!

"Oh, I forgot to say she would lie down an' fill her forward deck green, an' snore away into a twenty-knot gale forty-five to the minute, three an' a half knots an hour, the engines runnin' sweet an' true as a bairn breathin' in its sleep. Bell was skipper; an' forbye there's no love lost between crews an' owners, we were fond o' the auld Blind Deevil an' his dog, an' I'm thinkin' he liked us. He was worth the windy side o' twa million sterlin', an' no friend to his own blood-kin. Money's an awfu' thing—overmuch—for a lonely man.

"I'd taken her out twice, there an' back again, when word came o' the Breslau's breakdown, just as I prophesied. Calder was her engineer—he's not fit to run a tug down the Solent—and he fairly lifted the engines off the bed-plates, an' they fell down in heaps, by what I heard. So she filled from the after stuffin'-box to the after bulkhead, an' lay star-gazing, with seventy-nine squealin' passengers in the saloon, till the Camaralzaman o' Ramsey & Gold's Cartagena line gave her a tow to the tune o' five thousand seven hunder an' forty pound, wi' costs in the Admiralty Court. She was helpless, ye'll understand, an' in no case to meet ony weather. Five thousand seven hunder an' forty pounds, with costs, an' exclusive o' new engines! They'd ha' done better to ha' kept me on the old timin'.

"But, even so, the new Board were all for retrenchment. Young Steiner, the Jew, was at the bottom of it. They sacked men right an' left, that would not eat the dirt the Board gave 'em. They cut down repairs; they fed crews wi' leavin's an' scrapin's; and, reversin', McRimmon's practice, they hid their defeeciencies wi' paint an' cheap gildin'. Quem Deus vult perrdere prrius dementat, ye remember.

"In January we went to drydock, an' in the next dock lay the Grotkau, their big freighter that was the Dolabella o' Piegan, Piegan & Walsh's line in '84—a Clyde-built iron boat, a flat-bottomed, pigeon-breasted, under-engined, bull-nosed bitch of a five thousand ton freighter, that would neither steer, nor steam, nor stop when ye asked her. Whiles she'd attend to her helm, whiles she'd take charge, whiles she'd wait to scratch herself, an' whiles she'd buttock into a dockhead. But Holdock and Steiner had bought her cheap, and painted her all over like the Hoor o' Babylon, an' we called her the Hoor for short." (By the way, McPhee kept to that name throughout the rest of his tale; so you must read accordingly.) "I went to see young Bannister—he had to take what the Board gave him, an' he an' Calder were shifted together from the Breslau to this abortion—an' talkin' to him I went into the dock under her. Her plates were pitted till the men that were paint, paint, paintin' her laughed at it. But the warst was at the last. She'd a great clumsy iron twelve-foot Thresher propeller—Aitcheson designed the Kites'—and just on the tail o' the shaft, behind the boss, was a red weepin' crack ye could ha' put a penknife to. Man, it was an awful crack!

"'When d' ye ship a new tail-shaft?' I said to Bannister.

"He knew what I meant. 'Oh, yon's a superfeecial flaw,' says he, not lookin' at me.

"'Superfeecial Gehenna!' I said. 'Ye'll not take her oot wi' a solution o' continuity that like.'

"'They'll putty it up this evening,' he said. 'I'm a married man, an'—ye used to know the Board.'

"I e'en said what was gied me in that hour. Ye know how a drydock echoes. I saw young Steiner standin' listenin' above me, an', man, he used language provocative of a breach o' the peace. I was a spy and a disgraced employ, an' a corrupter o' young Bannister's morals, an' he'd prosecute me for libel. He went away when I ran up the steps—I'd ha' thrown him into the dock if I'd caught him—an' there I met McRimmon, wi' Dandie pullin' on the chain, guidin' the auld man among the railway lines.

"'McPhee,' said he, 'ye're no paid to fight Holdock, Steiner, Chase & Company, Limited, when ye meet. What's wrong between you?'

"'No more than a tail-shaft rotten as a kail-stump. For ony sakes go an' look, McRimmon. It's a comedietta.'

"'I'm feared o' yon conversational Hebrew,' said he. 'Whaur's the flaw, an' what like?'

"'A seven-inch crack just behind the boss. There's no power on earth will fend it just jarrin' off.'

"'When?'

"'That's beyon' my knowledge,' I said.

"'So it is; so it is,' said McRimmon. 'We've all oor leemitations. Ye're certain it was a crack?'

"'Man, it's a crevasse,' I said, for there were no words to describe the magnitude of it. 'An' young Bannister's sayin' it's no more than a superfeecial flaw!'

"'Weell, I tak' it oor business is to mind oor business. If ye've ony friends aboard her, McPhee, why not bid them to a bit dinner at Radley's?'

"'I was thinkin' o' tea in the cuddy,' I said. 'Engineers o' tramp freighters cannot afford hotel prices.'

"'Na! na!' says the auld man, whimperin'. 'Not the cuddy. They'll laugh at my Kite, for she's no plastered with paint like the Hoor. Bid them to Radley's, McPhee, an' send me the bill. Thank Dandie, here, man. I'm no used to thanks.' Then he turned him round. (I was just thinkin' the vara same thing.) 'Mister McPhee,' said he, 'this is not senile dementia.'

"'Preserve 's!' I said, clean jumped oot o' mysel'. 'I was but thinkin' you're fey, McRimmon.'

"Dod, the auld deevil laughed till he nigh sat down on Dandie. 'Send me the bill,' says he. 'I'm long past champagne, but tell me how it tastes the morn.'

"Bell and I bid young Bannister and Calder to dinner at Radley's. They'll have no laughin' an' singin' there, but we took a private room—like yacht-owners fra' Cowes."

McPhee grinned all over, and lay back to think.

"And then?" said I.

"We were no drunk in ony preceese sense o' the word, but Radley's showed me the dead men. There were six magnums o' dry champagne an' maybe a bottle o' whisky."

"Do you mean to tell me that you four got away with a magnum and a half a piece, besides whisky?" I demanded.

McPhee looked down upon me from between his shoulders with toleration.

"Man, we were not settin' down to drink," he said. "They no more than made us wutty. To be sure, young Bannister laid his head on the table an' greeted like a bairn, an' Calder was all for callin' on Steiner at two in the morn an' painting him galley-green; but they'd been drinkin' the afternoon. Lord, how they twa cursed the Board, an' the Grotkau, an' the tail-shaft, an' the engines, an' a'! They didna talk o' superfeecial flaws that night. I mind young Bannister an' Calder shakin' hands on a bond to be revenged on the Board at ony reasonable cost this side o' losing their certificates. Now mark ye how false economy ruins business. The Board fed them like swine (I have good reason to know it), an' I've obsairved wi' my ain people that if ye touch his stomach ye wauken the deil in a Scot. Men will tak' a dredger across the Atlantic if they 're well fed, an' fetch her somewhere on the broadside o' the Americas; but bad food's bad service the warld over.

"The bill went to McRimmon, an' he said no more to me till the week-end, when I was at him for more paint, for we'd heard the Kite was chartered Liverpool-side. 'Bide whaur ye're put,' said the Blind Deevil. 'Man, do ye wash in champagne? The Kite's no leavin' here till I gie the order, an'—how am I to waste paint onher, wi' the Lammergeyer docked for who knows how long an' a'?'

"She was our big freighter—McIntyre was engineer—an' I knew she'd come from overhaul not three months. That morn I met McRimmon's head-clerk—ye'll not know him—fair bitin' his nails off wi' mortification.

"'The auld man's gone gyte,' says he. 'He's withdrawn the Lammergeyer.'

"'Maybe he has reasons,' says I.

"'Reasons! He's daft!'

"'He'll no be daft till he begins to paint,' I said.

"'That's just what he's done—and South American freights higher than we'll live to see them again. He's laid her up to paint her—to paint her—to paint her!' says the little clerk, dancin' like a hen on a hot plate. 'Five thousand ton o' potential freight rottin' in drydock, man; an' he dolin' the paint out in quarter-pound tins, for it cuts him to the heart, mad though he is. An' the Grotkau—the Grotkau of all conceivable bottoms—soaking up every pound that should be ours at Liverpool!'

"I was staggered wi' this folly—considerin' the dinner at Radley's in connection wi' the same.

"Ye may well stare, McPhee,' says the head-clerk. 'There's engines, an' rollin' stock, an' iron bridgesd' ye know what freights are noo? an' pianos, an' millinery, an' fancy Brazil cargo o' every species pourin' into the Grotkau—the Grotkau o' the Jerusalem firm—and the Lammergeyer's bein' painted!'

"Losh, I thought he'd drop dead wi' the fits.

"I could say no more than 'Obey orders, if ye break owners,' but on the Kite we believed McRimmon was mad; an' McIntyre of the Lammergeyer was for lockin' him up by some patent legal process he'd found in a book o' maritime law. An' a' that week South American freights rose an' rose. It was sinfu'!

"Syne Bell got orders to tak' the Kite round to Liverpool in water-ballast, and McRimmon came to bid's good-bye, yammerin' an' whinin' o'er the acres o' paint he'd lavished on the Lammergeyer.

"'I look to you to retrieve it,' says he. 'I look to you to reimburse me! 'Fore God, why are ye not cast off? Are ye dawdlin' in dock for a purpose?'

"'What odds, McRimmon?' says Bell. 'We'll be a day behind the fair at Liverpool. The Grotkau's got all the freight that might ha' been ours an' the Lammergeyer's.' McRimmon laughed an' chuckled—the pairfect eemage o' senile dementia. Ye ken his eyebrows wark up an' down like a gorilla's.

"'Ye're under sealed orders,' said he, tee-heein' an' scratchin' himself. 'Yon's they'—to be opened seriatim.

"Says Bell, shufflin' the envelopes when the auld man had gone ashore: 'We're to creep round a' the south coast, standin' in for orders his weather, too. There's no question o' his lunacy now.'

"Well, we buttocked the auld Kite along—vara bad weather we made—standin' in all alongside for telegraphic orders, which are the curse o' skippers. Syne we made over to Holyhead, an' Bell opened the last envelope for the last instructions. I was wi' him in the cuddy, an' he threw it over to me, cryin': 'Did ye ever know the like, Mac?'

"I'll no say what McRimmon had written, but he was far from mad. There was a sou'wester brewin' when we made the mouth o' the Mersey, a bitter cold morn wi' a grey-green sea and a grey-green sky—Liverpool weather, as they say; an' there we lay choppin', an' the crew swore. Ye canna keep secrets aboard ship. They thought McRimmon was mad, too.

"Syne we saw the Grotkau rollin' oot on the top o' flood, deep an' double deep, wi' her new-painted funnel an' her new-painted boats an' a'. She looked her name, an', moreover, she coughed like it. Calder tauld me at Radley's what ailed his engines, but my own ear would ha' told me twa mile awa', by the beat o' them. Round we came, plungin' an' squatterin' in her wake, an' the wind cut wi' good promise o' more to come. By six it blew hard but clear, an' before the middle watch it was a sou'wester in airnest.

"'She'll edge into Ireland, this gait,' says Bell. I was with him on the bridge, watchin' the Grotkau's port light. Ye canna see green so far as red, or we'd ha' kept to leeward. We'd no passengers to consider, an' (all eyes being on the Grotkau) we fair walked into a liner rampin' home to Liverpool. Or, to be preceese, Bell no more than twisted the Kite oot from under her bows, and there was a little damnin' betwix' the twa bridges. "Noo a passenger"—McPhee regarded me benignantly—"wad ha' told the papers that as soon as he got to the Customs. We stuck to the Grotkau's tail that night an' the next twa days—she slowed down to five knot by my reckonin' and we lapped along the weary way to the Fastnet."

"But you don't go by the Fastnet to get to any South American port, do you?" I said.

"We do not. We prefer to go as direct as may be. But we were followin' the Grotkau, an' she'd no walk into that gale for ony consideration. Knowin' what I did to her discredit, I couldna blame young Bannister. It was warkin' up to a North Atlantic winter gale, snow an' sleet an' a perishin' wind. Eh, it was like the Deil walkin' abroad o' the surface o' the deep, whuppin' off the top o' the waves before he made up his mind. They'd bore up against it so far, but the minute she was clear o' the Skelligs she fair tucked up her skirts an' ran for it by Dunmore Head. Wow, she rolled!

"'She'll be makin' Smerwick,' says Bell.

"She'd ha' tried for Ventry by noo if she meant that,' I said.

"'They'll roll the funnel oot o' her, this gait,' says Bell. 'Why canna Bannister keep her head to sea?'

"It's the tail-shaft. Ony rollin''s better than pitchin' wi' superfeecial cracks in the tail-shaft. Calder knows that much,' I said.

"'It's ill wark retreevin' steamers this weather,' said Bell. His beard and whiskers were frozen to his oilskin, an' the spray was white on the weather side of him. Pairfect North Atlantic winter weather!

"One by one the sea raxed away our three boats, an' the davits were crumpled like ram's horns.

"'Yon's bad,' said Bell, at the last. 'Ye canna pass a hawser wi'oot a boat.' Bell was a vara judeecious man—for an Aberdonian.

"I'm not one that fashes himself for eventualities outside the engine-room, so I e'en slipped down betwixt waves to see how the Kite fared. Man, she's the best geared boat of her class that ever left Clyde! Kinloch, my second, knew her as well as I did. I found him dryin' his socks on the main-steam, an' combin' his whiskers wi' the comb Janet gied me last year, for the warld an' a' as though we were in port. I tried the feed, speered into the stoke-hole, thumbed all bearin's, spat on the thrust for luck, gied 'em my blessin', an' took Kinloch's socks before I went up to the bridge again.

"Then Bell handed me the wheel, an' went below to warm himself. When he came up my gloves were frozen to the spokes an' the ice clicked over my eyelids. Pairfect North Atlantic winter weather, as I was sayin'.

"The gale blew out by night, but we lay in smotherin' cross-seas that made the auld Kite chatter from stem to stern. I slowed to thirty-four, I mind—no, thirty-seven. There was a long swell the morn, an' the Grotkau was headin' into it west awa'.

"'She'll win to Rio yet, tail-shaft or no tail-shaft,' says Bell.

"'Last night shook her,' I said. 'She'll jar it off yet, mark my word.'

"We were then, maybe, a hunder and fifty mile westsou'west o' Slyne Head, by dead reckonin'. Next day we made a hunder an' thirty—ye'll note we were not racin-boats—an' the day after a hunder an' sixty-one, an' that made us, we'll say, Eighteen an' a bittock west, an' maybe Fifty-one an' a bittock north, crossin' all the North Atlantic liner lanes on the long slant, always in sight o' the Grotkau, creepin' up by night and fallin' awa' by day. After the gale it was cold weather wi' dark nights.

"I was in the engine-room on Friday night, just before the middle watch, when Bell whustled down the tube: 'She's done it'; an' up I came.

"The Grotkau was just a fair distance south, an' one by one she ran up the three red lights in a vertical line—the sign of a steamer not under control.

"'Yon's a tow for us,' said Bell, lickin' his chops. 'She'll be worth more than the Breslau. We'll go down to her, McPhee!'

"'Bide a while,' I said. 'The seas fair throng wi' ships here.'

"'Reason why,' said Bell. 'It's a fortune gaun beggin'. What d' ye think, man?'

"'Gie her till daylight. She knows we're here. If Bannister needs help he'll loose a rocket.'

"'Wha told ye Bannister's need? We'll ha' some rag-an'-bone tramp snappin' her up under oor nose,' said he; an' he put the wheel over. We were goin' slow.

"'Bannister wad like better to go home on a liner an' eat in the saloon. Mind ye what they said o' Holdock & Steiner's food that night at Radley's? Keep her awa', man—keep her awa'. A tow's a tow, but a derelict's big salvage.'

"'E-eh! 'said Bell. 'Yon's an inshot o' yours, Mac. I love ye like a brother. We'll bide whaur we are till daylight'; an' he kept her awa'.

"Syne up went a rocket forward, an' twa on the bridge, an' a blue light aft. Syne a tar-barrel forward again.

"'She's sinkin',' said Bell. 'It's all gaun, an' I'll get no more than a pair o' night-glasses for pickin' up young Bannister—the fool!'

"' Fair an' soft again,' I said. 'She's signallin' to the south of us. Bannister knows as well as I that one rocket would bring the Breslau. He'll no be wastin' fireworks for nothin'. Hear her ca'!'

"The Grotkau whustled an' whustled for five minutes, an' then there were more fireworks—a regular exhibeetion.

"'That's no for men in the regular trade,' says Bell. 'Ye're right, Mac. That's for a cuddy full o' passengers.' He blinked through the night-glasses when it lay a bit thick to southward.
"'What d' ye make of it?' I said.
"'Liner,' he says. 'Yon's her rocket. Ou, ay; they've waukened the gold-strapped skipper, an'—noo they've waukened the passengers. They're turnin' on the electrics, cabin by cabin. Yon's anither rocket! They're comin' up to help the perishin' in deep watters.'
"'Gie me the glass,' I said. But Bell danced on the bridge, clean dementit. 'Mails-mails-mails!' said he. 'Under contract wi' the Government for the due conveyance o' the mails; an' as such, Mac, yell note, she may rescue life at sea, but she canna tow!—she canna tow! Yon's her night-signal. She'll be up in half an hour!'
"'Gowk!' I said, 'an' we blazin' here wi' all oor lights. Oh, Bell, ye're a fool!'
"He tumbled off the bridge forward, an' I tumbled aft, an' before ye could wink our lights were oot, the engine-room hatch was covered, an' we lay pitch-dark, watchin' the lights o' the liner come up that the Grotkau'd been signallin' to. Twenty knot an hour she came, every cabin lighted, an' her boats swung awa'. It was grandly done, an' in the inside of an hour. She stopped like Mrs. Holdock's machine; down went the gangway, down went the boats, an' in ten minutes we heard the passengers cheerin', an' awa' she fled.
"'They'll tell o' this all the days they live,' said Bell. 'A rescue at sea by night, as pretty as a play. Young Bannister an' Calder will be drinkin' in the saloon, an' six months hence the Board o' Trade 'll gie the skipper a pair o' binoculars. It's vara philanthropic all round.'
"We'll lay by till day—ye may think we waited for it wi' sore eyes an' there sat the Grotkau, her nose a bit cocked, just leerin' at us. She looked paifectly ridiculous.
"'She'll be fillin' aft,' says Bell; 'for why is she down by the stern? The tail-shaft's punched a hole in her, an'—we 've no boats. There's three hunder thousand pound sterlin', at a conservative estimate, droonin' before our eyes. What's to do?' An' his bearin's got hot again in a minute: he was an incontinent man.
"'Run her as near as ye daur,' I said. 'Gie me a jacket an' a lifeline, an' I'll swum for it.' There was a bit lump of a sea, an' it was cold in the wind—vara cold; but they'd gone overside like passengers, young Bannister an' Calder an' a', leaving the gangway down on the lee-side. It would ha' been a flyin' in the face o' manifest Providence to overlook the invitation. We were within fifty yards o' her while Kinloch was garmin' me all over wi' oil behind the galley; an' as we ran past I went outboard for the salvage o' three hunder thousand pound. Man, it was perishin' cold, but

I'd done my job judgmatically, an' came scrapin' all along her side slap on to the lower gratin' o' the gangway. No one more astonished than me, I assure ye. Before I'd caught my breath I'd skinned both my knees on the gratin', an' was climbin' up before she rolled again. I made my line fast to the rail, an' squattered aft to young Bannister's cabin, whaaur I dried me wi' everything in his bunk, an' put on every conceivable sort o' rig I found till the blood was circulatin'. Three pair drawers, I mind I found—to begin upon—an' I needed them all. It was the coldest cold I remember in all my experience.

"Syne I went aft to the engine-room. The Grotkau sat on her own tail, as they say. She was vara shortshafted, an' her gear was all aft. There was four or five foot o' water in the engine-room slummockin' to and fro, black an' greasy; maybe there was six foot. The stoke-hold doors were screwed home, an' the stoke-hold was tight enough, but for a minute the mess in the engine-room deceived me. Only for a minute, though, an' that was because I was not, in a manner o' speakin', as calm as ordinar'. I looked again to mak' sure. 'T was just black wi' bilge: dead watter that must ha' come in fortuitously, ye ken."

"McPhee, I'm only a passenger," I said, "but you don't persuade me that six foot o' water can come into an engine-room fortuitously."

"Who's tryin' to persuade one way or the other?" McPhee retorted. "I'm statin' the facts o' the case—the simple, natural facts. Six or seven foot o' dead watter in the engine-room is a vara depressin' sight if ye think there's like to be more comin'; but I did not consider that such was likely, and so, yell note, I was not depressed."

"That's all very well, but I want to know about the water," I said.

"I've told ye. There was six feet or more there, wi' Calder's cap floatin' on top."

"Where did it come from?"

"Weel, in the confusion o' things after the propeller had dropped off an' the engines were racin' an' a', it's vara possible that Calder might ha' lost it off his head an' no troubled himself to pick it up again. I remember seem' that cap on him at Southampton."

"I don't want to know about the cap. I'm asking where the water came from and what it was doing there, and why you were so certain that it wasn't a leak, McPhee?"

"For good reason-for good an' sufficient reason."

"Give it to me, then."

"Weel, it's a reason that does not properly concern myself only. To be preceese, I'm of opinion that it was due, the watter, in part to an error o' judgment in another man. We can a' mak' mistakes."

"Oh, I beg your pardon?"

"I got me to the rail again, an', 'What's wrang?' said Bell, hailin'.

"'She'll do,' I said. 'Send's o'er a hawser, an' a man to steer. I'll pull him in by the lifeline.'

"I could see heads bobbin' back an' forth, an' a whuff or two o' strong words. Then Bell said: 'They'll not trust themselves—one of 'em—in this waiter—except Kinloch, an' I'll no spare him.'

"'The more salvage to me, then,' I said. 'I'll make shift solo.'

"Says one dock-rat, at this: 'D' ye think she's safe?'

"'I'll guarantee ye nothing,' I said, 'except maybe a hammerin' for keepin' me this long.'

"Then he sings out: 'There's no more than one lifebelt, an' they canna find it, or I'd come.'

"'Throw him over, the Jezebel,' I said, for I was oot o' patience; an' they took haud o' that volunteer before he knew what was in store, and hove him over, in the bight of my lifeline. So I e'en hauled him upon the sag of it, hand over fist—a vara welcome recruit when I'd tilted the salt watter oot of him: for, by the way, he could na swim.

"Syne they bent a twa-inch rope to the lifeline, an' a hawser to that, an' I led the rope o'er the drum of a hand-winch forward, an' we sweated the hawser inboard an' made it fast to the Grotkau's bitts.

"Bell brought the Kite so close I feared she'd roll in an' do the Grotkau's plates a mischief. He hove anither lifeline to me, an' went astern, an' we had all the weary winch work to do again wi' a second hawser. For all that, Bell was right: we'd along tow before us, an' though Providence had helped us that far, there was no sense in leavin' too much to its keepin'. When the second hawser was fast, I was wet wi' sweat, an' I cried Bell to tak' up his slack an' go home. The other man was by way o' helpin' the work wi' askin' for drinks, but I e'en told him he must hand reef an' steer, beginnin' with steerin', for I was goin' to turn in. He steered—oh, ay, he steered, in a manner o' speakin'. At the least, he grippit the spokes an' twiddled 'em an' looked wise, but I doubt if the Hoor ever felt it. I turned in there an' then, to young Bannister's bunk, an' slept past expression. I waukened ragin' wi' hunger, a fair lump o' sea runnin', the Kite snorin' awa' four knots an hour; an' the Grotkau slappin' her nose under, an' yawin' an' standin' over at discretion. She was a most disgracefu' tow. But the shameful thing of all was the food. I raxed me a meal fra galley-shelves an' pantries an' lazareetes an' cubby-holes that I would not ha' gied to the mate of a Cardiff collier; an' ye ken we say a Cardiff mate will eat clinkers to save waste. I'm sayin' it was simply vile! The crew had written what they thought of it on the new paint o' the fo'c'sle, but I had not a decent soul wi' me to complain on. There was nothin' for me to do save watch the hawsers an' the Kite's tail squatterin' down in white watter when she lifted to a sea; so I got steam on the after donkey-pump, an' pumped oot the engine-room. There's no sense in leavin' waiter loose in a ship. When she was dry, I went doun the shaft-tunnel, an' found she was leakin' a little through the stuffin'box, but nothin' to make wark. The propeller had e'en jarred off, as I knew it must, an' Calder had been waitin' for it to go wi' his hand on the gear. He told me as much when I met him ashore. There was nothin' started or strained. It had just slipped awa' to the bed o' the Atlantic as easy as a man dyin' wi' due warning—a most providential business for all concerned. Syne I took stock o' the Grotkau's upper works. Her boats had been smashed on the davits, an' here an' there was the rail missin', an' a ventilator or two had fetched awa', an' the bridge-rails were bent by the seas; but her hatches were tight, and she'd taken no sort of harm. Dod, I came to hate her like a human bein', for I was eight weary days aboard, starvin'—ay, starvin'—within a cable's length o' plenty. All day I laid in the bunk reading the' Woman-Hater,' the grandest book Charlie Reade ever wrote, an' pickin' a toothful here an' there. It was weary, weary work. Eight days, man, I was aboard the Grotkau, an' not one full meal did I make. Sma' blame her crew would not stay by her. The other man? Oh I warked him wi' a vengeance to keep him warm.

"It came on to blow when we fetched soundin's, an' that kept me standin' by the hawsers, lashed to the capstan, breathin' twixt green seas. I near died o' cauld an' hunger, for the Grotkau towed like a barge, an' Bell howkit her along through or over. It was vara thick up-Channel, too. We were standin' in to make some sort o' light, an' we near walked over twa three fishin'-boats, an' they cried us we were overclose to Falmouth. Then we were near cut down by a drunken foreign fruiter that was blunderin' between us an' the shore, and it got thicker an' thicker that night, an' I could feel by the tow Bell did not know whaur he was. Losh, we knew in the morn, for the wind blew the fog oot like a candle, an' the sun came clear; and as surely as McRimmon gied me my cheque, the shadow o' the Eddystone lay across our tow-rope! We were that near—ay, we were that near! Bell fetched the Kite round with the jerk that came close to tearin' the bitts out o' the Grotkau, an' I mind I thanked my Maker in young Bannister's cabin when we were inside Plymouth breakwater.

"The first to come aboard was McRimmon, wi' Dandie. Did I tell you our orders were to take anything we found into Plymouth? The auld deil had just come down overnight, puttin' two an' two together from what Calder had told him when the liner landed the Grotkau's men. He had preceesely hit oor time. I'd hailed Bell for something to eat, an' he sent it o'er in the same boat wi' McRimmon, when the auld man came to me. He grinned an' slapped his legs and worked his eyebrows the while I ate.

"'How do Holdock, Steiner & Chase feed their men?' said he.

"'Ye can see,' I said, knockin' the top off another beer-bottle. 'I did not sign to be starved, McRimmon.'

"'Nor to swum, either,' said he, for Bell had tauld him how I carried the line aboard. 'Well, I'm thinkin' you'll be no loser. What freight could we ha' put into the Lammergeyer would equal salvage on four hunder thousand pounds—hull an' cargo? Eh, McPhee? This cuts the liver out o' Holdock, Steiner, Chase & Company, Limited. Eh, McPhee? An' I'm sufferin' from senile dementia now? Eh, MCPhee? An' I'm not daft, am I, till I begin to paint the Lammergeyer? Eh, McPhee? Ye may weel lift your leg, Dandie! I ha' the laugh o' them all. Ye found watter in the engine-room?'

"'To speak wi'oot prejudice,' I said, 'there was some watter.'

"'They thought she was sinkin' after the propeller went. She filled wi' extraordinary rapeedity. Calder said it grieved him an' Bannister to abandon her.'

"I thought o' the dinner at Radley's, an' what like o' food I'd eaten for eight days.

"'It would grieve them sore,' I said.

"'But the crew would not hear o' stayin' and workin' her back under canvas. They're gaun up an' down sayin' they'd ha' starved first.'

"'They'd ha' starved if they'd stayed,' said I.

"'I tak' it, fra Calder's account, there was a mutiny a'most.'

"'Ye know more than I, McRimmon' I said. 'Speakin' wi'oot prejudice, for we're all in the same boat, who opened the bilgecock?'

"'Oh, that's it—is it?' said the auld man, an' I could see he was surprised. 'A bilgecock, ye say?'

"'I believe it was a bilgecock. They were all shut when I came aboard, but some one had flooded the engine-room eight feet over all, and shut it off with the worm-an'-wheel gear from the second gratin' afterwards.'

"'Losh!' said McRimmon. 'The ineequity o' man's beyond belief. But it's awfu' discreditable to Holdock, Steiner & Chase, if that came oot in court.'

"'It's just my own curiosity,' I said.

"'Aweel, Dandie's afflicted wi' the same disease. Dandie, strive against curiosity, for it brings a little dog into traps an' suchlike. Whaur was the Kite when yon painted liner took off the Grotkau's people?'

"'Just there or thereabouts,' I said.

"'An' which o' you twa thought to cover your lights?' said he, winkin'.

"'Dandle,' I said to the dog, 'we must both strive against curiosity. It's an unremunerative business. What's our chance o' salvage, Dandie?'

"He laughed till he choked. 'Tak' what I gie you, McPhee, an' be content,' he said. 'Lord, how a man wastes time when he gets old. Get aboard the Kite, mon, as soon as ye can. I've clean forgot there's a Baltic charter yammerin' for you at London. That'll be your last voyage, I'm thinkin', excep' by way o' pleasure.'

"Steiner's men were comin' aboard to take charge an' tow her round, an' I passed young Steiner in a boat as I went to the Kite. He looked down his nose; but McRimmon pipes up: 'Here's the man ye owe the Grotkau to—at a price, Steiner—at a price! Let me introduce Mr. McPhee to you. Maybe ye've met before; but ye've vara little luck in keepin' your men—ashore or afloat!'

"Young Steiner looked angry enough to eat him as he chuckled an' whustled in his dry old throat.

"'Ye've not got your award yet,' Steiner says.

"'Na, na,' says the auld man, in a screech ye could hear to the Hoe, 'but I've twa million sterlin', an' no bairns, ye Judeeas Apella, if ye mean to fight; an' I'll match ye p'und for p'und till the last p'und's oot. Ye ken me, Steiner! I'm McRimmon o' McNaughten & McRimmon!'

"'Dod,' he said betwix' his teeth, sittin' back in the boat, 'I've waited fourteen year to break that Jewfirm, an' God be thankit I'll do it now.'

"The Kite was in the Baltic while the auld man was warkin' his warks, but I know the assessors valued the Grotkau, all told, at over three hunder and sixty thousand—her manifest was a treat o' richness—an' McRimmon got a third for salvin' an abandoned ship. Ye see, there's vast deeference between towin' a ship wi' men on her an' pickin' up a derelict—a vast deeference—in pounds sterlin'. Moreover, twa three o' the Grotkau's crew were burnin' to testify about food, an' there was a note o' Calder to the Board, in regard to the tail-shaft, that would ha' been vara damagin' if it had come into court. They knew better than to fight.

"Syne the Kite came back, an' McRimmon paid off me an' Bell personally, an' the rest of the crew pro rata, I believe it's ca'ed. My share—oor share, I should say—was just twenty-five thousand pound sterlin'."

At this point Janet jumped up and kissed him.

"Five-and-twenty thousand pound sterlin'. Noo, I'm fra the North, and I'm not the like to fling money awa' rashly, but I'd gie six months' pay—one hunder an' twenty pounds—to know who flooded the engine-room of the Grotkau. I'm fairly well acquaint wi' McRimmon's eediosyncrasies, and he'd no hand in it. It was not Calder, for I've asked him, an' he wanted to fight me. It would be in the highest degree unprofessional o' Calder—not fightin', but openin' bilgecocks—but for a while I thought it was him. Ay, I judged it might be him—under temptation."

"What's your theory?" I demanded.

"Weel, I'm inclined to think it was one o' those singular providences that remind us we're in the hands o' Higher Powers.".

"It couldn't open and shut itself?"

"I did not mean that; but some half-starvin' oiler or, maybe, trimmer must ha' opened it awhile to mak' sure o' leavin' the Grotkau. It's a demoralisin' thing to see an engine-room flood up after any accident to the gear—demoralisin' and deceptive both. Aweel, the man got what he wanted, for they went aboard the liner cryin' that the Grotkau was sinkin'. But it's curious to think o' the consequences. In a' human probability, he's bein' damned in heaps at the present moment aboard another tramp freighter; an' here am I, wi' five-an'-twenty thousand pound invested, resolute to go to sea no more—providential's the preceese word—except as a passenger, ye'll understand, Janet."

****

McPhee kept his word. He and Janet went for a voyage as passengers in the first-class saloon.

They paid seventy pounds for their berths; and Janet found a very sick woman in the second-class saloon, so that for sixteen days she lived below, and chatted with the stewardesses at the foot of the second-saloon stairs while her patient slept. McPhee was a passenger for exactly twenty-four hours.

Then the engineers' mess—where the oilcloth tables are—joyfully took him to its bosom, and for the rest of the voyage that company was richer by the unpaid services of a highly certificated engineer.

AN ERROR IN THE FOURTH DIMENSION

Before he was thirty, he discovered that there was no one to play with him. Though the wealth of three toilsome generations stood to his account, though his tastes in the matter of books, bindings, rugs, swords, bronzes, lacquer, pictures, plate, statuary, horses, conservatories, and agriculture were educated and catholic, the public opinion of his country wanted to know why he did not go to office daily, as his father had before him.

So he fled, and they howled behind him that he was an unpatriotic Anglomaniac, born to consume fruits, one totally lacking in public spirit. He wore an eyeglass; he had built a wall round his country house, with a high gate that shut, instead of inviting America to sit on his flower-beds; he ordered his clothes from England; and the press of his abiding city cursed him, from his eyeglass to his trousers, for two consecutive days.

When he rose to light again, it was where nothing less than the tents of an invading army in Piccadilly would make any difference to anybody. If he had money and leisure, England stood ready to give him all that money and leisure could buy. That price paid, she would ask no questions. He took his cheque-book and accumulated things—warily at first, for he remembered that in America things own the man. To his delight, he discovered that in England he could put his belongings under his feet; for classes, ranks, and denominations of people rose, as it were, from the earth, and silently and discreetly took charge of his possessions. They had been born and bred for that sole purpose—servants of the cheque-book. When that was at an end they would depart as mysteriously as they had come.

The impenetrability of this regulated life irritated him, and he strove to learn something of the human side of these people. He retired baffled, to be trained by his menials. In America, the native demoralises the English servant. In England, the servant educates the master. Wilton Sargent strove to learn all they taught as ardently as his father had striven to wreck, before capture, the railways of his native land; and it must have been some touch of the old bandit railway blood that bade him buy, for a song, Holt Hangars, whose forty-acre lawn, as every one knows, sweeps down in velvet to the quadruple tracks of the Great Buchonian Railway. Their trains flew by almost continuously, with a bee-like drone in the day and a flutter of strong wings at night. The son of Merton Sargent had good right to be interested in them. He owned controlling interests in several thousand miles of track,—not permanent way,—built on altogether different plans, where locomotives eternally whistled for grade-crossings, and parlor-cars of fabulous expense and unrestful design skated round curves that the Great Buchonian would have condemned as unsafe in a construction-line. From the edge of his lawn he could trace the chaired metals falling away, rigid as a bowstring, into the valley of the Prest, studded with the long perspective of the block signals, buttressed with stone, and carried, high above all possible risk, on a forty-foot embankment.

Left to himself, he would have builded a private car, and kept it at the nearest railway-station, Amberley Royal, five miles away. But those into whose hands he had committed himself for his English training had little knowledge of railways and less of private cars. The one they knew was something that existed in the scheme of things for their convenience. The other they held to be "distinctly American"; and, with the versatility of his race, Wilton Sargent had set out to be just a little more English than the English.

He succeeded to admiration. He learned not to redecorate Holt Hangars, though he warmed it; to leave his guests alone; to refrain from superfluous introductions; to abandon manners of which he had great store, and to hold fast by manner which can after labour be acquired. He learned to let other people, hired for the purpose, attend to the duties for which they were paid. He learned—this he got from a ditcher on the estate—that every man with whom he came in contact had his decreed position in the fabric of the realm, which position he would do well to consult. Last mystery of all, he learned to golf—well: and when an American knows the innermost meaning of "Don't press, slow back, and keep your eye on the ball," he is, for practical purposes, denationalised.

His other education proceeded on the pleasantest lines. Was he interested in any conceivable thing in heaven above, or the earth beneath, or the waters under the earth? Forthwith appeared at his table, guided by those safe hands into which he had fallen, the very men who had best said, done, written, explored, excavated, built, launched, created, or studied that one thing—herders of books and prints in the British Museum; specialists in scarabs, cartouches, and dynasties Egyptian; rovers and raiders from the heart of unknown lands; toxicologists; orchid-hunters; monographers on flint implements, carpets, prehistoric man, or early Renaissance music. They came, and they played with him. They asked no questions; they cared not so much as a pin who or what he was. They demanded only that he should be able to talk and listen courteously. Their work was done elsewhere and out of his sight.

There were also women.

"Never," said Wilton Sargent to himself, "has an American seen England as I'm seeing it"; and he thought, blushing beneath the bedclothes, of the unregenerate and blatant days when he would steam to office, down the Hudson, in his twelve-hundred-ton ocean-going steam-yacht, and arrive, by gradations, at Bleecker Street, hanging on to a leather strap between an Irish washerwoman and a German anarchist. If any of his guests had seen him then they would have said: "How distinctly American!" and—Wilton did not care for that tone. He had schooled himself to an English walk, and, so long as he did not raise it, an English voice. He did not gesticulate with his hands; he sat down on most of his enthusiasms, but he could not rid himself of The Shibboleth. He would ask for the Worcestershire sauce: even Howard, his immaculate butler, could not break him of this.

It was decreed that he should complete his education in a wild and wonderful manner, and, further, that I should be in at that death.

Wilton had more than once asked me to Holt Hangars, for the purpose of showing how well the new life fitted him, and each time I had declared it creaseless. His third invitation was more informal than the others, and he hinted of some matter in which he was anxious for my sympathy or counsel, or both. There is room for an infinity of mistakes when a man begins to take liberties with his nationality; and I went down expecting things. A seven-foot dog-cart and a groom in the black Holt Hangars livery met me at Amberley Royal. At Holt Hangars I was received by a person of elegance and true reserve, and piloted to my luxurious chamber. There were no other guests in the house, and this set me thinking.

Wilton came into my room about half an hour before dinner, and though his face was masked with a drop-curtain of highly embroidered indifference, I could see that he was not at ease. In time, for he was then almost as difficult to move as one of my own countrymen, I extracted the tale—simple in its extravagance, extravagant in its simplicity. It seemed that Hackman of the British Museum had been staying with him about ten days before, boasting of scarabs. Hackman has a way of carrying really priceless antiquities on his tie-ring and in his trouser pockets. Apparently, he had intercepted something on its way to the Boulak Museum which, he said, was "a genuine Amen-Hotepa queen's scarab of the Fourth Dynasty." Now Wilton had bought from Cassavetti, whose reputation is not above suspicion, a scarab of much the same scarabeousness, and had left it in his London chambers. Hackman at a venture, but knowing Cassavetti, pronounced it an imposition. There was long discussion—savant versus millionaire, one saying: "ut I know it cannot be"; and the other: "But I can and will prove it." Wilton found it necessary for his soul's satisfaction to go up to town, then and there,—a forty-mile run,—and bring back the scarab before dinner. It was at this point that he began to cut corners with disastrous results. Amberley Royal station being five miles away, and putting in of horses a matter of time, Wilton had told Howard, the immaculate butler, to signal the next train to stop; and Howard, who was more of a man of resource than his master gave him credit for, had, with the red flag of the ninth hole of the links which crossed the bottom of the lawn, signalled vehemently to the first down-train; and it had stopped. Here Wilton's account became confused. He attempted, it seems, to get into that highly indignant express, but a guard restrained him with more or less force—hauled him, in fact, backyards from the window of a locked carriage. Wilton must have struck the gravel with some vehemence, for the consequences, he admitted, were a free fight on the line in which he lost his hat, and was at last dragged into the guard's van and set down breathless.

He had pressed money upon the man, and very foolishly had explained everything but his name. This he clung to, for he had a vision of tall head-lines in the New York papers, and well knew no son of Merton Sargent could expect mercy that side the water. The guard, to Wilton's amazement, refused the money on the grounds that this was a matter for the Company to attend to. Wilton insisted on his incognito, and, therefore, found two policemen waiting for him at St. Botolph terminus. When he expressed a wish to buy a new hat and telegraph to his friends, both policemen with one voice warned him that whatever he said would be used as evidence against him; and this had impressed Wilton tremendously.

"They were so infernally polite," he said. "If they had clubbed me I wouldn't have cared; but it was, 'Step this way, sir,' and, 'Up those stairs, please, sir,' till they jailed me—jailed me like a common drunk, and I had to stay in a filthy little cubby-hole of a cell all night."

"That comes of not giving your name and not wiring your lawyer," I replied. "What did you get?"

"Forty shillings, or a month," said Wilton, promptly,—"next morning bright and early. They were working us off, three a minute. A girl in a pink hat—she was brought in at three in the morning—got ten days. I suppose I was lucky. I must have knocked his senses out of the guard. He told the old duck on the bench that I had told him I was a sergeant in the army, and that I was gathering beetles on the track. That comes of trying to explain to an Englishman."

"And you?"

"Oh, I said nothing. I wanted to get out. I paid my fine, and bought a new hat, and came up here before noon next morning. There were a lot of people in the house, and I told 'em I'd been unavoidably detained, and then they began to recollect engagements elsewhere. Hackman must have seen the fight on the track and made a story of it. I suppose they thought it was distinctly American—confound 'em! It's the only time in my life that I've ever flagged a train, and I wouldn't have done it but for that scarab. 'T wouldn't hurt their old trains to be held up once in a while."

"Well, it's all over now," I said, choking a little. "And your name didn't get into the papers. It is rather transatlantic when you come to think of it."

"Over!" Wilton grunted savagely. "It's only just begun. That trouble with the guard was just common, ordinary assault—merely a little criminal business. The flagging of the train is civil, infernally civil,—and means something quite different. They're after me for that now."

"Who?"

"The Great Buchonian. There was a man in court watching the case on behalf of the Company. I gave him my name in a quiet corner before I bought my hat, and—come to dinner now; I'll show you the results afterwards." The telling of his wrongs had worked Wilton Sargent into a very fine temper, and I do not think that my conversation soothed him. In the course of the dinner, prompted by a devil of pure mischief, I dwelt with loving insistence on certain smells and sounds of New York which go straight to the heart of the native in foreign parts; and Wilton began to ask many questions about his associates aforetime—men of the New York Yacht Club, Storm King, or the Restigouche, owners of rivers, ranches, and shipping in their playtime, lords of railways, kerosene, wheat, and cattle in their offices. When the green mint came, I gave him a peculiarly oily and atrocious cigar, of the brand they sell in the tessellated, electric-lighted, with expensive-pictures of the nude adorned bar of the Pandemonium, and Wilton chewed the end for several minutes ere he lit it. The butler left us alone, and the chimney of the oak-panelled diningroom began to smoke.

"That's another!" said he, poking the fire savagely, and I knew what he meant. One cannot put steam-heat in houses where Queen Elizabeth slept. The steady beat of a night-mail, whirling down the valley, recalled me to business. "What about the Great Buchonian?" I said.

"Come into my study. That's all—as yet."

It was a pile of Seidlitz-powders-coloured correspondence, perhaps nine inches high, and it looked very businesslike.

"You can go through it," said Wilton. "Now I could take a chair and a red flag and go into Hyde Park and say the most atrocious things about your Queen, and preach anarchy and all that, y' know, till I was hoarse, and no one would take any notice. The Police damn 'em!—would protect me if I got into trouble. But for a little thing like flagging a dirty little sawed-off train,—running through my own grounds, too,—I get the whole British Constitution down on me as if I sold bombs. I don't understand it."

"No more does the Great Buchonian—apparently." I was turning over the letters. "Here's the traffic superintendent writing that it's utterly incomprehensible that any man should... Good heavens, Wilton, you have done it!" I giggled, as I read on.

"What's funny now?" said my host.

"It seems that you, or Howard for you, stopped the three-forty Northern down."

"I ought to know that! They all had their knife into me, from the engine-driver up."

"But it's the three-forty—the Induna—surely you've heard of the Great Buchonian's Induna!"

"How the deuce am I to know one train from another? They come along about every two minutes."

"Quite so. But this happens to be the Induna—the one train of the whole line. She's timed for fifty-seven miles an hour. She was put on early in the Sixties, and she has never been stopped—"

"I know! Since William the Conqueror came over, or King Charles hid in her smoke-stack. You're as bad as the rest of these Britishers. If she's been run all that while, it's time she was flagged once or twice."

The American was beginning to ooze out all over Wilton, and his small-boned hands were moving restlessly.

"Suppose you flagged the Empire State Express, or the Western Cyclone?"

"Suppose I did. I know Otis Harvey—or used to. I'd send him a wire, and he'd understand it was a ground-hog case with me. That's exactly what I told this British fossil company here."

"Have you been answering their letters without legal advice, then?"

"Of course I have."

"Oh, my Sainted Country! Go ahead, Wilton."

"I wrote 'em that I'd be very happy to see their president and explain to him in three words all about it; but that wouldn't do. 'Seems their president must be a god. He was too busy, and—well, you can read for yourself—they wanted explanations. The stationmaster at Amberley Royal—and he grovels before me, as a rule—wanted an explanation, and quick, too. The head sachem at St. Botolph's wanted three or four, and the Lord High Mukkamuk that oils the locomotives wanted one every fine day. I told 'em—I've told hem about fifty times—I stopped their holy and sacred train because I wanted to board her. Did they think I wanted to feel her pulse?"

"You didn't say that?"

"Feel her pulse'? Of course not."

"No. 'Board her.'"

"What else could I say?"

"My dear Wilton, what is the use of Mrs. Sherborne, and the Clays, and all that lot working over you for four years to make an Englishman out of you, if the very first time you're rattled you go back to the vernacular?"

"I'm through with Mrs. Sherborne and the rest of the crowd. America's good enough for me. What ought I to have said? 'Please,' or 'thanks awf'ly or how?"

There was no chance now of mistaking the man's nationality. Speech, gesture, and step, so carefully drilled into him, had gone away with the borrowed mask of indifference. It was a lawful son of the Youngest People, whose predecessors were the Red Indian. His voice had risen to the high, throaty crow of his breed when they labour under excitement. His close-set eyes showed by turns unnecessary fear, annoyance beyond reason, rapid and purposeless flights of thought, the child's lust for immediate revenge, and the child's pathetic bewilderment, who knocks his head against the bad, wicked table. And on the other side, I knew, stood the Company, as unable as Wilton to understand.

"And I could buy their old road three times over," he muttered, playing with a paper-knife, and moving restlessly to and fro.

"You didn't tell 'em that, I hope!"

There was no answer; but as I went through the letters, I felt that Wilton must have told them many surprising things. The Great Buchonian had first asked for an explanation of the stoppage of their Induna, and had found a certain levity in the explanation tendered. It then advised "Mr. W. Sargent" to refer his solicitor to their solicitor, or whatever the legal phrase is.

"And you didn't?" I said, looking up.

"No. They were treating me exactly as if I had been a kid playing on the cable-tracks. There was not the least necessity for any solicitor. Five minutes' quiet talk would have settled everything."

I returned to the correspondence. The Great Buchonian regretted that, owing to pressure of business, none of their directors could accept Mr. W. Sargent's invitation to run down and discuss the difficulty. The Great Buchonian was careful to point out that no animus underlay their action, nor was money their object. Their duty was to protect the interests of their line, and these interests could not be protected if a precedent were established whereby any of the Queen's subjects could stop a train in mid-career. Again (this was another branch of the correspondence, not more than five heads of departments being concerned), the Company admitted that there was some reasonable doubt as to the duties of express-trains in all crises, and the matter was open to settlement by process of law till an authoritative ruling was obtained—from the House of Lords, if necessary.

"That broke me all up," said Wilton, who was reading over my shoulder. "I knew I'd struck the British Constitution at last. The House of Lords—my Lord! And, anyway, I'm not one of the Queen's subjects."

"Why, I had a notion that you'd got yourself naturalised."

Wilton blushed hotly as he explained that very many things must happen to the British Constitution ere he took out his papers.

"How does it all strike you?" he said. "Isn't the Great Buchonian crazy?"

"I don't know. You've done something that no one ever thought of doing before, and the Company don't know what to make of it. I see they offer to send down their solicitor and another official of the Company to talk things over informally. Then here's another letter suggesting that you put up a fourteen-foot wall, crowned with bottle-glass, at the bottom of the garden."

"Talk of British insolence! The man who recommends that (he's another bloated functionary) says that I shall 'derive great pleasure from watching the wall going up day by day'! Did you ever dream of such gall? I've offered 'em money enough to buy a new set of cars and pension the driver for three generations; but that doesn't seem to be what they want. They expect me to go to the House of Lords and get a ruling, and build walls between times. Are they all stark, raving mad? One 'ud think I made a profession of flagging trains. How in Tophet was I to know their old Induna from a waytrain? I took the first that came along, and I've been jailed and fined for that once already."

"That was for slugging the guard."

"He had no right to haul me out when I was half-way through a window."

"What are you going to do about it?"

"Their lawyer and the other official (can't they trust their men unless they send 'em in pairs?) are coming hereto-night. I told 'em I was busy, as a rule, till after dinner, but they might send along the entire directorate if it eased 'em any."

Now, after-dinner visiting, for business or pleasure, is the custom of the smaller American town, and not that of England, where the end of the day is sacred to the owner, not the public. Verily, Wilton Sargent had hoisted the striped flag of rebellion!

"Isn't it time that the humour of the situation began to strike you, Wilton?" I asked.

"Where's the humour of baiting an American citizen just because he happens to be a millionaire—poor devil." He was silent for a little time, and then went on: "Of course. Now I see!" He spun round and faced me excitedly. "It's as plain as mud. These ducks are laying their pipes to skin me."

"They say explicitly they don't want money!"

"That's all a blind. So's their addressing me as W. Sargent. They know well enough who I am. They know I'm the old man's son. Why didn't I think of that before?"

"One minute, Wilton. If you climbed to the top of the dome of St. Paul's and offered a reward to any Englishman who could tell you who or what Merton Sargent had been, there wouldn't be twenty men in all London to claim it."

"That's their insular provincialism, then. I don't care a cent. The old man would have wrecked the Great Buchonian before breakfast for a pipe-opener. My God, I'll do it in dead earnest! I'll show 'em that they can't bulldoze a foreigner for flagging one of their little tinpot trains, and—I've spent fifty thousand a year here, at least, for the last four years."

I was glad I was not his lawyer. I re-read the correspondence, notably the letter which recommended him—almost tenderly, I fancied—to build a fourteen-foot brick wall at the end of his garden, and half-way through it a thought struck me which filled me with pure joy.

The footman ushered in two men, frock-coated, grey-trousered, smooth-shaven, heavy of speech and gait. It was nearly nine o'clock, but they looked as newly come from a bath. I could not understand why the elder and taller of the pair glanced at me as though we had an understanding; nor why he shook hands with an unEnglish warmth.

"This simplifies the situation," he said in an undertone, and, as I stared, he whispered to his companion: "I fear I shall be of very little service at present. Perhaps Mr. Folsom had better talk over the affair with Mr. Sargent."

"That is what I am here for," said Wilton.

The man of law smiled pleasantly, and said that he saw no reason why the difficulty should not be arranged in two minutes' quiet talk. His air, as he sat down opposite Wilton, was soothing to the last degree, and his companion drew me up-stage. The mystery was deepening, but I followed meekly, and heard Wilton say, with an uneasy laugh:

"I've had insomnia over this affair, Mr. Folsom. Let's settle it one way or the other, for heaven's sake!"

"Ah! Has he suffered much from this lately?" said my man, with a preliminary cough.

"I really can't say," I replied.

"Then I suppose you have only lately taken charge here?"

"I came this evening. I am not exactly in charge of anything."

"I see. Merely to observe the course of events in case—" He nodded.

"Exactly." Observation, after all, is my trade.

He coughed again slightly, and came to business.

"Now,—I am asking solely for information's sake,—do you find the delusions persistent?"

"Which delusions?"

"They are variable, then? That is distinctly curious, because—but do I understand that the type of the delusion varies? For example, Mr. Sargent believes that he can buy the Great Buchonian."

"Did he write you that?"

"He made the offer to the Company—on a half-sheet of note-paper. Now, has he by chance gone to the other extreme, and believed that he is in danger of becoming a pauper? The curious economy in the use of a half-sheet of paper shows that some idea of that kind might have flashed through his mind, and the two delusions can coexist, but it is not common. As you must know, the delusion of vast wealth—the folly of grandeurs, I believe our friends the French call it—is, as a rule, persistent, to the exclusion of all others."

Then I heard Wilton's best English voice at the end of the study:

"My dear sir, I have explained twenty times already, I wanted to get that scarab in time for dinner. Suppose you had left an important legal document in the same way?"

"That touch of cunning is very significant," my fellow-practitioner—since he insisted on it—muttered.

"I am very happy, of course, to meet you; but if you had only sent your president down to dinner here, I could have settled the thing in half a minute. Why, I could have bought the Buchonian from him while your clerks were sending me this." Wilton dropped his hand heavily on the blue-and-white correspondence, and the lawyer started.

"But, speaking frankly," the lawyer replied, "it is, if I may say so, perfectly inconceivable, even in the case of the most important legal documents, that any one should stop the three-forty express—the Induna—Our Induna, my dear sir."

"Absolutely!" my companion echoed; then to me in a lower tone: "You notice, again, the persistent delusion of wealth. I was called in when he wrote us that. You can see it is utterly impossible for the Company to continue to run their trains through the property of a man who may at any moment fancy himself divinely commissioned to stop all traffic. If he had only referred us to his lawyer—but, naturally, that he would not do, under the circumstances. A pity—a great pity. He is so young. By the way, it is curious, is it not, to note the absolute conviction in the voice of those who are similarly afflicted,—heart-rending, I might say, and the inability to follow a chain of connected thought."

"I can't see what you want," Wilton was saying to the lawyer.

"It need not be more than fourteen feet high—a really desirable structure, and it would be possible to grow pear trees on the sunny side." The lawyer was speaking in an unprofessional voice. "There are few things pleasanter than to watch, so to say, one's own vine and fig tree in full bearing. Consider the profit and amusement you would derive from it. If you could see your way to doing this, we could arrange all the details with your lawyer, and it is possible that the Company might bear some of the cost. I have put the matter, I trust, in a nutshell. If you, my dear sir, will interest yourself in building that wall, and will kindly give us the name of your lawyers, I dare assure you that you will hear no more from the Great Buchonian."

"But why am I to disfigure my lawn with a new brick wall?"

"Grey flint is extremely picturesque."

"Grey flint, then, if you put it that way. Why the dickens must I go building towers of Babylon just because I have held up one of your trains-once?"

"The expression he used in his third letter was that he wished to 'board her,'" said my companion in my ear. "That was very curious—a marine delusion impinging, as it were, upon a land one. What a marvellous world he must move in—and will before the curtain falls. So young, too—so very young!"

"Well, if you want the plain English of it, I'm damned if I go wall-building to your orders. You can fight it all along the line, into the House of Lords and out again, and get your rulings by the running foot if you like," said Wilton, hotly. "Great heavens, man, I only did it once!"

"We have at present no guarantee that you may not do it again; and, with our traffic, we must, in justice to our passengers, demand some form of guarantee. It must not serve as a precedent. All this might have been saved if you had only referred us to your legal representative." The lawyer looked appealingly around the room. The dead-lock was complete.

"Wilton," I asked, "may I try my hand now?"

"Anything you like," said Wilton. "It seems I can't talk English. I won't build any wall, though." He threw himself back in his chair.

"Gentlemen," I said deliberately, for I perceived that the doctor's mind would turn slowly, "Mr. Sargent has very large interests in the chief railway systems of his own country."

"His own country?" said the lawyer.

"At that age?" said the doctor.

"Certainly. He inherited them from his father, Mr. Sargent, who was an American."

"And proud of it," said Wilton, as though he had been a Western Senator let loose on the Continent for the first time.

"My dear sir," said the lawyer, half rising, "why did you not acquaint the Company with this fact—this vital fact—early in our correspondence? We should have understood. We should have made allowances."

"Allowances be damned. Am I a Red Indian or a lunatic?"

The two men looked guilty.

"If Mr. Sargent's friend had told us as much in the beginning," said the doctor, very severely, "much might have been saved." Alas! I had made a life's enemy of that doctor.

"I hadn't a chance," I replied. "Now, of course, you can see that a man who owns several thousand miles of line, as Mr. Sargent does, would be apt to treat railways a shade more casually than other people."

"Of course; of course. He is an American; that accounts. Still, it was the Induna; but I can quite understand that the customs of our cousins across the water differ in these particulars from ours. And do you always stop trains in this way in the States, Mr. Sargent?"

"I should if occasion ever arose; but I've never had to yet. Are you going to make an international complication of the business?"

"You need give yourself no further concern whatever in the matter. We see that there is no likelihood of this action of yours establishing a precedent, which was the only thing we were afraid of. Now that you understand that we cannot reconcile our system to any sudden stoppages, we feel quite sure that—"

"I sha'n't be staying long enough to flag another train," Wilton said pensively.

"You are returning, then, to our fellow-kinsmen across the-ah-big pond, you call it?"

"No, sir. The ocean—the North Atlantic Ocean. It's three thousand miles broad, and three miles deep in places. I wish it were ten thousand."

"I am not so fond of sea-travel myself; but I think it is every Englishman's duty once in his life to study the great branch of our Anglo-Saxon race across the ocean," said the lawyer.

"If ever you come over, and care to flag any train on my system, I'll—I'll see you through," said Wilton.

"Thank you—ah, thank you. You're very kind. I'm sure I should enjoy myself immensely."

"We have overlooked the fact," the doctor whispered to me, "that your friend proposed to buy the Great Buchonian."

"He is worth anything from twenty to thirty million dollars—four to five million pounds," I answered, knowing that it would be hopeless to explain.

"Really! That is enormous wealth. But the Great Buchonian is not in the market."

"Perhaps he does not want to buy it now."

"It would be impossible under any circumstances," said the doctor.

"How characteristic!" murmured the lawyer, reviewing matters in his mind. "I always understood from books that your countrymen were in a hurry. And so you would have gone forty miles to town and back—before dinner—to get a scarab? How intensely American! But you talk exactly like an Englishman, Mr. Sargent."

"That is a fault that can be remedied. There's only one question I'd like to ask you. You said it was inconceivable that any man should stop a train on your road?"

"And so it is-absolutely inconceivable."

"Any sane man, that is?"

"That is what I meant, of course. I mean, with excep—"

"Thank you."

The two men departed. Wilton checked himself as he was about to fill a pipe, took one of my cigars instead, and was silent for fifteen minutes. Then said he: "Have you got a list of the Southampton sailings on you?"

Far away from the greystone wings, the dark cedars, the faultless gravel drives, and the mint-sauce lawns of Holt Hangars runs a river called the Hudson, whose unkempt banks are covered with the palaces of those wealthy beyond the dreams of avarice. Here, where the hoot of the Haverstraw brick-barge-tug answers the howl of the locomotive on either shore, you shall find, with a complete installation of electric light, nickel-plated binnacles, and a calliope attachment to her steam-whistle, the twelve-hundred-ton ocean-going steam-yacht Columbia, lying at her private pier, to take to his office, at an average speed of seventeen knots an hour,—and the barges can look out for themselves,—Wilton Sargent, American.

MY SUNDAY AT HOME

If the Red Slayer think he slays,
    Or if the slain think he is slain,

  They know not well the subtle ways

   I keep and pass and turn again.

EMERSON.

It was the unreproducible slid r, as he said this was his "fy-ist" visit to England, that told me he was a New-Yorker from New York; and when, in the course of our long, lazy journey westward from Waterloo, he enlarged upon the beauties of his city, I, professing ignorance, said no word. He had, amazed and delighted at the man's civility, given the London porter a shilling for carrying his bag nearly fifty yards; he had thoroughly investigated the first-class lavatory compartment, which the London and Southwestern sometimes supply without extra charge; and now, half-awed, half-contemptuous, but wholly interested, he looked out upon the ordered English landscape wrapped in its Sunday peace, while I watched the wonder grow upon his face. Why were the cars so short and stilted? Why had every other freight-car a tarpaulin drawn over it? What wages would an engineer get now? Where was the swarming population of England he had read so much about? What was the rank of all those men on tricycles along the roads? When were we due at Plymouth I told him all I knew, and very much that I did not. He was going to Plymouth to assist in a consultation upon a fellow-countryman who had retired to a place called The Hoe—was that up-town or down-town—to recover from nervous dyspepsia. Yes, he himself was a doctor by profession, and how any one in England could retain any nervous disorder passed his comprehension. Never had he dreamed of an atmosphere so soothing. Even the deep rumble of London traffic was monastical by comparison with some cities he could name; and the country—why, it was Paradise. A continuance of it, he confessed, would drive him mad; but for a few months it was the most sumptuous rest-cure in his knowledge.

"I'll come over every year after this," he said, in a burst of delight, as we ran between two ten-foot hedges of pink and white may. "It's seeing all the things I've ever read about. Of course it doesn't strike you that way. I presume you belong here? What a finished land it is! It's arrived. 'Must have been born this way. Now, where I used to live—Hello I what's up?"

The train stopped in a blaze of sunshine at Framlynghame Admiral, which is made up entirely of the name-board, two platforms, and an overhead bridge, without even the usual siding. I had never known the slowest of locals stop here before; but on Sunday all things are possible to the London and Southwestern. One could hear the drone of conversation along the carriages, and, scarcely less loud, the drone of the bumblebees in the wallflowers up the bank. My companion thrust his head through the window and sniffed luxuriously.

"Where are we now?" said he.

"In Wiltshire," said I.

"Ah! A man ought to be able to write novels with his left hand in a country like this. Well, well! And so this is about Tess's country, ain't it? I feel just as if I were in a book. Say, the conduc—the guard has something on his mind. What's he getting at?"

The splendid badged and belted guard was striding up the platform at the regulation official pace, and in the regulation official voice was saying at each door:

"Has any gentleman here a bottle of medicine? A gentleman has taken a bottle of poison (laudanum) by mistake."

Between each five paces he looked at an official telegram in his hand, refreshed his memory, and said his say. The dreamy look on my companion's face—he had gone far away with Tess—passed with the speed of a snap-shutter. After the manner of his countrymen, he had risen to the situation, jerked his bag down from the overhead rail, opened it, and I heard the click of bottles. "Find out where the man is," he said briefly. "I've got something here that will fix him—if he can swallow still."

Swiftly I fled up the line of carriages in the wake of the guard. There was clamour in a rear compartment—the voice of one bellowing to be let out, and the feet of one who kicked. With the tail of my eye I saw the New York doctor hastening thither, bearing in his hand a blue and brimming glass from the lavatory compartment. The guard I found scratching his head unofficially, by the engine, and murmuring: "Well, I put a bottle of medicine off at Andover—I'm sure I did."

"Better say it again, any'ow'," said the driver. "Orders is orders. Say it again."

Once more the guard paced back, I, anxious to attract his attention, trotting at his heels.

"In a minute—in a minute, sir," he said, waving an arm capable of starting all the traffic on the London and Southwestern Railway at a wave. "Has any gentleman here got a bottle of medicine? A gentleman has taken a bottle of poison (laudanum) by mistake."

"Where's the man?" I gasped.

"Woking. 'Ere's my orders." He showed me the telegram, on which were the words to be said. "'E must have left 'is bottle in the train, an' took another by mistake. 'E's been wirin' from Woking awful, an', now I come to think of, it, I'm nearly sure I put a bottle of medicine off at Andover."

"Then the man that took the poison isn't in the train?"

"Lord, no, sir. No one didn't take poison that way. 'E took it away with 'im, in 'is 'ands. 'E's wirin' from Wokin'. My orders was to ask everybody in the train, and I 'ave, an' we're four minutes late now. Are you comin' on, sir? No? Right be'ind!"

There is nothing, unless, perhaps, the English language, more terrible than the workings of an English railway-line. An instant before it seemed as though we were going to spend all eternity at Framlynghame Admiral, and now I was watching the tail of the train disappear round the curve of the cutting.

But I was not alone. On the one bench of the down platform sat the largest navvy I have ever seen in my life, softened and made affable (for he smiled generously) with liquor. In his huge hands he nursed an empty tumbler marked "L.S.W.R."—marked also, internally, with streaks of blue-grey sediment. Before him, a hand on his shoulder, stood the doctor, and as I came within ear-shot, this is what I heard him say: "Just you hold on to your patience for a minute or two longer, and you'll be as right as ever you were in your life. I'll stay with you till you're better."

"Lord! I'm comfortable enough," said the navvy. "Never felt better in my life."

Turning to me, the doctor lowered his voice. "He might have died while that fool conduct-guard was saying his piece. I've fixed him, though. The stuff's due in about five minutes, but there's a heap to him. I don't see how we can make him take exercise."

For the moment I felt as though seven pounds of crushed ice had been neatly applied in the form of a compress to my lower stomach.

"How—how did you manage it?" I gasped.

"I asked him if he'd have a drink. He was knocking spots out of the car—strength of his constitution, I suppose. He said he'd go 'most anywhere for a drink, so I lured onto the platform, and loaded him up. 'Cold-blooded people, you Britishers are. That train's gone, and no one seemed to care a cent."

"We've missed it," I said.

He looked at me curiously.

"We'll get another before sundown, if that's your only trouble. Say, porter, when's the next train down?"

"Seven forty-five," said the one porter, and passed out through the wicket-gate into the landscape. It was then three-twenty of a hot and sleepy afternoon. The station was absolutely deserted. The navvy had closed his eyes, and now nodded.

"That's bad," said the doctor. "The man, I mean, not the train. We must make him walk somehow—walk up and down."

Swiftly as might be, I explained the delicacy of the situation, and the doctor from New York turned a full bronze-green. Then he swore comprehensively at the entire fabric of our glorious Constitution, cursing the English language, root, branch, and paradigm, through its most obscure derivatives. His coat and bag lay on the bench next to the sleeper. Thither he edged cautiously, and I saw treachery in his eye.

What devil of delay possessed him to slip on his spring overcoat, I cannot tell. They say a slight noise rouses a sleeper more surely than a heavy one, and scarcely had the doctor settled himself in his sleeves than the giant waked and seized that silk-faced collar in a hot right hand. There was rage in his face-rage and the realisation of new emotions.

"I'm—I'm not so comfortable as I were," he said from the deeps of his interior. "You'll wait along o' me, you will." He breathed heavily through shut lips.

Now, if there was one thing more than another upon which the doctor had dwelt in his conversation with me, it was upon the essential law-abidingness, not to say gentleness, of his much-misrepresented country. And yet (truly, it may have been no more than a button that irked him) I saw his hand travel backwards to his right hip, clutch at something, and come away empty.

"He won't kill you," I said. "He'll probably sue you in court, if I know my own people. Better give him some money from time to time."

"If he keeps quiet till the stuff gets in its work," the doctor answered, "I'm all right. If he doesn't... my name is Emory—Julian B. Emory—193 'Steenth Street, corner of Madison and— "

"I feel worse than I've ever felt," said the navvy, with suddenness. "What-did-you-give-me-the-drink-for?"

The matter seemed to be so purely personal that I withdrew to a strategic position on the overhead bridge, and, abiding in the exact centre, looked on from afar.

I could see the white road that ran across the shoulder of Salisbury Plain, unshaded for mile after mile, and a dot in the middle distance, the back of the one porter returning to Framlynghame Admiral, if such a place existed, till seven forty-five. The bell of a church invisible clanked softly. There was a rustle in the horse-chestnuts to the left of the line, and the sound of sheep cropping close.

The peace of Nirvana lay upon the land, and, brooding in it, my elbow on the warm iron girder of the footbridge (it is a forty-shilling fine to cross by any other means), I perceived, as never before, how the consequences of our acts run eternal through time and through space. If we impinge never so slightly upon the life of a fellow-mortal, the touch of our personality, like the ripple of a stone cast into a pond, widens and widens in unending circles across the aeons, till the far-off Gods themselves cannot say where action ceases. Also, it was I who had silently set before the doctor the tumbler of the first-class lavatory compartment now speeding Plymouthward. Yet I was, in spirit at least, a million leagues removed from that unhappy man of another nationality, who had chosen to thrust an inexpert finger into the workings of an alien life. The machinery was dragging him up and down the sunlit platform. The two men seemed to be learning polka-mazurkas together, and the burden of their song, borne by one deep voice, was: "What did you give me the drink for?"

I saw the flash of silver in the doctor's hand. The navvy took it and pocketed it with his left; but never for an instant did his strong right leave the doctor's coat-collar, and as the crisis approached, louder and louder rose his bull-like roar: "What did you give me the drink for?"

They drifted under the great twelve-inch pinned timbers of the footbridge towards the bench, and, I gathered, the time was very near at hand. The stuff was getting in its work. Blue, white, and blue again, rolled over the navvy's face in waves, till all settled to one rich clay-bank yellow and—that fell which fell.

I thought of the blowing up of Hell Gate; of the geysers in the Yellowstone Park; of Jonah and his whale: but the lively original, as I watched it foreshortened from above, exceeded all these things. He staggered to the bench, the heavy wooden seat cramped with iron cramps into the enduring stone, and clung there with his left hand. It quivered and shook, as a breakwater-pile quivers to the rush of landward-racing seas; nor was there lacking when he caught his breath, the "scream of a maddened beach dragged down by the tide." His right hand was upon the doctor's collar, so that the two shook to one paroxysm, pendulums vibrating together, while I, apart, shook with them.

It was colossal-immense; but of certain manifestations the English language stops short. French only, the caryatid French of Victor Hugo, would have described it; so I mourned while I laughed, hastily shuffling and discarding inadequate adjectives. The vehemence of the shock spent itself, and the sufferer half fell, half knelt, across the bench. He was calling now upon God and his wife, huskily, as the wounded bull calls upon the unscathed herd to stay. Curiously enough, he used no bad language: that had gone from him with the rest. The doctor exhibited gold. It was taken and retained. So, too, was the grip on the coat-collar.

"If I could stand," boomed the giant, despairingly, "I'd smash you—you an' your drinks. I'm dyin'—dyin'—dyin'!"

"That's what you think," said the doctor. "You'll find it will do you a lot of good"; and, making a virtue of a somewhat imperative necessity, he added: "I'll stay by you. If you'd let go of me a minute I'd give you something that would settle you."

"You've settled me now, you damned anarchist. Takin' the bread out of the mouth of an English workin'man! But I'll keep 'old of you till I'm well or dead. I never did you no 'arm. S'pose I were a little full. They pumped me out once at Guy's with a stummick-pump. I could see that, but I can't see this 'ere, an' it's killin' of me by slow degrees."

"You'll be all right in half-an-hour. What do you suppose I'd want to kill you for?" said the doctor, who came of a logical breed.

"'Ow do I know? Tell 'em in court. You'll get seven years for this, you bodysnatcher. That's what you are—a bloomin' bodysnatcher. There's justice, I tell you, in England; and my Union'll prosecute, too. We don't stand no tricks with people's insides 'ere. They give a woman ten years for a sight less than this. An' you'll 'ave to pay 'undreds an' 'undreds o' pounds, besides a pension to the missus. You'll see, you physickin' furriner. Where's your licence to do such? You'll catch it, I tell you!"

Then I observed what I have frequently observed before, that a man who is but reasonably afraid of an altercation with an alien has a most poignant dread of the operations of foreign law. The doctor's voice was flute-like in its exquisite politeness, as he answered:

"But I've given you a very great deal of money—fif-three pounds, I think."

"An' what's three pound for poisonin' the likes o' me? They told me at Guy's I'd fetch twenty-cold-on the slates. Ouh! It's comin' again."

A second time he was cut down by the foot, as it were, and the straining bench rocked to and fro as I averted my eyes.

It was the very point of perfection in the heart of an English May-day. The unseen tides of the air had turned, and all nature was setting its face with the shadows of the horse-chestnuts towards the peace of the coming night. But there were hours yet, I knew—long, long hours of the eternal English twilight—to the ending of the day. I was well content to be alive—to abandon myself to the drift of Time and Fate; to absorb great peace through my skin, and to love my country with the devotion that three thousand miles of intervening sea bring to fullest flower. And what a garden of Eden it was, this fatted, clipped, and washen land! A man could camp in any open field with more sense of home and security than the stateliest buildings of foreign cities could afford. And the joy was that it was all mine alienably—groomed hedgerow, spotless road, decent greystone cottage, serried spinney, tasselled copse, apple-bellied hawthorn, and well-grown tree. A light puff of wind—it scattered flakes of may over the gleaming rails—gave me a faint whiff as it might have been of fresh cocoanut, and I knew that the golden gorse was in bloom somewhere out of sight. Linneeus had thanked God on his bended knees when he first saw a field of it; and, by the way, the navvy was on his knees, too. But he was by no means praying. He was purely disgustful.

The doctor was compelled to bend over him, his face towards the back of the seat, and from what I had seen I supposed the navvy was now dead. If that were the case it would be time for me to go; but I knew that so long as a man trusts himself to the current of Circumstance, reaching out for and rejecting nothing that comes his way, no harm can overtake him. It is the contriver, the schemer, who is caught by the Law, and never the philosopher. I knew that when the play was played, Destiny herself would move me on from the corpse; and I felt very sorry for the doctor.

In the far distance, presumably upon the road that led to Framlynghame Admiral, there appeared a vehicle and a horse—the one ancient fly that almost every village can produce at need. This thing was advancing, unpaid by me, towards the station; would have to pass along the deep-cut lane, below the railway-bridge, and come out on the doctor's side. I was in the centre of things, so all sides were alike to me. Here, then, was my machine from the machine. When it arrived; something would happen, or something else. For the rest, I owned my deeply interested soul.

The doctor, by the seat, turned so far as his cramped position allowed, his head over his left shoulder, and laid his right hand upon his lips. I threw back my hat and elevated my eyebrows in the form of a question. The doctor shut his eyes and nodded his head slowly twice or thrice, beckoning me to come. I descended cautiously, and it was as the signs had told. The navvy was asleep, empty to the lowest notch; yet his hand clutched still the doctor's collar, and at the lightest movement (the doctor was really very cramped) tightened mechanically, as the hand of a sick woman tightens on that of the watcher. He had dropped, squatting almost upon his heels, and, falling lower, had dragged the doctor over to the left.

The doctor thrust his right hand, which was free, into his pocket, drew forth some keys, and shook his head. The navvy gurgled in his sleep. Silently I dived into my pocket, took out one sovereign, and held it up between finger and thumb. Again the doctor shook his head. Money was not what was lacking to his peace. His bag had fallen from the seat to the ground. He looked towards it, and opened his mouth-O-shape. The catch was not a difficult one, and when I had mastered it, the doctor's right forefinger was sawing the air. With an immense caution, I extracted from the bag such a knife as they use for cutting collops off legs. The doctor frowned, and with his first and second fingers imitated the action of scissors. Again I searched, and found a most diabolical pair of cock-nosed shears, capable of vandyking the interiors of elephants. The doctor then slowly lowered his left shoulder till the navvy's right wrist was supported by the bench, pausing a moment as the spent volcano rumbled anew. Lower and lower the doctor sank, kneeling now by the navvy's side, till his head was on a level with, and just in front of, the great hairy fist, and—there was no tension on the coat-collar. Then light dawned on me.

Beginning a little to the right of the spinal column, I cut a huge demilune out of his new spring overcoat, bringing it round as far under his left side (which was the right side of the navvy) as I dared. Passing thence swiftly to the back of the seat, and reaching between the splines, I sawed through the silk-faced front on the left-hand side of the coat till the two cuts joined.

Cautiously as the box-turtle of his native heath, the doctor drew away sideways and to the right, with the air of a frustrated burglar coming out from under a bed, and stood up free, one black diagonal shoulder projecting through the grey of his ruined overcoat. I returned the scissors to the bag, snapped the catch, and held all out to him as the wheels of the fly rang hollow under the railway arch.

It came at a footpace past the wicket-gate of the station, and the doctor stopped it with a whisper. It was going some five miles across country to bring home from church some one,—I could not catch the name,—because his own carriage-horses were lame. Its destination happened to be the one place in all the world that the doctor was most burningly anxious to visit, and he promised the driver untold gold to drive to some ancient flame of his—Helen Blazes, she was called.

"Aren't you coming, too?" he said, bundling his overcoat into his bag.

Now the fly had been so obviously sent to the doctor, and to no one else, that I had no concern with it. Our roads, I saw, divided, and there was, further, a need upon me to laugh.

"I shall stay here," I said. "It's a very pretty country."

"My God!" he murmured, as softly as he shut the door, and I felt that it was a prayer.

Then he went out of my life, and I shaped my course for the railway-bridge. It was necessary to pass by the bench once more, but the wicket was between us. The departure of the fly had waked the navvy. He crawled on to the seat, and with malignant eyes watched the driver flog down the road.

"The man inside o' that," he called, "'as poisoned me. 'E's a bodysnatcher. 'E's comin' back again when I'm cold. 'Ere's my evidence!"

He waved his share of the overcoat, and I went my way, because I was hungry. Framlynghame Admiral village is a good two miles from the station, and I waked the holy calm of the evening every step of that way with shouts and yells, casting myself down in the flank of the good green hedge when I was too weak to stand. There was an inn,—a blessed inn with a thatched roof, and peonies in the garden,—and I ordered myself an upper chamber in which the Foresters held their courts for the laughter was not all out of me. A bewildered woman brought me ham and eggs, and I leaned out of the mullioned window, and laughed between mouthfuls. I sat long above the beer and the perfect smoke that followed, till the lights changed in the quiet street, and I began to think of the seven forty-five down, and all that world of the "Arabian Nights" I had quitted.

Descending, I passed a giant in moleskins who filled the low-ceiled taproom. Many empty plates stood before him, and beyond them a fringe of the Framlynghame Admiralty, to whom he was unfolding a wondrous tale of anarchy, of bodysnatching, of bribery, and the Valley of the Shadow from the which he was but newly risen. And as he talked he ate, and as he ate he drank, for there was much room in him; and anon he paid royally, speaking of Justice and the Law, before whom all Englishmen are equal, and all foreigners and anarchists vermin and slime.

On my way to the station, he passed me with great strides, his head high among the low-flying bats, his feet firm on the packed road-metal, his fists clinched, and his breath coming sharply. There was a beautiful smell in the air—the smell of white dust, bruised nettles, and smoke, that brings tears to the throat of a man who sees his country but seldom—a smell like the echoes of the lost talk of lovers; the infinitely suggestive odour of an immemorial civilisation. It was a perfect walk; and, lingering on every step, I came to the station just as the one porter lighted the last of a truckload of lamps, and set them back in the lamp-room, while he dealt tickets to four or five of the population who, not contented with their own peace, thought fit to travel. It was no ticket that the navvy seemed to need. He was sitting on a bench, wrathfully grinding a tumbler into fragments with his heel. I abode in obscurity at the end of the platform, interested as ever, thank Heaven, in my surroundings. There was a jar of wheels on the road. The navvy rose as they approached, strode through the wicket, and laid a hand upon a horse's bridle that brought the beast up on his hireling hind legs. It was the providential fly coming back, and for a moment I wondered whether the doctor had been mad enough to revisit his practice.

"Get away; you're drunk," said the driver.

"I'm not," said the navvy. "I've been waitin' 'ere hours and hours. Come out, you beggar inside there!"

"Go on, driver," said a voice I did not know—a crisp, clear, English voice.

"All right," said the navvy. "You wouldn't 'ear me when I was polite. Now will you come?"

There was a chasm in the side of the fly, for he had wrenched the door bodily off its hinges, and was feeling within purposefully. A well-booted leg rewarded him, and there came out, not with delight, hopping on one foot, a round and grey-haired Englishman, from whose armpits dropped hymn-books, but from his mouth an altogether different service of song.

"Come on, you bloomin' bodysnatcher! You thought I was dead, did you?" roared the navvy. And the respectable gentleman came accordingly, inarticulate with rage.

"Ere's a man murderin' the Squire," the driver shouted, and fell from his box upon the navvy's neck.

To do them justice, the people of Framlynghame Admiral, so many as were on the platform, rallied to the call in the best spirit of feudalism. It was the one porter who beat the navvy on the nose with a ticket-punch, but it was the three third-class tickets who attached themselves to his legs and freed the captive.

"Send for a constable! lock him up!" said that man, adjusting his collar; and unitedly they cast him into the lamp-room, and turned the key, while the driver mourned over the wrecked fly.

Till then the navvy, whose only desire was justice, had kept his temper nobly. Then he went Berserk before our amazed eyes. The door of the lamp-room was generously constructed, and would not give an inch, but the window he tore from its fastenings and hurled outwards. The one porter counted the damage in a loud voice, and the others, arming themselves with agricultural implements from the station garden, kept up a ceaseless winnowing before the window, themselves backed close to the wall, and bade the prisoner think of the gaol. He answered little to the point, so far as they could understand; but seeing that his exit was impeded, he took a lamp and hurled it through the wrecked sash. It fell on the metals and went out. With inconceivable velocity, the others, fifteen in all, followed, looking like rockets in the gloom, and with the last (he could have had no plan) the Berserk rage left him as the doctor's deadly brewage waked up, under the stimulus of violent exercise and a very full meal, to one last cataclysmal exhibition, and—we heard the whistle of the seven forty-five down.

They were all acutely interested in as much of the wreck as they could see, for the station smelt to Heaven of oil, and the engine skittered over broken glass like a terrier in a cucumber-frame. The guard had to hear of it, and the Squire had his version of the brutal assault, and heads were out all along the carriages as I found me a seat.

"What is the row?" said a young man, as I entered. "'Man drunk?"

"Well, the symptoms, so far as my observation has gone, more resemble those of Asiatic cholera than anything else," I answered, slowly and judicially, that every word might carry weight in the appointed scheme of things. Up till then, you will observe, I had taken no part in that war.

He was an Englishman, but he collected his belongings as swiftly as had the American, ages before, and leaped upon the platform, crying: "Can I be of any service? I'm a doctor."

From the lamp-room I heard a wearied voice wailing "Another bloomin' doctor!"

And the seven forty-five carried me on, a step nearer to Eternity, by the road that is worn and seamed and channelled with the passions, and weaknesses, and warring interests of man who is immortal and master of his fate.

THE BRUSHWOOD BOY

Girls and boys, come out to play
  The moon is shining as bright as day!

  Leave your supper and leave your sleep,

  And come with your playfellows out in the street!

  Up the ladder and down the wall—

A CHILD of three sat up in his crib and screamed at the top of his voice, his fists clinched and his eyes full of terror. At first no one heard, for his nursery was in the west wing, and the nurse was talking to a gardener among the laurels. Then the housekeeper passed that way, and hurried to soothe him. He was her special pet, and she disapproved of the nurse.

"What was it, then? What was it, then? There's nothing to frighten him, Georgie dear."

"It was—it was a policeman! He was on the Down—I saw him! He came in. Jane said he would."

"Policemen don't come into houses, dearie. Turn over, and take my hand."

"I saw him—on the Down. He came here. Where is your hand, Harper?"

The housekeeper waited till the sobs changed to the regular breathing of sleep before she stole out.

"Jane, what nonsense have you been telling Master Georgie about policemen?"

"I haven't told him anything."

"You have. He's been dreaming about them."

"We met Tisdall on Dowhead when we were in the donkey-cart this morning. P'r'aps that's what put it into his head."

"Oh! Now you aren't going to frighten the child into fits with your silly tales, and the master know nothing about it. If ever I catch you again," *etc.*

****

A child of six was telling himself stories as he lay in bed. It was a new power, and he kept it a secret. A month before it had occurred to him to carry on a nursery tale left unfinished by his mother, and he was delighted to find the tale as it came out of his own head just as surprising as though he were listening to it "all new from the beginning." There was a prince in that tale, and he killed dragons, but only for one night. Ever afterwards Georgie dubbed himself prince, pasha, giant-killer, and all the rest (you see, he could not tell any one, for fear of being laughed at), and his tales faded gradually into dreamland, where adventures were so many that he could not recall the half of them. They all began in the same way, or, as Georgie explained to the shadows of the night-light, there was "the same starting-off place"—a pile of brushwood stacked somewhere near a beach; and round this pile Georgie found himself running races with little boys and girls. These ended, ships ran high up the dry land and opened into cardboard boxes; or gilt-and-green iron railings that surrounded beautiful gardens turned all soft and could be walked through and overthrown so long as he remembered it was only a dream. He could never hold that knowledge more than a few seconds ere things became real, and instead of pushing down houses full of grown-up people (a just revenge), he sat miserably upon gigantic door-steps trying to sing the multiplication-table up to four times six.

The princess of his tales was a person of wonderful beauty (she came from the old illustrated edition of Grimm, now out of print), and as she always applauded Georgie's valour among the dragons and buffaloes, he gave her the two finest names he had ever heard in his life—Annie and Louise, pronounced "Annieanlouise." When the dreams swamped the stories, she would change into one of the little girls round the brushwood-pile, still keeping her title and crown. She saw Georgie drown once in a dream-sea by the beach (it was the day after he had been taken to bathe in a real sea by his nurse); and he said as he sank: "Poor Annieanlouise! She'll be sorry for me now!" But "Annieanlouise," walking slowly on the beach, called, "'Ha! ha!' said the duck, laughing," which to a waking mind might not seem to bear on the situation. It consoled Georgie at once, and must have been some kind of spell, for it raised the bottom of the deep, and he waded out with a twelve-inch flower-pot on each foot. As he was strictly forbidden to meddle with flower-pots in real life, he felt triumphantly wicked.

****

The movements of the grown-ups, whom Georgie tolerated, but did not pretend to understand, removed his world, when he was seven years old, to a place called "Oxford-on-a-visit. "Here were huge buildings surrounded by vast prairies, with streets of infinite length, and, above all, something called the "buttery," which Georgie was dying to see, because he knew it must be greasy, and therefore delightful. He perceived how correct were his judgments when his nurse led him through a stone arch into the presence of an enormously fat man, who asked him if he would like some, bread and cheese. Georgie was used to eat all round the clock, so he took what "buttery" gave him, and would have taken some brown liquid called "auditale" but that his nurse led him away to an afternoon performance of a thing called "Pepper's Ghost." This was intensely thrilling. People's heads came off and flew all over the stage, and skeletons danced bone by bone, while Mr. Pepper himself, beyond question a man of the worst, waved his arms and flapped a long gown, and in a deep bass voice (Georgie had never heard a man sing before) told of his sorrows unspeakable. Some grown-up or other tried to explain that the illusion was made with mirrors, and that there was no need to be frightened. Georgie did not know what illusions were, but he did know that a mirror was the looking-glass with the ivory handle on his mother's dressing-table. Therefore the "grown-up" was "just saying things" after the distressing custom of "grown-ups," and Georgie cast about for amusement between scenes. Next to him sat a little girl dressed all in black, her hair combed off her forehead exactly like the girl in the book called "Alice in Wonderland," which had been given him on his last birthday. The little girl looked at Georgie, and Georgie looked at her. There seemed to be no need of any further introduction.

"I've got a cut on my thumb," said he. It was the first work of his first real knife, a savage triangular hack, and he esteemed it a most valuable possession.

"I'm tho thorry!" she lisped. "Let me look pleathe."

"There's a di-ack-lum plaster on, but it's all raw under," Georgie answered, complying.

"Dothent it hurt?"—her grey eyes were full of pity and interest.

"Awf'ly. Perhaps it will give me lockjaw."

"It lookth very horrid. I'm tho thorry!" She put a forefinger to his hand, and held her head sidewise for a better view.

Here the nurse turned, and shook him severely. "You mustn't talk to strange little girls, Master Georgie."

"She isn't strange. She's very nice. I like her, an' I've showed her my new cut."

"The idea! You change places with me."

She moved him over, and shut out the little girl from his view, while the grown-up behind renewed the futile explanations.

"I am not afraid, truly," said the boy, wriggling in despair; "but why don't you go to sleep in the afternoons, same as Provost of Oriel?"

Georgie had been introduced to a grown-up of that name, who slept in his presence without apology. Georgie understood that he was the most important grown-up in Oxford; hence he strove to gild his rebuke with flatteries. This grown-up did not seem to like it, but he collapsed, and Georgie lay back in his seat, silent and enraptured. Mr. Pepper was singing again, and the deep, ringing voice, the red fire, and the misty, waving gown all seemed to be mixed up with the little girl who had been so kind about his cut. When the performance was ended she nodded to Georgie, and Georgie nodded in return. He spoke no more than was necessary till bedtime, but meditated on new colors and sounds and lights and music and things as far as he understood them; the deep-mouthed agony of Mr. Pepper mingling with the little girl's lisp. That night he made a new tale, from which he shamelessly removed the Rapunzel-Rapunzel-let-down-your-hair princess, gold crown, Grimm edition, and all, and put a new Annieanlouise in her place. So it was perfectly right and natural that when he came to the brushwood-pile he should find her waiting for him, her hair combed off her forehead more like Alice in Wonderland than ever, and the races and adventures began.

Ten years at an English public school do not encourage dreaming. Georgie won his growth and chest measurement, and a few other things which did not appear in the bills, under a system of cricket, foot-ball, and paper-chases, from four to five days a week, which provided for three lawful cuts of a ground-ash if any boy absented himself from these entertainments. He became a rumple-collared, dusty-hatted fag of the Lower Third, and a light half-back at Little Side foot-ball; was pushed and prodded through the slack backwaters of the Lower Fourth, where the raffle of a school generally accumulates; won his "second-fifteen" cap at foot-ball, enjoyed the dignity of a study with two companions in it, and began to look forward to office as a sub-prefect. At last he blossomed into full glory as head of the school, ex-officio captain of the games; head of his house, where he and his lieutenants preserved discipline and decency among seventy boys from twelve to seventeen; general arbiter in the quarrels that spring up among the touchy Sixth—and intimate friend and ally of the Head himself. When he stepped forth in the black jersey, white knickers, and black stockings of the First Fifteen, the new match-ball under his arm, and his old and frayed cap at the back of his head, the small fry of the lower forms stood apart and worshipped, and the "new caps" of the team talked to him ostentatiously, that the world might see. And so, in summer, when he came back to the pavilion after a slow but eminently safe game, it mattered not whether he had made nothing or, as once happened, a hundred and three, the school shouted just the same, and women-folk who had come to look at the match looked at Cottar—Cottar, major; "that's Cottar!" Above all, he was responsible for that thing called the tone of the school, and few realise with what passionate devotion a certain type of boy throws himself into this work. Home was a faraway country, full of ponies and fishing and shooting, and men-visitors who interfered with one's plans; but school was the real world, where things of vital importance happened, and crises arose that must be dealt with promptly and quietly. Not for nothing was it written, "Let the Consuls look to it that the Republic takes no harm," and Georgie was glad to be back in authority when the holidays ended. Behind him, but not too near, was the wise and temperate Head, now suggesting the wisdom of the serpent, now counselling the mildness of the dove; leading him on to see, more by half-hints than by any direct word, how boys and men are all of a piece, and how he who can handle the one will assuredly in time control the other.

For the rest, the school was not encouraged to dwell on its emotions, but rather to keep in hard condition, to avoid false quantities, and to enter the army direct, without the help of the expensive London crammer, under whose roof young blood learns too much. Cottar, major, went the way of hundreds before him. The Head gave him six months' final polish, taught him what kind of answers best please a certain kind of examiners, and handed him over to the properly constituted authorities, who passed him into Sandhurst. Here he had sense enough to see that he was in the Lower Third once more, and behaved with respect toward his seniors, till they in turn respected him, and he was promoted to the rank of corporal, and sat in authority over mixed peoples with all the vices of men and boys combined. His reward was another string of athletic cups, a good-conduct sword, and, at last, Her Majesty's commission as a subaltern in a first-class line regiment. He did not know that he bore with him from school and college a character worth much fine gold, but was pleased to find his mess so kindly. He had plenty of money of his own; his training had set the public school mask upon his face, and had taught him how many were the "things no fellow can do." By virtue of the same training he kept his pores open and his mouth shut.

The regular working of the Empire shifted his world to India, where he tasted utter loneliness in subaltern's quarters,—one room and one bullock-trunk,—and, with his mess, learned the new life from the beginning. But there were horses in the land-ponies at reasonable price; there was polo for such as could afford it; there were the disreputable remnants of a pack of hounds; and Cottar worried his way along without too much despair. It dawned on him that a regiment in India was nearer the chance of active service than he had conceived, and that a man might as well study his profession. A major of the new school backed this idea with enthusiasm, and he and Cottar accumulated a library of military works, and read and argued and disputed far into the nights. But the adjutant said the old thing: "Get to know your men, young un, and they 'll follow you anywhere. That's all you want—know your men." Cottar thought he knew them fairly well at cricket and the regimental sports, but he never realised the true inwardness of them till he was sent off with a detachment of twenty to sit down in a mud fort near a rushing river which was spanned by a bridge of boats. When the floods came they went forth and hunted strayed pontoons along the banks. Otherwise there was nothing to do, and the men got drunk, gambled, and quarrelled. They were a sickly crew, for a junior subaltern is by custom saddled with the worst men. Cottar endured their rioting as long as he could, and then sent down-country for a dozen pairs of boxing-gloves.

"I wouldn't blame you for fightin'," said he, "if you only knew how to use your hands; but you don't. Take these things, and I'll show you." The men appreciated his efforts. Now, instead of blaspheming and swearing at a comrade, and threatening to shoot him, they could take him apart, and soothe themselves to exhaustion. As one explained whom Cottar found with a shut eye and a diamond-shaped mouth spitting blood through an embrasure: "We tried it with the gloves, sir, for twenty minutes, and that done us no good, sir. Then we took off the gloves and tried it that way for another twenty minutes, same as you showed us, sir, an' that done us a world o' good. 'T wasn't fightin', sir; there was a bet on."

Cottar dared not laugh, but he invited his men to other sports, such as racing across country in shirt and trousers after a trail of torn paper, and to single-stick in the evenings, till the native population, who had a lust for sport in every form, wished to know whether the white men understood wrestling. They sent in an ambassador, who took the soldiers by the neck and threw them about the dust; and the entire command were all for this new game. They spent money on learning new falls and holds, which was better than buying other doubtful commodities; and the peasantry grinned five deep round the tournaments.

That detachment, who had gone up in bullock-carts, returned to headquarters at an average rate of thirty miles a day, fair heel-and-toe; no sick, no prisoners, and no court martials pending. They scattered themselves among their friends, singing the praises of their lieutenant and looking for causes of offense.

"How did you do it, young un?" the adjutant asked.

"Oh, I sweated the beef off 'em, and then I sweated some muscle on to 'em. It was rather a lark."

"If that's your way of lookin' at it, we can give you all the larks you want. Young Davies isn't feelin' quite fit, and he's next for detachment duty. Care to go for him?"

"'Sure he wouldn't mind? I don't want to shove myself forward, you know."

"You needn't bother on Davies's account. We'll give you the sweepin's of the corps, and you can see what you can make of 'em."

"All right," said Cottar. "It's better fun than loafin' about cantonments."

"Rummy thing," said the adjutant, after Cottar had returned to his wilderness with twenty other devils worse than the first. "If Cottar only knew it, half the women in the station would give their eyes—confound 'em!—to have the young un in tow."

"That accounts for Mrs. Elery sayin' I was workin' my nice new boy too hard," said a wing commander.

"Oh, yes; and 'Why doesn't he come to the bandstand in the evenings?' and 'Can't I get him to make up a four at tennis with the Hammon girls?'" the adjutant snorted. "Look at young Davies makin' an ass of himself over mutton-dressed-as-lamb old enough to be his mother!"

"No one can accuse young Cottar of runnin' after women, white or black," the major replied thoughtfully. "But, then, that's the kind that generally goes the worst mucker in the end."

"Not Cottar. I've only run across one of his muster before—a fellow called Ingles, in South Africa. He was just the same hard trained, athletic-sports build of animal. Always kept himself in the pink of condition. Didn't do him much good, though. 'Shot at Wesselstroom the week before Majuba. Wonder how the young un will lick his detachment into shape."

Cottar turned up six weeks later, on foot, with his pupils. He never told his experiences, but the men spoke enthusiastically, and fragments of it leaked back to the colonel through sergeants, batmen, and the like.

There was great jealousy between the first and second detachments, but the men united in adoring Cottar, and their way of showing it was by sparing him all the trouble that men know how to make for an unloved officer. He sought popularity as little as he had sought it at school, and therefore it came to him. He favoured no one—not even when the company sloven pulled the company cricket-match out of the fire with an unexpected forty-three at the last moment. There was very little getting round him, for he seemed to know by instinct exactly when and where to head off a malingerer; but he did not forget that the difference between a dazed and sulky junior of the upper school and a bewildered, browbeaten lump of a private fresh from the depot was very small indeed. The sergeants, seeing these things, told him secrets generally hid from young officers. His words were quoted as barrack authority on bets in canteen and at tea; and the veriest shrew of the corps, bursting with charges against other women who had used the cooking-ranges out of turn, forbore to speak when Cottar, as the regulations ordained, asked of a morning if there were "any complaints."

"I'm full o' complaints," said Mrs. Corporal Morrison, "an' I'd kill O'Halloran's fat sow of a wife any day, but ye know how it is. 'E puts 'is head just inside the door, an' looks down 'is blessed nose so bashful, an' 'e whispers, 'Any complaints' Ye can't complain after that. I want to kiss him. Some day I think I will. Heigh-ho! she'll be a lucky woman that gets Young Innocence. See 'im now, girls. Do ye blame me?"

Cottar was cantering across to polo, and he looked a very satisfactory figure of a man as he gave easily to the first excited bucks of his pony, and slipped over a low mud wall to the practice-ground. There were more than Mrs. Corporal Morrison who felt as she did. But Cottar was busy for eleven hours of the day. He did not care to have his tennis spoiled by petticoats in the court; and after one long afternoon at a garden-party, he explained to his major that this sort of thing was "futile priffle," and the major laughed. Theirs was not a married mess, except for the colonel's wife, and Cottar stood in awe of the good lady. She said "my regiment," and the world knows what that means. None the less when they wanted her to give away the prizes after a shooting-match, and she refused because one of the prize-winners was married to a girl who had made a jest of her behind her broad back, the mess ordered Cottar to "tackle her," in his best calling-kit. This he did, simply and laboriously, and she gave way altogether.

"She only wanted to know the facts of the case," he explained. "I just told her, and she saw at once."

"Ye-es," said the adjutant. "I expect that's what she did. Comin' to the Fusiliers' dance to-night, Galahad?"

"No, thanks. I've got a fight on with the major." The virtuous apprentice sat up till midnight in the major's quarters, with a stop-watch and a pair of compasses, shifting little painted lead-blocks about a four-inch map.

Then he turned in and slept the sleep of innocence, which is full of healthy dreams. One peculiarity of his dreams he noticed at the beginning of his second hot weather. Two or three times a month they duplicated or ran in series. He would find himself sliding into dreamland by the same road—a road that ran along a beach near a pile of brushwood. To the right lay the sea, sometimes at full tide, sometimes withdrawn to the very horizon; but he knew it for the same sea. By that road he would travel over a swell of rising ground covered with short, withered grass, into valleys of wonder and unreason. Beyond the ridge, which was crowned with some sort of street-lamp, anything was possible; but up to the lamp it seemed to him that he knew the road as well as he knew the parade-ground. He learned to look forward to the place; for, once there, he was sure of a good night's rest, and Indian hot weather can be rather trying. First, shadowy under closing eyelids, would come the outline of the brushwood-pile; next the white sand of the beach-road, almost overhanging the black, changeful sea; then the turn inland and uphill to the single light. When he was unrestful for any reason, he would tell himself how he was sure to get there—sure to get there—if he shut his eyes and surrendered to the drift of things. But one night after a foolishly hard hour's polo (the thermometer was 94° in his quarters at ten o'clock), sleep stood away from him altogether, though he did his best to find the well-known road, the point where true sleep began. At last he saw the brushwood-pile, and hurried along to the ridge, for behind him he felt was the wide-awake, sultry world. He reached the lamp in safety, tingling with drowsiness, when a policeman—a common country policeman—sprang up before him and touched him on the shoulder ere he could dive into the dim valley below. He was filled with terror,—the hopeless terror of dreams,—for the policeman said, in the awful, distinct voice of dream-people, "I am Policeman Day coming back from the City of Sleep. You come with me." Georgie knew it was true—that just beyond him in the valley lay the lights of the City of Sleep, where he would have been sheltered, and that this Policeman-Thing had full power and authority to head him back to miserable wakefulness. He found himself looking at the moonlight on the wall, dripping with fright; and he never overcame that horror, though he met the Policeman several times that hot weather, and his coming was the forerunner of a bad night.

But other dreams-perfectly absurd ones-filled him with an incommunicable delight. All those that he remembered began by the brushwood-pile. For instance, he found a small clockwork steamer (he had noticed it many nights before) lying by the sea-road, and stepped into it, whereupon it moved with surpassing swiftness over an absolutely level sea. This was glorious, for he felt he was exploring great matters; and it stopped by a lily carved in stone, which, most naturally, floated on the water. Seeing the lily was labelled "Hong-Kong," Georgie said: "Of course. This is precisely what I expected Hong-Kong would be like. How magnificent!" Thousands of miles farther on it halted at yet another stone lily, labelled "Java."; and this, again, delighted him hugely, because he knew that now he was at the world's end. But the little boat ran on and on till it lay in a deep fresh-water lock, the sides of which were carven marble, green with moss. Lilypads lay on the water, and reeds arched above. Some one moved among the reeds—some one whom Georgie knew he had travelled to this world's end to reach. Therefore everything was entirely well with him. He was unspeakably happy, and vaulted over the ship's side to find this person. When his feet touched that still water, it changed, with the rustle of unrolling maps, to nothing less than a sixth quarter of the globe, beyond the most remote imagining of man—a place where islands were coloured yellow and blue, their lettering strung across their faces. They gave on unknown seas, and Georgie's urgent desire was to return swiftly across this floating atlas to known bearings. He told himself repeatedly that it was no good to hurry; but still he hurried desperately, and the islands slipped and slid under his feet; the straits yawned and widened, till he found himself utterly lost in the world's fourth dimension, with no hope of return. Yet only a little distance away he could see the old world with the rivers and mountain-chains marked according to the Sandhurst rules of mapmaking. Then that person for whom he had come to the Lily Lock (that was its name) ran up across unexplored territories, and showed him away. They fled hand in hand till they reached a road that spanned ravines, and ran along the edge of precipices, and was tunnelled through mountains. "This goes to our brushwood-pile," said his companion; and all his trouble was at an end. He took a pony, because he understood that this was the Thirty-Mile Ride and he must ride swiftly, and raced through the clattering tunnels and round the curves, always downhill, till he heard the sea to his left, and saw it raging under a full moon, against sandy cliffs. It was heavy going, but he recognised the nature of the country, the dark-purple downs inland, and the bents that whistled in the wind. The road was eaten away in places, and the sea lashed at him-black, foamless tongues of smooth and glossy rollers; but he was sure that there was less danger from the sea than from "Them," whoever "They" were, inland to his right. He knew, too, that he would be safe if he could reach the down with the lamp on it. This came as he expected: he saw the one light a mile ahead along the beach, dismounted, turned to the right, walked quietly over to the brushwood-pile, found the little steamer had returned to the beach whence he had unmoored it, and—must have fallen asleep, for he could remember no more. "I'm gettin' the hang of the geography of that place," he said to himself, as he shaved next morning. "I must have made some sort of circle. Let's see. The Thirty-Mile Ride (now how the deuce did I know it was called the Thirty-Mile, Ride?) joins the sea-road beyond the first down where the lamp is. And that atlas-country lies at the back of the Thirty-Mile Ride, somewhere out to the right beyond the hills and tunnels. Rummy things, dreams. 'Wonder what makes mine fit into each other so?"

He continued on his solid way through the recurring duties of the seasons. The regiment was shifted to another station, and he enjoyed road-marching for two months, with a good deal of mixed shooting thrown in, and when they reached their new cantonments he became a member of the local Tent Club, and chased the mighty boar on horseback with a short stabbing-spear. There he met the mahseer of the Poonch, beside whom the tarpon is as a herring, and he who lands him can say that he is a fisherman. This was as new and as fascinating as the big-game shooting that fell to his portion, when he had himself photographed for the mother's benefit, sitting on the flank of his first tiger.

Then the adjutant was promoted, and Cottar rejoiced with him, for he admired the adjutant greatly, and marvelled who might be big enough to fill his place; so that he nearly collapsed when the mantle fell on his own shoulders, and the colonel said a few sweet things that made him blush. An adjutant's position does not differ materially from that of head of the school, and Cottar stood in the same relation to the colonel as he had to his old Head in England. Only, tempers wear out in hot weather, and things were said and done that tried him sorely, and he made glorious blunders, from which the regimental sergeant-major pulled him with a loyal soul and a shut mouth. Slovens and incompetents raged against him; the weak-minded strove to lure him from the ways of justice; the small-minded—yea, men whom Cottar believed would never do "things no fellow can do"—imputed motives mean and circuitous to actions that he had not spent a thought upon; and he tasted injustice, and it made him very sick. But his consolation came on parade, when he looked down the full companies, and reflected how few were in hospital or cells, and wondered when the time would come to try the machine of his love and labour.

But they needed and expected the whole of a man's working-day, and maybe three or four hours of the night. Curiously enough, he never dreamed about the regiment as he was popularly supposed to. The mind, set free from the day's doings, generally ceased working altogether, or, if it moved at all, carried him along the old beach-road to the downs, the lamp-post, and, once in a while, to terrible Policeman Day. The second time that he returned to the world's lost continent (this was a dream that repeated itself again and again, with variations, on the same ground) he knew that if he only sat still the person from the Lily Lock would help him, and he was not disappointed. Sometimes he was trapped in mines of vast depth hollowed out of the heart of the world, where men in torment chanted echoing songs; and he heard this person coming along through the galleries, and everything was made safe and delightful. They met again in low-roofed Indian railway-carriages that halted in a garden surrounded by gilt-and-green railings, where a mob of stony white people, all unfriendly, sat at breakfast-tables covered with roses, and separated Georgie from his companion, while underground voices sang deep-voiced songs. Georgie was filled with enormous despair till they two met again. They foregathered in the middle of an endless, hot tropic night, and crept into a huge house that stood, he knew, somewhere north of the railway-station where the people ate among the roses. It was surrounded with gardens, all moist and dripping; and in one room, reached through leagues of whitewashed passages, a Sick Thing lay in bed. Now the least noise, Georgie knew, would unchain some waiting horror, and his companion knew it, too; but when their eyes met across the bed, Georgie was disgusted to see that she was a child—a little girl in strapped shoes, with her black hair combed back from her forehead.

"What disgraceful folly!" he thought. "Now she could do nothing whatever if Its head came off."

Then the Thing coughed, and the ceiling shattered down in plaster on the mosquito-netting, and "They" rushed in from all quarters. He dragged the child through the stifling garden, voices chanting behind them, and they rode the Thirty-Mile Ride under whip and spur along the sandy beach by the booming sea, till they came to the downs, the lamp-post, and the brushwood-pile, which was safety. Very often dreams would break up about them in this fashion, and they would be separated, to endure awful adventures alone. But the most amusing times were when he and she had a clear understanding that it was all make-believe, and walked through mile-wide roaring rivers without even taking off their shoes, or set light to populous cities to see how they would burn, and were rude as any children to the vague shadows met in their rambles. Later in the night they were sure to suffer for this, either at the hands of the Railway People eating among the roses, or in the tropic uplands at the far end of the Thirty-Mile Ride. Together, this did no much affright them; but often Georgie would hear her shrill cry of "Boy! Boy!" half a world away, and hurry to her rescue before "They" maltreated her.

He and she explored the dark-purple downs as far inland from the brushwood-pile as they dared, but that was always a dangerous matter. The interior was filled with "Them," and "They" went about singing in the hollows, and Georgie and she felt safer on or near the seaboard. So thoroughly had he come to know the place of his dreams that even waking he accepted it as a real country, and made a rough sketch of it. He kept his own counsel, of course; but the permanence of the land puzzled him. His ordinary dreams were as formless and as fleeting as any healthy dreams could be, but once at the brushwood-pile he moved within known limits and could see where he was going. There were months at a time when nothing notable crossed his sleep. Then the dreams would come in a batch of five or six, and next morning the map that he kept in his writing case would be written up to date, for Georgie was a most methodical person. There was, indeed, a danger—his seniors said so—of his developing into a regular "Auntie Fuss" of an adjutant, and when an officer once takes to old-maidism there is more hope for the virgin of seventy than for him.

But fate sent the change that was needed, in the shape of a little winter campaign on the Border, which, after the manner of little campaigns, flashed out into a very ugly war; and Cottar's regiment was chosen among the first.

"Now," said a major, "this'll shake the cobwebs out of us all—especially you, Galahad; and we can see what your hen-with-one-chick attitude has done for the regiment."

Cottar nearly wept with joy as the campaign went forward. They were fit—physically fit beyond the other troops; they were good children in camp, wet or dry, fed or unfed; and they followed their officers with the quick suppleness and trained obedience of a first-class foot-ball fifteen. They were cut off from their apology for a base, and cheerfully cut their way back to it again; they crowned and cleaned out hills full of the enemy with the precision of well-broken dogs of chase; and in the hour of retreat, when, hampered with the sick and wounded of the column, they were persecuted down eleven miles of waterless valley, they, serving as rearguard, covered themselves with a great glory in the eyes of fellow-professionals. Any regiment can advance, but few know how to retreat with a sting in the tail. Then they turned to made roads, most often under fire, and dismantled some inconvenient mud redoubts. They were the last corps to be withdrawn when the rubbish of the campaign was all swept up; and after a month in standing camp, which tries morals severely, they departed to their own place in column of fours, singing:

"'E's goin' to do without 'em—

Don't want 'em any more;

'E's goin' to do without 'em,

As 'e's often done before.

'E's goin' to be a martyr

On a 'ighly novel plan,

An' all the boys and girls will say,

'Ow! what a nice young man-man-man!

Ow! what a nice young man!'"

There came out a "Gazette" in which Cottar found that he had been behaving with "courage and coolness and discretion" in all his capacities; that he had assisted the wounded under fire, and blown in a gate, also under fire. Net result, his captaincy and a brevet majority, coupled with the Distinguished Service Order.

As to his wounded, he explained that they were both heavy men, whom he could lift more easily than any one else. "Otherwise, of course, I should have sent out one of my men; and, of course, about that gate business, we were safe the minute we were well under the walls." But this did not prevent his men from cheering him furiously whenever they saw him, or the mess from giving him a dinner on the eve of his departure to England. (A year's leave was among the things he had "snaffled out of the campaign," I to use his own words.) The doctor, who had taken quite as much as was good for him, quoted poetry about "a good blade carving the casques of men," and so on, and everybody told Cottar that he was an excellent person; but when he rose to make his maiden speech they shouted so that he was understood to say, "It isn't any use tryin' to speak with you chaps rottin' me like this. Let's have some pool."

****

It is not unpleasant to spend eight-and-twenty days in an easy-going steamer on warm waters, in the company of a woman who lets you see that you are head and shoulders superior to the rest of the world, even though that woman may be, and most often is, ten counted years your senior. P.O. boats are not lighted with the disgustful particularity of Atlantic liners. There is more phosphorescence at the bows, and greater silence and darkness by the hand-steering gear aft.

Awful things might have happened to Georgie but for the little fact that he had never studied the first principles of the game he was expected to play. So when Mrs. Zuleika, at Aden, told him how motherly an interest she felt in his welfare, medals, brevet, and all, Georgie took her at the foot of the letter, and promptly talked of his own mother, three hundred miles nearer each day, of his home, and so forth, all the way up the Red Sea. It was much easier than he had supposed to converse with a woman for an hour at a time. Then Mrs. Zuleika, turning from parental affection, spoke of love in the abstract as a thing not unworthy of study, and in discreet twilights after dinner demanded confidences. Georgie would have been delighted to supply them, but he had none, and did not know it was his duty to manufacture them. Mrs. Zuleika expressed surprise and unbelief, and asked—those questions which deep asks of deep. She learned all that was necessary to conviction, and, being very much a woman, resumed (Georgie never knew that she had abandoned) the motherly attitude.

"Do you know," she said, somewhere in the Mediterranean, "I think you're the very dearest boy I have ever met in my life, and I'd like you to remember me a little. You will when you are older, but I want you to remember me now. You'll make some girl very happy."

"Oh! Hope so," said Georgie, gravely; "but there's heaps of time for marryin' an' all that sort of thing, ain't there?"

"That depends. Here are your bean-bags for the Ladies' Competition. I think I'm growing too old to care for these tamashas."

They were getting up sports, and Georgie was on the committee. He never noticed how perfectly the bags were sewn, but another woman did, and smiled—once. He liked Mrs. Zuleika greatly. She was a bit old, of course, but uncommonly nice. There was no nonsense about her.

A few nights after they passed Gibraltar his dream returned to him. She who waited by the brushwood-pile was no longer a little girl, but a woman with black hair that grew into a "widow's peak," combed back from her forehead. He knew her for the child in black, the companion of the last six years, and, as it had been in the time of the meetings on the Lost Continent, he was filled with delight unspeakable. "They," for some dreamland reason, were friendly or had gone away that night, and the two flitted together over all their country, from the brushwood-pile up the Thirty-Mile Ride, till they saw the House of the Sick Thing, a pin-point in the distance to the left; stamped through the Railway Waiting-room where the roses lay on the spread breakfast-tables; and returned, by the ford and the city they had once burned for sport, to the great swells of the downs under the lamp-post. Wherever they moved a strong singing followed them underground, but this night there was no panic. All the land was empty except for themselves, and at the last (they were sitting by the lamp-post hand in hand) she turned and kissed him. He woke with a start, staring at the waving curtain of the cabin door; he could almost have sworn that the kiss was real.

Next morning the ship was rolling in a Biscay sea, and people were not happy; but as Georgie came to breakfast, shaven, tubbed, and smelling of soap, several turned to look at him because of the light in his eyes and the splendour of his countenance.

"Well, you look beastly fit," snapped a neighbour. "Any one left you a legacy in the middle of the Bay?"

Georgie reached for the curry, with a seraphic grin. "I suppose it's the gettin' so near home, and all that. I do feel rather festive this mornin. 'Rolls a bit, doesn't she?"

Mrs. Zuleika stayed in her cabin till the end of the voyage, when she left without bidding him farewell, and wept passionately on the dock-head for pure joy of meeting her children, who, she had often said, were so like their father.

Georgie headed for his own country, wild with delight of his first long furlough after the lean seasons. Nothing was changed in that orderly life, from the coachman who met him at the station to the white peacock that stormed at the carriage from the stone wall above the shaven lawns. The house took toll of him with due regard to precedence—first the mother; then the father; then the housekeeper, who wept and praised God; then the butler, and so on down to the under-keeper, who had been dogboy in Georgie's youth, and called him "Master Georgie," and was reproved by the groom who had taught Georgie to ride.

"Not a thing changed," he sighed contentedly, when the three of them sat down to dinner in the late sunlight, while the rabbits crept out upon the lawn below the cedars, and the big trout in the ponds by the home paddock rose for their evening meal.

"Our changes are all over, dear," cooed the mother; "and now I am getting used to your size and your tan (you're very brown, Georgie), I see you haven't changed in the least. You're exactly like the pater."

The father beamed on this man after his own heart,—"youngest major in the army, and should have had the V.C., sir,"—and the butler listened with his professional mask off when Master Georgie spoke of war as it is waged to-day, and his father cross-questioned.

They went out on the terrace to smoke among the roses, and the shadow of the old house lay long across the wonderful English foliage, which is the only living green in the world.

"Perfect! By Jove, it's perfect!" Georgie was looking at the round-bosomed woods beyond the home paddock, where the white pheasant boxes were ranged; and the golden air was full of a hundred sacred scents and sounds. Georgie felt his father's arm tighten in his.

"It's not half bad—but hodie mihi, cras tibi, isn't it? I suppose you'll be turning up some fine day with a girl under your arm, if you haven't one now, eh?"

"You can make your mind easy, sir. I haven't one."

"Not in all these years?" said the mother.

"I hadn't time, mummy. They keep a man pretty busy, these days, in the service, and most of our mess are unmarried, too."

"But you must have met hundreds in society—at balls, and so on?"

"I'm like the Tenth, mummy: I don't dance."

"Don't dance! What have you been doing with yourself, then—backing other men's bills?" said the father.

"Oh, yes; I've done a little of that too; but you see, as things are now, a man has all his work cut out for him to keep abreast of his profession, and my days were always too full to let me lark about half the night."

"Hmm!"—suspiciously.

"It's never too late to learn. We ought to give some kind of housewarming for the people about, now you've come back. Unless you want to go straight up to town, dear?"

"No. I don't want anything better than this. Let's sit still and enjoy ourselves. I suppose there will be something for me to ride if I look for it?"

"Seeing I've been kept down to the old brown pair for the last six weeks because all the others were being got ready for Master Georgie, I should say there might be," the father chuckled. "They're reminding me in a hundred ways that I must take the second place now."

"Brutes!"

"The pater doesn't mean it, dear; but every one has been trying to make your home-coming a success; and you do like it, don't you?"

"Perfect! Perfect! There's no place like England—when you 've done your work."

"That's the proper way to look at it, my son."

And so up and down the flagged walk till their shadows grew long in the moonlight, and the mother went indoors and played such songs as a small boy once clamoured for, and the squat silver candlesticks were brought in, and Georgie climbed to the two rooms in the west wing that had been his nursery and his playroom in the beginning. Then who should come to tuck him up for the night but the mother? And she sat down on the bed, and they talked for a long hour, as mother and son should, if there is to be any future for the Empire. With a simple woman's deep guile she asked questions and suggested answers that should have waked some sign in the face on the pillow, and there was neither quiver of eyelid nor quickening of breath, neither evasion nor delay in reply. So she blessed him and kissed him on the mouth, which is not always a mother's property, and said something to her husband later, at which he laughed profane and incredulous laughs.

All the establishment waited on Georgie next morning, from the tallest six-year-old, "with a mouth like a kid glove, Master Georgie," to the under-keeper strolling carelessly along the horizon, Georgie's pet rod in his hand, and "There's a four-pounder risin' below the lasher. You don't 'ave 'em in Injia, Mast-Major Georgie." It was all beautiful beyond telling, even though the mother insisted on taking him out in the landau (the leather had the hot Sunday smell of his youth) and showing him off to her friends at all the houses for six miles round; and the pater bore him up to town and a lunch at the club, where he introduced him, quite carelessly, to not less than thirty ancient warriors whose sons were not the youngest majors in the army and had not the D.S.O. After that it was Georgie's turn; and remembering his friends, he filled up the house with that kind of officer who live in cheap lodgings at Southsea or Montpelier Square, Brompton—good men all, but not well off. The mother perceived that they needed girls to play with; and as there was no scarcity of girls, the house hummed like a dovecote in spring. They tore up the place for amateur theatricals; they disappeared in the gardens when they ought to have been rehearsing; they swept off every available horse and vehicle, especially the governess-cart and the fat pony; they fell into the trout-ponds; they picnicked and they tennised; and they sat on gates in the twilight, two by two, and Georgie found that he was not in the least necessary to their entertainment.

"My word!" said he, when he saw the last of their dear backs. "They told me they've enjoyed 'emselves, but they haven't done half the things they said they would."

"I know they've enjoyed themselves—immensely," said the mother. "You're a public benefactor, dear."

"Now we can be quiet again, can't we?"

"Oh, quite. I've a very dear friend of mine that I want you to know. She couldn't come with the house so full, because she's an invalid, and she was away when you first came. She's a Mrs. Lacy."

"Lacy! I don't remember the name about here."

"No; they came after you went to India—from Oxford. Her husband died there, and she lost some money, I believe. They bought The Firs on the Bassett Road. She's a very sweet woman, and we're very fond of them both."

"She's a widow, didn't you say?"

"She has a daughter. Surely I said so, dear?"

"Does she fall into trout-ponds, and gas and giggle, and 'Oh, Major Cottah!' and all that sort of thing?"

"No, indeed. She's a very quiet girl, and very musical. She always came over here with her music-books—composing, you know; and she generally works all day, so you won't—"

"'Talking about Miriam?" said the pater, coming up. The mother edged toward him within elbow-reach. There was no finesse about Georgie's father. "Oh, Miriam's a dear girl. Plays beautifully. Rides beautifully, too. She's a regular pet of the household. Used to call me—" The elbow went home, and ignorant but obedient always, the pater shut himself off.

"What used she to call you, sir?"

"All sorts of pet names. I'm very fond of Miriam."

"Sounds Jewish—Miriam."

"Jew! You'll be calling yourself a Jew next. She's one of the Herefordshire Lacys. When her aunt dies—" Again the elbow.

"Oh, you won't see anything of her, Georgie. She's busy with her music or her mother all day. Besides, you're going up to town tomorrow, aren't you? I thought you said something about an Institute meeting?" The mother spoke.

"Go up to town now! What nonsense!" Once more the pater was shut off.

"I had some idea of it, but I'm not quite sure," said the son of the house. Why did the mother try to get him away because a musical girl and her invalid parent were expected? He did not approve of unknown females calling his father pet names. He would observe these pushing persons who had been only seven years in the county.

All of which the delighted mother read in his countenance, herself keeping an air of sweet disinterestedness.

"They'll be here this evening for dinner. I'm sending the carriage over for them, and they won't stay more than a week."

"Perhaps I shall go up to town. I don't quite know yet." Georgie moved away irresolutely. There was a lecture at the United Services Institute on the supply of ammunition in the field, and the one man whose theories most irritated Major Cottar would deliver it. A heated discussion was sure to follow, and perhaps he might find himself moved to speak. He took his rod that afternoon and went down to thrash it out among the trout.

"Good sport, dear!" said the mother, from the terrace.

"Fraid it won't be, mummy. All those men from town, and the girls particularly, have put every trout off his feed for weeks. There isn't one of 'em that cares for fishin'—really. Fancy stampin' and shoutin' on the bank, and tellin' every fish for half a mile exactly what you're goin' to do, and then chuckin' a brute of a fly at him! By Jove, it would scare me if I was a trout!"

But things were not as bad as he had expected. The black gnat was on the water, and the water was strictly preserved. A three-quarter-pounder at the second cast set him for the campaign, and he worked down-stream, crouching behind the reed and meadowsweet; creeping between a hornbeam hedge and a foot-wide strip of bank, where he could see the trout, but where they could not distinguish him from the background; lying almost on his stomach to switch the blue-upright sidewise through the checkered shadows of a gravelly ripple under overarching trees. But he had known every inch of the water since he was four feet high. The aged and astute between sunk roots, with the large and fat that lay in the frothy scum below some strong rush of water, sucking as lazily as carp, came to trouble in their turn, at the hand that imitated so delicately the flicker and wimple of an egg-dropping fly.

Consequently, Georgie found himself five miles from home when he ought to have been dressing for dinner. The housekeeper had taken good care that her boy should not go empty, and before he changed to the white moth he sat down to excellent claret with sandwiches of potted egg and things that adoring women make and men never notice. Then back, to surprise the otter grubbing for fresh-water mussels, the rabbits on the edge of the beechwoods foraging in the clover, and the policeman-like white owl stooping to the little fieldmice, till the moon was strong, and he took his rod apart, and went home through well-remembered gaps in the hedges. He fetched a compass round the house, for, though he might have broken every law of the establishment every hour, the law of his boyhood was unbreakable: after fishing you went in by the south garden back-door, cleaned up in the outer scullery, and did not present yourself to your elders and your betters till you had washed and changed.

"Half-past ten, by Jove! Well, we'll make the sport an excuse. They wouldn't want to see me the first evening, at any rate. Gone to bed, probably." He skirted by the open French windows of the drawing-room. "No, they haven't. They look very comfy in there."

He could see his father in his own particular chair, the mother in hers, and the back of a girl at the piano by the big potpourri-jar. The gardens looked half divine in the moonlight, and he turned down through the roses to finish his pipe.

A prelude-ended, and there floated out a voice of the kind that in his childhood he used to call "creamy" a full, true contralto; and this is the song that he heard, every syllable of it:

Over the edge of the purple down,

Where the single lamplight gleams,

Know ye the road to the Merciful Town

That is hard by the Sea of Dreams—

Where the poor may lay their wrongs away,

And the sick may forget to weep?

But we—pity us! Oh, pity us!

We wakeful; ah, pity us!—

We must go back with Policeman Day—
    Back from the City of Sleep!

Weary they turn from the scroll and crown,
    Fetter and prayer and plough
They that go up to the Merciful Town,
    For her gates are closing now.
It is their right in the Baths of Night
    Body and soul to steep
But we—pity us! ah, pity us!
    We wakeful; oh, pity us!—
We must go back with Policeman Day—
    Back from the City of Sleep!

Over the edge of the purple down,
    Ere the tender dreams begin,
Look—we may look—at the Merciful Town,
    But we may not enter in!
Outcasts all, from her guarded wall
    Back to our watch we creep:
We—pity us! ah, pity us!
    We wakeful; oh, pity us!—

We that go back with Policeman Day—

Back from the City of Sleep

At the last echo he was aware that his mouth was dry and unknown pulses were beating in the roof of it. The housekeeper, who would have it that he must have fallen in and caught a chill, was waiting to catch him on the stairs, and, since he neither saw nor answered her, carried a wild tale abroad that brought his mother knocking at the door.

"Anything happened, dear? Harper said she thought you weren't—"

"No; it's nothing. I'm all right, mummy. Please don't bother."

He did not recognise his own voice, but that was a small matter beside what he was considering. Obviously, most obviously, the whole coincidence was crazy lunacy. He proved it to the satisfaction of Major George Cottar, who was going up to town tomorrow to hear a lecture on the supply of ammunition in the field; and having so proved it, the soul and brain and heart and body of Georgie cried joyously: "That's the Lily Lock girl—the Lost Continent girl—the Thirty-Mile Ride girl—the Brushwood girl! I know her!"

He waked, stiff and cramped in his chair, to reconsider the situation by sunlight, when it did not appear normal. But a man must eat, and he went to breakfast, his heart between his teeth, holding himself severely in hand.

"Late, as usual," said the mother. "'My boy, Miss Lacy."

A tall girl in black raised her eyes to his, and Georgie's life training deserted him—just as soon as he realised that she did not know. He stared coolly and critically. There was the abundant black hair, growing in a widow's peak, turned back from the forehead, with that peculiar ripple over the right ear; there were the grey eyes set a little close together; the short upper lip, resolute chin, and the known poise of the head. There was also the small well-cut mouth that had kissed him.

"Georgie—dear!" said the mother, amazedly, for Miriam was flushing under the stare.

"I—I beg your pardon!" he gulped. "I don't know whether the mother has told you, but I'm rather an idiot at times, specially before I've had my breakfast. It's—it's a family failing." He turned to explore among the hot-water dishes on the sideboard, rejoicing that she did not know—she did not know.

His conversation for the rest of the meal was mildly insane, though the mother thought she had never seen her boy look half so handsome. How could any girl, least of all one of Miriam's discernment, forbear to fall down and worship? But deeply Miriam was displeased. She had never been stared at in that fashion before, and promptly retired into her shell when Georgie announced that he had changed his mind about going to town, and would stay to play with Miss Lacy if she had nothing better to do.

"Oh, but don't let me throw you out. I'm at work. I've things to do all the morning."

"What possessed Georgie to behave so oddly?" the mother sighed to herself. "Miriam's a bundle of feelings—like her mother."

"You compose—don't you? Must be a fine thing to be able to do that. ['Pig-oh, pig!' thought Miriam.] I think I heard you singin' when I came in last night after fishin'. All about a Sea of Dreams, wasn't it? [Miriam shuddered to the core of the soul that afflicted her.] Awfully pretty song. How d' you think of such things?"

"You only composed the music, dear, didn't you?"

"The words too. I'm sure of it," said Georgie, with a sparkling eye. No; she did not know.

"Yeth; I wrote the words too." Miriam spoke slowly, for she knew she lisped when she was nervous.

"Now how could you tell, Georgie?" said the mother, as delighted as though the youngest major in the army were ten years old, showing off before company.

"I was sure of it, somehow. Oh, there are heaps of things about me, mummy, that you don't understand. Looks as if it were goin' to be a hot day—for England. Would you care for a ride this afternoon, Miss Lacy? We can start out after tea, if you'd like it."

Miriam could not in decency refuse, but any woman might see she was not filled with delight.

"That will be very nice, if you take the Bassett Road. It will save me sending Martin down to the village," said the mother, filling in gaps.

Like all good managers, the mother had her one weakness—a mania for little strategies that should economise horses and vehicles. Her men-folk complained that she turned them into common carriers, and there was a legend in the family that she had once said to the pater on the morning of a meet: "If you should kill near Bassett, dear, and if it isn't too late, would you mind just popping over and matching me this?"

"I knew that was coming. You'd never miss a chance, mother. If it's a fish or a trunk I won't." Georgie laughed.

"It's only a duck. They can do it up very neatly at Mallett's," said the mother, simply. "You won't mind, will you? We'll have a scratch dinner at nine, because it's so hot."

The long summer day dragged itself out for centuries; but at last there was tea on the lawn, and Miriam appeared.

She was in the saddle before he could offer to help, with the clean spring of the child who mounted the pony for the Thirty-Mile Ride. The day held mercilessly, though Georgie got down thrice to look for imaginary stones in Rufus's foot. One cannot say even simple things in broad light, and this that Georgie meditated was not simple. So he spoke seldom, and Miriam was divided between relief and scorn. It annoyed her that the great hulking thing should know she had written the words of the song overnight; for though a maiden may sing her most secret fancies aloud, she does not care to have them trampled over by the male Philistine. They rode into the little red-brick street of Bassett, and Georgie made untold fuss over the disposition of that duck. It must go in just such a package, and be fastened to the saddle in just such a manner, though eight o'clock had struck and they were miles from dinner.

"We must be quick!" said Miriam, bored and angry.

"There's no great hurry; but we can cut over Dowhead Down, and let 'em out on the grass. That will save us half an hour."

The horses capered on the short, sweet-smelling turf, and the delaying shadows gathered in the valley as they cantered over the great dun down that overhangs Bassett and the Western coaching-road. Insensibly the pace quickened without thought of mole-hills; Rufus, gentleman that he was, waiting on Miriam's Dandy till they should have cleared the rise. Then down the two-mile slope they raced together, the wind whistling in their ears, to the steady throb of eight hoofs and the light click-click of the shifting bits.

"Oh, that was glorious!" Miriam cried, reining in. "Dandy and I are old friends, but I don't think we've ever gone better together."

"No; but you've gone quicker, once or twice."

"Really? When?"

Georgie moistened his lips. "Don't you remember the Thirty-Mile Ride—with me—when 'They' were after us—on the beach-road, with the sea to the left—going toward the lamp-post on the downs?"

The girl gasped. "What—what do you mean?" she said hysterically.

"The Thirty-Mile Ride, and—and all the rest of it."

"You mean—? I didn't sing anything about the Thirty-Mile Ride. I know I didn't. I have never told a living soul.'"

"You told about Policeman Day, and the lamp at the top of the downs, and the City of Sleep. It all joins on, you know—it's the same country—and it was easy enough to see where you had been."

"Good God!—It joins on—of course it does; but—I have been—you have been—Oh, let's walk, please, or I shall fall off!"

Georgie ranged alongside, and laid a hand that shook below her bridle-hand, pulling Dandy into a walk. Miriam was sobbing as he had seen a man sob under the touch of the bullet.

"It's all right—it's all right," he whispered feebly. "Only—only it's true, you know."

"True! Am I mad?"

"Not unless I'm mad as well. Do try to think a minute quietly. How could any one conceivably know anything about the Thirty-Mile Ride having anything to do with you, unless he had been there?"

"But where? But where? Tell me!"

"There—wherever it may be—in our country, I suppose. Do you remember the first time you rode it—the Thirty-Mile Ride, I mean? You must."

"It was all dreams—all dreams!"

"Yes, but tell, please; because I know."

"Let me think. I—we were on no account to make any noise—on no account to make any noise." She was staring between Dandy's ears, with eyes that did not see, and a suffocating heart.

"Because 'It' was dying in the big house?" Georgie went on, reining in again.

"There was a garden with green-and-gilt railings—all hot. Do you remember?"

"I ought to. I was sitting on the other side of the bed before 'It' coughed and 'They' came in."

"You!"—the deep voice was unnaturally full and strong, and the girl's wide-opened eyes burned in the dusk as she stared him through and through. "Then you're the Boy—my Brushwood Boy, and I've known you all my life!"

She fell forward on Dandy's neck. Georgie forced himself out of the weakness that was overmastering his limbs, and slid an arm round her waist. The head dropped on his shoulder, and he found himself with parched lips saying things that up till then he believed existed only in printed works of fiction. Mercifully the horses were quiet. She made no attempt to draw herself away when she recovered, but lay still, whispering, "Of course you're the Boy, and I didn't know—I didn't know."

"I knew last night; and when I saw you at breakfast— "

"Oh, that was why! I wondered at the time. You would, of course."

"I couldn't speak before this. Keep your head where it is, dear. It's all right now—all right now, isn't it?"

"But how was it I didn't know—after all these years and years? I remember—oh, what lots of things I remember!"

"Tell me some. I'll look after the horses."

"I remember waiting for you when the steamer came in. Do you?"

"At the Lily Lock, beyond Hong-Kong and Java?"

"Do you call it that, too?"

"You told me it was when I was lost in the continent. That was you that showed me the way through the mountains?"
"When the islands slid? It must have been, because you're the only one I remember. All the others were 'Them.'
"Awful brutes they were, too."
"I remember showing you the Thirty-Mile Ride the first time. You ride just as you used to—then. You are you!"
"That's odd. I thought that of you this afternoon. Isn't it wonderful?"
"What does it all mean? Why should you and I of the millions of people in the world have this—this thing between us? What does it mean? I'm frightened."
"This!" said Georgie. The horses quickened their pace. They thought they had heard an order. "Perhaps when we die we may find out more, but it means this now."
There was no answer. What could she say? As the world went, they had known each other rather less than eight and a half hours, but the matter was one that did not concern the world. There was a very long silence, while the breath in their nostrils drew cold and sharp as it might have been a fume of ether.
"That's the second," Georgie whispered. "You remember, don't you?"
"It's not!"—furiously. "It's not!"
"On the downs the other night-months ago. You were just as you are now, and we went over the country for miles and miles."
"It was all empty, too. They had gone away. Nobody frightened us. I wonder why, Boy?"
"Oh, if you remember that, you must remember the rest. Confess!"
"I remember lots of things, but I know I didn't. I never have—till just now."
"You did, dear."
"I know I didn't, because—oh, it's no use keeping anything back! because I truthfully meant to."
"And truthfully did."
"No; meant to; but some one else came by."
"There wasn't any one else. There never has been."
"There was—there always is. It was another woman—out there—on the sea. I saw her. It was the 26th of May. I've got it written down somewhere."
"Oh, you've kept a record of your dreams, too? That's odd about the other woman, because I happened to be on the sea just then."
"I was right. How do I know what you've done when you were awake—and I thought it was only you!"
"You never were more wrong in your life. What a little temper you've got! Listen to me a minute, dear." And Georgie, though he knew it not,

committed black perjury. "It—it isn't the kind of thing one says to any one, because they'd laugh; but on my word and honour, darling, I've never been kissed by a living soul outside my own people in all my life. Don't laugh, dear. I wouldn't tell any one but you, but it's the solemn truth."

"I knew! You are you. Oh, I knew you'd come some day; but I didn't know you were you in the least till you spoke."

"Then give me another."

"And you never cared or looked anywhere? Why, all the round world must have loved you from the very minute they saw you, Boy."

"They kept it to themselves if they did. No; I never cared."

"And we shall be late for dinner—horribly late. Oh, how can I look at you in the light before your mother—and mine!"

"We'll play you're Miss Lacy till the proper time comes. What's the shortest limit for people to get engaged? S'pose we have got to go through all the fuss of an engagement, haven't we?"

"Oh, I don't want to talk about that. It's so commonplace. I've thought of something that you don't know. I'm sure of it. What's my name?"

"Miri—no, it isn't, by Jove! Wait half a second, and it'll come back to me. You aren't—you can't? Why, those old tales—before I went to school! I've never thought of 'em from that day to this. Are you the original, only Annieanlouise?"

"It was what you always called me ever since the beginning. Oh! We've turned into the avenue, and we must be an hour late."

"What does it matter? The chain goes as far back as those days? It must, of course—of course it must. I've got to ride round with this pestilent old bird-confound him!"

""'Ha! ha!" said the duck, laughing'—do you remember that?"

"Yes, I do—flower-pots on my feet, and all. We've been together all this while; and I've got to say good bye to you till dinner. Sure I'll see you at dinner-time? Sure you won't sneak up to your room, darling, and leave me all the evening? Good-bye, dear—good-bye."

"Good-bye, Boy, good-bye. Mind the arch! Don't let Rufus bolt into his stables. Good-bye. Yes, I'll come down to dinner; but—what shall I do when I see you in the light!"

Printed in Great Britain
by Amazon

7ac8c488-8f6a-4f6a-a4d1-f4bd86bda8afR01